The Water at the End of the World

Michael Easterling

VALLEY OAK PUBLICATIONS

To Lisa, my collaborator in this, and all things good.

Part One

Qomermoya

Chapter 1

I pa always told me I had the power. Fool that I was, I did not believe her because it did not feel like power to me.

  The Capac Inca, now he was someone with power! Power over the seasons, over Inti, the sun, and Qillamama, the moon. And over men, he had the power of life and death; armies marched to the four corners of the world to do his bidding.

  But this power Ipa spoke of was, to me, no more than a vague uneasiness, perhaps a tingling in my hands, though upon occasion—nearly as rare as a coastal rain—I saw things no one else could see. Atakachau! I remember one of the first times that happened. We were waiting for the arrival of the Capac Inca and his retinue. I say "we," the families of our village called Qomermoya. It was a day of celebration for it was a great honor to be in the presence of the Capac Inca, though we knew he was but passing through and not stopping.

  For months, we had prepared for his visit—this in addition to our long days in the fields and with the herds of llamas. While the men re-thatched the roofs of our wasis where we slept, we women patched the walls with mud. While they had repaired the retaining walls of our terraced fields, we washed and mended all our clothing as well as the chusis we slept upon. Of course, Ipa had complained when the tokoyrikoq came to inspect our village three days before the Capac Inca's arrival. She hated the way he fingered our chusis and poked through our hair looking for lice. "As if that filthy know-nothing could tell me one thing about cleaning that I don't know better," she had grumbled then spat on the ground behind his back. Yet even she had been pleased when the tokoyrikoq had complimented Weqo Churu, our chieftain, on the cleanliness of our village.

  Now as we stood in the roadway awaiting the Capac Inca, our village looked the model of industry, and we, in our best garments, the dutiful citizens of the glorious kingdom of Tahuantinsuyu. The young men, my brother Charapa among them, played a lively tune on their flutes while people danced in the roadway, including a few men who had been drinking too much chicha and whose jerky stumbling was the cause of much amusement.

  It was then I saw it, or felt it—at first, I was not sure which. I do know everything was suddenly very dark. I looked up, but no clouds hid Inti; in fact, there were no clouds anywhere, not even to the south where the snowcapped peaks were usually hidden in mists. Yet in my mind, the valley was as dark as if a black storm had swept down from the mountains.

Alarmed, I looked at the others, but no one acted as if anything was amiss; the laughter, dancing, and playing of music continued as before. Yet for me the darkness only increased. It bore down upon me, and I felt a squeezing inside my chest as if the darkness possessed fingers to pry apart my heart. I was too overmastered to speak, but a prayer leapt from my heart to Inti, a pleading for deliverance. I followed my prayer upward with my eyes, and Inti appeared bright even in the darkness.

It was then I saw them: seven magnificent birds winging eastward. Though they were high up, I could still see their lustrous feathers of yellow and blue, and their long, pointed tails straight out behind them. Never had I seen birds such as these! My heart swelled with their beauty, and perhaps because of this, the darkness released its grip, and just for a moment, I felt the joy of longing fulfilled.

I watched until the fleeting birds were the size of tiny chamana seeds then looked to find Ipa among the crowd only to discover her watching me. I wanted to ask if she had seen the birds, but before I could say anything, the blare of a puturutu sounded in the distance.

Everyone went quiet. Then someone shouted, "The Capac Inca is coming!" and others took up the cry, "Atakachau! Atakachau! The Capac Inca!"

I looked at Ipa and smiled. She shifted Kusi, my baby brother, from one hip to the other then motioned me to join her.

"Yana, why are you smiling?" she said.

"It's not the Capac Inca."

"How do you know? A vision?"

I shook my head. "I think someone has had too much chicha. Only a chasqui would blow a puturutu."

I was right. As everyone studied the hill the road ran down, a head soon appeared above the ridge line, bobbing up and down, followed by the body of a young man running. Everyone groaned in disappointment. "False alarm!" someone cried. "It's just a chasqui!"

The chasqui, an official messenger, was a tall, weightless youth running at the edge of his endurance. We all quickly stepped out of the road to allow him to pass, and he whisked by without so much as a glance at any of us.

"He must have a very important message he must be trying to remember, or else he would have at least greeted us," I said to Ipa. "A chasqui would be a good job for Charapa. He can memorize anything."

Ipa looked at me askance, and I immediately realized the absurdity of what I had said. Then we both laughed. My brother did have an amazing memory, but as for running, he was like the turtle he was named after.

"Are you laughing at me?" said Charapa, who had a habit of suddenly appearing at awkward moments.

"Yana was just praising your ability to remember things," Ipa said.

Smiling, I pointed to the figure of the chasqui receding in the distance. "With your ability to memorize, you'd make a good chasqui, don't you think?"

Charapa made a face as if he had swallowed sour chicha. My brother hated physical labor, especially running. Though he did his share of work, it was always with great reluctance and perhaps out of fear of Weqo Churu. Charapa preferred to be out watching the herds of llamas where he had time to sit and dream.

An excited murmur passed through the crowd. "There!" someone shouted, pointing down the road. "Look! There!"

A score of heads bounced upon the ridge line, then bodies began to pour over the crest like excited ants out of a hole. It was the strangest sight! The mass of men looked like ground doves pecking for seed.

"What are they doing?" I said.

"They're the road cleaners," Ipa answered. "Wherever the Capac Inca travels, they go before him, making sure the road is smooth and clean."

As the men came nearer, I could see them pulling up tufts of grass or picking up stones and throwing them off to the side. A group out front suddenly broke away from the others and ran ahead to suddenly stop near to where we were standing. Like the chasqui, they paid us no mind, but flung stones as if we were not there. We quickly moved back from the road to avoid being hit.

"There are so many of them!" I exclaimed.

"About two hundred," Charapa responded. I did not doubt my brother's estimate. Like his memory, this was another of Charapa's talents, this thing for numbers and counting.

As the road cleaners moved past, we returned to the edge of the road, eager to see who would come next. We didn't have long to wait. Two columns of soldiers appeared along the ridge. Marching in step down the slope, they resembled a giant caterpillar. Those in front carried bows. These archers wore yacollas, long cloaks brightly patterned with reds the color of kantuta flowers and yellows like the flowers of the mutuy bush. Upon their chests, bronze breast plates flashed in Inti's light. Behind the archers, strode the lancers. The plainness of their yacollas was compensated by the vivid hues of the feathers that decorated the shafts of their long spears, and each lancer held a shield patterned with the same geometric design.

More men appeared behind the soldiers. Like the soldiers, they marched in two columns, but closer together, and each column bore a thick pole.

"Watch!" whispered Ipa, "those are the litter bearers."

There was a sudden shaft of light as when a strand of Inti's hair pierces a cloud. Then Inti himself slowly rose above the horizon.

"Atakachau!" I exclaimed. "How can there be two Intis in the sky at the same time?"

"That's the Capac Inca's litter," Ipa explained, "It's covered with plates of gold and silver—jewels, too!"

"It's so bright! It does look like Inti!" Charapa exclaimed.

"Of course it does!" said Ipa. "The litter carries the Capac Inca, Inti's son!"

"Look how smoothly the litter glides toward us," I said, "like it's floating upon a calm stream."

"That's because of the litter bearers," Ipa explained. "See how they're all the same height? They're all Qollohuayans, people who live near Lake Titikaka. They are known for their strength and the grace of their walk," and because it was important to her, she added, "and for the healing skills of their camascas."

"There are so many men to carry one litter," I said.

"Forty," was Charapa's quick response.

The brilliance of the sparkling litter hurt my eyes, so I half closed them and focused instead upon the curtain covering the middle section. Yet it too was dazzling: a brilliant red to match the gold and silver. I wondered what it was made of.

"The curtain is made of bird feathers," said Ipa, seeming to know my thoughts.

I tore my gaze from the litter to stare at her. "What kind of bird has feathers like that?"

She waved her hand toward the east. "One that lives far away in the jungle where it's hot all the time, and the little people live."

Turning to look once more at the curtains, I suddenly had a disturbing thought. "How will we see the Capac Inca if the curtains are drawn?" I said.

"We won't," Ipa answered. "That's the way he travels. There are holes in the curtain. He can see us, but we can't see him."

My disappointment was a rock in my stomach. As glorious as the litter was, it was the one who sat within it that I was hoping to see.

Everyone grew silent as the soldiers marched by. They were fierce-looking men with heavy shoulders and bulging muscles. Then as the litter bearers approached, we began to make the appropriate gestures of obeisance: heads lowered; arms outstretched; palms upward.

"Hail, mighty lord, Inti's son!" someone shouted. Others joined in, adding more words of praise, "Inti's son! The whole world harkens unto you! Hail, O wise Father!"

Though I bowed my head like everyone else, I watched the approaching litter out of the corner of my eye. Over and over, I chanted, "Hail, mighty lord, Inti's son!" but in my mind, I prayed the Capac Inca would throw back the curtains and let us behold him.

Then my prayer was answered! A long arm ringed with golden bracelets reached through the front curtain and flung it aside, then the side curtain nearest to us.

"Stop!" shouted a voice within the litter.

There were gasps of amazement. Was the Capac Inca going to favor us with a visit? Forgetting my place, I straightened up and stood looking directly at the Capac Inca. Thank Inti, he did not notice this disrespect, for his eyes were fixed upon a small boy seated next to him. Like the Capac Inca, the boy wore a headdress of feathers and gold upon his head. I knew at once I was seeing Topa Inca, the Capac Inca's son. He was cloaked in a magnificent mantle made of feathers as splendid as those of the litter's curtain, only these were yellow and blue. I gasped, for they were the same color as the feathers of the strange birds I thought I had seen earlier!

All of a sudden, my thoughts were a muddle. I felt like one of Ipa's curing dolls whose head was made of rags and stuffed with coarse llama wool. It was then Topa Inca looked directly at me, and for a moment our eyes met. It was long enough for me to see the pain and sadness in his eyes.

Then the most astonishing thing happened! Topa Inca, the son of the Capac Inca, the heir to the throne of Tahuantinsuyu, the descendant of Inti, bringer of light, leaned forward and vomited!

Chapter 2

Weqo Churu was forever scolding me: "Know your place! Don't think you know better than your elders!" Had I listened, I would have followed his lead and, like the others, backed away from the two divine beings, one of whom was acting more like a very sick little boy. Instead I stood and watched as Topa Inca continued to heave up the contents of his stomach. He looked very ill, and his face was a strange color—more yellow than brown.

Suddenly I knew I must help him, if only in a small way. I turned and ran to our wasi. Chumpi, my llama, bleated forlornly from his hated pen. For once I ignored him and quickly crawled through the wasi entrance. Inside I snatched a scrap of cloth used as a towel for Kusi's baths. Outside again, I dipped the towel into a clay bowl that still held some water left from our morning meal. Then, as fast as I could, I ran back toward the road. Ahead I could see that the litter had been lowered to the ground, and the Capac Inca stood next to it. As I approached the litter, two guards suddenly leapt in front of me. I was so startled, I slipped, which was fortunate, for as I slid upon my rump, the butt-end of a lance swished just above my head.

"Stop that!" the Capac Inca shouted.

Both guards backed away as ordered, but kept their eyes hard upon me.

"You!" shouted the Capac Inca again.

I looked up; the Capac Inca was motioning for me to approach. Quickly I stood and walked toward him. This time the guards let me pass, albeit reluctantly. With head lowered, I handed the towel to the Capac Inca. Out of the corner of my eye, I watched as he briefly examined it before handing it to Topa Inca, who was now sitting alongside the road, a yellow-brown mash of half-digested food covered his chin and spilling down the front of his beautiful feathered mantle.

Suddenly one of the guards grabbed me by the collar of my lliqlla. Lifting me nearly off my feet, he shoved me away, and once again I fell on my butt. Ipa quickly handed Kusi to Charapa then came forward and helped me to my feet. I expected her to scold me for my rash behavior, but instead she glared at the guard and hissed at him through her teeth. Then she dusted off my lliqlla before straightening the kantuta flowers she had earlier arranged in my hair.

As she fussed, I watched as an old man hurried forward from the rear of the Capac Inca's train. Bent with age, he walked with a rocking motion as if crossing a stream on a narrow log. Over one shoulder hung a woven carrying bag, and in one hand he held a small clay jar with a lid.

"It's about time!" muttered the Capac Inca.

The old man walked silently past the Capac Inca, making no sign of obeisance. He knelt beside Topa Inca, took my towel, snapped it in the air a few times, then finished wiping Topa Inca's face. Then he removed the lid from the jar and brought it to Topa Inca's lips. Topa Inca shrank away, but the old man rapped his knuckles sharply on Topa Inca's head. In response, Topa Inca drank from the jar, making a face. From his bag, the old man took something that looked like dried fruit, and Topa Inca immediately grabbed it and popped it into his mouth.

"That's probably a tea made from coca leaves," Ipa whispered, pointing to the jar. "It soothes a stomach, but can be bitter if too strong."

Leaving his son in the care of the old man, the Capac Inca addressed the guards, "Since we are stopped, I will inspect this village."

A man I hadn't noticed before—an Inca lord judging by his fine clothes—cautiously voiced a protest. "But Capac Inca, if we are to make Tambo Puquio by nightfall—"

The Capac Inca cut him off with the wave of his hand. "A good ruler must always know how his people are faring!" he declaimed, then looking around asked, "Who is the chieftain of this village?"

Looking a little sick himself, Weqo Churu approached the Capac Inca with head bowed. "I am, wise Father."

"Show me around your village," the Capac Inca ordered.

Though Weqo Churu looked ill at ease, everyone else chattered excitedly. How wonderful that the Capac Inca was interested in our village! Not that there was much to see, for Qomermoya was small—only ten families. Still the Capac Inca showed such curiosity, inspecting everything, he well might have been a tokoyrikoq. He went about, removing lids from storage jars and sifting the contents of grains through his fingers; he examined cookware for cleanliness; he sampled the large jars of fermenting chicha; and at every wasi, he stood and inspected the new thatch of the roofs.

At one point, he unexpectedly turned and pointed his finger at Taruka, a short, heavy-chested youth of Charapa's age. "You, boy! Are you getting enough to eat?"

Quiet by nature, Taruka reacted as if the Capac Inca had hit him with a war club. His mouth opened, but no words came out. Charapa immediately stepped forward. "We could use more guinea pigs, wise Father," he said.

Beside me, Ipa groaned, but for the first time since his arrival, the Capac Inca smiled. He stepped forward and grabbed Charapa by the small roll of fat around his waist.

"You look like you're getting enough to eat! Maybe you're eating all the guinea pigs!"

Charapa's face turned the color of ripe molle berries, but everyone else laughed.

Returning to the roadway, the Capac Inca stopped beside Topa Inca, who now was feeling well enough to stand. The Capac Inca spoke quietly to a nearby guard, who, in response, ran toward the rear of the Capac Inca's train. Turning to face us, the Capac Inca placed one hand upon the shoulder of Weqo Churu, who looked like he was about to be executed.

"Citizens of Tahuantinsuyu, I compliment you upon your fine village. Your industry proves that the way of the Inca is best. When together we labor, everyone prospers!" The Capac Inca turned toward Weqo Churu. "I commend you for your leadership."

Though a small smile appeared on Weqo Churu's face, I saw his legs were shaking.

Taking his hand from Weqo Churu's shoulder, the Capac Inca again addressed us. "And to reward you all for your hard work..." He looked to where the guard he had sent away was now hurrying forward, leading a llama by a rope. Two other guards quickly removed the packs balanced across the llama's back. "I give you this llama. Offer its blood to Inti, then feast upon the meat in celebration of my visit!"

What a tremendous gift! All that fresh meat! "Atakachau! Atakachau!" we all cheered.

"Now I know why the Capac Inca is called 'the lover of the poor,'" I said to Charapa, who never looked happier. Next to guinea pig, fresh llama was his favorite food.

The Capac Inca raised his hand for silence. "Remember, when subjects and chieftains cordially obey the Capac Inca, Tahuantinsuyu enjoys prosperity and peace!" The Capac Inca once again smiled. Then as he turned toward his litter, Topa Inca grabbed his hand. Talking quietly to his father,

Topa Inca pointed toward me. The Capac Inca nodded his head then motioned for me to approach.

Surprised, I went forward, careful to avert my eyes. I could hear Ipa following behind me.

"Look at me," commanded the Capac Inca.

I raised my head. Up close, I could see the Capac Inca had kind eyes.

"What is your name?" he said.

"Yana Mayu."

He frowned. "That's an unusual name." Women were usually named for desirable attributes, not for a river.

"I named her, wise Father," said Ipa, "from a dream I had the night before her quicochicoy. In the dream, I saw a black river. The dream was so powerful, I felt she should be named after the river."

The Capac Inca, understanding, nodded. A dream occurring at an auspicious time—in this case my quicochicoy, the ceremony honoring my first menstruation—was very significant and a portent of the future. It was to honor Ipa's dream that I was given my adult name.

"Well, Yana Mayu, my son, Topa, would like to give you something in return for your kind assistance."

First Topa Inca returned to me the towel, which smelled heavily of vomit. Then he carefully pulled a beautiful yellow feather from his mantle. My heart began to pound as I realized I was to receive one of these lovely treasures. Topa Inca held out the feather toward me, and I took it, mumbling my thanks. Then the Capac Inca and Topa Inca returned to their litter. The bearers eased it onto their shoulders. Someone began to strike a drum, and the bearers moved forward in time to the beat. Another litter, carrying the noble I had seen earlier, followed behind the Inca's. Then came more soldiers and finally a large train of llamas, each llama carrying a load.

"Can I look at your feather?" Charapa said.

Carefully I placed the feather in the hollow of my hand. Others crowded around eager to see.

"I've never seen a feather like that," someone remarked.

I had, on the seven birds I thought had seen earlier, but I said nothing.

"I'll wrap the quill with thread and you can tie it to a string and wear it as a necklace," Ipa said. "It will bring you good luck."

Weqo Churu, who had been talking to one of the Capac Inca's guard, suddenly shouted, "I need a young man to carry these to Tambo Puquio!"

He pointed to the two packs that had been removed from the llama and now lay beside the road.

Charapa may have been named for the turtle, but he could move like a puma when he wished. He jumped behind me to hide.

"Taruka!" shouted Weqo Churu.

Charapa breathed a sigh of relief.

Then Weqo Churu shook his head. "No, not Taruka." Weqo Churu looked directly at the group of people gathered around me. I tried to better conceal Charapa by dropping my hands to my side, but Weqo Churu pointed directly at me and shouted, "Charapa!"

Charapa groaned. "Atatau! I'll miss the celebration, the dances, the stories," and most importantly, "and all that delicious llama!" He groaned again.

Reluctantly, Charapa made his way to the road. He struggled to lift the heavy packs–two woven bags tied together at the corners–but eventually he slipped his head between them so that one bag rested on his chest and the other on his back. Then, he waited until the last llama in the Capac Inca's train passed before following behind. But as he trudged along, he looked back over his shoulder. Even from a distance, I could see the pain and sadness in his eyes, but his was different than that of an Inca boy with an upset stomach. Charapa's pain was that of a young man who realized he has almost no power in this world.

Chapter 3

That evening we feasted on succulent meat, for the Capac Inca's generous gift was a young llama, not old and tough. Like everyone else, I ate until I thought my stomach like to burst. Still my discomfort did not keep me from dancing to the music of the flutes and drums, which gave me an appetite for more llama. Many acted as I did, going back for second helpings, sometimes third, until the llama was reduced to a pile of picked over bones. Then too tired to dance anymore, we all sat around a small fire while above us the congenial stars glimmered in response to our happiness. Some peopled talked quietly while others were content just to sit and pick their teeth with a llaulli thorn and occasionally sip chicha.

Leaning back upon my elbows, I bumped against a sleeping elder, so instead sat cross-legged and closed my eyes. I listened to the quiet voices, and their murmuring helped to still the thumping of the drums, silent now, but still pulsing within my head. I opened my eyes and looked up at the stars, which seemed but an arm's length away. Again, I closed my eyes, but not quite shut so that the brilliant stars radiated long, shimmering rays of light. The small wind who journeyed down our valley each night suddenly grew stronger. No longer warm from dancing, I pulled my lliqlla tightly about me then rubbed my arms until warm again. I did not want the celebration to end. I could not have imagined anything better than to be warm, to be full of good food, and, most importantly, to be with the people I loved. And this too: to be up so late at night! Nights without celebrations seemed so long, with little to do but sleep until Inti's return.

I had my ocarina with me and began to play a tune, but softly so as not to disturb the others. Still, one by one, people stopped talking to listen to the melody. I blew a little louder. Someone started to sing and others joined in:

> Oh, Inti,
> Where do you journey
> When day has ended?
> Oh, Inti,
> by deep roads
> beneath where I sleep.

Oh, Inti,
The darkness
Brings me such sadness.
To the east
Will I go
To greet your return.

After the song was over, we sat in silence. No one made to retire, even though tomorrow would come too soon and with it another long day of hard labor.

"Ipa, tell us a story!" demanded a child. It was like setting a spark to dry wood. Suddenly, all the children were pleading: "Ipa, Ipa, tell us a story!"

Slowly, Ipa stood up. Though Qillamama had completed her journey across the sky, the fire illuminated Ipa's face.

"You little foxes! Don't think you can fool me! You only want me to tell you a story so you don't have to go to bed."

The children laughed at having been caught out.

"I ought to tell on you to the Capac Inca. Then he'd throw you all into the Uatay Uaci Zancay for your deceit!"

Tullu, the child sitting next to me, shivered. "Ooo! That's the prison with the hungry, wild animals!"

I sneaked my hand up under her lliqlla and wiggled my fingers across her stomach. "Where they'll throw you in with the poisonous snakes!"

She squealed in delight.

To everyone's surprise, Ipa began to twirl an aillo over her head. I'd never seen her hold this weapon before, but she handled it with skill. The children grew silent as the two stones, joined by a short piece of rope, whirled faster and faster. If Ipa didn't have everyone's attention before, she did now. Even the sleeping elders woke at the sound of the aillo's menacing whirr. Suddenly, Ipa slammed the stones to the ground with a solid whump!

Everyone was stunned by this performance. Ipa let the silence build for a moment before she spoke. "Well, since the Capac Inca is not here to give you the punishment you deserve, I'll tell you a story of someone who was imprisoned in a cave for being disobedient and cruel. And may it be a lesson to you!"

"Kachi!" a child shouted.

"Shhh!" someone else ordered. We had all heard this story before, but it was a good one.

"Today, you were privileged to see the Capac Inca," Ipa said. "Now I want to tell you about the very first Capac Inca, and how the city of Qosqo, where the Capac Inca lives, came to be.

"Long, long ago the world was in darkness, so Wiraqocha, the great creator, placed Inti in the sky along with Qillamama and all the stars. He created Pachamama, the earth, and placed people and animals upon her. Finally, on an island in Lake Titikaka, he made two brothers and named them Manka and Kachi. Wiraqocha commanded these two brothers to find a fertile valley and there build a great city. To Manka, the older of the two, Wiraqocha gave a staff of pure gold to test the richness of the soil. If the soil was good, the staff would sink deep into it, and the brothers would know they had found the right place.

"The brothers' journey began underground, deep within Pachamama. For days and days, they traveled down dark tunnels, which twisted and turned like the web of a spider. Eventually they came to a large cave with a small opening through which Inti's light streamed. The brothers crawled through the opening, and when they stood up, they saw tall mountains covered in snow and green valleys where clear rivers flowed. The brothers walked over the tall mountains, and when they came to a valley, Manka planted the golden staff into the soil, but none was rich enough to hold it.

"Finally they came to a valley that surpassed all the others in beauty. Inti's warm light, filtered by the rising mists, made the valley look as if it were made of gold. Herds of snow-white llamas grazed upon golden grass, and there were many handsome people tilling the fields. "Manka pushed the golden staff into the soil, and the ground swallowed it up! Thus, the brothers knew they had found the place to build their city."

Ipa picked up the aillo and began to whirl it above her head. She held the aillo by one stone, letting the other spin on its rope, far from her hand.

"Now the people of the valley feared the brother whose name was Kachi for he was conceited and cruel."

Ipa twirled the aillo a little faster.

"Kachi thought the beautiful valley his plaything. He killed the beautiful llamas with his aillo just for fun."

She spun the aillo faster still.

"He shattered the sacred places, the huacas, with his stones!"

Ipa stepped forward. Now the aillo whirred alarmingly above our heads! "But most of all he liked to kill the people!"

With a snap of her wrist, Ipa brought the stone of the aillo smashing down upon the head of a small boy. A woman screamed, but the stone bounced harmlessly off the boy's head. Before anyone could react, Ipa struck the startled boy again. Then everyone began to laugh at Ipa's trick. She had replaced one of the stones of the aillo with a soft ball of llama wool!

Ipa continued above the laughter. "Manka, fearing the anger of both the gods and the people of the valley, thought of a plan to stop his brother's cruelty. He ordered Kachi to retrieve a cup made of gold that he had left inside the cave. This Kachi agreed to do, but only because he was very fond of gold. When Kachi got to the cave, he ordered the gatekeeper to guard the entrance while he went inside to get the golden cup. But Manka had already made other plans with the gatekeeper, and while Kachi was inside the cave, the gatekeeper dropped a great boulder in front of the entrance, trapping Kachi. Kachi pushed against the rock with all his strength, but the rock would not budge. He kicked the rock, but the boulder still did not move. Finally, in a rage, he beat against the rock with his mighty fists, but to no avail.

"When the people of the valley heard how Manka had tricked Kachi, they helped Manka build a great city which Manka named Qosqo. The people liked Manka so much, they made him the ruler, and that is how Manka became the very first Capac Inca."

Ipa had finished her story. For a while, no one spoke. Tullu had fallen asleep. Then a child asked, "What happened to Kachi? Did he get out of the cave?"

"No one knows for certain," Ipa said, "but south of Qosqo there is a village called Tambo Toco that is surrounded by hills riddled with caves. The people who live in Tambo Toco say that on some nights, like tonight when it's very dark, they can hear coming from inside the mountain the voice of a man screaming!"

I know I was not the only one who felt a chill down my back, thinking of screams coming out of a mountain.

"Erraaarr!" Someone roared. Children screamed. Even a few adults jumped up, alarmed. Weqo Churu, whose roar it was, stood with a big grin on his face. Then, everyone laughed at being fooled a second time.

"What happened?" Tullu said, suddenly awake.

"I think Weqo Churu just announced it's time to go to bed."

Chapter 4

"Yana, if you don't get your miserable llama off me, I'm going to slice him up and make him into charqui!"

Half asleep, I tried to think why Ipa would want to dry meat in the middle of the night. Then I felt a gentle puff of air against my face, bringing with it a not unpleasant smell of half-digested grass. Chumpi, my llama, had managed to wiggle through the entryway into our wasi once again. He was now lying on the ground between Ipa and myself, his long neck resting upon my chest while Ipa was pinned by Chumpi's broad flank.

Pushing Chumpi's face away, I slowly sat up. "Chumpi, you're getting too old for this."

"Too fat, you mean," muttered Ipa. "How can such a big llama get through such a small opening?"

I looked at the entryway. The heavy curtain was twisted aside, allowing the cold air to enter in. I could also see it was almost daylight and knew we had slept late. I pushed off the top half of my chusi and stood up. Chumpi stood also, and I scratched him along his neck. "Chumpi just wanted to know why we are being such sleepyheads."

Ipa slowly sat up, her back creaking like a dead tree branch in the wind. "It's the curse of old age that you wake up feeling like you drank too much chicha the night before when you hadn't drunk any at all."

"Here, let me help you up."

Ipa pushed my hand away. "Save your kindnesses for Topa Inca. I'll get up when I'm ready. Now go fetch some water for tea."

Quickly I wrapped my lliqlla around me and clasped it together at my throat with a topu.

"And take old buzzard breath with you!" Ipa commanded.

"Chumpi's breath doesn't smell bad," I said.

"Yes, and one's own farts don't stink!"

I crawled through the opening, knowing Chumpi would follow. Kusi, wide awake, beckoned me with waving arms. I lifted him out of his play pit where he slept nights and pressed his shivering body against mine. Kusi knew that any cry he made would bring a sharp reprimand from Ipa, but as I pressed his cold body against me and warmed his face with mine, he quietly whimpered.

I hated that my little brother had to sleep outside. I thought it cruel, even though I understood the reason: to toughen him to the harshness of our climate. His little nose felt like ice. I rubbed mine against his, and Kusi gurgled happily.

"Yana, the water!" Ipa yelled from inside the wasi.

I pried Kusi's fingers from my lliqlla and set him back in his play pit. Selecting a clay jar with a handle, I swung it back and forth as I strode toward the stream. Chumpi appeared beside me, and I placed the heavy jar upon his back. "Good! you're going to help me carry the water." Chumpi stepped forward so quickly, I nearly dropped the jar.

I had to travel a long way down stream to find a pool deep enough to immerse the jar. Never had I seen the stream with so little water in it. Setting the jar on the bank, I studied my reflection in the water. I still had kantuta flowers clinging to my hair. I removed the wilted blossoms and tossed them out into the stream where they floated upon the surface, drifting aimlessly in the sluggish current. Then I washed my face. The cold water sent a shiver down my back. Chumpi, who hated getting wet, cautiously lowered his head for a drink. I splashed water on him, and he jumped back, alarmed.

"You and Kusi are a pair, both afraid of a little cold."

Chumpi shook his head then wandered upstream beyond the range of my splashing. Briefly I watched his rolling gait, then feeling thirsty myself, drank deeply from the stream. As I wiped my lips with the back of my hand, I said a prayer to Pachamama, thanking her for her gift of water. I also prayed to Intuillapa, asking him to send down water from his river in the night sky so that our stream would flow freely once more.

Lifting the water jar, I started back. The jar was heavier by the addition of the water, so I stopped halfway along to rest. Qomermoya, late to awaken, was now showing signs of life. Several children hurried toward me, carrying jars to fetch water. In the air was the smoke of burning llama dung. Rested, I again hoisted the water jar and brought it to the place where we prepared our meals, just outside our wasi. Ipa sat before the clay oven, feeding pellets of dried llama dung onto the small flame.

"Remember there's only you and me this morning," Ipa said, as I poured water into a fire-hardened clay pot, blackened from smoke.

"And Kusi," I reminded her.

"Since when does Kusi get his own cup of tea? He can sip some of mine."

From a recess in the wall of our wasi, I removed a jar containing dried bilyea leaves, which I crushed in my hands and brushed into the water for tea. To this I also added dried capuli berries for sweetness. I placed the pot atop the oven then lifted Kusi from his play pit and warmed him in my arms while waiting for the water to boil.

"I doubt Charapa will race back from Tambo Puquio this morning to help with the repair of the irrigation ditches," Ipa said. She chuckled. "That lazy boy! I'm sure we'll not see him until just before evening meal, when the day's work is done."

I defended Charapa. "Since Father left to serve in the Capac Inca's army, Charapa has worked hard, tending our family's field."

Ipa clucked her tongue. "You know as well as I do that Weqo Churu has ordered Taruka to work alongside Charapa until your father returns. The way Charapa likes to talk and Taruka to listen, I bet it's Taruka who does most of the work."

Ipa pulled her hands away from the fire where she had been warming them. "That Taruka may not say much, but he's a good worker." Ipa looked up at me. "He'll make some woman a good husband."

I kept my face expressionless, not wanting to encourage such talk. It had been only a year since my first menstruation. "I don't want to marry yet. Maybe when I'm sixteen." I said sixteen to appease Ipa, but I hoped to put off marriage as long as possible –until eighteen, the age at which I would be required to marry.

"Atatau! You young women make me sick! When I was sixteen, I was already pregnant with my second child!"

I quickly changed the subject. "After our tea, I'll air out the chusis."

"No! I need you to weave. We must produce three more lengths of cloth before the Coya Raymi festival if we are to pay our tribute to the Capac Inca. Warp your loom with the black thread you've been spinning. Do it quickly so that after morning meal you can take your loom with you as you go to watch the llama herds."

Though I knew better than to argue with Ipa, I didn't want her to have to air the chusis; crawling in and out of the wasi aggravated the rheumatism in her back. I knew if I worked quickly, I could do both jobs before morning meal.

But Ipa knew what I was thinking. "I can manage. I'm not dead yet!"

I looked down upon Ipa's head with its few strands of gray hair. Her face was deeply lined, which, to me, only increased her beauty. Once again I realized how much I loved her. Ipa was my father's aunt, and when my mother died giving birth to Kusi, Ipa had come to live with us. It was Ipa who made my brother and me feel we were still a family, and she helped to fill the empty place in my heart made by my mother's death.

I had loved my mother dearly. She had been so kind—perhaps too kind, for as Ipa once said, it is only those who harden themselves to life who survive. Yet surely my mother had fought hard against death so that Kusi could be born. Though it had been more than a year since my mother began her journey on the underground road, I still sometimes heard her cries of pain, especially as I lay at night unable to sleep. It was only by running to the stream and plunging my face into the icy water that I could silence those heart-rending cries.

"What I miss most is being able to weave," Ipa said, examining her bent and twisted fingers. "I loved how swiftly the beautiful cloth grew before my hands." As she rubbed her swollen knuckles, something happened I had not seen before: Ipa's eyes actually filled with tears.

"Ipa?"

"Atatau!" she cried, dropping her hands. To cover her embarrassment, she threw a rock at Chumpi, who, for once, was lying well outside the cooking area. "Self-pity makes me want to puke!" Ipa pointed a crooked finger up at me. "Remember, Yana, you can't water maize with tears! Now, pour our tea. The water's hot enough!"

I handed Kusi to her then carefully filled two cups. The little tea that remained I poured into the cup belonging to my father. Ipa handed Kusi back to me then slowly pushed herself onto her feet. I followed as she carried my father's cup to our huaca, a special recess in the wall of our wasi where dwelled the figures of the spirits who protected our family. A small llama carved from quishuar wood represented Urcuchillay whose two eyes could be seen at night, looking down, watching over our llama herds. A long, smooth stone placed upright honored Pachamama from whom came all life. The last figure was of special significance now that my father was again away serving in the Capac Inca's army. It was a piece of bronze in the shape of Inti, a gift from my father's commanding officer who gave these awards only to soldiers who had shown themselves brave in battle. My father had wedged the image into the crevice of a jagged piece of snow-white quartz. The effect was that of Inti rising above a snowy mountain peak. Before this lovely representation, Ipa placed my father's cup then stepped back and extended her right arm, palm upward.

"O spirits," she intoned, "you who have given your children glorious life, protect us. May we live in health, sheltered from danger, and may those we love return safely to us." Ipa didn't mention my father or brother by name lest an evil spirit hear their names in passing and place a curse upon them. Yet as we stood in silence, I wondered about my father. Where was he? What was he doing? Perhaps at this very moment, he was also drinking tea and offering a portion of it to the gods asking, in turn, for our safety. When my father left to join the army, shortly after Kusi's ratuchicoy, the ceremony given at his first haircut, I felt as if part of my heart had been taken from me. Every day I prayed for his safe return. I prayed as well for the health and safety of the other members of our small family, for I could not bear to surrender any more of my heart.

Our prayers concluded, Ipa and I returned to sip our tea beside the oven with Kusi sitting between us. Suddenly Chumpi emitted the clicking noise a llama makes when alarmed. Looking up, we saw Weqo Churu staring down at us. Though actually a kind man, Weqo Churu looked like a fierce bird of prey. Perhaps it was because his bent nose resembled the beak of a hawk, or because, like an owl, his dark eyes were burrowed beneath his protruding brow.

He spoke no greeting, but got straight to the point. "Ipa, I need your skills as our camasca this morning. Ukumari is bent over with the cramps. He thinks he's dying and smells as bad as if he had. I need him to help clean the irrigation ditches today."

"Atatau! It's because that glutton gorged himself on too much llama last night. I saw him going back for a fourth helping. Now, he's all plugged up. I'll make him a laxative of checche root–that'll clean him out in no time." Ipa chuckled. "He won't like the taste though."

"It'll serve him right," Weqo Churu said, smiling briefly before becoming serious again. "Sumaq Uya is not doing so well. She never complains, but her daughter says she can barely walk. Her daughter also thinks Sumaq Uya is having bad dreams because she mutters in her sleep."

Ipa sighed "I think Sumaq Uya might be preparing to walk the underground road." Ipa started to stand. Whereas Ipa rarely accepted my help, she gladly took hold of Weqo Churu's offered hand.

"I'll gather some chilca leaves," she said. "A poultice of the leaves helps to draw up the blood and relieves the pain of old bones. That should help Sumaq Uya to move about more easily. Then when she's feeling better, she may be willing to talk about her dreams." Ipa turned to me. "Yana, fetch me the bag with my medicines."

I quickly crawled into the wasi. Ipa always kept her medicines near where she slept. Outside, I handed her the large woven bag.

"I'll be back before morning meal," she said. "Remember what I said about warping your loom."

As she walked away toward Ukumari's wasi, I expected Weqo Churu to follow. Instead he moved closer to me and fixed me with his most hawk-like stare.

"That was a foolish thing you did yesterday. You were lucky you slipped, otherwise that guard would have taken your head off. Next time keep out of the way of your betters, especially Incas. Between you and that disrespectful brother of yours saying we could use more guinea pig..." He shook his head. "Both of you must learn to control your impulses, otherwise you'll bring disgrace upon us all!" Weqo Churu jabbed me in the shoulder with a stiff finger. "Remember, you are a Hatunruna, a commoner! The less Hatunrunas interact with Incas, the better off we are! Do you understand?"

I nodded, trying to look contrite, but in my heart, I felt anger. The real reason Weqo Churu was scolding me was because he feared the censure of those above him. Why couldn't he admit that good things had come from my showing Topa Inca a little kindness?

Then I realized I was not being fair to Weqo Churu, for he was a good chieftain and showed it in many ways. For one, he never played favorites with any member of our village, and not because to do so was forbidden by the Incas, for some chieftains were clever about getting around this law. Weqo Churu did not play favorites because he was fair-minded. When he assigned work, he made sure all shared equally in the difficult tasks. Our village was like a group of musicians playing together harmoniously because no one felt unfairly put upon.

"I'm sorry, Weqo Churu. I will try harder to think first and control my impulsiveness." I meant what I told him. I would try, though I didn't know if I would succeed.

"Very well," he responded gruffly. He turned away then quickly turned back again. "That yellow feather of yours—ask Ipa about the birds with such feathers. She's seen them."

He hurried away before I could ask him to tell me more. His comment reminded me I had not told Ipa of the seven magnificent birds I thought I had seen. She and I would have much to talk about at morning meal.

I set Kusi back in his play pit, then started my first task: making a pot of locro for morning meal. I built up the fire in the oven then set a small clay pot, half filled with water, atop it. To the water I added potatoes, peppers, and small piece of charqui made from guinea pig. I sliced fresh nasturtium root and added it to the other ingredients. I threw a couple of slices to Chumpi who had been watching me, hoping for a tidbit. I was glad Ipa wasn't there to scold me for wasting food.

Next I began my warp. I took the tension poles of my loom and set them into the ground and attached a crosspiece to keep them upright. Then I wound thread between the poles moving in and out so the crossing threads would prevent the warp from tangling. This took a long time, for the cloth was to be a chusi. Because a sleeper lies upon one half of his chusi and pulls the remainder over him, a chusi must be twice as long as a person is tall. Several times I stopped my work to stir the pot of locro and to add llama dung to the fire. By the time my warp was tied on, my fingers were aching. I interwove slender sticks crossways to further prevent the threads from tangling then rolled up the warp, careful to maintain the tension. Later I would stretch the tension poles apart by tying one stick to a pole or tree and the other stick to a wide strap that goes around my back. By leaning back upon the strap, I could maintain the tension on the warp as I wove threads crossways through it.

This done, I inspected the locro once again. The strings of meat had started to separate and the potatoes to soften. The fire was nearly out so I left the pot on the oven to stay warm while I quickly gathered the items for Kusi's bath. Seeing this, Kusi slapped his hands excitedly upon the edge of his play pit and jumped up and down. I realized it would not be long before he would be able to crawl out of the pit by himself.

Lifting up Kusi, I spied Chumpi eyeing the pot of locro. "I know what you're thinking, Chumpi!"

Chumpi looked at me with his ears upright and forward as if to say, "Who, me?"

I think you better come with me and Kusi," I told him.

Though he couldn't answer back, I am certain Chumpi understood me, for a llama is a very intelligent animal. Our lives are intertwined with the lives of llamas, for without them we would not be able to survive. That is why we call llamas our silent brothers.

At the stream, I removed Kusi's clothing then warmed the icy water in my mouth before spraying it over him. I was careful not to wet the top of his head which, for reasons of health, was never washed. I wet a piece of paqpa root and rubbed it between my hands to make a lather, then rubbed the lather over Kusi's body. He laughed delightedly as I tickled him under his arms and across the soles of his feet. I loved to hear my little brother's laughter. The way his cheeks dimpled and his eyes shone reminded me of my mother. I lathered up more of the paqpa root and blew the suds at him. It was a game we always played. He tried to bat away the tiny bubbles before they touched his face.

It was when I was rinsing off the soap, again by warming the water first in my mouth, that Ipa found us.

"Atatau! What are you doing?" Quickly, she dipped both of her hands into the stream and hurled handfuls of water over Kusi's body. When the first icy wave hit him, Kusi went rigid, his eyes wide. Then he let out an ear-piecing scream.

"It's cold!" I cried.

"Of course, it's cold! That's how streams are. Show me a warm stream, and I'll use that instead." She continued to fling handfuls of water—even getting Kusi's head wet—until icy water streamed off his arms and legs and pooled on the flat rock he sat upon.

When Ipa paused to catch her breath, I whisked Kusi into the air, holding him there for a moment to let some of the water drain off, then quickly wrapped a towel around him and began to rub him dry. As he grew warm, he ceased crying. Kusi's crying was as painful to me as his laughter was pleasing.

"Foolish girl!" Ipa said. "You think you're being kind to him by coddling him, but you're not. The cold water strengthens him, so when he grows older, he'll be able to withstand cold and not fear it. Do you want him always to act like a baby?"

Ipa's scolding stung me like the icy water stung Kusi. "You're just like Weqo Churu. Now I suppose you're going to tell me I was stupid to show kindness to Topa Inca." I quickly reached down for the paqpa root, intending to take it and walk away, but Ipa gripped my arm and squeezed it hard, then harder still until I was forced to look at her.

When she had my attention, she released my arm. Though her face looked stern, her voice was gentle when she spoke. "Do not be angry with me, Yana. I'm old and not much use, but still there are things I can teach you. You must understand that sometimes a kindness given now may result in greater suffering later on. Someday, you may have to hurt someone, perhaps someone you love, for their own good. You must be prepared to do that if necessary."

I hung my head, sorry I had spoken to her in anger. Ipa was only trying to teach me to be the adult I was supposed to be.

"About Weqo Churu," she continued, "he has much to worry about, especially since there's been so little rain, and the harvest was poor. He also fears that attracting the attention of the Incas will bring disgrace upon our village. I think he worries too much. For myself, I am glad you offered Topa Inca the towel to clean himself. The boy needs kindness because..." she hesitated, as if deciding whether to say more, "...because he is dying."

Disbelief must have shown in my face, for she repeated herself.

"Yes, Topa Inca is dying."

I couldn't believe my ears. Kusi, too young to understand my distress, playfully grabbed my nose, and I took his tiny hand away and held it in mine. "How do you know?"

She motioned to Kusi. "I'll tell you as you get him dressed."

I placed the towel upon a flat rock, stood Kusi upon the towel, and pulled over his head his unku, a sleeveless garment that fell to his knees.

"While the Capac Inca was inspecting our village" Ipa said, "I had a talk with the old Qollohuayan, the man you saw giving Topa Inca some medicine. Atakachau! he's a great camasca! I never talked to anyone who knew so much about medicinal plants. And he's also a Yacarca, one who can summon the voice of the gods from fire!"

I stared at Ipa, hoping she wouldn't stray off onto her favorite subject: methods of healing.

"Anyway, it was he who told me Topa Inca is dying. The vomiting we saw? It happens frequently, and Topa Inca is growing weak due to a lack of nourishment. In Qosqo, the Wilka Uma sacrifices two hundred white llamas a day on Topa Inca's behalf. Along with feeding the blood of these animals to the gods, he examines the animals' organs, but none of the organs have revealed the nature of Topa Inca's illness. They have even bled Topa Inca several times, yet still he grows weaker. That is why the Capac Inca is taking Topa Inca to Tambo Puquio, for he hopes the baths there will help him. The camasca I talked to believes they will do him no good, but is glad, nevertheless, that the Capac Inca is away from Qosqo. In Qosqo, the Wilka Uma, who is covetous of his power, has prevented the camasca from summoning the voices from fire. The camasca told me he hopes to perform a ceremony while at Tambo Puquio and hear for himself what the gods have to say about Topa Inca's sickness."

All this explained to me the sadness I had seen in Topa Inca's eyes. And something else: "It is because Topa Inca is ill that we've had so little rain and a poor harvest."

Ipa smiled. "I see not all of my teaching has been wasted. Yes, sickness in people and sickness in Pachamama are one and the same thing. To cure one is to cure the other. When someone like Topa Inca, who is a descendant of Inti, is sick then Pachamama suffers more than usual. And because Pachamama suffers, we of Tahuantinsuyu suffer as well."

"Then if we heal either Pachamama or Topa Inca, the rains will return. What exactly must we do?"

Ipa shook her head. "That's just it. All the usual observances are not working. Something special must be done only no one knows what."

"What happens if Topa Inca dies? Who will be the next Capac Inca?"

"I'm afraid if Topa Inca dies, matters could get worse: a prolonged drought and perhaps famine. It is best not to dwell on uncertainties, but to hope Topa Inca recovers. In the meantime, we will pray for him and offer sacrifices to the gods on his behalf. As to who would become the next Capac Inca, don't worry your head about that. The Capac Inca has more sons than our village has llamas."

True, I thought, but perhaps none he loves as much as the sad little boy with the beautiful mantle of yellow feathers. Which reminded me: "Ipa, Weqo Churu told me you've seen the birds with yellow feathers like the one Topa Inca gave me."

She grinned. "Did he? He just wants you to hear about what happens to foolish girls who disobey." She picked up the paqpa root. "All right, I'll tell you while we eat our meal. My old stomach is making noises like bees trapped in a jar."

Chapter 5

The locro was delicious even though the meat was a little tough. I had to chew it tender before Kusi could eat it, which he did greedily. I let him sip some of the broth while I chewed some more.

"Atatau!" Ipa exclaimed, pulling a bit of meat from her mouth. "You come into this world with no teeth, and you leave with no teeth. I think I'll stick with the broth. Old people don't need meat anyway."

She sipped from her bowl, set it down, then licked the small salt cube that was always available at mealtimes.

"Ah! Nothing brings out the flavor of food like salt!"

This must have reminded her of something, for she sat with a distant look in her eyes. I sipped from my bowl and waited for her to speak.

"Let me to tell you how I came to see the birds with the yellow feathers. As you know, my father was also a camasca and had a great interest in plants. When he had learned all there was to know about the local plants, he traveled to other places to find new plants and to talk to other camascas about their uses. The Capac Inca has always encouraged the exchange of knowledge among camascas, even if in general, he disapproves of people traveling far from their villages. The Capac Inca has even sent camascas to faraway places to study the medicinal plants used by different people.

"So when my father was given an opportunity to join a group of camascas traveling to the jungle to study the plants of that region, he naturally seized it. As you know, the jungle is far away, across the mountains to the east. It's a very unpleasant place, hot even though it rains all the time. There are many dangerous animals like jaguars and bears. And not only large animals, but poisonous snakes and reptiles. There's even a tiny little frog whose poison will kill you like that!" Ipa snapped her fingers.

"The people who live there are very primitive–like animals really–and they're not friendly except a few who wish to trade with us. Yet they know how to survive in that awful place and can attack strangers without being seen. That is why they have never been conquered by the armies of the Capac Inca. Some of them even capture people and eat them!

"Still, there is a great variety of plant life in the jungle. The trees grow as thick as grass, and beneath them grow strange plants with beautiful flowers, many of which produce strong medicines. My father, through trading, had come to know of some of these plants and their uses, especially coca, but he had never seen the place where the plants grew or talked to a camasca who lived in the jungle. To go on this journey was a tremendous opportunity for him and for the people of our village who would profit from his increased knowledge.

"But my father had one problem: a foolish daughter. Of all my brothers and sisters, I was the one most like my father, for I also had a great interest in plants and wanted to know their uses. It gave my father great pleasure to teach me, and he was surprised how quickly I learned.

"I asked my father to take me with him to the jungle. He told me children were not allowed and not to ask again. This blunt response was like a slap in the face, for I already thought myself a great camasca. Atatau! For such a small girl, I had a big head. What did I know, really? I hadn't even menstruated yet.

"I obeyed my father and never again asked to go with him. Nevertheless, I went about moping and feeling sorry for myself.

"Then I had an idea! I would secretly follow my father and the other camascas and not show myself until they were too far from our village for my father to order me back. Thus, he would be forced to let me continue along with him.

"Atatau! How selfish I was to take advantage of my father this way. But that is what I did. By the time my father was ready to leave, so was I, for I had secreted away food—enough to last me many days. It was easy to follow the camascas, for the road across the highlands was well marked, and I was able to stay behind and not be seen. At night, I'd sneak up to their camp and spy on them before finding a place to bed down in the shelter of boulders. I dared not light a fire, but had thought to bring food I could eat without cooking: charqui and maize cakes. You see I was clever, if wicked.

"Once by a stream, I sneaked up really close to their camp, and hid behind a big huayau tree. It was a pleasant scene that greeted my eyes. Several camascas, my father among them, were discussing plants they had gathered throughout the day. Others were soaking their feet in a shallow pool of water. Off to one side, near where the pack llamas were grazing, three camascas played music while a fourth demonstrated a curing dance. Everyone was so immersed in their activities, I think I could have helped myself from the pot of delicious smelling locro bubbling over a wood fire, and no one would have noticed.

"Yet as I watched, I began to wonder what effect my appearance would have upon this happy fellowship. As I slipped downstream to find a place for the night, I began to doubt the wisdom of my plan. I realized it wouldn't do to just suddenly burst in upon the company of camascas. I would have to wait for an advantageous moment. But as it turned out the moment of my discovery was chosen for me.

"As they started into the mountains, the way become steep. That steepness, along with the fact that several of the camascas were old, slowed the company's progress. Several times I had to wait beside the road to avoid getting too close and being seen.

"After one such period of waiting, I again trailed along behind. I'd just picked a beautiful red flower I'd not seen before, and as I walked along examining it, I forgot about the others. Suddenly I came around a sharp bend and ran right into the camascas. They had all stopped, and were anxiously examining an injured llama. My appearance produced a few curious looks, but, save for my father, none of great surprise. After all, I could have been a local person, traveling from a nearby village. But the look on my father's face was quite different from the others. At first, he looked confused. He rubbed his eyes as if to clear them of a strange vision. I smiled at him to assure him I was real.

"It was then that my father's face became a storm. Dark clouds swirled in his eyes. His eyebrows bent down like tree branches under the weight of snow. Across his cheekbones, the skin stretched taut as when a mighty wind rams the surface of a lake. Worst of all, his mouth opened and thunder came out.

"'You're not allowed here!' he roared. Then leaping across the short distance that separated us, he grabbed me by the top of my lliqlla and lifted me off the ground. Suddenly I was flying through the air in the direction I had come. I hit the rocky ground, and the air gushed from my lungs. It seemed an eternity before I could breathe again. Then as I tasted blood from a cut on my lip, I became aware of voices talking excitedly, though none my father's. I was also aware that something strange had happened when I collided with the ground. My childhood had left my body, but unlike the air, I could not suck it back in again. It seemed that I was seeing the world for the first time. I cupped one hand around loose stones. Here's what the world truly is, I thought. It feels like a sharp rock and tastes like blood.

"I wanted to cry, but found that had been taken from me also. I heard footsteps approaching and closed my eyes out of fear, for I knew it was my father, coming to hurt me again. Oddly, I did not care. Then I felt his two arms between me and the ground. Once more I was lifted up, but this time my father gently carried me a short distance then sat down with me lying across his lap. I did not open my eyes, but could hear a trickle of water close by. I flinched as he pressed snow against the cut on my lip, but didn't cry out.

"Suddenly I felt a spray of warm water on my face. It washed away the dirt and returned to my world some things not sharp and hard. I opened my eyes and looked up at my father. A few drops of water dripped off his chin. Thankfully, the storm had passed from his face.

"One of the camascas, old in years, came and placed an arm on my father's shoulder, but before he could say anything, my father spoke: 'I will take her home.'

"Quick to protest, I sat up, 'No! I can go home by myself. You must continue on to the jungle with the others.'

"The old camasca silenced me by placing a calloused finger across my lips. 'There is nothing bad that happens without some good,' he said. 'The llama has broken its leg. This is very bad, but tonight we can eat fresh llama, and we can dry the remaining meat for our journey. Still, someone will have to carry the llama's packs.'

"I leaped to my feet. 'Let me do it!' I cried.

"The old man looked at me skeptically.

"I turned to my father. 'Please, Father, let me carry the packs! I know I can carry them! I won't complain, and I'll cook your meals, and–'

"My father cut me off with a wave of his hand, but I saw a look of relief on his face.

"'Do you think she'll complain?' the old camasca asked my father.

"My father shook his head.

"'Then, perhaps she has arrived at the right time.'

"In the days and weeks that followed, I came to curse the day I chose to disobey my father and follow him. The packs weighed nearly as much as I did. How I managed to carry them over the mountains, I don't know, for no one even looked at me, let alone helped me carry the load. Once going over the highest pass, the old camasca gave me some coca leaves to chew, which helped with my altitude sickness. All told, my experience resulted in more pain than pleasure, though I did see many wonderful things. I never saw a jaguar, but I saw a jungle chieftain wearing a robe made of a jaguar's hide. And I got to look down upon the jungle forest and see how the trees covered Pachamama like water fills the ocean. And once we stopped at a spring where salt leached out of the surrounding clay bluffs. There hundreds of birds feasted upon the salt and other minerals. Some were small with thick bills, and with feathers colored a brilliant green like unripe lucumas. Some of the birds were big–longer than a man's arm. Two types of these looked exactly alike except in color. One type was brilliant red like the curtain of the Capac Inca's litter; the color of the other was–"

"Yellow," I interrupted. "The same yellow as Topa Inca's mantle. And the top of their wings was blue. When they flew, their long tails stretched out behind them straight as an arrow."

Ipa looked at me, blinking. "How did you know that? Did Weqo Churu tell you?"

I shook my head. "I saw them yesterday, or I think I did." Then I told her about my strange experience of the day before; how the sky had gone dark and only returned to normal with the passing of the birds.

"Was this just before the arrival of the Capac Inca?" Ipa said.

I nodded.

"I thought I saw a strange expression on your face, but in the excitement of the Capac Inca's visit, I forgot to ask you about it."

Ipa looked away and tapped her chin, as she often did while thinking. "Did anyone else see the birds?"

"I don't think so. No one said anything about them."

Ipa nodded. "Then the birds were not real, but a vision."

"How do you know that?" I said, suddenly feeling uncomfortable.

She began to count upon her fingers "One, no one saw the birds but you. Two, I have lived my whole life in Qomermoya, and never have I seen those birds except the one time I went to the jungle with my father. And three, I've known since you were a small child that you have the gift of visions, whether you believe you do or not." Ipa again tapped her chin. "But what does this vision mean?"

I let her think about that while I thought about the story she had told me. One thought soon came to mind. "You said your story is about what happens to someone who disobeys, but I think matters worked out well. Both you and your father got to go to the jungle and to learn about plants that grow there."

Ipa shook her head. "The truth of a thing is often difficult to see. Sometimes it depends on your perspective. Yes, I got to see the jungle, but that was insignificant compared to the really important thing that happened to me: I grew up."

Ipa straightened one of her legs. "Yet think about it from my father's point of view. Had the llama not broken its leg, my father would have been forced to take me home, for, being the loving father he was, he would not have let me return alone. And what about my mother and my brothers and sisters? I had told no one of my plan to follow my father. Was it right that I caused them to worry needlessly when I suddenly disappeared?"

"But isn't it strange that the llama broke its leg at the very moment you met up with the camascas?"

Ipa smiled. "Yes, I thought of that, too. Perhaps I was meant to go with my father. It is certain I never again had the opportunity to see the jungle. Like I said, the truth of a thing is often difficult to see."

Ipa looked at our empty bowls encrusted with dried broth. "Atatau! What are we doing wasting the day with all this prattle? Take your loom and go help watch the llamas. Even the younger boys will be needed today to help clear the ditches." Ipa pointed an angry finger at Chumpi. "And take that llama with you. If that beggar takes one more step closer, I'm going to throw a pot at his head!"

Chumpi, who had been creeping toward a few nasturtium roots I had set aside, turned and made a hasty retreat. Smiling, I lifted Kusi, and placed him in his play pit. But as I turned to get my loom, Ipa's voice stopped me.

"Yana, that vision of yours. I think it means..." She took me by the arm and turned me so she could look me straight in the eyes. "I know this will make me sound like a crazy, old woman, but I think it means that your fate and Topa Inca's are now somehow tied together."

Chapter 6

Though everything in Tahuantinsuyu belonged to the Capac Inca, in practice the land and the llamas were divided three ways. A third of the llamas we tended belonged to the wilka camayocs, the priests. These llamas were pure of color—usually white or black—and were used as sacrifices to the gods. Chumpi with his wide belt of brown, and splotches of black and tan would have made an unsuitable sacrifice, for which I was grateful.

Another third of the llamas belonged to the Capac Inca. Though these were used mostly for transporting goods, they were also used to feed the Capac Inca's family along with the other members of the Inca nobility. And, in time of need, the Capac Inca sent llamas to any village whose own llamas had died of disease.

Finally, there were the llamas that belonged to our village. Though each family was permitted to have its own small herd, in Qomermoya we shared the llamas collectively—except for a few like Chumpi who were pets. This arrangement worked well, for it eliminated any resentment that might have resulted from one family's llamas dying while another's did not.

Herding the llamas had become hard work, for the grass in the pasture had withered due to the lack of rain, forcing us to move the herd high up into the mountains where the slopes were too steep and rocky to be terraced into fields for crops. From up there, the terraces looked like steps made by giants while our wasis appeared no bigger than the small square patterns in the fabric I was weaving.

As the llamas spread out across the face of the mountain—Chumpi among them—I watched that none sneaked down to feast upon the crops growing on the terraces, or strayed too far from the herd to fall victim to a hungry puma. Luckily I was assisted by my two young cousins, Wachwa and Llakato. Though they were twins, they were as different from one another as a valley is from a mountain. Wachwa was short and fat, but could move very fast when he wanted to. Llakato, though tall and thin, never seemed to go anywhere in a hurry, though there was no mountain slope too steep for him to climb.

When they weren't chasing after llamas, my cousins played chuncara, a dice game using colored beans, while I worked at my loom. And as I worked, I thought about what Ipa had said about my fate and Topa Inca's somehow being tied together. I hoped she was wrong, for I did not want anything to change. My life was like the beautiful cloth rapidly growing upon my loom; it consisted of many individual threads tightly woven together: my village, my family, Chumpi, the work of my hands. Ipa hoped I would someday become a camasca, like her, but I had no such ambitions. I only wanted for nothing loosened in the fabric of my life. If I could have changed the pattern in any way, it would have been to weave into it my father's presence once more.

A sudden breeze revealed a few slack threads, so I shifted my weight slightly to equalize the tension of the warp. Llakato with his long, slow steps trod past me to head off a young llama edging toward the fields. I watched until he had the llama moving back toward the main herd, then resumed weaving. If anyone in our family would have wanted his life linked with Topa Inca's, it would have been Charapa, for he seemed to have a hunger for excitement, and this brought to mind the many times Charapa had defied convention, often with humorous results. These reminiscences, along with the work of my loom and an occasional pursuit of a wayward llama, caused the day to pass quickly, and soon it was time to herd the llamas back down to our village.

Once the llamas were safely in their pen for the night, Chumpi and I returned to our wasi where, to my surprise, Ipa was baking a guinea pig for our evening meal. "I needed to examine its organs to see if Sumaq Uya would get better," she explained.

Having watched Ipa many times, I was familiar with how to use guinea pigs to determine a person's illness. First two guinea pigs, one male and one female, were placed atop the sick person's chest. In this way, the state of the person's sonqo–her organs, such as the heart and lungs, which make up her life force–were communicated to the guinea pigs. Then the guinea pigs were torn open and their organs examined. A heart which continued to beat was always a good sign, as well as a healthy liver and pancreas.

"What did they tell you?" I said.

Ipa shook her head. "The signs were not good; both guinea pigs had small livers, and their hearts stopped beating immediately. I think all I can do for Sumaq Uya now is to make her comfortable until she begins her journey on the underground road. Since Sumaq Uya insisted I take one of the guinea pigs, I decided to bake it for evening meal. Charapa will be pleased. The guinea pig will help to make up for the roasted llama he missed last night."

"It's an extravagance to have fresh meat two nights in a row," I said. "You should have made the guinea pig into charqui and saved the meat for later."

Ipa stared at me, not believing her ears.

Then I smiled and squeezed her arm to let her know I was teasing. "I know you like to do special things for Charapa."

It was Ipa's turn to smile. "It's hard not to spoil Charapa. He's used to it because your mother spoiled him as a baby. That's why he's always so restless, and that's why I don't want you spoiling Kusi or he'll grow up to be dissatisfied with his life as well. Now let go of my arm and go comb that walking fleabag you call Chumpi. We need some more variegated wool for the next chusi you're going to weave."

From the woven bag in which I kept my weaving tools, I removed a long comb made of llaulli thorns held between two flat pieces of wood. As usual, Chumpi was sitting as close as he dared to our food preparation area. I knelt beside him and began to comb his hair. In response to the soothing stroke of the comb, Chumpi began to hum contently. I felt very content as well. As I combed Chumpi, I watched the other women in our village preparing food, as men, tired from work, sat nearby, drinking chicha. Taruka, returning from the stream where he had washed away the dirt from a day spent clearing irrigation ditches, made no response to my greeting. Yet I noticed his look of surprise when he caught a whiff of the roasting guinea pig.

When I had combed out a large ball of wool, I twisted a few hairs onto a spindle then, standing, began to spin the loose fiber into thread. As I watched the spindle turn, I thought about Charapa. He should have returned from Tambo Puquio by now. He seemed to have lingered upon the road just as Ipa had predicted. Thinking of him walking along in the twilight, I quietly sang a familiar song.

> Oh, to be wandering,
> Free upon the plain;
> Only the wind and ichu grass
> Brushing against my legs;
>
> Oh, to be wandering,
> Like my brother the mountain stag;

Sheltered beneath a starlit sky
Wrapped only by wind and rain.

Sad the Kullku's cry,
Sweet my glad heart's song;
Oh, to be wandering,
Always wandering on.

While I sang, Inti began his nightly journey underground. The other families had finished their meals while we still waited for Charapa. Eventually Ipa called to me. "Let's eat. We can't wait any longer for that lazy boy."

I put away my spindle and helped Ipa dish up the food. She had baked quinoa along with the guinea pig. As she lifted the lid of the baking dish, the piquant aroma of meat seasoned with peppers came out with the steam. Kusi, watching from his play pit, slapped the ground excitedly as Ipa stirred the juices through the quinoa.

"I knew Charapa wouldn't arrive before the men finished work," said Ipa, "but I surely expected him for evening meal. Yana, take a moment and go see if you can see him."

I hurried out to the road. There was just enough light to see to where it crossed the stream. I returned to find Ipa sitting on the ground, feeding Kusi. She looked up and I shook my head.

"Atatau!" she exclaimed. "If he shows up, he'll just have to eat his dinner cold. Serve him right!"

We ate in silence. By the time we finished, it was dark. Fortunately, Qillamama provided enough light for us to see to wash our dishes. Charapa's portion of the guinea pig would remain in the baking dish, to be enjoyed as a part of morning meal.

Before we crawled into our wasi, Ipa gave me the necklace she had made, incorporating the yellow feather Topa Inca had given me. "I know it's too dark for you to see it very well, but I used black thread which I think makes a pleasing contrast to the yellow feather."

I held the necklace up to catch Qillamama's light. "It's beautiful, Ipa. Thank you."

"I had meant to give it to you earlier, but what with worrying about your brother, I forgot."

I was grateful for the gift, for it lessened my disappointment in Charapa's not returning. Both Ipa and I had been looking forward to hearing Charapa share his experiences in Tambo Puquio, even though much of what he said likely would not have been true exactly. But that was as it should be. A good storyteller always embellishes his story, and Charapa was certainly a good storyteller.

Inside the wasi, we lay upon our chusis. "Do you think something bad may have happened to Charapa?" I said.

Ipa snorted. "What could have happened? Perhaps when he got to Tambo Puquio he was ordered to do other work, but most likely…"

Ipa didn't need to finish the sentence. Most likely, Charapa had found some excuse to stay at Tambo Puquio and thus turn his bit of servitude into an adventure.

I turned on to my side. "Weqo Churu is not going to be happy."

Ipa snorted again.

Chapter 7

The next day, just as we prepared to eat our evening meal, Charapa returned, sneaking up to our wasi by way of the stream so no one would notice him. By comparison to the night before, our evening meal was decidedly plain. Ipa had made motepatasca, a soup using whole kernels of maize and dried chili peppers. Along with this, there were small cakes made of ground quinoa also flavored with peppers. But Charapa was so excited, he hardly noticed what he was eating. In fact, to my amazement, he tossed one of his cakes to Chumpi. Never before had I seen him give Chumpi even a crumb!

"Atakachau! What a good time I had in Tambo Puquio!" he declared.

"A good time?" Ipa said. "Are the irrigation ditches in Tambo Puquio that much easier to clean than ours?"

Charapa dropped his head. "Cleaning ditches is the same everywhere. I had more important work."

Ipa and I laughed.

"It's true! You wouldn't believe the amount of baggage the Capac Inca brought with him. It took most of the day to unload it all because several of the Capac Inca's servants were sick."

"You mean they were drunk on the Capac Inca's special chicha," I said.

Ipa added, "I'm sure they were glad to sit around and drink while you did their work."

Like a turtle, Charapa would pull his head into his body when he was sulky, and this is what he did now.

Ipa placed her hand under his chin and lifted his head. "We're glad you had a good time, Charapa. We're making fun only because listening to you makes us happy, too."

Charapa stretched his head out a little and smiled.

"Besides," she added, releasing his chin, "it's not us you have to convince you were working. It's Weqo Churu."

Charapa seized the stirring spoon and hit himself over the head with it. "I'm sorry, Weqo Churu," he cried. "I'm sorry I didn't hurry back to clean the irrigation ditches!" He hit himself again. "Weqo Churu, don't hit me! I forgot you were more important than the Capac Inca!" He hit himself a third time, even harder, then rolling up his eyes, he toppled over sidewise. He failed, however, to consider where he would land, and his head fell right into Ipa's bowl of motepatasca. I laughed so hard, I snorted food through my nose.

"Shhh! Shhh!" Ipa hissed. "Not so loud! Everyone can hear you." But she was also laughing at Charapa's antics.

Charapa wiped his face then exchanged his bowl for Ipa's, but she switched them back. "Eat," she ordered, "you've come a long way today."

Charapa reversed the bowls again. "I'm not hungry. The woman in charge of preparing the food for the Incas gave me sweet maize cakes to eat along the way back."

Both Ipa and I were silenced by this information. Sweet maize cakes were a delicacy reserved for only the most special occasions, like weddings.

"You did have a good time!" Ipa said.

Grinning, Charapa produced two sweet maize cakes, one for Ipa and one for myself.

"Atakachau!" I exclaimed and immediately broke off a small piece and popped it into my mouth. The honey sweetness dissolved delightfully upon my tongue. I broke off another piece and fed it to Kusi who then tried to take the whole cake from my hand. Even Chumpi sensed something special. He stood up and voiced a high-pitched bleat.

"Forget it, fleabag!" shouted Ipa, and we all laughed again.

Offended, Chumpi flattened back his ears then turned his back on us.

"Chumpi, don't mind us," I said. "We're just being silly. Besides, llamas don't like sweet maize cakes." Which, of course, was not true.

When the last delicious crumb was gone, I let Kusi suck the sticky sweetness from my fingers. Charapa seemed to get as much pleasure watching us eat the cakes as he would from eating them himself, and he waited patiently until the cakes were gone before posing a question.

"Ipa, have you ever been to Tambo Puquio?"

"Yana," Ipa said, "I fear Charapa is about to bore us with tall tales about his merry escapades in Tambo Puquio." She sighed. "Turn around so I can lean my tired back against yours."

When she had made herself comfortable, Charapa said, "Well, have you?"

"Once I visited Tambo Puquio, but it was long, long time ago. You'll have to help me remember what it was like."

"It's beautiful, not like this place." He looked about with disdain in his eyes. "The wasi of the Capac Inca is bigger than all the wasis in our village put together, and it's not built with bricks of dried mud, but of cut stone, and each one is shaped so skillfully that they fit together like this." He interlocked his fingers tightly together.

"His wasi is set amidst gardens filled with flowers. Most of the flowers are real, but some are made of gold and silver. And there are animals made of gold, also. I swear I saw a golden deer as big as a live one, and its eyes were green gemstones!"

"How did you see all this?" Ipa said. "I remember the Capac Inca's residence was surrounded by a high wall to keep Hatunrunas out."

"It is!" He sat up straight and drew back his shoulders. "But they let me inside. Like I said, many of the Capac Inca's servants were sick, so I was allowed to carry stacks of chusis to the colcas where they are stored. Ipa, their chusis are made out of vicuña! I've never felt anything so soft!" He rubbed his fingers as if again feeling their softness.

"I bet the wasis of the Capac Inca's servants are not made of cut stone," I said. "I bet they're no better than ours."

Charapa shrugged as if this was of no importance. "But let me tell you about the baths! There are streams and pools all throughout the garden. Some of the streams have been diverted to make small waterfalls. And the pools are shaded by great trees with bright orange blossoms."

"Pisonay trees," said Ipa.

"I don't know their names, but when the blossoms fall, they float upon the water. And here's the best part: some of the streams are hot! They are so hot, cold water has to be added to the pools before anyone can bathe. And the hot water in each pool is a different temperature, so the Capac Inca can choose the temperature he wishes for his baths. The very hottest pools have clouds of steam rising from them!"

I turned to Ipa. "You said if I could show you a stream that was warm, you'd use it for Kusi's baths. Does that mean we'll now have to travel to Tambo Puquio every time Kusi needs bathing?"

Ignoring me, Ipa said, "I could see why you wanted to stay in Tambo Puquio an extra day, Charapa. You saw things very few others are permitted to see. Now as you work in the fields, you'll have something special to think about."

A small cloud passed across Charapa's face, taking with it his smile.

"Tell me," Ipa continued, "did you see the old camasca, the one we saw treating Topa Inca after he vomited?"

Charapa's face immediately brightened. "Did I ever! I kept hearing rumors that Topa Inca is very sick, maybe even dying. I didn't believe them until I saw the camasca perform a special ceremony."

Ipa gasped. "They didn't let you watch, did they?"

Charapa shook his head. "I didn't see the ceremony up close. It was performed atop the temple to Inti, which is a stone tower you can't see from outside of the walls. But I made a few friends, and last night, just before Inti prepared to make his underground journey, they took me to a place on a hill that overlooks the temple. Hiding within some bushes, we could see and hear everything."

Ipa waved a finger at Charapa. "You should not have been watching!" She dropped her hand. "But since you did, use that good memory of yours and tell me exactly what you saw, and don't leave out any details."

Charapa leaned forward. "Well, first the Capac Inca climbed the stairs leading to the top of the tower. He wore a mantle made of bright red feathers. He also wore the same headdress we saw him wearing the other day. Behind the Capac Inca came the old camasca. The camasca wore a red yacolla that came nearly to the ground and was tied by a sort of belt with a long fringe. He was followed by two young women dressed alike in lliqllas of pure white. One was carrying plates of food while the other held two cups of drink.

"In the center of the tower was an altar made of stone, piled high with sticks of wood. I was told that each piece of wood had the image of an animal carved into it. The women placed the food and drink around the edge of the altar before going back down the steps. Then the camasca lifted his hands and started shouting in a language I never heard before. From somewhere came the beating of a drum, and the camasca began to dance around the altar in time to the beat."

"What was the Capac Inca doing while the camasca danced?" Ipa said.

"He just stood and watched. The camasca continued to chant in that strange language, repeating the same words over and over. As he circled the altar, he kept throwing his arms into the air. I guess he was summoning fire, for suddenly the wood on the altar began to burn. The fire quickly grew and must have been very hot, for the Capac Inca was forced to move back. But the camasca didn't seem to notice the heat, and kept circling the altar and chanting. Occasionally he took something from the woven bag he carried and threw it onto the fire. I'm not certain, but I think he might have been throwing small birds.

"Then nothing seemed to happen for a long time. The camasca just kept circling the fire which slowly burned down. I guess I was tired, for I closed my eyes. I might even have fallen asleep. But I remember that, even with my eyes closed, there was a sudden brightness. I opened my eyes. The fire had burned down to coals, but there was a spot in the center of the altar that flared up with sparks shooting into the sky. The fire died down again, but just for a moment. Then it flared up once more.

"You won't believe what happened next, but I swear it's true, for I heard it with my own ears. The fire started to talk!"

Ipa leaned forward. "Did it talk in the strange language the camasca used?"

Charapa shook his head. "No, I could understand exactly what it said."

"What did the voice of the fire sound like?" Ipa said. "Did it sound like the camasca's?"

"No! The camasca has a voice like an old man's, but the voice of the fire was beautiful, deep, and strong!"

"How do you know it wasn't the Capac Inca talking?" I said.

"Because I could see his face as well as the face of the camasca, and neither said anything when the fire was speaking. I tell you the voice came out of the fire! And every time it spoke, the flames got bigger, and when it stopped talking, the flames died down again."

Smiling, Ipa leaned back. "All right, Charapa, what did the voice say?"

Charapa took a deep breath then began to imitate the voice he'd heard. "'Capac Inca, your son must drink of the water at the end of the world!'" Then in his own voice, Charapa said, "The voice of the fire spoke these words three times just like that. 'Capac Inca, your son must drink of the water at the end of the world!' Then the fire died to a flame so small, it barely illuminated the faces of the Capac Inca and the camasca."

"What was the Capac Inca's response to the voice of the fire?" Ipa said.

"That was strange. After the fire died down, the Capac Inca said something to the camasca that I couldn't hear. The camasca responded by shaking his head, which seemed to make the Capac Inca angry because he quickly moved toward the camasca and stood over him. I thought the Capac Inca was going to hit him! Then the Capac Inca said something else, and this time the camasca pointed to the dying flame. The Capac Inca then raised his fist above the camasca. The Capac Inca is so big and tall, he could have crushed the camasca with one blow, but the camasca took no more notice of the Capac Inca than if he had been a fly. It was as if, to him, the Capac Inca wasn't even there.

"Finally, the Capac Inca turned away and sat upon the wall that ringed the tower. The camasca went to the altar and prayed in a low voice as he fed the fire the food and drink left by the women. Then he gave one of the empty plates to the Capac Inca. The plate was different from the others and reminded me of the one you use, Ipa, to catch the blood when you are bleeding a sick person."

"What did the Capac Inca do with this plate?" she said.

"He took it to the edge of the tower where he stood awhile, looking in our direction. I was frightened, for I thought maybe he could see us hiding in the bushes. Atatau! My heart was beating so hard I was sure my chest was going to burst.

"Then the Capac Inca did a strange thing. He hurled the plate. It whirred above my head and shattered on a rock right behind us!"

Chapter 8

Though it was nearly dark, neither Ipa nor I moved, for we were caught in the spell created by Charapa's story. His description of the ceremony was vivid in my mind, and I struggled to make sense of what it all meant. Finally, Charapa asked Ipa the question which had been in my mind also.

"Ipa, where is the water at the end of the world?"

She snorted. "It is nowhere."

"What!"

"It is everywhere," Ipa continued.

Charapa frowned. "Ipa, you make no sense. The water has to be somewhere, otherwise why did the camasca say Topa Inca had to drink it. How can anyone drink water that's nowhere and everywhere?"

"I can't give you a simple answer, Charapa. I wish I could. Do you think you know where the water is?"

Charapa stared at the ground. There were lines of tension around his mouth. Perhaps he had an idea where the water at the end of the world might be found, but if so, he didn't share his idea with us.

"I envy you, Charapa," I said. "I would have loved to have seen a fire that talks!"

"Yes, it was astonishing! That camasca must be very powerful. No wonder the Capac Inca didn't hit him."

I could feel Ipa pushing against my back as she struggled to stand.

"I can't wait to tell Taruka all about it," Charapa said, "though I might make him wait until our village has a night of storytelling. That will give me time to remember a few more details."

"Or make them up," I said.

Charapa grinned.

I thought Ipa had gotten up to start washing dishes. Instead, she was making a clatter as she rummaged through our cookware. "Ipa what are you looking for?"

Ipa produced a small clay jar with a lid. Standing a way from us, she held the jar with one hand while lifting the lid up and down.

"Charapa, where is the water at the end of the world?"

I gasped. The jar had spoken! Both Charapa and I jumped to our feet.

"Charapa," the jar said again, "where is the water at the end of the world?" It was as if I was hearing a voice at the edge of a dream, not able to tell if it was real, or part of the dream. I watched the jar closely. Each time Ipa lifted the lid, a word came out. This time the jar had an angry edge to its voice.

"Charaaaapa! WHERE is the WATER at the end of the WORLD?"

I looked at Charapa and he looked as frightened as I. Instinctively, we moved closer to each other.

Ipa thrust the jar toward us. "Charaaaapa! WHERE is the WATER at the end of the WORLD?"

"Aaaiii!" we screamed. Charapa grabbed me by my arm and turned to flee, but tripped over Chumpi, lying in our path. We both went down and lay in the dirt too stunned to move.

Ipa started to laugh. At first her laughter was high and thin like a long note played on a flute. Then she emitted several short blasts like the blare of a chasqui's puturutu. Finally, she let loose with a whole string of whoops as she slapped her hand against her thigh.

Frightened by our screams and Ipa's laughter, Kusi began to cry. Ipa, still laughing, put down the jar and picked up Kusi. She patted him on the back as she walked to where we still lay in the dirt.

"You should have seen your faces," she said. "Last time I saw a face like that was when Weqo Churu accidentally bit into a dung beetle!"

Charapa and I looked at each other and shook our heads in disgust. Somehow we'd been tricked.

"Are you two planning to lie there all night?" Ipa said, a big grin on her face. "Go down to the stream and clean yourselves."

Charapa sat up. "But how did–"

"Go! I'll tell you once you're clean."

We rose stiffly and stumbled toward the stream where we washed away the grains of dirt embedded in our skin and soothed our scratched faces. By the time we returned, Ipa had finished cleaning up and was bundling Kusi in his small chusi.

"Sit down by the jar, and I'll show you how I made it talk." She chuckled as she placed Kusi in his play pit. "Don't worry. The jar won't attack you."

We both sat down. Charapa picked up the jar, opened the lid, and cautiously looked inside.

Ipa sat down before us. "Hand me the jar, Charapa" she ordered. "Now watch." She lifted the lid three times, and the jar spoke the syllables of Charapa's name, but being closer to Ipa, I now noticed something different: the jar's voice seemed to come from Ipa, though her lips never moved.

"Do that again!" Charapa said.

Ipa obliged him. Then she set the jar down and leaned forward. "Charapa," she said, "where is the water at the end of the world?"

"That's amazing," I said, "you're talking, but your lips aren't moving."

"How did you do that?" Charapa said.

"With practice," Ipa answered. "Atakachau! It's been a long time, but I haven't lost the touch."

"But the voice of the jar and yours are different," Charapa said.

"That comes with practice, too. Listen."

Ipa spoke, using the deep resonant voice of the jar. Then she spoke in a high, pinched voice, and Charapa and I laughed because it seemed to come out of her nose.

"A skilled camasca can speak using a variety of different voices," she said.

Charapa looked troubled. "So the voice I heard coming out of the fire was a trick?"

Ipa let silence be her answer.

"But I saw the fire flare up as it spoke!"

"Do you remember the camasca's assistants, the women who carried the offerings of food and drink? I guess that in the center of the altar there was the end of a long metal tube, only you couldn't see it because it was covered over by the burning wood. From inside the tower, an assistant could hear the false voice of the camasca and would simultaneously blow through the tube, causing the fire to flare up as the camasca spoke."

"Atatau!" Charapa exclaimed. "No wonder the Capac Inca looked so angry. He probably knew the whole thing was nothing but a trick!"

"Does that mean that there is no water at the end of the world," I said.

Ipa shook her head. "No, not at all. I am not a great camasca like the one who summoned the voice from the fire, but the most important skill of any camasca is to create trust, for if a patient has faith in his camasca, then half the camasca's healing work is done for him. A fire that talks is powerful magic and a way of commanding respect. You thought the voice was real, didn't you, Charapa?"

Charapa nodded.

"The voice of the fire, though not real, nevertheless gave power to the words it spoke, and it was the words, and not how they were produced, that were important."

"Then there is a water at the end of the world," I said.

"Yes, perhaps," Ipa replied.

"But where is it?" Charapa said.

But before Ipa could answer, Chumpi made a clicking noise, announcing a visitor.

"It sounded like a celebration was going on here," Weqo Churu said, appearing out of the darkness.

"I was just showing Charapa and Yana a little magic, a jar that talks."

Weqo Churu smiled. "I remember a long time ago when you did that with a llama. I thought an evil spirit had entered its body. I was so scared, I nearly soiled my unku."

Ipa laughed, remembering.

"Ipa," Weqo Churu said, "I just talked to Sumaq Uya, and she says she's feeling better. Her bones don't trouble her so much. Thank you for tending to her."

Ipa nodded. "A tea of chilca leaves did the trick. And how is Ukumari? Was he able to work?"

"Yes, thanks to the drink you gave him, though none of us could stand to work downwind from him." Then Weqo Churu got to the real reason for his visit. "I saw Charapa sneaking into the village this evening. I wanted to let him know that we finished cleaning the irrigation ditches."

Ipa and I laughed at Charapa's sigh of relief.

"All except for one," Weqo Churu said. "The one that supplies water to the upper terraces on the north side."

"Atatau!" Charapa cried. "That's the hardest one to clean. Every time it rains, the rocks wash down and fill it up!"

"That's why I saved it for you, Charapa. I'm certain with the rest you've had, you're now eager to get back to work. You best get an extra early start, for I want that ditch cleared by day's end."

Weqo Churu turned to Ipa. "Perhaps at our next celebration, you could bring your talking jar. I don't believe any of the children have seen one."

"I just may do that," Ipa said. "I'd forgotten how much fun it is."

"I will look forward to it." Then addressing us all, Weqo Churu said,

"May the gods grant you a peaceful rest."

"And you," Ipa and I replied.

Ipa slowly stood up. "Well, Kusi is fast asleep, and we should be also." Then she laughed. "Oh, if you could have seen the look on your faces!"

Chapter 9

I stood up and rubbed my back, sore from holding the tension of the warp. Yet I was glad to have accomplished so much; I was nearly done weaving another chusi.

The llamas, earlier scattered across the mountain side, were now grouping together as they did when it was nearly time to return to the village. A llama whose hair was variegated like Chumpi's came to stand next to me, and I found my comb and began to comb him. Behind me I heard a clatter upon the loose scree and assumed it was one of my cousins. I tried to guess which by the sound of his footsteps. Judging by the slow pace, I decided it had to be Llakato. But I was wrong. It was neither of my cousins. It was Charapa.

I was surprised to see him, yet glad for him that he had finished his work early. I pointed to a trio of llamas still high above us. I expected Charapa to go after them, but instead he sat down upon a rock. Dirt outlined the creases in his forehead, and his cheeks were streaked with sweat.

I set my comb aside. "You look tired. I'll herd the llamas down while you sit and rest."

"I'm leaving," he announced, staring at the ground.

Not understanding, I said nothing.

He looked up. "Didn't you hear me, Yana? I said I'm leaving Qomermoya."

"You can't! It's forbidden!"

"I don't care! I don't care if they throw me in the Uatay Uaci Zancay. It couldn't be worse than living here. There's nothing for me here." For emphasis, he began to pound the palm of one hand with his fist. "It is always the same thing! I get up in the morning and go clean ditches, or plant potatoes, or repair walls. And it will be the same every day for the next forty years until I'm too old to do anything but sit and make sandals. In our society, a Hatunruna may as well be in prison. He can never be free from a life of drudgery."

"There's always the army," I said. "With courage a man can advance and be made a leader. Look at Father; he's now a chungacamayoc, a soldier who commands ten other men."

Charapa shot me look of disgust. "I'm no soldier!" He hung his head. "All I'm good at is remembering things and counting."

"You could be a quipucamayoc!" I blurted out, not thinking. Charapa even didn't bother to answer since it was a foolish suggestion: being a record keeper was a job for an old man.

"Yana, I wish you could have seen Tambo Puquio. It was so beautiful! I talked to one of the Capac Inca's servants, a gardener. He spends every day among the flowers, and the golden animals, and the waterfalls, and the warm pools. Did I tell you about the golden deer with the blue gemstones for eyes?"

"They were green last time," I said, but Charapa wasn't listening.

"The servants of the Incas have better clothes than we do and more varieties of things to eat. But it's not just the clothes and the food that make their lives better. They have more opportunities. The gardener told me he sometimes travels to gather special plants for the garden. Can you imagine, Yana, being allowed to travel and see different places and how other people live? Can you imagine what it would be like to be one of the servants who work for the Incas? How interesting life would be?"

"But how can you be a servant? It is a position that is inherited. Only if Father were a servant could you be one."

Charapa smiled. "Not necessarily. Not if I found the water at the end of the world."

I stared at him, not believing my ears.

"Don't you see, Yana? If I found the water that cured Topa Inca, the Capac Inca would give me anything I wanted. I could become one of his personal servants and travel with him everywhere he went and live in Qosqo, the golden city."

I shook my head, appalled by his foolishness.

Seeing my reaction, Charapa rushed to head off any objections. "It's not just me I thinking about, Yana. Think of our family! If I found the water at the end of the world, the Capac Inca would be so grateful, he'd release Father from his military service. And think of our village! The Capac Inca would give us more llamas, more guinea pigs, and clothes made of vicuña. Think of what it would be like to have a topu made of gold to pin your lliqlla together rather than that beat-up, copper one you wear."

"I don't need a topu made of gold! We don't need more llamas and guinea pigs! We have all we need now! All this is just an excuse for you to go off on an adventure. You got a taste for it when you went to Tambo Puquio, and now you want to go off and leave us to do your work!"

Tired of arguing, Charapa stood up. He had with him a woven bag that looked heavy. I realized it probably contained food, enough for many days.

"You're leaving right now, aren't you?"

Charapa made no reply, but adjusted the strap of his bag.

"No!" I screamed, running to him. "I'll not let you!" I pushed him in the chest, and he stumbled back, surprised. "I'll tell Weqo Churu! He'll hunt you down faster than the time it takes to cook locro!"

Charapa didn't say anything, but looked at me with great sad eyes. I turned from those eyes and sat upon a rock and covered my face with my hands. I should tell Weqo Churu, I thought. Ipa was right: sometimes you must hurt a person you love for their own good. Often in the weeks that followed, I regretted not having run down the mountain at that very moment and told Weqo Churu of Charapa's plan. But I was weak. I had seen the sorrow in my brother's eyes and knew I could not tell on him.

Charapa placed a hand upon my shoulder. "I came to tell you I was leaving so you wouldn't worry. I will be back before the time of planting potatoes. Weqo Churu can certainly get along without me until then." He withdrew his hand and straightened up. "And when I return, it will be with a herd of llamas for our village."

I looked up at him, his face a blur through my tears. "But you don't even know where the water at the end of the world is!"

Charapa smiled a knowing smile.

"Tell me!" I demanded.

"If I told you, you would have to tell Weqo Churu when he asked you."

He was right. From birth, we were instructed to obey the three principal rules: do not steal; do not lie; do not be lazy. Nevertheless, I suddenly realized where he was going.

"You're going to the ocean!" Charapa and I had often talked about the ocean and speculated upon its appearance. Perhaps Charapa was right. The ocean was the water where the land ended.

Charapa, still smiling, refused to confirm my suspicions.

"What will I tell Ipa when you don't return for evening meal?"

"You won't have to tell her anything. She's gone to be with Sumaq Uya and won't return until after you're asleep. By tomorrow morning, I'll be too far away for Weqo Churu to catch me."

I nodded, understanding. My clever brother had seen an opportunity and seized upon it.

"Now I must go. There's Llakato and Wachwa coming to see why you're not helping with the herd." Yet Charapa lingered, perhaps troubled by my sadness. In truth, I felt as if I were losing another piece of my heart. "Don't worry, Yana. It will all work out just fine. I promise."

I stood up and hugged him tightly, not wanting to let him go. Charapa squeezed me in return then pulled away and started climbing the slope. I watched him while I fought for control, for I did not want to have to explain my tears to my cousins. Was it my imagination or did Charapa's footsteps sound lighter than when I heard them earlier?

I rolled up my weaving and gathered my tools. When again I looked up, I saw Charapa was near to the top of the ridge. The sadness in my heart welled up and threatened to spill out as tears once more. I fought the sadness by scurrying up the slope to where the three llamas still lingered. But before I reached them, I heard the sound of Charapa's flute carried down to me by the wind. I stood and listened to the familiar melody:

> Sad the Kullku's cry,
> Sweet my glad heart's song;
> Oh, to be wandering,
> Always wandering on.

Chapter 10

I f Charapa had known where his wandering was to take him, he never would have promised to return by planting time. Then again, he never would have left Qomermoya in the first place. But my brother was a dreamer, and never in dreams is the future clear.

When Weqo Churu discovered Charapa had left, and the reason, he became so angry, I feared he might drop a rock on my head. Ipa explained to him about the voice Charapa had heard in the fire. Weqo Churu ordered us not to repeat the story for fear that other young men would likewise run off in search of the water at the end of the world. Then he forbade everyone in our village to speak of Charapa. I think Weqo Churu wanted Charapa to cease to exist.

But to Ipa and myself, Charapa did exist, and we spoke of him in silent ways. Each morning we poured a little tea into his cup and placed it alongside my father's in our family's huaca. We stopped flavoring our food with peppers, a small but sincere entreaty to the gods for Charapa's safe return. And sometimes when the ache for him seemed unbearable, we comforted ourselves by baking a guinea pig, Charapa's favorite food.

When Charapa left Qomermoya, it was Chahua-huarquiz, that time of the year when the irrigation ditches were cleaned. As the days passed, the rhythm of our village continued with little variation, save that Sumaq Uya finally passed from this life to walk the underground road. For three days, we did not flavor our food with either salt or peppers until she completed her journey to the mountain top, there to await rebirth.

One evening, shortly after we broke our fast, Qillamama rose above the mountains, her lovely face round and full. Such a time is bad for planting, but each night thereafter Qillamama hid a little of her beauty until her face was cloaked in darkness. Then it was Yapaquiz, the time of planting of ocas and potatoes. By the Capac Inca's decree, we were required to plant the fields belonging to the wilka camayocs first. Though nearly everyone but infants participated in the planting, each family usually worked as a unit. The men of each family turned over the soil using foot plows called tacllas, and the women broke up the soil using handheld hoes called lampas. Behind them came the younger children who sowed the ground with tubers of ocas or the moist eyes of potatoes. Older children carried water from the stream to water the plantings. It was pleasant work with cheerful banter between families and the drinking of chicha when throats got dry.

Of course, in my family it was different, for there was no father nor mother. Weqo Churu chose Taruka to do the plowing that should have been done by my brother. Kneeling, I followed behind Taruka and broke apart the dry clods. Then behind us came children borrowed from larger families.

Taruka and I were a match in that we both liked to work hard and see the rows of plowed earth grow behind us. His quiet nature suited my mood, for if I could not talk of Charapa, there was little else I wished to speak of. Instead I played a game in my mind. Each morning I guessed the location in the field we would likely reach by the end of the day's plowing. I told myself that when I reached that spot, Charapa would be there to greet me. All day my excitement mounted as I moved closer and closer toward a reunion with my brother. But day after day I came to that place only to find Charapa not there.

When we finished planting the fields of the wilka camayocs, we sowed those belonging to the Capac Inca. I continued to play my game, though with less enthusiasm, as every day ended with my brother not returning. Still, the next day Inti would rise above the eastern mountains, and my hope would be renewed.

By the time we finally began to plant the fields that were allotted to each family, my feelings concerning Charapa had undergone a change. Though I longed to see him more than ever, I also began to feel angry. It was just as I told Charapa: he would go off adventuring while we got stuck with his work. Yet if Taruka felt any resentment at having to work our fields, he was kind enough not to mention it, though I was certain that other members of our village thought Charapa's absence from the work of planting inexcusable.

By the time we finished planting our fields, the fields of the wilka camayocs were already starting to green. Because of this, a pure white llama was sacrificed to Inti. After its throat was slit, its blood was collected and sprinkled over the newly planted fields, for blood empowers the soil with its life energy. Before the llama's organs were offered to the gods, Ipa examined them to determine if Pachamama would grant us a good harvest. The organs revealed nothing to indicate whether it would be good or bad. Once the organs were burned and prayers offered, we feasted on llama and a locro made with dried potatoes called chuños then danced a line dance called the guayyaya, though with less exuberance than usual because of the uncertain prospects concerning the harvest. The subdued dancing matched my mood, for I was unhappy that we had finished planting. Now where could I go to meet my brother? Then one day I learned my brother was in a place I dare not go.

I was not there when the chasqui brought the message to Weqo Churu. Following the planting, I had returned to my task of watching the llama herd. But later I was told that when he turned from talking to the chasqui, Weqo Churu looked like a man who has been hit upon the head with a war club.

He went to our wasi, and when he told Ipa of the chasqui's message, a great cry left her body. It was the cry that lives deep inside a person and does not emerge until someone she loves suddenly dies. Her cry, like the wind, swept through our village and up the mountain side. I heard it where I sat working upon my loom and knew in an instant it was Ipa's voice. Then I was flying down the mountain even before her wail ceased to echo off the rocks.

I found her lying on the ground outside our wasi, her head cradled in the lap of Qapia Weqe whose wasi was next to ours. Qapia Weqe's daughter stood comforting Kusi who was biting his tiny fist, his face wet with tears. Seeing me, Kusi let out a scream and held out his arms for me to take him.

"What has happened?" I said, pressing Kusi tightly to my chest.

Qapia Weqe did not answer, but looked to Weqo Churu who stood away from the circle of women gathered around Ipa. I hurried to him.

"Weqo Churu, what has happened?"

He turned his troubled eyes upon me and spoke in a hoarse whisper only I could hear. "Charapa has been imprisoned."

His words struck with the force of an aillo winding tighter and tighter around my chest. I wanted to cry out like Ipa, but could not draw breath.

"Breathe!" Weqo Churu commanded, pressing his fist into my chest.

I gulped air like a fish out of water. Then I began to cry, though little sound came with the tears that coursed down my cheeks. Kusi, thinking it a game, batted my tears as they dribbled off my chin. I took his tiny hand in mine and pressed his fingers to my cheek.

Weqo Churu took me by the arm and led me farther from the others. "It seems the water your brother brought to the Capac Inca was not the water at the end of the world. The Capac Inca, angered at being tricked, ordered Charapa placed in prison."

I shuddered. "Not the Uatay Uaci Zancay!"

"Don't be stupid!" he hissed. "Charapa is not a murderer, and the Capac Inca is not a cruel man. There are other prisons in Qosqo, and Charapa is being held in one of those until his punishment is determined. I have been ordered to go to Qosqo to meet with one of the Capac Inca's officials."

"Let me go with you!"

"No!" His voice was sharp, like the snap of a rope. The women who had been attending Ipa turned to look at us. Weqo Churu lowered his voice. "You and your brother have done enough damage. I am going, and you will stay here and look after Ipa. She is more important to our village than ten of you and your brother." Weqo Churu shook his head. "Atatau! I should have tracked down that little troublemaker when I discovered he left, but I was sure he would come crawling back as soon as he ran out of food."

"I'm sorry Weqo Churu. This is all my fault. I should have told you immediately when Charapa left. We have brought disgrace upon our village."

Weqo Churu nodded. "Now you see what comes of disobedience. As I told you before, nothing good comes from Hatunrunas interfering in the affairs of the Incas. I only hope our village is not also punished because of Charapa's stupidity. Now go look after Ipa while I arrange for Ukumari to take charge while I'm gone. It will take me..." slowly, he counted on his fingers, "three or four days to reach Qosqo."

"What should I say to the others concerning Charapa?"

"You will tell them nothing."

"But—"

"Just do as I tell you for once! I will explain Charapa's imprisonment to everyone when I get back. Now go look after Ipa. She has received a terrible shock."

By now the women had placed Ipa inside our wasi. I put Kusi in his play pit and crawled inside. Except for Qapia Weqe, all the others had left to prepare evening meal.

"She's been unconscious ever since she cried out," Qapia Weqe said, looking worried.

I stood looking down at Ipa whose chusi had been pulled up to her neck. Her face was gray; her hair limp. I watched the shallow rise and fall of her chest.

"Will she be all right?" I said.

Qapia Weqe was startled by my question. "Don't you know?"

I realized she was expecting me to know what to do. Most everyone in our village assumed Ipa had been teaching me to be a camasca, which was true, in a way, only now I wish I had paid more attention to her instructions. I closed my eyes and said a silent prayer, asking for guidance.

"I must go and prepare evening meal for my family," Qapia Weqe said.

I didn't want her to leave. I didn't want to be alone with Ipa. Yet I knew Qapia Weqe knew even less than I about what should be done. It was at times like this when we relied upon Ipa and her skills as our camasca.

"Later I will bring back food for you and Ipa," she said.

"Thank you, Qapia Weqe," I whispered, though I didn't feel like eating and wondered if Ipa would be able.

Qapia Weqe crawled through the entryway, then immediately stuck her head back in. "I will take Kusi with me. He can stay with us tonight. You have enough to do. You must look after Ipa and see she that gets well."

I nodded. It was the same order Weqo Churu had given me.

"Yana?" Qapia Weqe still had her head in the entryway. "Is it true Charapa has been thrown in prison because he lied to the Capac Inca?"

Contrary to Weqo Churu's wishes, word had gotten out. "Weqo Churu has ordered me not to talk about it to anyone."

"Atatau!" she exclaimed, shaking her head. Then she disappeared.

I knelt beside Ipa and held her hands. They felt like ice, and this frightened me. I did not need Weqo Churu to tell me she had received a great shock. I remember Ipa telling me just how dangerous shock was. People had died of it.

"You can't die," I whispered. My eyes filled with tears. "Everyone needs you."

Then I heard Ipa's voice in my head: "You can't water maize with tears!"

She was right. I had to do something useful. I tried to remember what Ipa had told me about treating someone who had received a bad shock. I recalled the first requirement was to keep the person warm. I took my chusi and laid it atop hers. Then I used my rubbing stick to start a fire right inside the wasi. Ipa had done this once when Charapa and I were both very sick. I made a fire big enough to warm the wasi, but not so large that the smoke could not dissipate through the small holes in the thatch. When the fire was going well, I sat back upon my heels and tried to remember what else Ipa had told me about shock. Once I had watched while Ipa had treated Penqali, another woman in our village, who, terrified by a landslide, had fainted. The first thing Ipa did was to take Penqali's pulse. Her pulse had been weak, and

Ipa had told me it was an indication that Penqali's blood had been taken by the landslide and replaced with water.

I placed a finger on the side of Ipa's neck. Her pulse was faint. This made me feel both worried and relieved: worried because shock was a dangerous condition, relieved to have confirmed the cause of Ipa's condition.

The next step Ipa had taken in treating Penqali was to restore Pachamama's vitality by feeding the area where the landslide had occurred with blood, the fluid that carries the force of life. Once Pachamama was restored to health, Penqali recovered from her shock.

I sprang to my feet, eager to act now that I knew what to do. I went to the corner of our wasi where our guinea pigs were penned. I selected the largest one and took it outside. Inti had begun his nightly journey beneath the ground, and out of the darkness, Qapia Weqe emerged, carrying two bowls of locro.

"Where was Ipa when she cried out?" I said.

"Right where you're standing," she replied.

Holding the guinea pig firmly by its neck I turned it upon its back. Ipa would have torn it open using her strong fingers, but I used the sharp edge of my topu. In my hurry to slit the guinea pig's throat, I also cut my hand. I shrugged off the pain. The more blood the better.

Qapia Weqe nodded approvingly as I sprinkled the ground with both the guinea pig's blood and my own. "Pachamama," I intoned, "receive this offering of life. May it restore you to fullness of health. And please return Ipa's blood to her. She is our camasca and we need her." It was a simple, ineloquent prayer, but heartfelt nonetheless.

Because I had forgotten to place the guinea pig upon Ipa's chest before killing it, an examination of its organs would have been fruitless. Still I thought I would know soon enough whether Ipa would recover. Before the guinea pig was completely drained of blood, I let some of it drip into one of the bowls of locro Qapia Weqe was holding. I'm not sure why I did this, only that it seemed the right thing to do, and I remembered Ipa telling me she often followed her intuition when treating a patient.

I gave Qapia Weqe the guinea pig in exchange for the bowls of locro.

"Has Ipa woken yet?" she said.

I shook my head.

"Then you must get back to treating her. Let me know if you need me to assist you."

I thanked her. Her faith in me made me feel good. I thought that this feeling must be one of the reasons why Ipa liked being a camasca. Then I shook my head. What was I thinking? I didn't really know what I was doing! What if feeding blood to Pachamama didn't cure Ipa of her shock? What would I do then?

I carried the bowls of locro into the wasi and set them down beside Ipa. Despite the warmth inside the wasi, Ipa felt as cold as before. How long would it take before Pachamama would give Ipa back her blood, I wondered? I tried to recall what else Ipa had done for Penqali, but nothing came to mind other than the feeding of Pachamama. Feeling at a loss, I reviewed what I had done so far. I had started by trying to warm Ipa. Unfortunately, the fire and the additional chusi had not appeared to have worked. I decided to rub her body the way I did Kusi with a towel after his bath.

I quickly moved toward Ipa's feet. I don't know why I started with her feet other than Ipa often complained of her feet always being the coldest part of her body. Lifting back the chusis, I began to rub her feet and calves. As I worked, I began to feel a tingling in my hands as sometimes occurred when I was upset. It was similar to the prickly feeling when a person's hand falls asleep, only this tingling also made my hands feel warm. I prayed the warmth in my hands would be given to Ipa's body. After a while I moved my hands upward to rub her thighs. Then I rewrapped her legs snugly in the chusis and rubbed one arm then the other. To my relief, her hands felt warmer. I moved to her head and, sitting cross-legged, held it in my lap. I did not rub her face but pressed both hands upon her cheeks. Now the tingling in my hands was painful, as if there was a fire within them. I reached down and unpinned Ipa's lliqlla then slid my hands beneath and rubbed her chest and stomach.

"Your hands feel very warm."

Startled, I looked down. Ipa was staring up at me.

"Praise the gods! You're awake!"

She smiled. "Why didn't you place the guinea pig on my chest before you killed it?"

"How did you know I killed—" I suddenly suspected Ipa of shamming. "Tell me, Ipa, how long have you been awake?"

"I never really lost consciousness."

"Then why didn't you say something? I've been out of my mind with worry!"

"It's not good for a person who's had a bad shock to talk. Besides, I wanted to see what you would do."

I uncrossed my legs and let her head fall to the ground with a thump. I moved quickly to the opening in the wasi.

"Yana!" Ipa called after me, but I ignored her.

Not caring if I should trip in the darkness, I strode from our wasi and did not stop until halfway to the stream. In my anger, I was not mindful of approaching footsteps.

"How is Ipa?"

The voice was Taruka's.

"Unfortunately, she'll live," I replied, before turning back to our wasi.

When I went back inside, I could see by the glow of the fire Ipa was sitting up and about to eat from one of the bowls of locro.

"Not that one!" I barked.

I quickly switched her bowl for the one containing the guinea pig's blood. Ipa though curious, said nothing until she sipped the locro.

"What is this, blood soup?"

I didn't reply.

"That was good thinking, Yana. Blood helps to restore a person's energy."

I said nothing.

"Are you angry with me?"

I let my silence be my answer.

Ipa chuckled. "Good! I prefer your anger to your sulkiness."

"Why did you let me worry myself sick when you were all right all along?"

"Because I wasn't all right. I needed to stay quiet and rest. If I had spoken would you have cared for me the way you did–which you did very well, by the way, except remembering to put the guinea pig on my chest before killing it–or would I have had to take responsibility for my own care while you hung over me, wringing your hands, waiting for me to tell you exactly what to do?"

"What if I had done something wrong? I could have made you even sicker!"

Ipa took another swallow of her locro then set it aside. "If you had started to slit my throat instead of the guinea pig's, I probably would have said something."

Regardless of my anger, I had to smile–at Ipa's humor, and also because she had complimented me on my care of her. I had always thought Ipa stingy with her praise, especially of Charapa and me.

"Did I really do well?" I said. "I tried to remember what you did for Penqali when she was frightened by the landslide."

"You did very well, Yana. Keeping me warm was the most important thing. And your hands! How did you get them so warm?"

The feeling in my hands was something I had never told her about. "My hands get hot and tingly when I'm upset. Sometimes they even shake."

Ipa nodded. "This thing in your hands is a special healing gift, Yana. It is another sign you would make a good camasca."

I sighed. "I've never wanted to be a camasca, but when you were unconscious—or faking unconsciousness—I was afraid you might die, and I wondered who would then replace you as camasca of our village and realized no one else is capable."

"I've always hoped you would be the one to take my place, but I've never pushed you because you always seemed unwilling. A person cannot be forced to become a camasca. A reluctant camasca would not make a good one. To be a good camasca, a person must truly have the desire to heal others and must also have a gift for it. You have the gift, Yana, more of a gift than I have."

I shook my head. "I could never be as good a camasca as you."

"Why do you say that? You already know most of the medicinal plants, and you certainly knew what to do for shock."

"That reminds me of something I was wondering about. At the time when you treated Penqali for shock, you said the landslide had replaced her blood with water. If I had bled you, would your blood have been clear like water?"

"First, I hope you never bleed a person suffering from shock. I know some camascas have a great regard for bloodletting. They tell me Topa Inca has been bled many times, but I think that is the wrong thing to do, especially in his case. Rarely is it necessary to bleed anyone and only when his blood is too strong."

"When is that?"

"Usually in the case of a head injury. The strong blood swells inside the skull, and the pressure sometimes kills the person. Yet it is very dangerous to release the blood, for to do it properly, a piece of the skull must be removed. I've done this twice and only with great reluctance. Fortunately, in both cases, the patient lived.

"But to answer your question—had you bled me, my blood would have appeared normal to the eye. 'Blood replaced with water' is only an expression. It just means that when a person is in shock, the blood becomes weaker. That's why it was clever of you to put the guinea pig's blood in the locro, to help thicken my blood. Now, does my apprentice have any more questions?"

I thought for a moment, weighing the possibility of her relapsing against my own need for peace of mind.

"Is this about Charapa?" she said.

I nodded. "What is going to happen to him?"

Ipa sighed. "I do not know. What Charapa did was wrong, and he cannot hope to escape punishment. Yet the severity of the punishment will depend on whether or not the Capac Inca believes Charapa was intentionally trying to trick him. The Capac Inca is wise, and I'm certain he will realize Charapa is just a foolish young man, not a malicious one. I only worry that the Capac Inca, blinded by his concern for his son, Topa Inca, might act uncharacteristically. Tomorrow we will offer maize and chicha to the gods and pray for the Capac Inca to act with wisdom."

"Ipa, I'm sorry I did not tell Weqo Churu immediately when Charapa left. I feel it is all my fault."

Ipa shook her head. "Do not assume all the blame. Even if you had told Weqo Churu that doesn't mean Charapa would not have tried to run away another time. As you know, once he gets something in his head, your brother can be quite determined."

I nodded in agreement.

"Yana, I want to tell you something which may be of comfort to you. When Weqo Churu told me Charapa had been imprisoned, I was, as you know, a little upset."

My mouth dropped open.

"All right, I was *very* upset. But while you cared for me, I was able to think clearly. You remember I told you I thought your fate and that of Topa Inca were tied together? Now I believe that more than ever, and I believe the gods have also imprisoned your brother for a reason."

"What makes you think the gods have a hand in this?"

"I cannot explain why exactly. Perhaps it is because I am a camasca, and after so many years of watching the gods choose who they will or will not make well, I can tell when they have an interest in someone. I think it significant that Charapa was the one Weqo Churu picked to go to Tambo Puquio. Who else from our village would have hung around to see the talking fire? And who else but Charapa would have gone looking for the water at the end of the world?"

"But why would the gods want Charapa to be imprisoned?"

"Atatau! If I knew that, I'd be a god myself. But I do know this: the gods always act for the best."

"Charapa being in prison is for the best? That's not very comforting."

"In my heart, I feel all will work out well for Charapa, eventually."

We were both quiet for a while. I thought about what Ipa said. Perhaps if Topa Inca and I were truly in some way connected, I could use that connection to free my brother. But how?

Ipa interrupted my thoughts. "Yana, I have never told you much about the dream I had just before your quicochicoy, but lately it has been much on my mind. Tomorrow, I will tell you about it in detail."

"Tell me now!" I demanded.

"No, not now! I am tired. I'm recovering from shock, remember? Nothing will change between now and tomorrow, so let us get some sleep." She lay back upon her chusi. "Atatau! Of the years I have to left to live, I think half were taken today."

I took the bowls outside and scraped their contents into a jar. I had not eaten any of mine, and Ipa had taken only a couple of sips of hers. Tomorrow I would reheat the locro for morning meal. I decided to go to the stream to rinse the bowls and to wash away the dried blood from the cut on my hand. When I crawled back into our wasi, Ipa was asleep, snoring. She had returned my chusi, but I did not pull it over me as the air was still warm from the fire. I stared at the glowing embers and thought about all that had happened since the chasqui delivered his message. Despite what Ipa said, I was still very worried about Charapa. Where was he? Was he alone? Had he eaten? Had he been given a chusi to keep himself warm? Would the gods keep him safe?

It was a long time before I fell asleep.

Chapter 11

I dreamt I was in a place of darkness, but also of beauty. I did not know by what means I saw this beauty in the darkness, for the light was strange to me: a lantern whose flame consumed neither wood nor fat. Still, by the lantern's glow, I could see a portion of my surroundings: a cavern—the walls, roof, floor all of rock.

The beauty was in the wall directly before me, for it was covered with crystals and sparkled like Intillapu's river in the night sky. I held the lantern high above my head, and the reflected light danced across the rough ceiling like snowflakes swirling in the wind. Crystals, as thick as my arm, thrust out from the wall, their facets smooth and polished as if cut by some charmed artisan. One of these crystals, larger than the rest, was as transparent as the slivers of ice that rimmed our stream in the morning, yet deep within it floated a dark cloud which, when I moved the lantern, flashed silvery beams.

But the crystals were not the only beauty, for a stream had carved a channel at the base of the wall and had worn its bed to the smoothness of river-polished pebbles. The water within this channel was so clear, it was all but invisible, save where it poured over a short ledge, making a sound like the wind cutting through the leaves of a molle tree. Overcome by thirst, I submerged my face in the stream and drank deeply. The water seemed without substance, a cold vapor that funneled down my throat, yet was so delicious and satisfying, I continued to drink past the quenching of my thirst just for the pleasure it gave me. When I discovered I could breathe underwater, I laughed with delight. Atakachau! In the water, I could drink, I could breathe, I could laugh!

I thought to try to sing when a sudden fear gripped me. I pulled my face from the stream and listened, but heard only the sound of the small waterfall. I picked up the lantern and lifted it as high as I could. Though the crystals magnified the light, I sensed there were great spaces the lantern failed to illuminate.

Cautiously, I moved away from the stream to stand in the center of a chamber in which I counted the entrances to four separate tunnels. I sniffed the air, but could smell nothing except damp earth and an acrid odor that emanated from my lantern.

Suddenly there was a change in the temperature. Though the air had been cool, now it was icy. I wrapped my lliqlla tightly about me, but the coldness had tendrils that burrowed beneath my lliqlla and sinuated across my skin. My apprehension grew and with it an urgency to hasten back to the wall of crystals, for I believed it a refuge from an approaching menace. But as I began to move, my legs felt as if they were pushing against the current of a strong river. I wanted to run, but it took all my strength just to lift one leg and place it before the other. I was shivering uncontrollably and losing sensation in both my arms and legs. I could no longer feel the handle of the lantern, and no sooner had I realized this than it fell from my hand, and the light went out.

Yet even with the light extinguished, it was not completely dark, for the crystals held their light and only gradually dimmed. The stream, a black line within the fading light, was the last thing I saw before darkness enveloped me. The stream was a black river, the river for which I was named.

I awoke and quickly sat up, my heart racing. At first I was uncertain whether I was truly awake, for it was pitch black within the wasi. Then to my relief, I felt my chusi beneath me. I pulled my lliqlla tight about me, for I was cold, having lain without a covering. When I tried to stand up, I found my trembling legs would not support me. I did not know whether I trembled from the cold or the power of my dream. On hands and knees, I crawled to the entryway. Outside, I placed my hand on the side of our wasi to steady myself as I slowly stood up. When certain I could stand without support, I groped about for a jar containing water, for I was very thirsty. But when I tilted back my head to drink, I saw Qillamama perched atop the roof of our wasi and my thirst, for the moment, was forgotten. Bathed by Qillamama's light my heart quieted. In gratitude, I took a small handful of quinoa seeds and offered it up to Qillamama.

"Qillamama," I intoned, "friend to the Hatunruna, thank you for the balm of your radiance."

With the aid of a gentle wind and a slight tilting of my hand, she received my offering. Then I quenched my thirst before going to sit beside Chumpi, who was awake, chewing his cud. Leaning back against him, I studied our village, bathed in Qillamama's light. The wasis appeared bluish-white save in the dark shadows beneath the eaves. Beyond the wasis, a bend in the stream sparkled in Quillamama's light. Farther still, the terraced fields, though duller in their reflection than the walls of the wasis, were rungs of a ladder climbing to the stars.

All this beauty only deepened my sense of peace, and with this peace came the realization that something had altered within me. I knew my dream had been more than a dream, a vision sent by the gods, and I the recipient because, as Ipa so firmly believed, I possessed a gift. No longer did I doubt her assertion that my life and Topa Inca's had become entwined, for the gods had revealed to me the existence of the water at the end of the world, for surely the crystalline river with its supernatural qualities could be nothing else! And there was the fact of my name, Yana Mayu, which described the image, still strong in my mind, of a black river clearly outlined even within the darkness. This to me was not only the final proof that the water at the end of the world existed, but also that the gods had revealed to me its existence so that I might find it.

The power of my dream lingered and made me feel as if I were balanced between the past and the future. The past was my childhood, all my life up until this moment, despite the fact that it had been over a year since my quicochicoy. Always in the past, I had had little power, and for that reason I had feared change, for it had often resulted in the loss of someone I loved. What power had I over my mother's death? What power over my father's having to serve in the Capac Inca's army? What power over Charapa's imprisonment? I realized I had always been a small knot of wood floating upon the water, subject to the push of the wind.

To my credit, I did not believe the future held for me some greatness. Rather it was by accepting my helplessness, I gained strength, for even if I was but a knot floating upon the water, I could at least face the wind pushing me along and thus play my part in the greater power that patterned the water's surface and churned its icy depths.

The choice before me now was whether to go on living as I had been, a girl frightened of change, denying the gifts I had been given, comfortable in my little world; or whether to become a true woman, accepting of my gifts, not hiding from change or what plans the gods might have in store for me, believing, as Ipa believed, that the gods acted for the best. The path toward womanhood was clearly before me, and I all I had to do was to seek the water at the end of the world and I would be upon it.

Yet all journeys require preparation, so with a feeling of contentment, I pulled my knees into my chest and postponed, for a little longer, any decision. For the time it took Qillamama to travel across the sky, I enjoyed the freedom of being neither a girl nor a woman.

Just before dawn, Ipa came and stood before me. "Your chusi is cold," she said. "How long have you been awake?"

"A long time. I've been thinking about a dream I had, a dream of a black river."

She looked at me intently. "The water that flows underground?"

"Yes."

I stood and motioned for her to take my place. I sat cross-legged before her then waited until she was resting comfortably against Chumpi before asking the question which was foremost in my mind. "Where do I find the water at the end of the world?"

She sighed. "Charapa asked me this same thing, remember? I told him the water was nowhere and everywhere."

I started to object, but she raised a hand. "I know this answer does not satisfy you, so let me try to explain." She leaned forward. "Sit up straight." She unclasped my topu and pushed back my lliqlla, exposing my shoulders to the cool morning air. "In life, there are two primary forces. One force moves to the center, and the other force moves away from center." She placed the palm of her hand against my chest. "The food you eat, the water you drink, the air you breathe, all move to your center, the sonqo, the area of the heart. There the sonqo takes these elements and combines them before moving them outward to the other parts of your body through your blood. The blood gives your body life; the fat within the blood gives energy. That which your body does not want is eliminated through your sweat, urine, and feces. This elimination is returned to Pachamama where it is used to grow plants. Then the movement toward your sonqo begins again as you eat, drink and breathe."

She removed her hand and sat back.

"It is the same with Pachamama as it is with you, only her blood is water. There is water in the clouds. As rain, it falls upon the mountains and gathers in the lakes and rivers. The water also seeps into the ground and flows in underground rivers. All waters feed Pachamama's sonqo which is Lake Titikaka.

"But Lake Titikaka also gives back the water, for by Inti's warmth, its water is taken and formed into clouds. The clouds make rain, and once again the rain falls and brings life to the mountains.

"So, you see there are two forces: one that moves the water toward Lake Titikaka; one that moves it away. But in this cycle where is there a beginning or an ending? How can there be a water at the end of the world when water is everywhere? Is the water at the end of the world in the sky? Surely, there is no land in the sky. Or is it nearer to Pachamama's sonqo, Lake Titikaka? Nothing is clear, so who can say where the world ends or the water begins?"

"I have seen the water at the end of the world," I said. "In a dream, the gods have shown me a beautiful river which flows underground."

"Yana, can you share your dream with me?"

I thought hard about her request. We both understood this dream was a gift to me, to share or not to share. If I told her of my dream then, for me, its power would diminish, and the only way I could restore the power of the dream would be to act upon it.

I looked to the east. A faint star hung above mountains clearly outlined by the predawn light. I took in a great breath and slowly released it. It was time to choose. I could not remain half-girl, half-woman.

So, I told Ipa of my dream, everything including the fear I had felt of an invisible presence with me in the cavern. By the time I was finished, Inti was in the sky and in the air smelled of burning llama dung as the women in our village went about preparing morning meal. Chumpi, tired of being a backrest, stood up and went to the stream to drink. Still Ipa and I continued to talk.

"Atakachau! What a wonderful dream!" Ipa exclaimed. "Truly the gods were speaking to you."

"Is it the same dream you had night before my quicochicoy?"

She nodded. "But my dream was not so detailed. I never saw the crystals or the separate tunnels. But cave was the same and the river within it, darker than the walls surrounding it, like the mountains against the lesser darkness of the night sky."

"What about my feeling of there being an unseen menace in the cave with me?"

She shook her head. "I don't remember anything like that."

I shivered remembering the icy touch upon my skin.

Ipa placed a hand upon my arm. "Don't worry so much about whatever was in the darkness. Perhaps it was nothing to be frightened of. As you know, when people die, they travel the underground road that takes them to the lakes high in the mountains where they are reborn. Perhaps the thing in your dream was such a traveler. If you are respectful of the dead, then they have no cause to harm you."

This made me feel better, for it made sense: the place where the world ends could also be the place where a person goes before he is reborn.

"Ipa, I want to find the place in my dream. I want to find the water at the end of the world and bring it to the Capac Inca. Once Topa Inca is cured by the water, the Capac Inca will surely release Charapa from prison."

Ipa released by arm. "Dreams can mean so many things."

"I know what this one means!"

She was startled by the passion in my voice. "So now you no longer doubt the validity of your visions? Good! But did the dream tell you exactly where the underground river is?"

I shook my head. "Not exactly, but…" Then I remembered the story she told. "What about the cave you told us about, the place where Manka and Kachi ended their underground journey? You said it was near Tambo Toco."

Ipa looked worried. "Yana, are you certain you wish to do this? To go looking for the water at the end of the world? Think of the danger. Even if you were to find the cave that would lead you to the water, how can you travel underground? What if you ran out of food or water? What if you became lost?"

I tried not to show the fear I felt in response to her questions. "Ipa, I know that many times I have acted rashly, but this is not one of those times. During the night, I thought about my dream for longer than it takes to cook potatoes three times. I understand your concerns, for I have them too. Just the thought of being underground terrifies me. Still I believe the gods gave this dream to me for a reason. They have shown me the water at the end of the world, and I don't believe they would have revealed it to me unless they wanted me to find it.

"You told me that my life and Topa Inca's are intertwined. I now believe you. The gods want me to bring the Capac Inca the water that will cure his son. I do not know how I can find the cave. I do not know how I can survive beneath the ground. But I have faith that, when the time comes, the gods will show me how I can do these things."

Ipa smiled. "Whatever happened to the girl who was afraid of a little cold water?"

I smiled in return. "She is trying to become a woman."

Ipa reached forward and grasped my shoulders with her strong fingers.

She did not speak, but communicated through the strength of her hands her love and concern for me. Yet I also sensed she was proud of me. She gave me a final squeeze before releasing me.

"Help me up!" she commanded. "I've been sitting so long I can't feel my butt."

I stood up and helped lift her.

"Atatau! There was a time when I could sit that way all day and not be stiff at all."

"I'll make some tea," I said "It'll warm you up."

"No, there's no time. We've much to do. We need to start baking sweet maize cakes."

I stared at her, not understanding.

"For your journey, of course! They are lightweight and filling, and they keep well. We also need to count how much charqui we have. Maybe Qapia Weqe can part with some. They had to kill that llama that got mange." She slapped her forehead. "Atatau! I've forgotten all about Kusi! Poor Qapia Weqe has enough to do without also having to take care of him also."

"I'll go get him," I said

But as I turned toward Qapia Weqe's wasi, Ipa turned me round to face her. She gently placed her hand upon my cheek.

"Every morning, I shall make offerings to the gods. Each night will I give them chicha. I shall pray for you with every breath I take. But remember this: if you cannot find this water beneath the ground, come home. No one will punish you for having tried, I promise!" She dropped her hand and looked in the direction of our family's huaca. "Now I'll have to place three cups of tea before our spirits each morning!"

Part Two

Tambo Toco

Chapter 12

The morning I was to leave Qomermoya, I awoke well before Inti appeared in the sky. Ipa, who had risen earlier, had made a bowl of locro for me. The plan was for me to leave before the others in the village awoke. Preparations for my journey had been completed; the two packs Chumpi would carry contained all necessary provisions.

Finished eating, I picked up Kusi and held him for a while. He pulled at my necklace, and I dangled the beautiful yellow feather before him. As I watched him stare in fascination, I felt a lump in my throat and had to force back tears. I tried to follow Ipa's example, for she looked as unconcerned as if it was just an ordinary day. She did, however, remind me of what she had said before.

"Remember, no one here will punish you for trying to find the water at the end of the world. And don't feel ashamed if you can't find it. The gods sometimes ask us to do things that are not humanly possible. Remember that, for I want you to return safely."

I nodded. I was trembling. Never before had I spent a night away from Qomermoya.

Ipa took Kusi from my arms. "Now go! The sooner you are gone, the sooner you will find the water at the end of the world and return."

I placed the packs atop Chumpi and led him by his halter. At the stream, I looked back, but Ipa had her back to me. Once across the stream, I released Chumpi, and we traveled up the valley quickly, for the way was open and Qillamama very bright.

Ipa had made no secret of my journey to Tambo Toco, though she did not mention the reason for my going. People assumed it was because I wished to pray for Charapa at the cave where Manka and Kachi had emerged from beneath the ground, for it was a place of great spiritual power. If Weqo Churu had been there, likely Ipa would have kept quiet about my leaving, but Ukumari was no match for her authority. In fact, he proved a useful ally, for he had spent a few months in the area of Tambo Toco, fixing roads as part of his service to the Capac Inca. From him, I learned of a little-frequented route to Tambo Toco that followed the Apurimac River. Although I would have made better time following the road Weqo Churu had taken to Qosqo, that way passed through the fertile valley of the Huatanay River, where my presence as a Hatunruna traveling without permission would certainly have been noticed and reported.

By the time Inti rose, Chumpi and I were well into the mountains. Chumpi, who usually scrambled on ahead of me, was slowed by the heavy packs he carried, and I sensed his frustration. Even with nothing to carry, I found the rocky terrain tiring, and it was not until late afternoon that we stood on the rim of the canyon where I could see the Apurimac River far below.

Then it started to rain. Considering how much we needed rain, I felt this a good omen, though it was not a storm, but a localized cloudburst, a frequent occurrence in the mountains at that time of year. With the rain came a biting wind. My lliqlla was woven with llama wool which provides warmth even when wet. Still, some rain found its way underneath my collar and trickled down my chest or back, depending which way the wind blew.

Battered by the rain, Chumpi looked bedraggled. The short hairs on his head were beaten down, and his long ears drooped like sodden leaves. Twining rivulets ran off his chin, creating a long, twisting beard. His mournful eyes asked: Why are we doing this? Why don't we find some place nice and dry like a wasi with an opening large enough for me to crawl through?

I rubbed the side of his neck. "I'm sorry, my friend, but there are no wasis here." I reached down to dislodge a stone wedged between my toes. I could not wear my sandals while it was raining for fear of ruining the soft llama leather. "Let's try to make it to the river before we camp. With any luck, it won't be raining down there."

This proved to be the case, though the air was chilly, for Inti was hidden not only by clouds, but by the steep hillside opposite the river. The Apurimac River was not as Ukumari described it. Though known to be swift and treacherous, the lack of rainfall had reduced it to a timid stream. This proved beneficial, since in that wild area of the canyon there was no trail. Instead, I made my way along the exposed shoreline, avoiding the dense brush made up of chilca, hanca hanca and thorny llaulli bushes.

Though tired, I nevertheless decided to push on until I found a good place to camp. We forded a side stream bordered with huayau trees. The trees offered shelter, should the rains return, and the use of downed branches for firewood. I made my way up this little stream, for I wanted to be away from the river should someone happen by. I chose a spot beneath a large huayau tree and leaned the packs against the trunk. Glad to be relieved of his burden, Chumpi rolled upon his back on the very spot where I wished to make a fire.

"Look at you!" I scolded, pointing to the dirt on his back. "If you think I'm going to comb you, forget it. I'm too tired."

Sitting up, he amiably twirled his ears then quickly stood and attacked a nearby patch of green grass. From the packs, I took the items I would need for the night. My chusi was damp, but my food was dry, thanks to the watertight gourds the women in our village had contributed for my journey. The women also had provided me with enough charqui to last three weeks. Three weeks seemed an eternity away from Qomermoya, and I vowed to find the water at the end of the world well before my supply of charqui ran out.

I made a fire, then hung my chusi in the branches above it. This served two purposes: the heat from the fire would dry my chusi, and the chusi would trap the smoke which helped to repel the biting insects. When I had a good bed of coals, I placed a small jar, half filled with water, upon them. Into the jar I crushed bilyea leaves. Besides bilyea, Ipa had provided me with a variety of dried herbs including coca. "Don't use the coca leaves unless you have to," she had instructed, "but they'll be invaluable should you need them. If you run out of food, chewing on a leaf will silence your hunger and give you energy. Also, chew a leaf or two if you become sick crossing any mountain passes."

As the water heated, I nibbled upon a sweet maize cake. I did not realize how hungry I was until I bit into it, then it was all I could do to keep from gobbling it down and reaching for another. Chumpi nosed my arm, and I broke off a small piece and gave it to him.

"Don't think I'm always going to share my cakes with you. I have to make them last."

Having issued this warning, I nevertheless thought a bit of maize cake a small trade for the pleasure of his company. There is an old saying: to be alone is the worst tragedy of life. Without Chumpi's companionship, I'm certain I would have been retracing my steps back to Qomermoya at that very moment, tired as I was. Even with Chumpi's company, I felt uneasy; it was too quiet. I missed rattle of bowls, the banging of stirring spoons against the rim of pots, the murmur of voices in conversation punctuated with bursts of sudden laughter.

When the tea was ready, I poured it into my cup. It tasted good and warmed me inside. Still I wished I had had some chicha, for it is a good drink to relax sore muscles.

Chumpi nosed my arm again. Having put aside the maize cakes, I could only offer to scratch his nose. He deemed this a poor substitute, and turned away and lay down nearby. I added more sticks to the fire. The fire reminded me of how, following a day of celebration, the people of my village would sit around a fire and talk quietly or listen as someone played a flute or an ocarina. From a pack, I took my ocarina and played a song, which I had always loved for the melody, if not the words.

> The fire you have started,
> It rings the mountains,
> It fractures the rock.
>
> Sparks fly up,
> Like Intuillapa's river
> They illuminate the night.
>
> Cruel Passion's daughter,
> You who made this fire,
> Fly to my arms
> And with one thousand tears,
> Quench this burning in my heart.

Obviously, this song had been composed by some lovesick youth whose sadness at not having his love returned had addled his brain. One thousand tears? What woman could cry so many, even if she wanted to?

I leaned away from the fire and looked to the sky where a few stars were visible through a scattering of faintly lit clouds. It was a beautiful sight, but I found it difficult to keep my eyes open. The stream running alongside my camp sang a lullaby. Further down the canyon the Apurimac River joined in. Just as I thought I could make out the words they were singing, I fell asleep.

Chapter 13

The next morning, I awoke just as the stars were beginning to fade. I said a prayer to the gods, asking for the safekeeping of my family, and for their aid in my finding the water at the end of the world. As I did not wish to rekindle the fire, I had no offering of tea, but I broke off a small piece of charqui and placed it in a notch of the huayau tree.

While I was waiting for Inti's light, I combed Chumpi's hair so the packs would ride comfortably upon his back. By the time I finished combing out all the tangles and bits of leaves and grass, it was light enough for us to see our way back down to the Apurimac River. A cold ground mist hovered above the water, and I walked quickly to warm myself. The way was difficult, for I had to clamber over the many large rocks along the river's edge. I walked until I could no longer ignore my hunger pains, then stopped to nibble on a piece of charqui while sitting in Inti's light. Inti's warmth did much to dispel my unease at being so far from home, and I was glad that, despite all the river rocks, Chumpi and I had made good progress since leaving camp. I thought it likely we would arrive in Tambo Toco in less time than Ukumari had estimated.

I was too fidgety to rest for long, so I put away my half-eaten charqui then quickly drank from the river. I noticed my chusi was damp from last night's dew, so I draped it over the packs atop Chumpi.

"Don't look so insulted," I told him, as I tied the chusi down with a piece of rope. "It won't take long to dry, and I promise to pack it away before it gets too hot."

As we continued upriver, I began to glimpse sections of a deer trail cutting through the tangle of brush lining the river. Farther on, the trail showed signs of someone having cut back the brush to accommodate the passing of human feet. This troubled me, for it meant people frequented this area. Still, I appreciated the increase in speed the trail provided.

Towards the middle of the afternoon, I came upon a village. It appeared smaller than Qomermoya, just five or six wasis set upon a hill above a shallow stream that entered the Apurimac River from the north. Regardless of its small size, my heart began to race as soon as I saw it. I hurried along, not seeing anyone until Chumpi and I crossed the stream. At a distance, a group of women sat, weaving. They did not see me and I thought I might slip by unnoticed until a barking dog announced my presence. I smiled and waved to the women. None waved back. A boy started to run toward me, but was called back. I waved again, and this time a few women cautiously acknowledged me. No one approached, and I went ahead at a trot and did not slow until I had gone a tupu, the distance a person can walk in the time it takes to cook potatoes.

A light rain prevented me from making a fire where I spent the night, but I managed to stay dry, sheltered beneath the overhang of a rock. I must have been very tired, for I did not wake until Inti returned to the sky. I quickly packed away my things, said a prayer and hurried along upriver. About the time my stomach was starting to complain, I came to a narrow gorge where the river voiced its power with an angry roar. Piles of stranded debris marked the height of the river at flood. Had it not been for the lack of rain, I doubt I could have gone any farther without growing wings. As it was, Chumpi and I were forced to scramble up a boulder-strewn incline, an arm's length from the roaring cascade that wet us with its spray.

I was soaked to the skin by the time we reached the top of the cascade where we found our way blocked by a small lake. The only way forward was to swim. I was not a strong swimmer, and though Chumpi was a better swimmer than I, I doubted whether he could manage with the heavy packs.

I sat down to think. My immediate thought was to return to Qomermoya. My second thought was to question my resolve. I looked about to see if there were any way I could avoid a swim. Across the lake to the right there was a narrow shoreline separated from me by the channel through which the lake water spilled. I realized it would take someone with legs longer than mine to leap across this. My next thought was to find a crossing back down below the cascade, yet I chafed at having to retrace my steps. Turning, I saw several floating logs drifting toward the outflow, and this gave me an idea. Using a long stick, I maneuvered the logs to shore. Curious, Chumpi watched as I lashed the logs together, using rope. I lifted the packs off Chumpi's back and placed them on my makeshift raft. The raft sat deeper in the water, yet still floated.

"We must hurry before the packs get waterlogged," I told Chumpi. I pushed the raft out into the water, then, holding on to one of the logs, propelled the raft forward with strong kicks. Behind me, Chumpi bleated in distress. "Come on, big baby! You're already wet!"

The water was not as deep as I feared, and my feet soon touched bottom. When the water was but waist high, I looked back, but did not see Chumpi. My heart sank.

"Chumpi!" I called. "Chumpi!"

I heard his bleat and turned about to see him already standing on the shore ahead of me. Leave it to Chumpi to find a way to avoid a soaking!

Shivering, I waded onto shore to be met by Chumpi, humming contentedly. "Don't look so smug!"

I wrung out the packs then my chusi. To my relief, the gourds had kept my food dry. Then I repacked my supplies and put the packs upon Chumpi. Finally, I untied my raft and used the rope to secure my chusi atop the packs where, once again, it could dry.

The packs, being wet, were heavier, and Chumpi twitched his ears in annoyance.

"Serves you right for acting so smug," I told him. Then to show there were no hard feelings, I gave him a whole sweet maize cake and ate one myself. It was an indulgence, yet I felt we both deserved a reward for our perseverance. It seemed Pachamama also wished to reward us, for beyond the lake, the river was wide and shallow as it meandered across a sandy bottom that made walking a pleasure. With Inti smiling upon me, my lliqlla was soon dry. I felt happier than any time since leaving Qomermoya. It was a feeling to be short-lived.

As we made our way around a bend in the river, I saw a suspension bridge spanning the canyon. Ukumari had told me that when I came upon this bridge I would be, at most, two days walk from Tambo Toco.

A bridge, however, being made of coiled rope and subject to rot, was often in need of repair, and though I was surprised to come upon men working, I should not have been. Fortunately, I saw the men before they saw me. Immediately I grabbed Chumpi and pulled him to the side where we hid behind a section of collapsed river bank. From where we stood, I could hear the voices of men calling to each other. I debated whether to go back and wait for the cover of darkness, or to stay where I was. If I tried to go back, there was a chance of being seen. Yet if I stayed put, Chumpi would likely grow restless and try to break away.

While I was debating what to do, the gods chose to decide for me. The rope I had used to tie my chusi atop Chumpi must have come loose, for a gust of wind caused the chusi to suddenly flutter high above Chumpi's head.

Alarmed I pulled it back down. The top of the bank was more than twice my
height so I didn't think it likely anyone had seen the chusi waving about, but
then I heard footsteps followed by a trickle of dirt that fell from above.
Looking up, I saw a young man smiling down at me.

"Why are you hiding down there, pretty woman?"

There was nothing to do but try to bluff my way out. "As you can see, I
need to retie my load." If this didn't answer his question exactly, at least it
was the truth. I quickly retied the chusi then, taking Chumpi by his halter,
started upriver, acting as if I had every right to be there. The man followed
along on a ledge above me until forced to move back where another section
of bank had given away.

As I neared the bridge, I heard the voices of men above me and to my
left. Suddenly a row of young men appeared above me. I waved and tried to
act casual, though I don't think I was ever more frightened in my life. An
older man walked out onto the bridge and leaned upon the rope hand rail. A
red llautu, a woven headband with a diadem of brightly-colored feathers,
identified him as an Inca.

"Stop!" he commanded. "Come up here at once!"

It was right at that moment when Chumpi chose to break away. I lunged
after him, but he was too quick, and I slipped and fell headlong into the river.
To the sound of men's laughter, I slowly pushed myself back onto my feet.

"Stay where you are!" the Inca ordered. He was quick to descend the
slope leading down to the river. Behind him, two young men followed, one
of them my discoverer. The Inca stopped at the water's edge and motioned
me to come toward him. His face was very grim, but the two young men
behind him were smiling.

"Who are you, and what are you doing here?" the Inca demanded.

"I am Yana Mayu, and I'm on a pilgrimage to Tambo Toco."

"And do you have permission?" He looked very angry. Though he was
not tall–not nearly as tall as the other two–he was powerfully built. He also
had a hawkish bend in his nose like Weqo Churu's.

I hung my head. Lacking permission to travel, I would be sent back to
Qomermoya, perhaps punished first.

My discoverer spoke up. "Look at her, Father. She's shaking from the
cold. If you must continue your interrogation, at least let her sit down."

Though I was trembling more from fear than the cold, I was grateful for
this consideration. I glanced at the man who made it. Not only did he smile

with his mouth, but also with his eyes.

The Inca pointed to a rock for me to sit on. When I was seated, he propped one foot up beside me and leaned forward. For what seemed an eternity, he didn't speak. Though I had averted my eyes out of respect, I could still feel his gaze hard upon me. In one hand, he held a metal tool which he tapped against the palm of his other hand.

Behind him I heard the voice of the other young man. "Why do you want to go to Tambo Toco?"

I looked up and wished I hadn't. Like my discoverer, this young man also had a look of amusement on his face, but in his case, it was not pleasant to see. As he ran his eyes over me, I longed to put a mountain between us.

I looked down at the ground. "I am going there to pray for my brother."

"Why must you pray for your brother?" The Inca said. "And look at me when you speak."

I lifted my head and spoke the truth to his face. "He is in prison."

I saw a flicker of anger in his eyes.

"It is not what you think! My brother is a good person." I explained how it was that Charapa came to be imprisoned, adding, "My brother is not a person who deceives. His only crime is being that of a dreamer."

The nobleman took his foot from the rock and stood up. "But why must you go to Tambo Toco? You could have prayed for your brother without leaving your village."

I didn't think it would help to tell him that I, too, was seeking the water at the end of the world. Instead, I told him something else, something also true. "I wish to pray for my brother at the place where Manka and Kachi came from beneath the ground. I have been told that prayers, spoken there, have great power."

My discoverer punched the other young man good-naturedly. "Did you hear that, Kacha? Everyone knows how powerful we are!"

For the first time the Inca smiled—just a little. "My sons are named Anka and Kacha," he said, pointing first to my discoverer, then the young man I did not like. "It is because their names sound similar to Manka and Kachi that they like to think of themselves as being fearless, invincible, and above the rules that govern ordinary mortals." He cleared his throat and spat on the ground. "But everyone knows they are foolish, self-deceivers who are not worthy to collect llama dung."

Anka laughed at this. I was liking him more and more.

To the Inca, I said, "Please, Father. Do not send me back to my village."

The Inca scratched the side of his head with his tool. "Allowances are made for those who wish to perform pilgrimages to sacred places." He pointed his tool at me. "I will allow you to continue on to Tambo Toco provided you promise me that once you have prayed for your brother you will return immediately to your village."

How could I promise him this? I had to find the water at the end of the world. I leaned forward and cradled my face in my hands. In doing so, my necklace slipped out from under my lliqlla.

The Inca was quick to grab it. "Where did you get this feather?" He tugged on my necklace so that it dug into the back of my neck.

"Topa Inca gave it to me."

"Atatau! Why would Topa Inca give such a beautiful feather to a Hatunruna?"

I quickly explained how I came to have the feather. When I finished, the Inca released my necklace with a sigh. "I feel there is more to your story than you're telling me. For your own good, I ought to beat you and send you home. Still, Topa Inca saw something good in you, and it is good that you love your brother and honor the gods. If you wish to continue on to Tambo Toco, I will not stop you."

I leapt up, feeling like a bird released from a cage. "Thank you, Father!"

"Do not thank me. I know the chieftain of Tambo Toco, and he is not soft-hearted like me. He'll probably give you a thrashing you will not forget. You will walk all the way home without stopping because you'll be too sore to sit or lie down."

Before I could think of a response, Anka said, "Are you certain you know the way to Tambo Toco?"

"I just follow the Apurimac upriver until I get there."

All three laughed.

"Which fork of the Apurimac?" Anka said.

I shook my head, not knowing.

"Atatau!" the Inca cried, "The foolishness of young people!" He turned away and began to climb back up the steep bank. Over his shoulder he said, "One of you better walk a little distance with this pilgrim and see she doesn't get lost."

I had a sudden fear that my escort would be Kacha, but my apprehension vanished when Anka spoke up.

"I will go with her," he said, looking not at me, but at his brother, as if challenging him to object. Kacha studied me for a moment with eyes that made my skin crawl. Then he shrugged and followed after his father.

It was then I remembered Chumpi and looked to see where he had run off to.

"It looks like your llama has made friends," Anka said, pointing to the ledge above us.

Chumpi had made his way up the opposite bank, across the bridge, and was now surrounded by several young men who were giving him tidbits of food.

"He's the friend of anyone who will feed him," I said.

"Chumpi!" I shouted, "Come down! We're leaving!"

Chumpi, ignoring me, nuzzled a man's chest, seeking more treats.

"Do you expect your llama to understand you?" Anka said.

I nodded. "Chumpi understands me very well, and that's why he's ignoring me. But once he sees I'm leaving, he'll follow."

Anka went before me, leading the way upriver. Beyond the bridge, the canyon narrowed, and the river flowed swiftly around rocks and boulders. I picked my way carefully along the shoreline, but Anka, with his long legs, hopped effortlessly from one rock to the next. After a while, I looked back. I could no longer see the bridge, and neither could I see Chumpi. Annoyed, I was just about to turn back when I heard him anxiously bleat, as if to say: "Don't leave me!" Of course, as soon as Chumpi caught sight of me, he acted as if nothing was amiss.

"Don't play that game with me!" I scolded. "The next time you desert me for some bits of food, I will give you to the wilka camayocs to be sacrificed!"

Not believing a word of what I said, he airily smacked his lips.

I laughed at his impudence, suddenly feeling very pleased myself.

Chapter 14

It troubled me that Anka was the son of an Inca, for that made him an Inca also. Yet he appeared to be a cheerful and good-natured man, and despite Weqo Churu's earlier warning, I didn't believe difficulties would arise from my associating with him—not that it seemed I had a choice.

We walked about a half a tupu before coming to a fork in the river. Anka led me along the left fork until we came to calm section of water interspersed with large rocks. Anka crossed the river by hopping from rock to rock. Perhaps it was because he was an Inca that he did not think it necessary to make the proper observances before crossing. I, on the other hand, knelt and said a prayer before taking Chumpi by his halter and wading across.

Anka waited for us, then, to my surprise, started back downriver until once again we reached the confluence of the two forks.

"This other is the fork you'll want to follow," Anka said, as he started up the trail that edged the river.

This was confusing to me. Why had Anka led me along the wrong fork when we could have just as easily crossed the river below the confluence? Was he playing a game with me? But his reason became clear when, a little farther on, I heard the rumble of falling water. On the opposite side, a rampaging stream poured out of a narrow canyon, dropping from tree height into the river below. The waterfall was thrilling to look upon, for a brilliant rainbow hung in the mist created by the rock-pounding torrent, but getting past the waterfall from the other side would have been impossible. I said a prayer, thanking the gods for sending me a guide.

Anka outpaced me, preventing me from asking more about the trail we were on. As Inti made his way across the sky, the distance between us only lengthened. I was glad when Inti finally passed behind a ridge, certain we would stop soon. But Anka continued on, and I staggered after him, reluctant to admit of my fatigue. It wasn't until Chumpi, who was as tired as I, stumbled and nearly fell, that I called to Anka.

"Anka!" I shouted, "are you planning to lead me all the way to Tambo Toco today?"

Anka turned about and retraced his steps. His ever-present smile disappeared when he saw how tired I was. "I'm sorry, Yana, I was only trying to lead you to a village not far ahead."

"I don't think Chumpi and I can go another step. We've walked much farther today than any day since we left home."

Anka looked around. "You wish to sleep here, in the open, away from the village?"

"I'd rather sleep in the open than collapse from exhaustion."

He grinned. "But aren't you afraid you might get eaten by a hungry puma?"

He was teasing, of course, for we both knew pumas rarely attacked people. "I'm less afraid of pumas than of people asking me questions about where I'm going."

Anka laughed then lifted the packs off Chumpi's back. "Where do you want these?"

I pointed to an open area next to a large rock. "Lean them against that rock, if you would."

He started rummaging through my packs. "So, what's to eat?"

I had not expected him to join me for evening meal, though I was not displeased. "Charqui," I answered.

"Atatau!" he exclaimed, making a face. "After you have rested, start a fire. I will be back in a little while with dinner."

I knew if I sat to rest I would fall asleep. I walked to the river and splashed cold water on my face then set about gathering wood. Chumpi, too tired to stand, sat with his legs tucked beneath him and stretched out his long neck to nibble blades of grass.

After I had the fire going, I sat beside it and failed in my struggle to stay awake. Anka's voice woke me.

"These ought to taste better than charqui," he announced, holding aloft two fish in one hand and a jar of chicha in the other. "I could have caught five times as many fish, some bigger than these."

I pointed to the jar. "And did you also catch a jar of chicha?"

Anka grinned. "The chicha I got from the villagers." He set down his load and reached into his bag. "I also got these."

He handed me more potatoes than we could possibly eat in one sitting. I laughed with pleasure at this bounty. Once I set the potatoes to bake, I started to clean the fish, using the sharp edge of my topu to cut into the flesh.

"Here, let me," Anka said, unsheathing the knife he carried. The magnificent blade, made of bronze, sparkled in the firelight. With a few expert strokes, Anka filleted the fish. The entrails he placed upon the fire as an offering to the gods.

I skewered the fish with sticks then set them aside until the potatoes were nearly baked. While we waited, we shared the chicha, but only after I made another offering, pouring a little upon the fire. Silently, I asked the gods to watch over my family, and again I thanked them for providing me with a guide.

I had but one cup, but Anka did not mind sharing it with a Hatunruna. In fact, he insisted I drink first. I took several large swallows and soon felt the beverage enter my muscles and begin to untie the knots. But chicha also loosens the tongue and makes the mind less cautious. It gave me the courage to ask personal questions of an Inca.

"Your father is a very important person, is he not?"

Anka sat up straight and tall. "My father is a great amauta!" he declared.

"What is an amauta?"

"He is someone who teaches at the Yachawasi, the academy for young Incas who will one day hold important positions within the government or the army." Anka pushed one of the potatoes closer to the fire with a stick. "My father teaches mathematics and engineering, but he believes that attending classes in the comfort of the Yachawasi is of little value. He wants his students to get out and apply what they learn. That's why we are working on the bridge, so his students can see how an actual bridge is constructed."

A sudden realization came to me. "Then those young men at the bridge are all Incas?"

Anka nodded. "Nearly half are either the sons of the Capac Inca or of his brother, the Wilka Uma, the high priest."

"Why don't you and these young men wear llautus like your father?"

Anka shrugged. "A llautu is not comfortable to wear when working. And many of the students you saw today are just boys. Not until they've entered puberty and celebrated their huarachicoy will they be allowed to wear a llautu." Anka smiled "Besides, my father thinks it's a good experience for his students to work and live like Hatunrunas."

"Do you always work with your father?"

He sighed. "Unfortunately, yes. I've lost count of the number of bridges my brother and I have worked on. I swear I could build a bridge with my eyes closed, but my father still doesn't think I'm good enough. It's his wish that I take his place when he retires."

Anka did not look happy about this. "Don't you want to be an amauta?"

"Yes, eventually. It's just that I've spent so much time studying with my father, I haven't done many of the things I would like to do. I would like to travel, perhaps join the army—not as an engineer, but as an actual soldier. Or perhaps just go traveling with my brother." He waved an arm. "Tahuantinsuyu is so vast, and there's so much to see."

I smiled, thinking how much Anka sounded like Charapa.

Anka continued. "And being an amauta is just so…" he scratched his cheek, "…so settled."

"What about your brother? Could he not take your father's place?"

An uncharacteristic frown appeared on Anka's face. "Kacha is not interested in mathematics or engineering. My father only brings him on these outings because…" He appeared uncertain whether to tell me more. Then he shrugged. "Understand, I love my brother. We have shared many fine adventures." His eyes sparkled, remembering. "One time, when we were just boys, we climbed over the walls which surround the garden of the Acllawasi, that's the palace of the sacred women where no man is allowed to enter save the Capac Inca himself. Atatau! If we had been caught!"

Anka lifted his head by his hair until his neck was stretched out. He looked so comical I had to laugh despite the fact it was no laughing matter. Had Anka and his brother been caught, they would have been strung up by their hair.

"Kacha has always been mischievous, but lately some of his antics have gotten him into serious trouble. I think there is something not right in his head. He's very ambitious, but doesn't like to work. He'd rather take from others, and sometimes he seems to find pleasure in hurting people. My father recognizes this about Kacha and insists he stay with us and not be left to get in more trouble."

Smiling, I gazed into the fire.

"What do you find so humorous?" Anka said.

I looked up. "I'm sorry. I mean no disrespect, it's just that listening to you talk—your dissatisfaction with your work, your fear of your brother disgracing your family—I thought these were the problems of Hatunrunas, not Incas."

"I guess no matter who you are, the problems are the same." He poked at a potato again. "I'm hungry enough to eat a whole llama." Before I could object, he added. "Not Chumpi, of course."

I tested a potato. "Almost done." I set the fish over the flames. We didn't speak as we watched them sizzle. The fire suddenly sent up sparks, and I sought to pacify the god of the fire with a sprinkling of chicha. The smell of the roasting fish was almost overwhelming, and I think I would have eaten the fish half raw had I not had the chicha to ease the ache in my stomach.

When the fish were done, we ate them, holding onto the skewers. I do not know if that was the best meal I had ever eaten. It seemed so, but hunger goes a long way toward flavoring a meal. Yet the fish were succulent, their flesh falling easily from the bone. There was nothing to flavor the potatoes other than salt, but the potatoes were the small, hard ones that only grow at the highest elevations and always taste as if they had been cooked in fat.

I ate until my stomach was as taut as a drum, and still there were more potatoes left. I offered these to Anka, but he waved them away. "Save them for your journey," he said.

Sated and sleepy, I struggled to keep my eyes open. Anka looked sleepy as well. He stared into the fire, which gave me the opportunity to study his face. Anka was very handsome, yet I noticed lines of tension in his face which I sensed reflected an inner worry. I got out my ocarina and began to play softly, and as I played I watched the lines in his face relax. I did not play a familiar tune, but something suggested by the sound of the river. My notes started high and spilled downward, like water gushing over rocks, then they became breathy and almost indistinguishable from the river's lively chatter. Resonant tones slipped down as if into a deep pool, there to be held under by the weight of near silence. A startled fish flicked its tail stirring them, and the notes rose upward, broke the surface, and lazily drifted in widening circles until swept out into the main current where they undulated through a ripple. Finally, the notes rose with the mist, hovering like a hummingbird greeting Inti's return from his subterranean wandering. Following the path of a golden beam, the hummingbird soared upward, her expectant song vanishing along with her.

I put my ocarina away then got maize cakes from one of my packs. Chumpi, who missed nothing, saw me offer one of the cakes to Anka. Chumpi stood up and trotted toward us. He stopped just outside of the ring of firelight, not knowing what to do. At home, he was not allowed to step inside of our eating area, but we were not at home.

"It's all right, Chumpi," I said, breaking my cake and offering him half. He chewed, smacked his lips, then seeing he would get no more from me, turned to Anka and nudged his arm.

"Chumpi, leave Anka alone!"

"That's all right," Anka said. "I'm really too full to eat any more." He gave Chumpi the remainder of his cake. As Chumpi chewed, Anka scratched him just above his nose. "It's funny, I've never had a llama of my own."

"I sometimes think Chumpi doesn't consider himself a llama, more of a human with two extra legs and a lot more hair."

Chumpi sat down next to me, and I leaned back against him.

"I'm envious," said Anka. "Your backrest is softer than mine."

"You're welcome to trade places," I offered.

"Isn't Chumpi big enough for two?"

His question surprised me. Could an Inca actually wish to sit so close to a Hatunruna? Then I had another thought. Was Anka attracted to me? Was such a thing possible? I did not know how to respond.

Anka, showing no sign of being offended by my reticence, moved back a little to rest his back against an upright boulder. When he was comfortably situated he said, "Is that true what my father thinks, that there is more to your story than you told him?"

My muscles tensed. I feared to respond lest a full disclosure of my intentions make Anka as upset as his father had been.

Anka must have been reading my mind. "Do not worry, Yana. Whatever you tell me will not be repeated."

I sighed. "At Tambo Toco, I shall pray for my brother, just as I told your father. But afterwards I must find the water at the end of the world." I explained to him why I felt I had to do this. I did not speak specifically of my dream, but by talking around it, conveyed my conviction that the gods had chosen me for this task.

"When I left Qomermoya, I little knew how to go about finding the water at the end of the world. I am still in the dark, but I have faith in the gods. Today when you discovered me hiding, I thought my journey had come to an end, especially when I could not promise your father I would return to my village once I prayed at Tambo Toco. But now I know the gods wanted you to discover me, for without your guidance, I would not have known which fork of the river to take."

As I was talking, Anka closed his eyes. I thought he might have fallen asleep. Then he spoke with sadness in his voice.

"Except for occasional travels with my father and his students, I have lived in my whole life in Qosqo. In Qosqo, there are temples everywhere. Many are magnificent, like small mountains rising up in the squares. Wilka camayocs are constantly making offerings to the gods. The very air smells of our veneration of the gods." He took a stick and stirred the coals. "Living in Qosqo, one cannot help sensing the presence of the gods everywhere. Still, I don't believe I would have the courage to undertake a quest such as yours just on faith."

He turned to look directly at me. "Listening to you has made me realize something about myself. Regardless of all my reckless adventures, I'm more of my father's son than I realize. I put my faith in those things I can build with my hands and in the knowledge I have acquired which allows me to build them.

"But you, Yana, are like a person who, on a night with no stars, is trying to cross a deep gorge. Unseeing, you step off the ledge with faith that a bridge will appear beneath your feet."

I smiled at this image. "Sometimes it feels that way. I don't think I was ever so frightened as when your father commanded me to stop. Yet that is what the gods wanted. Each time the gods help me, another step is placed on this bridge you speak of. And where there is one step, surely there will be others."

Anka tossed his stick aside. "When you find the water at the end of the world, how will you get it to the Capac Inca?"

"I am not sure." I smiled. "I haven't gotten that far on the bridge."

From around his neck Anka removed a necklace which had been hidden beneath his unku. As we had been talking, Qillamama had risen above the rim of the canyon, and a metal medallion, fastened to the necklace, glistened in her light.

"Look at this," Anka commanded, holding the necklace out to me.

I took the necklace and brought it close to my face. On the medallion was an image of Inti, more finely detailed than the one that had been given to my father. Obviously, it was the work of a great artist.

"Why is it so heavy?" I said.

"It is made of gold."

I quickly thrust the necklace back into his hand.

"No!" Anka cried. "I want you to have it!" He extended the necklace toward me again, but I shrank away as if it were a poisonous snake. "It is a serious crime for Hatunrunas to possess gold!"

Anka took my hand and pried open my fingers "Then hide it beneath your lliqlla. Eventually you may need it order to get an audience with the Capac Inca."

"Why? My brother received an audience."

Anka grinned. "Oh, really? It is more likely he gave what he thought was the water at the end of the world to someone who gave it to someone else, who gave it to a third person, who may have finally given it to the Capac Inca."

I realized I had been foolish in thinking that, by finding the water at the end of the world, I could just walk up to the Capac Inca and hand it to him.

"But how will the necklace help?" I said.

"If you find you cannot get an audience with the Capac Inca, then make your way to the Yachawasi, the academy for boys I told you about. Present this necklace and someone will summon me. Then at least I could help you gain admittance to the Cora Cora, the palace where the Capac Inca lives. And if I cannot help you, I'm sure my father can."

Such kindness and generosity on top of what Anka had already shown left me speechless. I was beginning to understand why Incas were called noble.

I placed the necklace over my head, careful to hide the gold medallion beneath my lliqlla. Then I started to remove my own necklace to give to Anka. It was my only possession comparable in value to the necklace he had given me.

"Don't!" Anka cried, seeing what I was doing. "Please, keep your necklace."

It hurt that he would not accept my gift in return for his. Tears come into my eyes.

Anka moved closer and took both of my hands. "I know what you're thinking, that it is wrong for me not to receive your gift in exchange for mine, but let me tell you this: I am a most fortunate man, for my father is a very respected teacher, and, as a consequence, our family has received many treasures. But tonight, Yana, you have given me a treasure of greater value. You have challenged me to look deep within myself. Thanks to you, I have much to think about."

It could not imagine what I said that could be of great value, but I saw true sincerity in Anka's eyes.

He released my hands and stood up. "Now, I must go."

My heart sank. "But wouldn't it be better to wait for Inti to light your way?"

He laughed. His laughter had become special to me. "Qillamama's light is more than enough to see by. Besides, tomorrow there's to be a competition to see which group of students can make a span of weight-bearing rope the fastest. My father won't forgive me if I'm not there to lead one of the teams."

One of my legs had gone to sleep, making it difficult for me to stand. Anka took my hand and helped me up. He held my hand for a moment before picking up the jar that had contained the chicha. Smiling, he absently turned the jar in his hands. "Yana, I don't know who you talked to, but Tambo Toco is not located along the Apurimac River."

Disbelief must have shown in my face, for Anka laughed once more.

"Tambo Toco is located upon a high plain. But don't worry, you're still going in the right direction." With his free hand, he pointed up the trail. "In about four tupus, you will cross a small stream. If you were to follow this stream, you would eventually reach Tambo Toco, but I know from experience that going that way requires the agility of a mountain goat. Farther along there is a much bigger stream, which has a name: Ccolpamayo. An easier route is marked with a rock cairn just past the Ccolpamayo. The trail is very steep, and sometimes disappears in the rocky scree, but if you just keep going in direction that Inti rises, you'll come to Tambo Toco." He turned to look at me. "Can you remember all that?"

I nodded.

He handed me the jar. "I told the chieftain of the village I would return this to him."

I took the jar with a feeling of sadness. A sudden breeze blew ashes in my face, forcing me to look away to keep from getting them in my eyes.

Anka gently turned my face back toward him. "When you come to Qosqo, whether you get an audience with the Capac Inca or not, come visit me."

He left me then. I watched until a turn in the trail hid him from view. My loneliness returned with his leaving, but was assuaged by the memory of his smile and of his laughter. Now I had another reason to find the water at the end of the world, so I might visit Anka in Qosqo.

Feeling tired, yet content, I turned to get my chusi from my pack, and in that moment, my contentment vanished, replaced with a feeling of terror.

Chapter 15

I stood stiff from fright, but heard no sound I could not account for. Yet the fear grew stronger, causing my skin to tingle and my heart to race.

Run! Escape! screamed a voice inside my head. But run to where? And from what?

Then I had a vision in which I saw myself with Anka's brother, Kacha. He was leaning over me as I lay on the ground unable to move my legs. His eyes were black stones, and I shrank from the evil lurking behind them.

I dropped the jar Anka had entrusted to me, and the sound of it breaking released me from this hideous vision. I ran to get the packs and flung them across Chumpi, still lying on the ground. He stretched his neck upward, but did not stand. I dared not raise my voice, so whispered in his ear. "Chumpi, we must leave this place, now!" Frantically, I pulled on his halter. Sometimes when a llama is too tired, he will not budge despite any amount of urging. Chumpi, bless him, sensed my alarm and stood up. Quickly, I adjusted the packs then looked about for anything I'd not packed. There were only the potatoes left from our meal. Leaving them, I took Chumpi by his halter and started upriver.

My sense of fear urged me to run, yet even with the aid of Qillamama's light, it was difficult to tell which were rocks before me and which were but shadows. Several times I stumbled and would have fallen had I not had Chumpi to hold onto. Struggling to control my fear, I slowed to a fast walk, for it would have done me no good to fall and break a leg. If I were being pursued, which I feared I was, my pursuer would have equal difficulty seeing his way.

In a short time, we came upon the village Anka had spoken of. All was quiet; not even a dog announced our presence. I thought to wake someone and explain to him my apprehensions. Then I heard footsteps not far behind me and knew there was no time. Yet even as I ran, I noticed how much the village reminded me of Qomermoya, and I felt a pang of homesickness and longed to be safe in my own wasi, snug in my chusi, listening to Ipa snoring.

I ran until my lungs were afire then slowed until the pain eased then ran again. Sometime during the night, I began to wonder if it would not be better to surrender myself to my pursuer rather than to run myself to death. But then the vision of Kacha standing over me returned, and I forced my aching legs to carry me forward. Only once did I stop, to get from my pack the coca leaves Ipa had given me, for I was in grave need of a stimulant. But once stopped, I again thought I heard footsteps and immediately forgot about the leaves and forced my legs into a run. Chumpi, ever faithful, kept pace with me.

Eventually Qillamama completed her journey across the night sky and began to pass behind the lip of the canyon. I was reaching the point when even fear could no longer impel me. I felt as if someone was using my head as a drum. The muscles of my legs had passed beyond fatigue to a disturbing numbness, save for my knees, which pained me with every step. My lips bled, as did my battered toes. I cried at seeing Qillamama begin to disappear, for how would I be able to see my way without her light? It did not occur to my muddled brain that my pursuer would have the same problem.

It was then I heard a sound that drove me to exertions I had not thought myself capable of. It was a whirring menace I knew well from that night Ipa used an aillo to add drama to her story of Manka and Kachi. Hearing it also, Chumpi bleated in fear. I tackled his back legs and bore him crashing to the ground just as the aillo struck the rocks before us with a sound like lightning cracking open the sky. The ear-splitting percussion was still reverberating through my skull as I leapt to my feet and pulled Chumpi up, praying he had not broken a leg in his fall. Then we ran forward like creatures driven by demons.

I ran until the air was sand scouring my lungs, until the muscles of my legs were searing coals. I ran until I had completely exhausted all powers within my body. And when I could go not one step farther, I fell to the ground, and Chumpi collapsed at my side. I managed to lift my head. Chumpi lay on his side, his chest heaving. I crawled to him and buried the side of my face in his hair.

"My friend," I whispered. "I am so very sorry." I noticed the packs he had uncomplainingly carried had fallen off, probably when I had tackled him. And then I noticed something else: I was free of the mad, driving fear!

Chapter 16

The sound of clattering rocks broke in upon my exhausted sleep. My heart pounded as I thought of the aillo. Then the ground quivered beneath me, and I realized the sound was of Pachamama trembling a little. It wasn't the first time she had disturbed my sleep in this manner. Strangely, I had always felt comforted by Pachamama trembling, perhaps because it was a dramatic reminder of her vitality. Of course, sometimes she shook herself like a dog flinging water from her fur, and that was truly terrifying, but such violence was rare.

The next time it was Chumpi who woke me, blowing in my face, urging me to wake up. Inti was already high in the sky, and I shielded my eyes from his brightness. My legs protested my efforts to stand. Blood pounded in my temples. My ears rang. My mouth was so dry, my lips stuck to my gums.

I staggered to the river and drank greedily then threw cold water on my face. Looking down, I saw the face of a strange woman reflected in the water. Her hair was a tangle of tree roots, and she could not have been filthier had she bathed in mud. Atatau! What would the people of Tambo Toco think of such a repulsive creature creeping into their village?

I needed to bathe, yet to do that properly, I first had to find my packs. Calling Chumpi to join me, I made my way back down the trail. As I had suspected, the packs had fallen off when I had tackled Chumpi; proof was the aillo lying nearby. Seeing it brought back the terror of last night, and I hurried back up the trail, leaving the aillo where it had struck the ground.

I stopped beside a calm spot in the river. An examination of the contents of the packs revealed two cracked gourds, but the jar I used to heat water had not broken. I started a fire then stripped off my lliqlla and washed it in the river, using sand to scrub the dirtiest parts. After spreading my lliqlla out to dry, I used hot water and the paqpa root I had packed to make a lather to wash my hair and body. To rinse, I jumped into the river. The river was fed by nearby snowfields and was much colder than the stream that ran through Qomermoya. I stayed in until my muscles started to cramp then ran back to the fire. Its warmth sent delightful shivers across my skin. I let the fire dry me before making tea and drinking it by the river's edge. The tea, in combination with Inti's warmth, did much to alleviate my aches and pains.

Considering my trial of the night before, I was in good spirits. The day held great promise, for soon I would be in Tambo Toco, and once there, I felt certain it would not take long to find the water at the end of the world.

While my lliqlla continued to dry, I combed the tangles out of Chumpi's hair, which produced clouds of dust, forcing me to go for another swim to rinse off the dirt. Chumpi watched as I splashed about, and I urged him to join me. He shook his head and went back to nibbling ichu grass. It did not take me long to dry a second time, for the day had become very warm. My lliqlla was only slightly damp when I put it back on.

Despite my efforts with a comb, Chumpi still looked as if he had been rolling in the dirt. "I should have forced you to go for a swim," I told him, as I placed the packs upon his back. "What will the people of Tambo Toco think when I arrive in the company of such a filthy llama?"

During our flight, Chumpi and I had passed the first of the streams Anka had mentioned. The stream called the Ccolpamayo was nearly as big as the Apurimac River, and we had to walk a fair distance upstream to find a safe crossing. Once back on the trail, it did not take long to find the rock cairn marking the beginning of the trail that led to Tambo Toco. Before starting up the trail, I drank deeply from the Apurimac River then thanked the river for her companionship of the last few days. I realized that if all went as hoped, I might never see the Apurimac River again, for my success at finding the water at the end of the world might allow me to return to Qomermoya along a well-traveled road.

Climbing up out of the river canyon was not difficult until the trail disappeared at the base of a scree. Then for every two steps forward, I slid back one. Chumpi with his narrow feet and long legs soon disappeared over the ridge above. I envied his ease, for I was feeling light-headed, and several times had to stop and catch my breath. When I finally reached the top, I was pleased to see Chumpi waiting for me beside a pool of water made where a seep filled a shallow depression. He did not look happy, and I quickly discerned why, for the terrain ahead was nothing but a jumble of rock with nary a blade of grass in sight. I didn't waste time feeling sorry for him. Like any llama, Chumpi could have gone for days without food or water.

I drank from the pool, then rested. The sky was that intense blue only seen high in the mountains. It felt good to be so high up, for it reminded me of herding llamas in the mountains surrounding Qomermoya. It seemed an eternity since I had left my village, though it had been less than four days.

The trail ahead stretched across a long plateau, flanked on the left by a rocky slope that rose to an arching spine on which rocks protruded evenly like the vertebrae of a monstrous animal. A little way ahead, the trail disappeared in the chaos of a boulder field to reemerge in the distance at the base of a craggy spire. In line with the spire, but far beyond, was a lofty peak covered with snow, and the sky above it appeared even more blue, if such a thing were possible.

For fun, I tried to cross the boulder field by hopping from rock to rock, as I'd seen Anka do. At first I worried the rocks would turn beneath me and cause me to fall. Consequently, I jumped stiff-legged and tense. Then I remembered how graceful Anka had appeared, his motions effortless. I relaxed my muscles and tried not to worry about falling. This made it easier, and I began to imagine myself a little bird, dipping and gliding along. I laughed with the pleasure this gave me. Chumpi thought it a game and ran along beside me. A rock turned beneath me and I screamed, but before losing my balance, jumped to another rock. A second rock turned, and again I jumped away, laughing. I continued dancing across the boulder field until finally a rock turned too quickly, and I fell, landing hard on my rump, but laughing so hard, I scarcely noticed the pain. I lay on the ground, catching my breath, until Chumpi nudged me, and I grabbed his halter to help pull myself up.

Looking back, I was surprised how far I had come from the spring. In the other direction, the spire was close enough so that I had to tilt my head back to see the top. A small cloud suddenly appeared just above it, followed by several others pushed along by a strong wind that cooled my flushed face. A trick of angle and distance made it appear as if the clouds were issuing from the top of the spire. The shape of one cloud reminded me of a condor, launching himself from his aerie, wings outstretched, a lifting wind at his back.

Soon I was walking in cloud shadow. The clouds were becoming increasingly dark, but the thought of a sudden downpour did nothing to lessen my feeling of joy. In a little while, I would be in Tambo Toco, a village I had never seen. There was something exciting about this, and for the first time I had a sense of why Charapa had not wanted to stay in our village, but to travel and meet new people and have new experiences. In my happiness, I improvised a song.

With the wind, I come,
With the rain, I come,
Like a little bird
Dipping and gliding.

Look!
See who enters Tambo Toco.
It's a little bird,
Dipping and gliding
With the wind
And the rain.
Dipping and gliding.

I walked along, singing my silly song until I saw Chumpi suddenly stop. I was immediately on the alert, for I feared he had caught the scent of a puma. I quickly picked up a large rock. There were plenty of boulders about, large enough to conceal a puma. I threw my rock, to make noise rather than with the hope of hitting anything. Suddenly Chumpi kicked up his back legs. He leaped about as if being attacked by a thousand wasps. The packs flapped up and down like wings, then slid off Chumpi's rump, briefly entangling his hind legs before he kicked himself free. Then he sprinted toward the spire.

"Chumpi!" I cried, running after him. The sound of my voice reverberated off the rocks, vibrated through my bones and pounded within my chest. Then I realized it was not my voice causing this. It was Pachamama's!

Within her body, a dragon awakes. To my left, the ground ripples, arches up, splits open, and the dragon emerges. His roar is a hammer beating upon my chest. My feet are yanked from beneath me. Momentarily I seem to float, then I hit the ground, bounce impossibly high, then strike the ground again, face first. My teeth snap together. Dust clouds my eyes. Dirt fills my nostrils.

The dragon gnashes its teeth: a horrible grinding, grinding, grinding! Pachamama screams as her bones are being crushed. I rattle upon the ground like a pebble vibrating upon the skin of a drum. Fine grains of sand sputter before my eyes like water thrown upon a hot rock. Behind me, the rocks I had danced upon are themselves dancing. The slope is also moving, a cascade of stones tumbling down, and I am helpless in their path.

My mind is a scream. Run! Run! Escape the river of rocks! Yet how can

I run when I cannot even stand!

For a moment, the shaking lessens. I see Chumpi, safe near the spire. He lifts his head, opens his mouth, but the sound of his bleating is lost as once again the dragon roars.

I am running now, though I do not remember standing. A rock streaks past my head. I try to run to where Chumpi stands in safety. It seems I am but an arm's length away when the first wave of rocks strikes the back of my legs, almost knocking me down. A rock glances off my head, yet in my panic I hardly feel it as I struggle to stay atop the torrent of rocks. Rocks now whirr past me like small gray birds fleeing before a grass fire. A cloud of dust engulfs me, blocking my view of Chumpi

Chumpi! Chumpi!

Just when I think I have fought free of the river of rocks, another stone strikes my head, this time with such force it spins me clear around. I am upon my back, floating, being carried along by a strong current. Warm liquid trickles down my face and neck. I feel something heavy upon my chest. Above me, there are fragments of blue sky as if I were looking up through the leaves of a tree. I feel a sudden urge to sleep and find myself back home in our wasi, my chusi pulled up to my chin. Ipa turns from a fire she has made and places her warm hands upon my face. I shiver delightfully at her touch.

You are safe. Go to sleep now.

I smile, close my eyes, and obey.

Chapter 17

I was alone, walking upon the underground road, the road the dead take to the mountains, there to be reborn. In the darkness, I trembled from fear and cold.

Then I saw a fire and the people of my village dancing around it. They raised their arms to a sky without stars. I wanted to dance with them, to warm my shivering body, but the harder I tried to reach them, the farther away they moved. I called to them, but the people, laughing and singing, did not hear me. They moved away, taking the fire with them, leaving me alone once more in the darkness.

I cried out from the pain in my body. My thirst was unbearable!

Crystals! As bright as Inti! I closed my eyes, but could not shut out their brightness. My face burned. The heat was worse than the cold, for it made my thirst all the worse. Gradually the crystals began to fade, save one, directly over my head, its shape not sharp-angled, but misshapen and ugly, a dragon's wicked tooth. A drop of water glistened on the very tip. I willed the drop to fall into my waiting mouth, but it refused.

Darkness returned. I heard a familiar sound, the splash of water as it falls over a ledge. Once again, I was in the presence of the water at the end of the world. I knelt and drank of its healing water then lay beside the stream and, in sleeping, dreamed of dragons and rivers of rocks.

The people of my village returned. They lifted me up and placed me inside our wasi, where Ipa was waiting. She lifted my head, and made me drink. The liquid tasted bitter, but warmed my body and dulled my pain. Then I fell into a sleep devoid of dreams.

It was Anka's smile that greeted me when I returned from the place of darkness. I wanted to ask how it was we had come to meet again, but my mouth refused to form the words. He gently lifted my head and gave me water to drink. It dribbled down my chin as I sought to satisfy my thirst. Then I lay back, closed my eyes to stop Anka's face from spinning, and immediately fell asleep.

The next time I awoke, I was alone. Above me, dried herbs and desiccated birds dangled from roof beams, which told me I was in the wasi of a camasca. But who was this camasca, and where was I? And where was Anka, or had I dreamt him? I thought to go seek answers to my questions, but instead fell asleep. When I awoke again, there was a stranger hovering over me, scrutinizing my face in a manner I recognized as being that of a camasca. As he observed me, I observed him. Though much younger than Ipa, his back was bent like an old man's. His back, along with the way his head stuck out, made me think of a vulture, but a vulture whose face was as unlined as a child's.

He pulled down one of my eyelids then the other. When I started to speak, he placed a finger over my mouth before leaning close and smelling my breath. Then he moved down to my feet and began to unwind the strips of cloth my feet were wrapped in. I cried out in pain.

"Shhh!" he commanded. He poured something upon my feet that burned at first, then numbed the pain. After rewrapping my feet, he returned to examine my head, gently probing with his fingers a soreness on the back side.

Satisfied, he sat back upon his heels. "You are truly favored by the gods." His voice surprised me; high, almost like a girl's. He seemed two people in one body: a man, bent with age; a girl, smooth of face, speaking with a sweet voice. This man-girl favored me with a smile. Later, as I grew to know him, I understood why he did not smile often. "I have never seen anyone so pummeled by rocks who didn't have broken bones. If any are broken, they're the bones in your toes, and for that there is little I can do. They will heal on their own."

I had so many questions, yet found it difficult to speak. I pointed to a cup, and the camasca lifted my head so I could drink. Only then did I find my voice. "Who are you and where am I?"

"My name is Mana Chanka." He set the cup aside. "Call me Chanka. And you're in the village of Tambo Toco. Now, do you remember this person?"

With difficulty, I turned my head in the direction Chanka indicated. Near the entrance Anka sat with his back against the wall. "Yes, Anka." I tried to smile; even that caused me pain.

"Now then," Chanka said, "I must ask you a question or two, then I want you to sleep some more," He pulled the chusi up to cover my exposed shoulders. "What do you remember?"

I closed my eyes and saw again the skin of Pachamama breaking open and the dragon emerging. Involuntarily I shuddered. When I spoke, my voice trembled. "I remember I was riding the back of a dragon, or so it seemed. He tossed me about to dislodge me. When I hit the ground, I tried to stand up, but the dragon knocked me down."

I struggled to control the fear the memory evoked. "I remember rocks, like a waterfall, pouring down upon me. I couldn't lift my legs high enough to free myself from the river of rocks." A sudden thought made my heart beat all the faster. "Will my feet be all right? Will I be able to walk?"

"Why do you ask?" Chanka said, a glint of amusement in his eyes. "Is there someplace you're in a hurry to get to?"

I swallowed, wondering how much Anka had told him.

Then Chanka became serious. "Your feet will be fine. I'd be surprised if you're not walking within a few days. It is your head that concerns me. You received a very severe blow. There was much blood on your clothes and on the rocks where they found you."

I carefully fingered the back of my head and traced the outline of a large swelling beneath the wrapping of cloth.

"Now, I'm going to give you a drink that will help you sleep," Chanka said.

"Wait! Can I talk to Anka a while?"

Chanka considered this. "You really need to sleep, but I think a little talking will not hurt."

Chanka moved to the far side of the wasi where there was another injured person, whom I judged to be a child. I could not see much of the child's face, which was heavily wrapped. Chanka put his ear to the child's chest. Apparently satisfied with what he heard, Chanka crawled out through the wasi's opening.

Anka moved to sit next to me. "Be glad you're not that boy. Chanka had to cut a piece out of his skull." Using his thumb and index finger, Anka made a circle the size of a small stone.

"What happened to him?" I said.

"He and his brother had gone inside their wasi to get out of the rain that had started just before Pachamama began to shake. The walls of the wasi collapsed, and the roof fell on them. His older brother was killed."

I thought of my brother Charapa. "That's very sad."

"Yes, but it could have been worse. Four other wasis collapsed, but among the people of Tambo Toco, there were no other serious injuries."

"Thanks to the gods."

"Yes, thanks to the gods."

"How did I get here? Did you rescue me?"

Anka grinned. "It was Chumpi who rescued you."

How could I have forgotten Chumpi? Alarmed, I started to sit up. "Where is he?"

Anka placed his hand upon my shoulder and gently pushed me back down. "He's fine. In fact, he's been getting a hero's welcome, being treated with maize cakes and lots of fresh vegetables. I doubt he'll go back to eating grass again."

I smiled. "So how did he save me?"

"Do you remember me telling you about the rope-making contest?"

I nodded.

"My father's team won, of course—his teams always do, even when he chooses the worst students to be on it. Anyway, the contest had just concluded when Pachamama began to shake. My father, at the time, was standing in the center of the bridge talking to my brother. As soon as Pachamama began to tremble, he shouted for us all to run onto the bridge. At first, frightened, no one moved until Pachamama began to shake again and rocks came raining down on us. I ran with all my strength, yet feared I would never reach the bridge. The bridge itself was tossing about like a stick on a lake in a storm, but where my father and brother stood, they were safe from falling rocks. Some of the students, afraid of the way the bridge was swinging wildly back and forth, blocked those behind from getting on it.

"In a voice louder than Pachamama's, my father again ordered everyone onto the bridge." Anka chuckled. "I think the students were more afraid of disobeying my father than they were of the swinging bridge. Of course, all this happened in less time than it's taking me to tell you about it.

"I remember clutching the hand lines of the bridge and looking down to the river below. Three students had been down there when the shaking began. I watched as a large section of the bank broke off and buried them. I remember thinking they were dead.

"The quaking finally stopped, and everything came to a rest except the section of bank that had fallen on the three students. It was still moving. Suddenly, three heads poked up through the collapsed bank. The students were favored by the gods, for the section that had fallen on them was mostly of sand. They looked so funny with just their heads sticking out and them spitting like angry llamas, we had to laugh. Of course, we were mostly

laughing to release our fear. The shaking had been terrifying, but thanks to
the gods, no one had been killed or even seriously injured. And the reason
no one had been hurt was because the bridge had kept us safe.

"Suddenly, all my father's students got very quiet. I knew they were
thinking the same thing: my father was right to insist upon excellence from
his students. We were alive because the bridge had been built so well. I'm
sure some of the students even thought my father had gotten Pachamama to
shake just to prove a point.

"My father, however, didn't give anyone a moment to think about this
lesson, but began shouting orders. He assigned a few students the job of
helping to dig out the three who had been buried. The rest of us were set to
clearing the road of rocks. It was hard work for some of the rocks were nearly
as tall as I am. We first had to cut down trees and fashion poles to use as
levers. We had not removed a third of the debris when Chumpi arrived. I
heard his bleats of distress before I saw him coming across on the bridge.
Since you were not with him, I knew something was wrong. As I raced to
meet him, Chumpi suddenly turned back toward the way he had come,
expecting me to follow. Of course, I couldn't go with him without first telling
my father.

"As I stood near the bridge, thinking about all I might need to take with
me, I failed to notice that Chumpi had returned to stand next to me." Anka
smiled. "Then do you know what happened?"

I was now wide awake. I had even managed to roll on to my side so I
could see Anka better. "Tell me."

"Your cantankerous friend bit me!" We both laughed.

"So what did you do?"

"Well, I remembered you telling me how Chumpi understood what you
said. I explained to him that I had to tell my father where I was going, and I
needed to get supplies to take with me. Also, I wanted my brother to go
along. Only then could I follow him."

"How did Chumpi react?"

"You're right. He does understand. He crossed back over the bridge and
lay down to wait. I sure he must have been very tired.

"I quickly explained to my father about Chumpi and my fear that
something bad had happened to you. I thought he might object to Kacha and
me leaving when there was still so much work to do, but he surprised me by
saying he would accompany us. I was grateful, for we would have the added

benefit of his experience. For my father, I think it was an opportunity to survey the damages brought about by Pachamama's shaking.

"Kacha, of course, was only too willing to go. It was the kind of adventure he and I were always looking for. As my brother and I gathered the necessary supplies, my father gave instructions to the students concerning the clearing of the road. Then we three were heading upriver with Chumpi leading the way. Unfortunately, Inti was about to begin his underground journey, and with all the dust in the air, darkness came quickly. But my father had thought to bring along two torches.

"Yet even with the torches to light our way, it was slow going, for landslides had covered the trail with rubble made slick by the dust that covered everything. In places, boulders had dammed the river, forming small lakes, forcing us to climb around them. This was dangerous because, every once in a while, a loose rock would come crashing down from above. Even my father, who was familiar with Pachamama's violent shaking, was amazed by just how much the terrain had been altered. The Apurimac River flowed through different channels, and cascades were created where none had been before." Anka shook his head. "Seeing the evidence of Pachamama's power, I feared we would not find you alive.

"Finally both our torches were used up, and we could go no farther until Qillamama rose above the mountains. Chumpi understood this, and joined us to rest. But as soon as Qillamama peeked over the canyon rim, he was on his feet, insisting that we continue on. I think right then a bond was created between Chumpi and my father. He kept saying how he wished his students were as devoted."

Behind Anka, Chanka entered the wasi. I was afraid he would make Anka stop talking so I could sleep, not that sleep would have been possible without hearing the remainder of Anka's story.

"Chanka," Anka said, "I was just about to tell Yana of the destruction of the village."

Chanka sat down. "Good. I would like to hear this again."

"About the time the stars were starting to fade, we came to the village. I couldn't believe it was the same place where I'd gotten the potatoes and chicha. The wasis were gone, buried under rocks. I'm certain if Pachamama had chosen the nighttime to do her shaking, everyone would have been killed. As it was, many perished, including the village's chieftain." He sighed. "It is troubling to think how quickly a life can end. The chieftain was a kind man who had refused payment for the chicha and potatoes he gave me. Yet more tragic was the death of a boy who had been playing in the stream when a tree toppled over and pinned him beneath the water. He was still there when we arrived, for the villagers were too busy searching for survivors to pull his body out of the water."

My eyes filled with tears.

"I'm sorry, Yana. I probably shouldn't be telling you all this when you are still recovering."

Chanka placed his hand upon Anka's shoulder. "Now that I'm not so busy with my patients, I will perform a ceremony of healing for you. I will feed Pachamama blood and fat, which will help to restore her and thereby prevent you from becoming sick due to the disturbing deaths you witnessed."

"Please pray also for my brother and my father who also witnessed the destruction."

Chanka nodded then waited for Anka to continue.

"Knowing the chieftain was dead, my father could not continue on, for he had to stay and help with the rescue of those still trapped. He immediately reorganized the efforts of those shifting through the rubble, for they were in danger of injury from the unstable rocks. Fortunately, the village's camasca had not been hurt in the shaking. He was a very busy man.

"Though my father could not accompany us, he insisted Kacha and I continue on. The village could have used our help, but there was no one, besides us, who knew to look for you." Anka smiled. "Also I think my father did not wish to see the torment it would have caused Chumpi had we not continued.

"About midday, it began to rain and the dust that covered everything turned to mud. Though tired, we didn't stop to rest, for I felt certain we had to be getting close to where you were. Imagine my surprise when we reached the Ccolpamayo and still Chumpi urged us on."

Anka grinned. "You complained about not being able to keep up with me. Now we were the ones struggling to match the distance you had traveled."

I smiled back, saying nothing about my terrifying flight, for I sensed he had not learned of it.

"The rock cairn that marked the trail to Tambo Toco, as well as the trail itself were gone. We had to rely on Chumpi to lead us over the loose scree. It wasn't until we ascended the ridge that we knew you had to be somewhere nearby, for Chumpi was more anxious than ever, urging us to walk faster by bleating and running back and forth. Though we tried to increase our pace, we could hardly walk, for nearly every rock turned beneath our feet, and if they didn't, we slipped anyway because of the mud.

"Finally, Chumpi came to the place near the base of a large spire where he stood, bleating ceaselessly. There was nothing to see but rocks and mud. Kacha and I looked at each other with the same thought: if you were under those rocks, you couldn't possibly be alive.

"Then I saw among the rubble something that glittered. It was the gold medallion I had given you. Furiously we tossed aside rocks. Fortunately, you were not buried deep. Still many of the rocks were heavy. The worst part for me was seeing all the blood mixed with the mud.

"When we had gotten all the rocks out of the way, we found, to our amazement, that your heart was still beating. I quickly wrapped the worst of your wounds, while Kacha fashioned a sling from rope. Then we carried you here to Tambo Toco. That was three days ago, Yana, and until this morning, you've been unconscious."

I turned upon my back and stared up at the thatch. I was alive because of the devotion of many people, including Chumpi whom I really did think of as a person. Grateful tears ran down my cheeks. I said a silent prayer thanking the gods for such friends.

I turned toward Anka. "It is you who saved me." I looked at Chanka. "And you, Chanka."

Anka shook his head. "It was Chumpi, really. We never would have found you if it hadn't been for him."

"But you didn't have to follow him." I slipped my hand from beneath my chusi and placed it upon Anka's. "There was so much to do at the bridge, or at the village, and you didn't even know if I was alive."

Anka laid his other hand atop mine. "Which was why I could not have rested until I found out. Besides, the gods would not have forgiven either me or Chanka if we had failed you, for we are both steps upon your bridge, the one leading you to the water at the end of the world."

Chanka said, "We will talk of that later. Now, I want to give Yana something to help her sleep."

I was about to object, saying I didn't need anything, but fell asleep first.

Chapter 18

The third day after I returned to the living, I was able to stand and move about the wasi in a pair of padded sandals that Chanka made for me. Only when I placed too much weight on my left foot did I feel a pain so sharp I could not help but cry out. Chanka said this was probably caused by a broken toe which would take a while to heal.

On the fifth day, I was strong enough to go outside, and I immediately went to see Chumpi. Anka accompanied me as I shuffled along toward the pen in which Chumpi was being kept. Anka explained how he had been forced to pen Chumpi to keep him from trying to crawl through the opening into Chanka's wasi where I slept.

Chumpi was as pleased to see me as I him. He greeted me by blowing into my face, then hummed ecstatically as I laid my head against his. I told him over and over how brave and intelligent he was and how grateful I was for his devotion. I presented him a maize cake I had saved from morning meal, but, to my amazement, he turned his nose up at it.

"Atatau!" I cried. "Since when do you turn down a maize cake?"

"I told you that people have been giving Chumpi special treats," Anka said.

"Well, I shall soon put an end to that or else there will be no living with him."

"That might not be so easy. What started out as a way to reward Chumpi for his heroics has become a way to honor Urcuchillay."

I also wanted to honor Urcuchillay, the god who, with his two great eyes, watched over llamas at night. Yet I doubted spoiling Chumpi the best way to do this. "Do you know what became of the packs Chumpi had carried?"

Anka shook his head. "They must have been buried in the rubble caused by Pachamama's shaking. Why?"

"I'd like something to trade for a guinea pig to sacrifice to the gods to thank them for giving my life back to me."

"Soon Chanka is going to sacrifice a llama on behalf of the whole village to thank the gods for sparing Tambo Toco from worse misfortunes and to seek the gods' help in healing Urpito."

As I ran my fingers through Chumpi's hair, I thought about Urpito, the boy who shared Chanka's wasi with me. I had begun to attend to him as soon as I was able, for his grieving mother had responsibilities to her large family. I talked to Urpito, hoping he could hear me, though I was uncertain whether he did. His soft, brown eyes stared fixedly at the roof of the wasi while I told him stories my mother told me when I was sick. And when I was too tired to talk, I sat beside him and held his hand and occasionally moistened his lips with a damp cloth. Through all this, Urpito did nothing but stare at the thatch with vacant eyes.

"I understand why Chanka is worried about Urpito," I said. "Being with Urpito has only increased my gratitude to the gods for saving me from worse injuries. I am also thankful for the many kindnesses of my new friends." I stepped away from Chumpi. "Anka, where is your brother Kacha? I must thank him for helping to rescue me."

Anka smiled. "My brother is a strange fellow. I thought he would have wanted to stay in Tambo Toco in order to get out of work. Perhaps he's trying to become a better person. The day after we brought you here, he went back to be with my father."

Or to avoid my accusations, I thought. Still, regardless of the reason, I was glad Kacha had gone, for I did not want to look into his eyes, even to thank him.

"I suppose you'll be leaving Tambo Toco soon also," I said.

"I see you're anxious to be rid of me."

I was about to object when I saw the laughter in his eyes.

"I should have left with my brother," he said, "but I can't bring myself to leave while you're still recovering."

Momentarily disregarding the fact that he was an Inca, I took his hand.

He moved closer. "So you like me a little after all," he whispered.

"I owe my life to you."

My response failed to please him. He released my hand and stepped away.

"I told Chanka I would not leave Tambo Toco before he sacrifices the llama," he said. "Or rather Chanka told me…" He did not complete his sentence, but looked away. "Still, that leaves me a few days to look after you, which is why I'm now going to insist you go and rest, for I don't want you to have a relapse and not be able to attend the celebration that will follow the sacrifice."

I said good-bye to Chumpi, assuring him I would come again soon. I leaned upon Anka's arm as we slowly walked back to Chanka's wasi. When I crawled through the entryway, I saw that Urpito was still staring up at the thatch. I moistened his lips with a wet cloth before lying down. Though I felt tired, sleep did not come. Likely this was for fear of dreaming, for each time I slept, the dragon returned and tossed me about.

I turned upon my side and thought about Anka. I did not want him to leave Tambo Toco. I did not want to leave either. Though Tambo Toco was not my home, I felt safe here. What would happen if I continued to seek the water at the end of the world? Would other dragons attack me?

I tossed the top of my chusi aside, got up and sat beside Urpito. I described for him my dream in which I saw the beautiful crystals. I told him about water at the end of the world, water so pure and clear it could be breathed as if it were air. I told myself I did this in the hope that Urpito would benefit from hearing my words. In truth, I spoke to give myself courage.

Chapter 19

By the day of the sacrifice, I was no longer experiencing dizziness, and had very little pain in my foot. Yet I was still troubled by terrifying dreams, so I was grateful to have Urpito to care for, as he took my mind off my fears. Thanks to the gods, Urpito was now sitting up and starting to walk. My job was to see that he did not overly exert himself. I did this by telling him stories, which he seemed to enjoy, smiling each time I said something funny. Still, he had yet to speak.

In the afternoon, the people of Tambo Toco gathered around a large stone altar upon which the llama was to be sacrificed. Chanka came from his wasi bearing Urpito. It was the first time most of the villagers had seen Urpito since the roof of his family's wasi had fallen on him and his brother, and his appearance was met with smiles and greetings. Never having seen Chanka walk any distance, I studied him as he carried Urpito. One of his legs was shorter than the other, and this caused him to rock side-to-side. The thought occurred to me that Chanka's physical defects were likely the reason he was a camasca, for in Tahuantinsuyu a person who was not able to perform normal work was expected to make contributions in other ways. Then I realized my thinking was backwards, for a camasca is not chosen by humans, but by the gods; Chanka's physical appearance was a sign that the gods had marked him as a healer.

Sumaq, Urpito's mother, came forward, and Chanka placed Urpito in her arms. Then Chanka went to the altar where he picked up a long knife that lay upon it. A young man dressed in a beautiful unku of many colors passed through the crowd leading a white llama. The chieftain of Tambo Toco and three other strong men lifted the llama onto the altar and held him down while Chanka plunged the knife into the llama's chest and lifted out the llama's beating heart. He held it up high so everyone could watch while he examined it. Then he inspected the llama's spleen and liver. Satisfied by what he saw, Chanka announced that Pachamama would not shake herself again for a very long time. Upon hearing this, everyone cheered, and the atmosphere suddenly became celebratory. A few people even started to dance, but Chanka reminded them of the serious observances still to be conducted: the burning of the llama's organs as an offering to Inti; the feeding of chicha and certain special foods to Pachamama to pacify her restless spirit; and a sacrifice of several guinea pigs to Qillamama to honor her and to ask her for the full recovery of Urpito.

I had gotten used to Chanka's unnaturally high voice, which had the benefit of carrying well. The prayers he uttered were simple, yet heartfelt in praise and gratitude to the gods. Listening to Chanka calmed my fears, and I realized that words as much as medicines had the power to heal. I had only Ipa to compare Chanka to, but I wondered if all camascas were as capable as he.

When Chanka finished, the men carried away the body of the llama to prepare it for the feast. Several jars of chicha appeared. Suddenly there was the twitter of flutes and the beating of drums and everyone talking, laughing, or singing.

I spotted Sumaq and Urpito, and went to them. "I was wondering if Urpito would like to meet Chumpi, my llama?"

Sumaq looked at Urpito. "Would you like that, little heart stealer?"

Urpito nodded.

The three of us walked to the pen which Chumpi, as a favored guest, had to himself. I took a small squash, broke it apart, and gave the pieces to Urpito to give to Chumpi. Urpito's eyes glowed as Chumpi took the food from his hand. When the food was gone, Urpito suddenly leaned forward and put his arms around Chumpi's neck, nearly causing Sumaq to drop him.

"Urpito!" Sumaq exclaimed. "What a big boy you are! Soon I won't be able to carry you."

"Perhaps Urpito would like to sit on top of Chumpi," I said.

As soon as Sumaq placed Urpito on Chumpi's back, Urpito started to bounce up and down.

"Careful, little one," Sumaq said. "You must not overdo it."

Ignoring his mother, Urpito continued to bounce.

"I best take him down," I said, reaching forward to take hold of Urpito.

"Nooo!" Urpito shouted.

Sumaq gasped for Urpito had finally spoken. But the speaking of one word was like a hole punched in a dam, releasing a torrent.

"I don't want to get down! Mother, make Chumpi go! I want to ride around!"

"Easy, Urpito!" Sumaq exclaimed, wiping a tear from her eye. "You're still not well yet."

"No, Mother! I want him to go!"

Sumaq looked at me. "Do you think it will be all right for Urpito to go for a short ride on Chumpi?"

I removed the railings of the pen. Then with Sumaq on one side of Chumpi, and I on the other, we walked in the direction of the celebration.

"Faster, Chumpi! I want to go faster!"

Sumaq and I laughed.

"He's going quite fast enough," Sumaq said. "If you don't settle down, I will give away the sweet maize cakes I've been saving for you."

"Nooo!" Urpito cried. "I'll be good."

Many people stopped their merrymaking to watch our little procession.

Waving his hand in the air, Urpito shouted, "Look at me! I'm riding Chumpi!"

Everyone had been worried about Urpito's inability to speak. To hear him carrying on now was an answer to prayers. With shouts of joy, they all rushed upon us.

With her eyes, Sumaq implored me to do something. I lifted Urpito off Chumpi and attempted to carry him away from the pressing crowd.

Suddenly Chanka was at my side. "Back everyone! Back! Give them room!" He held up his hands and the well-wishers became quiet. "I know you're grateful Urpito is doing so well, but he's not fully recovered and must not get too excited."

People nodded their understanding and began to move away. Sumaq took Urpito's from my arms.

"Now it's time for you to rest, little one," she told him.

"No, mother! I want to ride Chumpi some more."

"Shhh! Maybe tomorrow, if that's all right with Yana and Chumpi."

Urpito looked at me and pleaded with his gentle brown eyes.

"I'm sure Chumpi would love to give you a ride tomorrow," I told him.

Urpito smiled then turned to his mother. "Can I have those sweet maize cakes now?"

Sumaq stroked his cheek. "I think I'll let him sleep in our wasi tonight," she said. She shifted Urpito onto her hip. "I confess I never fed anything special to Chumpi because I thought it silly to waste good food on a llama. But tomorrow, I'm going to bring him something special to eat."

I nodded, smiling, yet thought that Chumpi would never eat ordinary grass again. I turned to see Chumpi receiving the attention of several people.

A man was trying to get Chumpi to drink some Chicha, but Chumpi turned away and begged a bright green lucuma fruit from a woman.

"Chumpi!" I scolded. I ran my hand down his side. "Atatau! If you get any fatter, you'll not be able to walk. I'm going to put you where these good people will not have to be pestered by you."

I took Chumpi by his halter and put him back in his pen where I stood absently running my fingers through his hair. When he turned to lie down, I leaned upon the railing, and stared at nothing in particular. I was not in the mood for a celebration. My reason had nothing to do with the good people of Tambo Toco, who had treated me with as much kindness as if I were one of their own. I just felt the need to be alone.

Then I had an inspiration: I would visit the famous caves of Tambo Toco! I had been too weak to visit them before, but knew the trail to the caves started near to where the celebration was taking place. I left Chumpi to enjoy his rest and walked through the crowd of celebrants, waving to some and calling out greetings to those I knew by name. No one seemed to notice that I did not stop. Soon, I was alone on the trail.

It felt good to be out walking with Inti's warmth bringing sweat to my face. The air was so still, the dust I kicked up hovered in the air. The trail meandered through a grove of glossy-leafed chachacomo trees. I spotted a woodpecker circling the tree in search of worms, and I stopped to admire his brilliant red head and the yellow and black feathers upon his breast. People also ate the worms the woodpecker was searching for, but I had never cared for their taste.

The trees obstructed my view, and I had only occasional glimpses of a mountain side pocked with openings. Eventually the trail circled a craggy outcropping, and beyond this I saw a large entrance to a cave. I slowed, not because I was tired, but in response to an inexplicable sensation of being in the presence of many people. I wondered if this large cave was the one Manka and Kachi had emerged from. I had always imagined them crawling out through a hole barely large enough for them to fit through.

I heard footsteps and turned. From behind the outcropping Chanka appeared. He smiled and waved his hand. I waved back and waited for him.

"I saw you heading this direction, and thought I would join you," he said.

"I'm afraid I was not in the mood for celebrating. I hope no one will be offended by my absence."

Chanka stopped. "I'm sorry, I have intruded upon your need to be alone."

"No, not at all," I said. "Actually, I'm grateful you're here." I pointed toward the cave. "Is this where Manka and Kachi came from underground?"

Chanka scratched his chin. "That is what everyone says, yet is difficult to know for sure; it happened so long ago. For myself, I find it difficult to believe this is the cave, for there are no—but wait, let me show you." He reached into the woven bag he carried and removed a rubbing stick. "The cave is large inside, and we will need light if we wish to see its extent."

While Chanka worked to start a fire, I found a piece of wood heavy with pitch.

"You go ahead of me, Yana, while I hold the torch for you."

It was obvious the cave had been visited often, for the ground before the opening had been tamped down by the passing of feet. Once inside, I could see nothing until Chanka came behind, carrying the torch. Then I gasped. Everywhere I looked, there were the bodies of the dead. I wish Charapa was here to tell me just how many. Chanka lifted his torch higher. More bodies became visible, row upon row as far as the light carried. I suddenly knew why I had felt the presence of others; the cave was where the people of Tambo Toco placed their dead.

"There are other caves similar to this," Chanka said, "though not as large."

"Do they also contain the bodies of your ancestors?"

"Most of them. Many generations of our ancestors have been interred in the caves."

Each person sat with arms wrapped around his knees. This created the strange impression of a person sitting there, thinking. As was the custom throughout Tahuantinsuyu, each person was attired in his best garments and each held at least one possession. Many women clutched drop spindles while others held mortars for grinding maize. Most men gripped tacllas, though a few held lances. There were girls with combs and boys with toy tops like the ones my cousins sent spinning along the ground.

"Are all the people in Tambo Toco placed in caves when they die?" In Qomermoya, we had no caves to inter our dead, so we used small buildings instead.

"All those who live long enough to celebrate their ratuchicoy," Chanka said. "But the ancestors are not what I wanted you to see. Walk with me."

Between the walls of the cave and the rows of bodies was a path and

Chanka led the way along it. Sometimes the path turned to avoid projections of rock, but kept to the periphery of the cave. The cave was so large, Chanka's torch was not bright enough to illuminate all of it. After we had gone a considerable distance, I looked back toward the entrance which now appeared as a small half-circle of light. Outlined by this light were the countless bodies of the dead.

It took us a long time to circle the cave. The farther we walked, the more I felt troubled by something, but it was not until we finally returned to the entrance that I realized what is was. "There are no openings into this cave except this one here."

"Ah, you noticed that." Chanka dropped the torch and smothered the flame by kicking dirt over it.

"But Manka and Kachi discovered the cave only after traveling for many days underground." I looked back inside the cave. "This cannot be the cave the brothers came out of."

"Let's find a place to sit. You have not fully regained your strength, and I need to rest my leg."

We sat in the shade of a tree. Leaning back against the trunk, I studied the entire mountain side upon which the cave we had explored was just one of many openings. In fact, the mountain looked like a piece of wood that had been bored by woodpeckers.

"So, which is the cave the Manka and Kachi came out of?"

"All the caves have been explored extensively," Chanka said, "even those high up where it seems only a bird could get to. None have openings other than the ones you see before you. There are no passages within any of them.

"But what about the screams of Kachi that sometimes can be heard?"

Chanka smiled. "The cave openings are like holes in a flute. At times the wind likes to play upon them. The music is strange and sometimes disturbing because it can sound like someone screaming. But it is only the music of the wind and not Kachi."

I leaned forward and put my face in my hands to hide my sudden tears. Chanka placed a hand upon the middle of my back. I brought his arm around my shoulders and leaned my head against his chest. I did not want to trouble Chanka with my sadness, yet could not resist my need to be held. The memory of my father and how he used to hold me and soothe my pains with his gentle voice brought more tears. I longed for my father's embrace to help assuage the pain of defeat, for as there were no underground passages within the caves, it would be impossible for me to find the water at end of the world. How could I have imagined that I had been chosen by the gods to save Topa Inca? The magnitude of my foolishness washed over me, and I felt immeasurably small. I had been a young woman playing at a game just like my cousins played with their tops.

Yet, in addition to my sadness, I felt a sense of relief. I had done all I could, and now I could go home. I recalled Ipa's words: "If you cannot find this water beneath the ground, come home. No one will punish you for trying, I promise." Perhaps Ipa had known all along I would fail. I pictured myself slinking home like a dog who had gotten thoroughly trounced in a fight.

The thought lit a fire in my breast. I sat back up. Now I wanted to scream like Kachi. I wanted to hammer my fists against all the little cave openings, which now looked like so many laughing eyes. I yearned for the power of the gods so I might bring down the whole mountain before me. I was so caught up in my anger, I was startled when Chanka spoke.

"Why do you think Pachamama shook so violently?"

I looked at him, wondering what this had to do with anything.

He continued, "Why do you suppose the river of rocks washed over you and still you lived?"

I shook my head.

"Pachamama had a reason for shaking, a reason for each person, a reason for each group of people. For our village, this has been a time of renewal. By the display of Pachamama's power, we have been brought closer together. Our prayers are more fervent, our love for each other stronger. In this way, Pachamama's shaking has been beneficial."

"What about the village Anka told us about?" I said "Was Pachamama's shaking beneficial for all those who died?"

Chanka sighed. "Long ago I gave up trying to understand all the reasons the gods act as they do. It is for each person, each village to determine what the shaking has meant. I content myself with just trying to understand the things I see. I cannot imagine what it must have been like for you to see a dragon coming out of the ground, to watch helplessly as a river of rocks poured down upon you. And yet you lived! What does all this mean to you?"

"That the gods are as powerful as I am weak!"

Chanka nodded his head in agreement.

My face colored. I had spoken sarcastically and had not meant to be taken seriously.

"I would amend your statement a little," he said. "The gods are as powerful as you were once weak."

I shook my head. "I do not understand."

"Anka told me the reason why you journeyed to Tambo Toco, and what it is you seek: the water at the end of the world." He turned to fix me with an intense stare. "When the gods choose someone to do their bidding, they first make her strong."

My face must have reflected my confusion.

"Did you honestly expect to just walk into Tambo Toco, find some water in a cave, and hope to cure Topa Inca with your little discovery?"

I turned from his gaze, feeling ashamed. "You think me naive, but what else could I have done? This is the only place I knew to look for the water at the end of the world."

Chanka put his hand upon my shoulder. "Do not feel bad. You did all you knew to do. And by coming to Tambo Toco, you have acted correctly."

I pulled away, angry. "But the water at the end of the world is not here!"

"What was it you told Anka about steps along a bridge?"

"Anka has spoken too much! He promised not to tell anyone I was seeking the water at the end of the world."

"I am certain he told me only out of concern for you."

"It was Anka, the bridge builder, who used that image. He said I was like a person stepping off a cliff with the belief that a bridge would suddenly appear beneath my feet. That is how it felt at the time. With each footstep, a step of the bridge appeared beneath me." I looked up at the cave openings. "But it no longer feels that way. I have stepped forward and fallen to the bottom of the canyon."

"Not true," replied Chanka. "Tambo Toco is just another step on your bridge."

For a moment, I felt a spark of hope, quickly followed by a much stronger feeling, that of dread. "Do you know where I can find the water at the end of the world?"

Chanka shook his head. "But I do know this: birds will lead you to it!"

Chapter 20

Birds had become woven into the fabric of my life. There were the beautiful blue and yellow birds I thought I had seen the day the Capac Inca had visited Qomermoya; there was my yellow feather, a gift from Topa Inca; I even thought I had been following little grey birds when trying to escape the flood of rocks during Pachamama's shaking. And now Chanka informed me that birds would lead me to the water at the end of the world!

Ignoring my look of puzzlement, Chanka straightened out his legs before him. "I thought it most unusual that you, a Hatunruna, were rescued by two Incas. Yet I knew that nothing happens without a reason. While you were unconscious, Anka told me of your plans. I had already heard about Topa Inca's illness and the rumor that only the water at the end of the world could cure him. Important news travels faster than a hawk can fly.

"That the gods would choose you to find this curative water, I could accept, for, as I said, I've given up trying to understand all the reasons for their actions. Still, I wondered that they should choose someone so young. To find the truth of this matter, I prepared a potion that I have used many times when treating patients. It allows me to journey into the spirit world and there, if necessary, contend with the evil spirits that inhabit a body and cause sickness. I prepare this potion using ayahuasca, a potentially dangerous plant that must be used with great care.

"I borrowed your necklace with the yellow feather, for I needed something of yours to take with me on my spirit journey. Sitting beside you with your necklace around my neck, I chanted softly while lightly tapping upon a drum. After a while, when I felt my mind beginning to separate from my body, I drank the potion.

"My plan was to meet with a spirit and hear from her lips your role in this matter concerning Topa Inca's illness. I thought she might also reveal the location of the water at the end of the world. In my journey, however, I saw no spirits though I sensed their presence. Instead I found myself in a place I've only heard of. At my feet were lush, broad-leafed plants covered with delicate flowers. These plants grew in the shadow of tall vine-covered trees with branches high up and spreading. The air was warm and humid, and

I knew I must be in the jungle, or someplace very near to it.

"There was also a road, and as I looked down it, I saw a woman approaching who, as she got closer, I recognized was you. I called to you, but it seemed you could neither hear nor see me. The road wound around the base of a rocky hillside much like the one you see before you, only without caves. Something must have caught your attention, for you left the road and hurried up the hillside. I followed to see what had attracted you. When I drew near, I saw you surrounded by birds. That is, I think they were birds, for they were whirling around you so swiftly, I could not distinguish their features. Faster and faster they spun like a great whirlwind that lifts up dirt and leaves, obscuring all that lies within it. This whirlwind, with you inside it, rose from the ground. It carried you away faster than I could follow. Higher and higher it rose until finally it appeared no bigger than a bird flying in the distance.

"Then came darkness, and I thought my journey had ended, but I was wrong. I was in a great cave. Though I could not see, I knew it was a cave by the familiar smell. I sensed you were there with me and heard your footsteps as you stumbled about in the darkness. I called to you, but again you could not hear me.

"It was then that my spirit journey ended. I felt weak and nauseous as I always do after using ayahuasca. I drank a tea strong with bilyea leaves to help purge my system of the drug. Soon I was feeling better in body, but was not clear in my mind concerning what I had seen."

As Chanka spoke of his journey into the spirit world, I imagined myself there with him. The image of the birds lifting me up thrilled me. "Earlier, you said birds would lead me to the water at the end of the world. Is that what the birds were doing when they swept me up into the sky? Taking me to the water?"

Chanka smiled. "Journeys into the spirit world are like dreams; they speak a language of their own. The images seem fantastic, sometimes frightening, but in truth they are but symbols."

Chanka stood up. "But enough for now. This is the time when you should be resting and enjoying yourself. Later, we will talk some more." He motioned toward the village. "Shall we go back? I'm very hungry. I might be dreaming again, but I believe I can smell roasting llama from here."

As we walked back to Tambo Toco, I savored the feeling of peace I always experienced following a great release of emotion. Rather than think about Chanka's spirit journey, I basked in the beauty surrounding me, for

Inti's light sparkled golden in the motes of dust we stirred up, and the trees, which were scattered across the high plain, partitioned Inti's slanting rays and cast long shadows dark purple in color.

It was nearly dark by the time we returned to the celebration. Though the feast had been going for quite some time, there was still plenty of food left. I thought myself not hungry until I smelled the roasted llama and a locro made with potatoes, maize, peppers, and guinea pig. Once I started to eat, it seemed I could not stop. People chided me good-naturedly as I went back for a third, even a fourth helping, and if I had not been so ashamed of my gluttony, I would have gone back a fifth time!

I ate, sitting beside Anka, and together we watched as a circle of men and women danced to the music of flutes and drums. Many a pretty woman sought Anka's eye as the circle dance brought them near, but he seemed unaware of their attentions. For some reason Anka was not his cheerful self. I sensed he was troubled in spirit, and I hoped I was not the cause.

The dancing came to an end. Some of the dancers collapsed upon the ground, exhausted, while others, not so tired, went to help themselves to more food. The chieftain of Tambo Toco suddenly stood over us. I could tell he had been drinking much chicha.

"Hey, you two! Are you going to sit there all night watching us entertain you? Now it is your turn. Do something to amuse us."

Anka thought for a moment before turning to me. "Do you still have your ocarina with you?"

I shook my head. "It was in one of the packs which was buried during the shaking."

Anka turned toward the chieftain. "I'm afraid we can do nothing. Yana lost her ocarina."

The chieftain turned and yelled. "Akakllu! Come here!"

A young man, one of the flute players, hurried to him.

"Do you have an ocarina Yana can play?" the chieftain said.

Akakllu offered me the choice of two. I selected the one nearer in size to the one I'd lost. Then Anka and I went to stand in the center of the dance circle.

Anka leaned over and whispered in my ear. "Do you know the song, *Two Ringed Doves?*"

It was a sad, but familiar song. I played part of a melody and Anka nodded. Then I began again, and this time Anka joined me, singing:

Two doves,
Two snow-white doves,
Winging the skies as one;
Two doves,
Two snow-white doves,
Joined together in love.

Anka had a unique voice. It had none of the usual nasal quality, but came from deep within his chest.

A hawk,
A black hawk,
Like a stone plummeting down;
Struck a dove,
Killed a dove,
His body crashing to the ground.

Akakllu, who stood nearby, joined in, blowing upon a conch shell. Its single note complimented the deepness of Anka's voice and imitated the call of a dove.

One dove,
One snow-white dove,
Found his body and cried;
One heart,
A broken heart,
Upon his breast, she died.

I trembled from the words and from the emotion in Anka's voice. I closed my eyes and tried to answer him through my playing. *I am still here, Anka.*

Pity the doves,
Pity their love,
The gods took pity and sent
Two rings,

Two jewel-like rings;
And placed them around their necks.

And by this gift,
This precious gift,
Let it be a sign;
Two doves,
Two snow-white doves,
Are forever joined as one.

Anka held the last note. Like a moth, it slowly fluttered away. Akakllu continued to sound long, mournful notes upon his conch shell. I closed my eyes, not wishing them to reveal the sadness I felt. But when I finally opened them, Anka was gone, and I did not see him again that night, though I waited until I fell asleep, sitting with my back against a rock.

When I awoke, most of the people had already gone to their wasis to sleep. Only a few young couples remained, softly serenading the stars with songs of longing. I stumbled away to Chanka's wasi and fell asleep the instant I lay upon the chusi.

And once more, the dragon entered my dreams. This time it was more than his great, arching back I saw. His head burst from beneath the ground, flinging dirt and rocks skyward. Eyes like molten copper fastened upon me. He had no mouth, but a terrible beak like that of a giant parrot, sharp and snapping.

I tried to run, but the ground shook and I was thrown upon rocks. Crawling, twisting, rolling, I narrowly escaped the dragon's slashing beak, while beneath me sharp stones lacerated my skin. Suddenly the dragon trapped me with his great tail. The weight of it was crushing; I could not pull air into my lungs. The dragon seized my arm in his beak. Screaming, I awoke just before he tore it off.

I sat up. My head spun, and it took all my willpower to slow my frantic breathing. As I wiped the sweat from my face, I stared into the darkness, hoping to see Urpito before remembering he now slept with his family. His absence added to my distress. Alone, I relived the dream over and over in my mind until, out of desperation, I gathered up the chusi and went outside. With the chusi wrapped around me, I waited for the night to end. Eventually I fell asleep, and it was the stirring of the village that woke me. I went to visit

Sumaq and was invited to stay for morning meal. After we ate and finished cleaning up, I gave Urpito his promised ride on Chumpi. As I led Chumpi about, Urpito called to others to witness his pleasure. His happiness did not lighten the heaviness in my heart, for the memory of the dream still lingered. And there was another reason for my distress: with the celebration over, Anka would be leaving this morning to rejoin his father and brother, and I would never see him again, for having failed to find the water at the end of the world, there was no longer a reason for me to visit Qosqo.

I did my best to hide from Urpito the tears welling up in my eyes, but could not spare myself the pain in my heart. I loved Anka. I had loved him ever since the night we shared a meal beside the Apurimac River, this despite knowing it was to be a love never fulfilled. Love between an Inca and a Hatunruna? Impossible! But what does the heart know about impossibility?

Yet when Anka had sung about the two doves, I knew he had been singing about us, and I was certain he loved me also. And now, we were parting forever. Like my mother, my father and my brother, Anka was to be another piece taken from my heart.

Then it occurred to me that this taking had been no more than what I had been given. My life had not been diminished because I had met Anka, and the pain I would feel at our parting was a small price to pay for the time we had shared. This thought comforted me, and I suppose represented a maturity in my thinking. Yes, I would lose those I love, but others would enter my life, enrich it, and help to fill those missing pieces in my heart.

I also admitted that Urpito's ride was, for my part, just a way of delaying the moment when I would have to say goodbye to Anka. Not wanting my selfishness to force Anka to delay his departure, I abruptly ended Urpito's ride, much to his disappointment. As a consolation, I left him with slices of potatoes to feed Chumpi while I went in search of Anka.

But as I approached Chanka's wasi, I saw Anka and Chanka arguing. I drew back, afraid, but Chanka spotted me.

"There you are," he shouted. "We were about to come looking for you."

I walked forward cautiously. "I had promised Urpito another ride on Chumpi," I said.

Anka suddenly turned away from me, and I felt sick.

"Also, I was putting off having to say good-bye to Anka."

From beneath my lliqlla, I removed the necklace Anka had lent me. Earlier I had polished the golden medallion and rewoven the cord that held it, adding a few red woodpecker feathers I had found.

"Here, Anka," I said, holding the necklace out to him.

Anka turned back toward me, but when he saw what I held, he grew angry again. I hurried to explain. "I must return it to you because I will not be coming to Qosqo and…" I did not need to finish my sentence; we both knew its conclusion: *I will never see you again.*

Anka took the necklace. Slowly he ran a finger down the cord, stopping to feel the softness of each feather. He looked at Chanka. There was something in his eyes I had never seen before: a look of defiance. But that look was lost on Chanka.

Then Anka grabbed my arm with such force, it hurt. Startled, I fought to control the sudden hammering in my chest.

Slowly, Anka relaxed the pressure of his grip, but still held onto me. He closed his eyes and took several deep breaths. When he again opened his eyes, I saw the gentle Anka I knew.

"We will meet again, Yana. Until then, please wear this." He placed the necklace again around my neck. I stared down at the medallion, tears filling my eyes: hopeful tears. He lifted my chin, and with one finger brushed away a tear upon my cheek. Then he leaned forward and whispered in my ear. "I promise you, Yana, we will meet again."

Chapter 21

For a second time, I had to watch Anka leave. As before, I stood looking on long after he had disappeared.

Out of the corner of my eye, I saw Chanka pick up a clay jar. "Here," he said, shoving the jar into my stomach, "quit sulking and make yourself useful!" He pointed in the direction of the stream. "Fetch some water for tea. We have work to do."

Even in my sadness at seeing Anka leave, I could not help but smile a little. I knew Chanka was trying to speak in a commanding voice, but instead he twittered like an angry little bird.

I hurried to the stream, curious about the nature of the work. When I returned, Chanka had a fire going. I set the jar to heat then sat next to him. From one of two bags, Chanka took a handful of stones colored a brilliant yellow.

"Take one," he commanded.

The stone had a powdery surface that coated my fingers.

"Smell it."

I brought it to my nose then quickly pulled it away.

Chanka laughed. "You should smell it when it's burning."

"Burning?"

Chanka nodded. "The problem with being underground for a long period of time is having a means to light your way. Did you ever wonder how Manka and Kachi could see to walk during the days they spent underground?"

"I hadn't thought of it. I imagine they just stumbled along in the dark until they saw the opening in the cave."

Chanka shrugged. "Perhaps."

He poured the stones back into the bag. I offered him the one I held, but he shook his head.

"But think about it," he said. "You came here expecting to find the water at the end of the world by retracing Manka and Kachi's steps. Were you planning to just stumble about in the dark also? You could have stumbled right past the water at the end of the world and never even seen it."

"I could've carried a torch."

Chanka shook his head. "What if you had to travel underground for many days? You would not be able to carry enough torches."

I rolled the yellow stone back and forth between my fingers. In truth, I had never given a thought as to how I would find my way in the darkness. I looked at Chanka who was smiling, waiting for me to respond. "I don't know why you're asking me these questions. I'm not going to travel beneath the ground. You told me the caves here have no passages."

Chanka did not answer, but held out his hand for the yellow stone then placed it in a small lantern made of fire-hardened clay. He picked up a twig, lit it in the fire, then placed it inside the lantern. The lantern was thin-walled and glowed with the light of the flame. But to my amazement, the lantern continued to glow after he removed the burning twig. He handed me the lantern by its handle. Inside, the yellow stone was burning slowly. An acrid smell came to my nose, burning my nostrils, and I was seized with a fit of coughing. Chanka laughed as I handed him back the lantern.

"Where did these stones come from?" I said, between coughs.

"From a mountain where Pachamama spits out fire. She also spits out these yellow stones. I have used the smoke the burning stones produce to rid chusis of lice. It works well, but leaves an unpleasant odor, as you can imagine. Now, I can see another use for them. One of those stones can burn for the time it takes to cook potatoes." He pointed to the bags. "I've estimated that these two bags of stones will provide you with enough light to travel for about eight days underground, maybe longer."

I felt a tightness in my chest. I closed my eyes, but really wanted to close my ears. Chanka tapped me on the shoulder. I ignored him. He poked harder, hurting me, forcing me to open my eyes and acknowledge him.

"Remember I asked you about Pachamama's shaking? What it meant to you?"

His mentioning of the shaking only increased the tightness in my chest.

"And I told you," he continued, "that when the gods choose someone to do their bidding, they first make her strong."

Suddenly, I became like that mountain which spits out the yellow stones, only I spat out angry words. "How can you say that? I am not strong! Why must I be the one to find the water at the end of the world? Let someone else find it. I'm…" Seeing in my mind the dragon erupting from the ground, I pulled my knees to my chest and wrapped my arms around them. "Chanka, I'm frightened!"

Chanka placed his hand upon my shoulder. "I know, but it's important to realize that out of fear comes strength."

I wanted to hit him. What did he know of fear?

"Because of the shaking, you now know what real fear is," he said. "The fear that comes from having been touched by the hand of death. If you can master that fear, then there is little you cannot achieve. I remember how miserable you were when you learned the caves of Tambo Toco had no passages, how you cried. But then you suddenly became angry, is that not so?"

I nodded.

"Your reaction excited me, for it showed me that your courage was already returning. Tell me, what were you thinking when you were so angry?"

I was ashamed to tell him. "My thoughts were evil, blasphemous. I have since asked the gods to forgive me." But my reluctance to tell him was more than just shame. With every word that left my mouth, I was committing myself to something I did not want.

Chanka waited, watching with sharp eyes. I grew uncomfortable under his stare and eventually confessed my blasphemy. "I wanted the power of the gods so that I could bring down the mountain and crush all those caves. I wanted the world to suffer for my being made the gods' plaything, a little stick on the water which they could push about."

Chanka threw back his head and laughed, a laugh like a child's and just as thoughtless. "Atakachau, Yana! And a good god you would make too!"

"You of all people should know it is wrong to disrespect the gods!"

He nodded in agreement, but still continued to smile broadly. "You are right. But tell me, what is disrespect?"

I did not understand why he should ask such a question.

"Most people tiptoe around the gods," he said, "acting like little ants always afraid they might be stepped on. It is good to respect the gods, but the gods want more than just respect." The smile left his face. He leaned forward and tapped me on the leg. "The gods challenge us and expect us to rise to the challenge! They hit us and hurt us, because they want us to fight!"

"Why should we fight against the gods?"

"Not *against* the gods, Yana, *for* them!"

I closed my eyes and rubbed my forehead. My thoughts seemed like so many moths beating against the inside of my head.

Chanka pressed on. "You said you were angry at the gods."

"Yes, because I thought they wanted me to find the water at the end of the world, only it's not here."

"Yes, but that was just part of your anger. I have a feeling you were also angry because you knew the gods wanted more of you."

Alarmed, I opened my eyes.

"The gods want you to continue on until you find the water at the end of the world, and this makes you angry because, since Pachamama's shaking, you've been afraid."

I pleaded with my eyes for him to stop. After a moment, he looked away.

"You must forgive me, Yana. I'm not being a very good camasca. I have become so excited by your story I have forgotten it is not mine." He took a deep breath then slowly released it. "Let me tell you something about myself. When I was young, I worked in the fields like the other men of our village. This was very difficult for me, for there is something wrong with my leg. To stand for long periods of time, causes great pain. To work all day in the field was agony. Our chieftain—another one, long since dead—forced me to continue to work, thinking I would become strong enough to conquer the pain. I think it was his way of teaching me courage. Atatau! My leg would hurt so much, I hated to be alive!

"Then one day when we were tilling the fields, the pain was far worse than it had ever been. Each time I pushed my taclla into the soil, it felt as if I were plunging a knife into my leg. Finally, I could take no more, and I threw down my taclla, refusing to turn over one more clod of dirt. This made the chieftain furious, and he advanced toward me, intent upon forcing me back to work. In response, I picked up my taclla, and brought it crashing down on the chieftain's head! It was a terrible thing to do. If I had killed him, I would have been stoned to death. Since he recovered, my punishment was the hiwaya, having a great stone dropped upon my back. That is why my back looks as it does."

The sympathy must have shown in my eyes, for Chanka held up his hand. "Do not feel sorry for me. From bad came good. With an injured back as well as a deformed leg, I truly could no longer work in the fields. The camasca we had at the time took me under his wing and taught me the healing arts. As it turned out, it seemed to be work for which I have some talent."

"You are a very good camasca," I said.

"Thank you, I have tried to be, and this brings me to the point of my story. The chieftain I hit was not a good chieftain. A good chieftain would have realized I would never have made a good farmer and found some other way for me to contribute to our village. Instead he forced me to work in the fields, because he thought it would make me courageous.

"Yana, I have told you what I think the gods are asking of you: to continue on until you find the water at the end of the world. That is what I think you should do. But I do not want to push you to do that which is too painful for you. That would be like the chieftain forcing me to work with the unbearable pain of my leg. You have already acted courageously by undertaking this quest for the water at the end of the world, by not becoming overwhelmed by the horror of your dreams, by helping Urpito even when you yourself have been recovering. You are a brave woman, a kind woman, and now if you decide to return to your village, the gods will understand."

I swallowed hard. "If I continue to search for the water at the end of the world, will I always be afraid?"

"Let me tell you something about fear: it is like your bridge. Take one step at a time. Fear is easier to manage in steps. It is only when we look to the future and imagine things that are not there that the fear overcomes us. I cannot say you will not feel fear. I cannot say you will not be hurt. If it is the will of the gods, you may even die. But this I can promise you: the gods will never abandon you, not even in death."

I took no comfort from his words because I did not wish to die. I realized, however, that what Chanka said about fear was true. Even though fear had been my constant companion since the shaking, I had still managed to do things, to tell Urpito stories and give him rides on Chumpi, to sometimes help Sumaq prepare meals, to play the ocarina at the celebration. It was only when I thought about the future and what might happen should I continue to search for the water at the end of the world that fear overwhelmed me. But were the things I imagined real? Perhaps I was trying to see all the steps on my bridge, rather than just concentrating on the one step at my feet.

I could tell that I was slowly changing my mind about continuing to search for the water at the end of the world. Still, I had reservations. "How can I find the water at the end of the world when not even you know where it is?"

Chanka smiled. "I have an idea about its location."

I closed my eyes and tried to look into my heart. It did not take me long to realize the decision I had made when I left Qomermoya was still the correct one; it was only that fear had weakened my resolve. If I were to quit now, it would not be because I was not meant to find the water at the end of the world, but because I was too afraid to look for it.

In my mind, I heard once more Chanka advise: *Take one step at a time. Fear is easier to manage in steps. It is only when we look to the future and imagine things not there that the fear overcomes us.*

I opened my eyes. "Then tell me where you think it is."

Chanka understood that I had made my decision to continue on. "You will find you have chosen to live fully as the gods intended."

I was not sure I wished to live fully as the gods intended. And if Chanka was correct, the gods had a cruel way of making a person stronger.

Chapter 22

Chanka and I had gotten so caught up in our conversation, we had forgotten about the water in the jar, which had mostly boiled away. I offered to get some more water, but Chanka shook his head.

"I have given much thought to the journey I made into the spirit world," he said. "Two aspects of it seem particularly significant. First, was the location of the road I saw you walking along. It was in the jungle or very near to it. Second, was the road itself, for you were not making your own way through the jungle, but following one made by others. It was near to this road that the birds found you and swept you away.

"I have talked to our chieftain as well as many of our elders. From them I've learned about the roads that lead into the jungle. There are not many. As you may know, the Capac Inca has not expanded the boundaries of Tahuantinsuyu far in that direction. The jungle is not a pleasant place. It's hot and humid, and the primitive people who live there are cunning defenders of their land." Chanka picked up the twig he had used to ignite the yellow stone and drew a small circle in the dirt. "This circle is the city of Qosqo. North of Qosqo are many villages and a road passes through them then curves west following the Wilkamayu River. Eventually, the Wilkamayu River flows into the jungle."

"Is this the road that will lead me to the water at the end of the world?"

"I don't think so. The elders reminded me of an ancient legend. Long before the Incas came to rule, there was a great people who must have shared some of the power of the gods, for they were able to dig a system of tunnels that went north and south, and east and west from the place that is now the city of Qosqo." In the dirt, he drew two perpendicular lines intersecting within his small circle. "No one knows why they did this or how far the tunnels extended. Perhaps these people used the tunnels to travel. It is said that one tunnel went south all the way to the ocean. I now believe it is in one of these tunnels you will find the water at the end of the world."

"How do you know if these ancient legends are true? How do you know if the tunnels exist?"

He smiled. "I never believed they did exist, until Anka told me about them."

"Anka?"

Chanka pointed with his stick. "As you can see, the tunnels intersect at Qosqo. The shape of the city resembles that of a puma. The puma's spirit protects Qosqo. The head of the puma is Saqsaywaman, a place where spirits live and guard the city. Beneath Saqsaywaman there are ancient tunnels. Most people do not know they exist, for they are kept secret."

"Then how did Anka know of them?"

"You should ask? The discovery of the tunnels was another adventure of Anka and his brother, Kacha. Though the main entrance to the tunnels is sealed off, and no one can enter without special permission, Anka and Kacha came upon another entrance, one that was outside Saqsaywaman and hidden among a jumble of rocks. Anka said it is very dangerous to explore the tunnels, not just because it is forbidden, but because the tunnels are many and interconnected, and a person can easily get lost, which is what happened to Anka and his brother. Eventually they managed to find their way out, but the experience was so frightening, not even they ventured back into the tunnels again."

"How do you expect me to find my way in these tunnels if they could not?" I said.

"I don't. I only told you what Anka told me so you would know the tunnels exist.

"I mentioned there is a road leading to the jungle that follows the Wilkamayu River. There is, however, another road, not as well traveled. It is used to transport goods to and from a coca plantation." Chanka drew another line in the dirt extending north of Qosqo. "This road follows a smaller river called the Jochoc. I am told the Jochoc winds through a steep canyon—much like the Apurimac River you traveled along to get here. Eventually, the road comes to the source of the river, a lake high in the mountains, then it continues across the mountains and down to the coca plantation at the edge of the jungle."

The line Chanka drew intersected the line he had drawn earlier representing the tunnel that went north from Qosqo. I pointed to this intersection of road and tunnel. "Do you think this is the place you saw in your spirit journey?"

Chanka nodded.

"I don't suppose you have ever traveled there."

"Of course not! With my leg, the farthest I have ever traveled is the caves here at Tambo Toco."

"I'm sorry, Chanka. I did not mean to offend you. I only wanted to know how you knew so much about this road."

"I have pieced together my knowledge from many sources, things I remember being told, conversations with the elders and others. For instance, I once talked with the man who was in charge of the distribution of coca leaves. He was the one who told me about the Jochoc River and the road along it."

Looking closely at the lines Chanka had drawn, I made a pleasing discovery. "Look! The quickest way for me to go is through Qosqo."

"No!" Chanka exclaimed. "You must not go that way!"

The sharpness in his voice startled me. "You are right, Chanka. I was not thinking. That way is too populated; too many people would ask me questions."

"It is not people asking questions that bothers me. In fact, you will need to ask questions from those you meet along the way, for the information I have given you is like a cloth loosely woven. It needs more threads to make it whole. No, the reason I don't want you to go through Qosqo is because of Anka."

"What do you have against Anka?" I said.

Chanka looked surprised.

"I saw you two arguing."

Chanka nodded. "Yes, he was insisting on accompanying you on your search for the water at the end of the world. I told him he must not do that."

The thought of Anka's company made my heart leap with joy. "Anka would be a great help to me! His presence would lessen my fear and increase my chance of success. Are you wanting me not to find the water at the end of the world?"

"I will tell you exactly what I told him: if he accompanies you on your journey, you will certainly fail to find the water at the end of the world!"

"How can—"

"Listen! It is obvious you have a great affection for each other, yes?"

I nodded. "I love Anka, and I'm almost certain he loves me."

"You should not doubt his love. If anything, it is too strong. I'm certain Anka cares more about you than he cares about whether you find the water at the end of the world. If he were to accompany you and you were to meet with danger, he would urge you to give up your search rather than risk injury.

He might even force you to stop, and you, with your affection for him and with your fears, would not be able to resist him. No, if you are to succeed, you must go alone, unencumbered by your affections and the affections of someone else. Only by going alone do you have a chance of succeeding."

Tears blurred my vision. "And if I go through Qosqo—"

"That is what Anka is expecting, I'm certain of it. Did you not see the look of defiance on his face? If you go in the direction of Qosqo, you will find him somewhere on the road waiting for you."

I wiped my wet cheek with the back of my hand. "I understand why you say I must go alone. But, Chanka, I'm so tired of being alone."

"Everyone is alone. We only disguise our loneliness with our affection for others." He made a mark in the dirt just below the circle that represented Qosqo. "Tambo Toco is here. In order to avoid Qosqo, you must travel northeast across the mountains until you reach the Wilkamayu River here." He indicated a place east of Qosqo. "Then you will follow the Wilkamayu in a northwest direction to its confluence with the Jochoc River. There you will find a village where the chieftain should be able to tell you more about the road into the jungle. I am sending Akakllu with you as far as the Wilkamayu River. Otherwise, you might lose your way, for the terrain is very rugged between here and there. How are you feeling? I would like you to start tomorrow."

So soon? I thought. "I no longer get dizzy when I walk, but I am not as strong as I was before Pachamama's shaking."

"I'll tell Akakllu to go slow until your strength returns." Seeing my reluctance, he added. "I wish I could give you more time, Yana, but yesterday a chasqui passed through Tambo Toco. He brought news that Topa Inca is getting worse. He no longer has the strength to rise from his chusi."

Chapter 23

The people of Tambo Toco were as generous in my leaving as they had been during my time of recovering. I was given a new lliqlla to wear, for my own had been torn in the shaking and looked ragged despite my efforts to mend it. My new lliqlla had a border of dark red squares. I had never worn anything so beautifully colored.

"Good!" said Chanka when he saw me in my new apparel. "The pattern of your lliqlla is like that worn by the Incas. Along with your yellow feather and the gold medallion, it gives you the appearance of someone important. People will be less inclined to question your right to travel alone."

"But I'm not important," I said, "and it's wrong for me to pretend that I am. It's a lie. Don't lie, don't steal, don't be lazy. These are what we've always been taught."

"Yes, that is the way the Hatunruna think: Don't! Don't! Don't! Do you think the Capac Inca conquered the world thinking, Don't! Don't! Don't? You are now in the service of the Capac Inca, are you not? Tell that to anyone who questions you. Be commanding! Be proud! It will take you a long way."

Though I did not argue the point, I did not think I could act in such a manner and would continue to avoid people whenever possible.

Besides the lliqlla, I was given new packs filled with the supplies I would need. Chanka also gave me coca leaves along with instructions similar to the ones Ipa had given me.

"Do not come to rely upon the leaves, especially early on when you are regaining your strength," Chanka said. "But later you may have use for them, especially if you have not eaten for a while and must have more energy."

He also gave me something Ipa hadn't: llipta, a resinous ball made from the ashes of burnt plants.

"Chew that along with the coca leaves," he said. "It will enhance the effect of the leaves and take away their bitterness."

Sumaq presented me with a unique clay jar, one she had made following Chanka's instructions.

"It is so you will have something to put the water at the end of the world in when you find it," she explained.

I held the jar and lifted its lid. The inside was glazed to prevent the water from seeping out through the otherwise porous clay. The outside was padded with a winding of yarn dyed gold using chilca root. The lid was also wrapped with the yarn and hinged to the lip of the jar using the same fiber.

"Once the jar is filled, you can seal it shut using pitch," Sumaq said. She gave me a small container of pitch along with thin strips of cloth to wind over the sticky resin.

"I will be very careful not to break this," I said. "I never would have thought to protect the jar by wrapping it with yarn. And it is so beautiful. The yellow threads make it look as if it's made of gold!"

Sumaq smiled. "I wanted it to be special, as a way of thanking you for looking after Urpito. He will be very sorry to see you go."

I knelt down in front of Urpito who stood beside his mother. "You will probably miss Chumpi more than me, won't you?"

He assured me he would not, though his grin said otherwise. "Someday, when I have my own llama, I will name him Chumpi." He looked up at his mother. "I will have my own llama, won't I?"

"Perhaps someday, little heartbreaker," she said.

I gently placed my hand atop his lightly bandaged head. "And every time I give a child a ride on Chumpi, I will remember Urpito, the brave boy who used to ride him."

I placed the jar in one of my packs, wrapping my chusi around it for good measure. Then it was time to leave Tambo Toco. I turned to Chanka. It was sad to think I would likely never see this wise man again. I put my arms around him and rested my head upon his chest.

He patted me on the back. "Remember, Yana, what I said about fear. Remember also, the gods will never forsake you."

I released him and looked into his gentle face. "If I were as wealthy as the Capac Inca, there is nothing I could give you equal to the life you have given back to me."

"Ah, but there is! After you have saved Topa Inca, return and tell me how it was done." He smiled. "Oh, Yana, how I envy you! To be able to travel so far in the service of the gods. Now go! Try to make good time. It is many days to the Jochoc River and many more until you find the tunnel. Go as quickly as you can. Topa Inca is depending on you."

I lifted the packs onto Chumpi's back then began to lead him through the village. Many people stopped what they were doing to say goodbye and offer me words of encouragement. Smiling, I returned their good-byes.

Akakllu, leading the way ahead of me, began to play on his flute the same tune Charapa had played when he left Qomermoya.

> Sad the Kullku's cry,
> Sweet my glad heart's song;
> Oh, to be wandering,
> Always wandering on.

Akakllu's playing was cheerful, the smiles of the well-wishers sincere, but my heart felt heavy.

Part Three

Alone

Chapter 24

Either Chanka forgot to tell Akakllu to moderate his pace until I had fully recovered my strength, or going slow was not within Akakllu's ability. Fortunately, the first part of our journey was downhill into a deep river canyon. It was when we got to the river and had to scramble over rocks that I began to tire. Over his shoulder, Akakllu explained that the river, called the Paruro, eventually flowed into the Apurimac, the river I had traveled along for much of my journey to Tambo Toco. His leading me this way made no sense, for we were now traveling opposite to the direction we needed to go. Still, I did not waste my breath asking questions and concentrated upon putting one foot in front of the other.

In two ways, Akakllu reminded me of Taruka, the young man of Qomermoya who had helped till our family's field in my brother Charapa's absence. Akakllu was of the same age as Taruka, and like him, a person of few words. There was no physical resemblance, however, for Taruka was short and thick-chested, whereas Akakllu was a tall, slender blade of grass much like my cousin, Llakato, though with none of my cousin's leisureliness.

After we traveled nearly a tupu, another river, nearly the equal of the Paruro, entered from the left.

"We'll cross here," Akakllu announced.

We both knelt beside the river, drank of its cold water, and prayed to the gods for a safe crossing. Then, as I had seen Anka do before, Akakllu began to cross the river by leaping from rock to rock. Even if I hadn't been so tired, I doubted whether I could have made the jumps. I removed my sandals then waded into the river, holding onto the rocks to keep my balance. This worked well until I reached the middle where the water was deeper. There I lost my hold, and the swift current swept me away. Chumpi, who had been following closely behind, bleated anxiously. Fortunately, I was able to grab hold of a projecting rock and pull myself from the current. I stumbled onto the far shore completely wet and shaking from cold and fatigue.

Akakllu had not waited for me, and I had not the energy to call him back. I squeezed water from my lliqlla then sat out of the wind and hugged myself to get warm, not caring whether Akakllu noticed I was following or not. Eventually he returned.

"This river I was following is the Parococha," he said before I could chide him for his desertion. "It flows from the north and we'll follow it for one... no, two... or maybe three tupus."

"You don't seem very certain," I said.

Akakllu shrugged.

"Well, I'm sorry, but I am too tired to go another step, let alone a tupu." Chumpi, who had gotten fat and lazy during his stay at Tambo Toco, was tired also.

"If you can walk but a little farther," Akakllu said, "there is a good place to make camp."

I forced my legs to follow him. The campsite was a good one, a large area of soft sand left when the high water of the river had receded. Though there were no trees for shade, this did not matter to me as I was still chilled from my soaking. Akakllu removed the packs from Chumpi, and I began to go through them.

"Are you hungry?" I said.

"I have my own food." He patted the woven bag he carried. "Chanka told me not to use any of yours."

"I notice several deep pools in the river. Perhaps you can catch some fish." Akakllu's look told me that if I wanted fish to eat, I would have to catch them myself. I sighed. "I will heat some water for tea."

There was plenty of driftwood scattered about, and soon I had a fire going. As I fed pieces of wood to the flames, Akakllu sat by the river and played his flute. Though I thought I played the ocarina rather well, I was nowhere near as good a musician as Akakllu. I admired the clarity of his notes, and his runs were as swift as the river and flowed as effortlessly.

When the tea was ready, I filled my cup and brought it to share with Akakllu. But Akakllu was lost in his playing. With eyes closed, he sat cross-legged, swaying to the rhythm of his music. I did not disturb him, but sipped tea as I leaned against a warm rock and enjoyed his performance.

Eventually he opened his eyes, saw me watching him, and immediately stopped playing.

"Pleased don't stop. You play beautifully."

He smiled and ran his fingers nervously over the air holes of his flute. Then from his bag he took the same ocarina I had played the night of the celebration and handed it to me.

I played him a simple tune, one that did not require too much dexterity.

"Again!" Akakllu commanded, when I had finished. "Play it over and over."

I played as ordered. He joined me, matching my notes as two people match their strides. But as I repeated the melody a second time, he began to vary his accompaniment. Sometimes his notes ranged below me, rising and falling in parallel with mine. Other times he twittered above, restless and energetic. I felt I was a big bird, perhaps a raven, slowly beating my wings with unending regularity while he, a swift swallow, soared and swooped and circled around me. Over and over we played, and each time his accompaniment was different.

I closed my eyes and, like Akakllu, lost myself to the music. After a while, I also ventured away from the basic melody. As I grew bolder, I too began to soar, though not as assuredly or as effortlessly as Akakllu. Even so, we became two birds in playful flight. Upon the wind of our notes, we rose in ever broadening circles. Then we tucked our wings and plummeted down, crisscrossing in flight before finally pulling up to glide contentedly side-by-side. Such flight was exhilarating, but also tiring. I began my final descent, touched down, and stopped to catch my breath. Immediately Akakllu launched into another song, one requiring great agility.

Inti stood upon the rim of the river canyon, his slanting rays of light reflected in the rippling water, creating a tapestry of constantly shifting patterns. I studied the patterns until my eyelids grew heavy. Lost in his playing, Akakllu didn't notice when I stood up. Too tired to eat, I lay upon my chusi on the soft sand. In the little time before sleep overtook me, I listened as Akakllu's notes were now accompanied by the squeak of bats in erratic flight above the darkening river.

The next morning, we rose just as it was growing light. As we packed away our things, I reminded Akakllu that I had yet to regain my strength, and requested he not walk so fast. He nodded, understanding, then started off as quickly as the day before. I bit back angry words and struggled to follow. Then I remember how Akakllu had adjusted his stride to the tune he played as we left Tambo Toco. I thought of a slow song, one about the snail who carries his home on his back.

"Akakllu, do you know the song, *Llakato, Llakato?*"

Akakllu took out his flute. But when he began to play *Llakato, Llakato*, it was a quick and lively rendition. Defeated, I varied my pace between a brisk walk and a slow run in order to keep up.

After we had gone about two tupus, the canyon opened up, revealing a wide cultivated valley. Before I could voice to Akakllu my desire to avoid contact with people, he ran ahead across the shallows toward a village perched upon a hillside. Then the sound of girls' laughter caused him to change course. It came from behind a great rock perched near the river's edge, As Akakllu circled around the rock, I followed cautiously, stopping before I could be seen. I listened as Akakllu offered a greeting then began to ask questions concerning the way ahead. Judging by her voice, she was an old woman who answered.

I waited, watching as Chumpi pulled up clumps of grass. I recalled Chanka saying how I looked like an Inca. Seized by an impulse, I decided to see if I could act like one. I pulled my two necklaces out where they could be seen then strode from behind the rock, stopping as soon as I saw the girls. I stood with Inti's light reflecting off the gold medallion.

The girls, who had been washing clothes, stopped what they were doing and stared at me. The old woman did not see me at first, but continued talking to Akakllu, giving directions with her hands. When she finally turned my direction, she stopped mid-sentence, her arms still raised. Then as fast as her old bones allowed, she stood and bowed toward me with arms extended in obeisance. The girls, dropping their washing into the river, quickly followed her example.

Confused, I also started to bow, then checked myself. "Arise!" I said in a voice not my own. Motioning toward Akakllu, who looked at me in disbelief, I commanded, "Continue giving Akakllu your directions, mother." Still everyone but Akakllu continued to hold their arms before them. "Arise!" I again ordered. One girl lifted her head momentarily then quickly looked back down. "Atatau!" I muttered, "Why aren't they listening?" I fled to the concealment provided by the rock. I felt both exhilarated and afraid at the same time. Their instant acceptance of my nobility astonished me. I remembered how Ipa had amazed Charapa and me with her talking jar, and now understood why she had enjoyed the deception, for the girls and the old woman were no less amazed by my sudden appearance than if I had been a talking jar. Still underneath my excitement was a feeling of unease.

I walked to Chumpi and started to lead him by his halter away from the river. Hearing Akakllu coming along behind me, I turned.

"Why did you do that?" Akakllu said. "You frightened them. I thought the old woman wasn't going to talk to me after you appeared with that." He pointed to the gold medallion still dangling visibly from my neck.

I did not know how to answer him, for he knew nothing of my conversation with Chanka. Instead, I posed a question. "Why were you asking directions? Haven't you been this way before?"

He looked away. "I have never been this far from Tambo Toco, but my uncle, who once worked on the road that follows the Wilkamayu River, gave me good directions. I was just confirming them with the old woman."

Behind Akakllu, a girl peeked from behind the rock then disappeared.

"So which way do we go?" I said.

Akakllu pointed northeast. "Up that mountain."

The way was not overly steep, but very long. Up and up we climbed, higher and higher until the fields of the valley were like green checkered patterns in a woven cloth. We reached the top to find ourselves upon a broad, wind-swept plain. To the northwest, the treeless plain stretched to the horizon. To the southwest, it narrowed then seemed to disappear.

Unexpectedly, Akakllu stopped to rest. Though tired, I was pleased that much of my former endurance had returned. I took two sweet maize cakes from a pack and offered one to Akakllu, who, despite Chanka's orders, was glad to receive it. Of course, Chumpi had to have some of mine. I sat on the ground next to Akakllu, facing northeast, the direction the old woman told us we must go. Storm clouds edged the horizon, and as we watched, a bolt of lightning illuminated the dark clouds.

Akakllu jumped up as if the bolt had struck him and began to stride across the pathless plain. I hurried to catch up. When we finally reached the edge of the plain, Akakllu pointed down into a canyon where another river could be seen. "When we reach the river, we'll camp for the night."

I looked at the dark clouds and knew we would be lucky to make camp before the storm overtook us. We descended down a ravine which, in times of heavy rain, channeled the run-off. This ravine provided a path through thickets of checche bushes whose pointy leaves liked to stick to our clothing. When the ravine became too steep to continue down, we followed a well-worn deer trail. Thunder reverberated up the canyon, and a few raindrops began to fall.

When we reached the river, we immediately started looking for shelter from the impending storm. Akakllu pointed to a depression in the hillside above, and we scrambled up slope to examine it more closely. Set into the hillside was a small recess. It was not big enough to sleep in, but could shelter us sitting up. Akakllu and I were considering whether to continue looking for a larger shelter when a sudden thunder was followed by a curtain of rain.

Quickly we stripped Chumpi of his packs and placed them as far back in the recess as possible. That left an area just big enough for Akakllu and me to sit out of the rain. Chumpi tried to push in beside us, but there was no room. "I'm sorry, Chumpi," I said. "I know how you hate to get wet, but as you can see, there isn't enough room for you also. Go find a place where you can be dry, and we'll come find you when the rain stops."

"Chumpi actually understood you," Akakllu said, as we watched Chumpi trot away down river.

The sudden downpour gave way to a steady rain. Raindrops spattered on the rocks before us, but did little more than wet our toes. Akakllu and I looked at each other, pleased with our cozy shelter. Then a gust of wind drove the rain sideways, right into our faces. There was little we could do but pull our legs tight to our chests and suffer in silence. Thunder continued to echo up the canyon, though increasingly muffled as the edge of the storm moved westward.

The rain lasted for about the time it takes hot water to soften charqui, then patches of blue could be glimpsed through lifting clouds. I stood up and stepped out of the shelter. My legs were stiff from squatting, my back sore from pushing back under the overhanging ledge. "The storm is nearly over. I'm going to go look for Chumpi."

Akakllu pulled the packs from the recess, and slung them over his shoulder. The ground was slick, and by the time we reached the base of the slope, our legs were covered in mud. We proceeded down river and had only gotten about three hundred paces when we came upon Chumpi, sitting beneath the overhang of a ledge large enough to shelter a whole village.

"Atatau!" Akakllu cried in disgust, dropping the packs on the ground before stomping away. It was easy to guess the reason for Akakllu's disgruntlement. While we were getting drenched in our inadequate shelter, Chumpi had been comfortable and dry.

But I could not be angry. I put an arm around Chumpi's neck. "To think we rudely drove you away. Next time it rains, we'll know to stick with you."

In response, Chumpi belched up a cud of grass.

I gathered up an armful of wood and started a fire beneath the rock ledge, which was blackened by previous fires. Akakllu returned, having washed some of the mud from his arms and legs. He squatted next to the fire and warmed his hands.

"I'm going to take a bath!" I announced.

"Inti has passed behind the mountain. It will soon be dark."

"I don't care. I won't be able to sleep unless I get this mud off me. By the way, what is the name of this river?"

"I don't remember if the old woman told me. Your dramatic entrance confused her. But I remembered she said it flows into the Huatanay River, which flows through Qosqo then eastward to join the Wilkamayu."

I took a piece of paqpa root along with my comb down to the river. The water was not very cold perhaps on account of the river being shallow. I made a lather of the paqpa root and rubbed it into my hair, then made more lather to wash my body. I rinsed by splashing the water over me. This reminded me of Ipa flinging water upon Kusi, and I realized it had been several days since I last said a prayer for my family. I prayed for the safekeeping of each family member then asked the gods to keep watch over Akakllu and me.

As the chill wind dried me, I combed out my hair, which was full of tangles. When I finally slipped back into my lliqlla, I felt restored.

Returning to the fire, I found, to my surprise, Akakllu heating water for tea. I added dried bilyea leaves to the water then sat next to the fire and chewed upon a piece of charqui while waiting for the water to boil.

"It is good to be clean," I declared.

Akakllu's response was a grunt.

"How much farther do we have to go before we reach the Huatanay River?"

Akakllu moved the jar higher upon the flames. "I don't think it is a great distance as the hawk flies, but the old woman said a large marsh lies between us and the river. I don't know how long it will take us to get around this marsh, but once we reach the Huatanay River, we will be able to travel quickly upon the highway my uncle helped to build. The road divides at the confluence of the Huatanay and Wilkamayu Rivers. In one direction, the road follows the Wilkamayu downriver. That is the way you will go. In the other direction, the road goes to Lake Titikaka. My uncle said the road is wide and paved with flat stones. If we are fortunate, we might make it to the confluence by tomorrow night."

"Then we must get an early start." I poured tea into my cup and the one Akakllu had brought with him. "As soon we finish this, we should go to sleep."

Akakllu took a few sips of tea, but mostly he sat staring into the fire. I stared also until my eyelids grew heavy. I had almost fallen asleep when Akakllu spoke.

"The Coya Raymi festival will be in three days."

I had forgotten all about this most important of festivals, which marked the time when the days begin to grow longer. The rainy season begins and with it growth of new crops. The Coya Raymi festival is preceded by a great amount of work as everything must be made clean. By tradition, this work is performed by men. "Then it is fortunate that you are here with me," I said. "Now you'll get out of having to help clean."

"Cleaning is a small price to pay for the celebration that follows. I was going to play a new song I had composed."

Then it occurred to me the sacrifice Akakllu had made. As my guide, he had lost the opportunity to share his cherished music with others.

"Would you play your new song for me?"

This time Akakllu chose an ocarina to play. To limber his fingers, he blew a few quick runs, which echoed within our rock shelter, making his one ocarina sound like many. Even Chumpi raised his head and pointed his ears in response to this wonderful swelling of sound.

"Now I will play my song."

At first, the song did not appeal to me. The music was very slow and without embellishment. It didn't seem much like music, yet sounded familiar. I stared into the fire, wondering what it reminded me of. Then the wind blew ash from the fire, and I knew. Akakllu's music depicted the wind, but not just any wind, only that wind which blows across high empty plains or across mountain slopes where there was nothing to resist the wind's movement. We had heard it earlier that day. The wind that blows across the empty plains is so incessant, one often forgets it's there until it stops. Listening to Akakllu's music, I imagined myself in the mountains above Qomermoya. Scattered across the steep slopes were the llamas, their backs to the wind that sliced through the ichu grass. Out of habit, I tucked my loose hair behind my ears as I had done countless times only to have the wind blow it free again a moment later.

Akakllu reached the end of his song and my vision dissolved. "That was wonderful. Your music is the wind you hear in high places."

Akakllu nodded, looking very pleased.

"Are there words that go with this music?"

Akakllu set aside his ocarina and began to sing.

> I walk across the plain.
> Only the dry ichu grass
> And the jagged stones greet me.
>
> I walk across the plain,
> The mountains forever distant.
>
> I walk across the plain,
> And suddenly hear your voice;
> I turn quickly,
> But, alas, it is only the wind.

The song expressed a tenderness I did not expect from Akakllu, and I realized how little I knew of this unassuming young man who spoke so eloquently through his music.

"I am sorry you will miss the Coya Raymi festival because of me. I'm sorry the people of Tambo Toco will miss hearing your lovely song."

"There will be other times." He stood up, unrolled his chusi then lay down upon it. "Besides how often do I get a chance to be pelted by rain while just a few steps away, someone's llama is nice and dry?"

Chapter 25

The next day, we came to the marsh the old woman had spoken of. It edged a large lake, partially encircling it with a wide expanse of dark green reeds. By comparison to Qomermoya, where greenery was often sparse, it seemed an extravagance. As Akakllu and I began to make our way around, keeping to higher ground and avoiding the muddy shoreline, we crossed a trail that disappeared into the reeds. Fearing we might end up knee-deep in mud, we went along the trail cautiously. Though dark and moist, the ground held our weight and was a pleasure to walk upon, for it was soft and springy. The trail was like a river winding through a narrow canyon, except that, in place of rocks, there were reeds, higher than our heads. Around us we heard the squawks and splashes of startled birds, but the reeds prevented us from seeing them. Chumpi, not liking this confined space, nudged me, urging me to walk faster.

We emerged from our canyon onto the rocky shore of the lake. Several men were out fishing in boats made of reeds bound together. We waved to them in passing before disappearing into another stand of reeds.

Akakllu spoke over his shoulder. "This trail clearly goes north."

I knew what he was thinking. To get around the marsh, we thought we would be forced to go far out of our way to the west.

"Perhaps we'll reach the Huatanay River soon," I said.

This prompted Akakllu to increase his pace. I did not mind, for I was feeling strong, and Chumpi certainly did not mind our hurrying to get through the reeds. When we came back into the open again, we startled a large flock of birds that had been feeding at the water's edge. With a rush of wings, they took to the air, and we stopped to watch. I had never seen birds such as these, and, judging from Akakllu's excited expression, he had never seen them either. Their bodies were as large as those of geese, and like geese they cried out when in flight. But their legs were much longer the those of geese as were their necks which seemed unusually thin. They had great crooked beaks, black in color.

But what was most astonishing about these birds was their color: pink, nearly orange, with striking black wing tips, and their legs blue gray with bright pink knees. They rose quickly on strong wings and circled right over our heads, a great swirling pink cloud. We watched as they glided away in the direction we had come, eventually to be hidden by the reeds.

I turned toward Akakllu. "What were they?"

But Akakllu, his face bright with excitement, was not listening. "Weren't they the most beautiful birds you've ever seen, Yana? Did you see the way Inti's light caught them as they turned together in flight? It was as if someone had suddenly painted the sky pink." He sighed. "Perhaps on my way back, I will see them again, though it was worth missing the Coya Raymi festival just to see them this once."

Near the water's edge we found a few of their feathers. I picked up two, planning to add them to my necklace with the yellow feather once I had time.

Not long after seeing the birds, we came to the Huatanay River and the great road that went along it. The road was as Akakllu's uncle had described to him: broad, straight, and surfaced with flat stones. We found a shady place beneath a huayau tree to sit, for it was late in the day, and we had not rested since morning meal.

"We have made good time," I said.

Akakllu nodded. Looking ahead along the road, he proudly announced, "This is the Capac-nan, the great highland road that my uncle helped build. It runs the entire length of Tahuantinsuyu."

Suddenly we heard the sound of running feet. We both jumped up. Coming toward us was a chasqui, his puturutu tied with a cord and flapping against his side.

As he drew near, Akakllu called out to him. "How far to the Wilkamayu River?"

The charqui did not slacken his pace, but shouted as he streaked past. "About a tupu!"

Akakllu turned to me. "We will be there before nightfall."

"In that case, there really is no need for you to accompany me any further. I could not possibly get lost following this magnificent road, and this way, if you hurry, you might make it back to Tambo Toco in time for the Coya Raymi festival. After all, isn't that why you've been leading me at such a fast pace?"

Embarrassed, Akakllu looked away.

I smiled. "It would be a shame if the people of Tambo Toco missed hearing your new song. What do you call it?"

"*Only the Wind*," he said in a small voice.

"If you leave now, you may have time to teach someone the words, or better yet, the accompaniment, for you sing very well."

Akakllu grinned. "Now that I've made the journey, I know a place or two where I can take a short cut. The trick will be not to return to Tambo Toco before the men have finished cleaning the village."

I laughed. "Then take some time by the marsh to look for those magnificent birds." I went to my packs and removed two sweet maize cakes. "These are for you."

Akakllu shook his head. "I have already taken some of your food when I wasn't supposed to."

I pressed them into his hand. "Take them. They are poor payment for all you've done for me."

"And this is for you," he said, reaching into his bag. He handed me the ocarina I had played the night Anka sang of the two doves. "I wanted to give it to you before, but it never seemed the right time."

Tears came to my eyes. "Thank you. I will play it at night, remembering how we played music together, sitting beside the Parococha River. That way, I will not feel so alone." I stepped forward and gave him a brief hug. "Now, go! You don't want to miss seeing those birds because of darkness."

Akakllu turned and started back down the trail at a jog. I tucked my gift away in one of my packs then walked down the bank to drink from the river. As I splashed water on my face, I thought about playing music when alone. Music seemed a poor substitute for human companionship. While I had been with Akakllu, it had not been difficult to forget why I was making this journey and what might lie ahead. Only when I woke in the night did the fear creep upon me. Now I would only have Chumpi and my fears for company.

I caught the familiar smell of burning llama dung long before I saw the village situated at the confluence of the Huatanay and Wilkamayu Rivers. What troubled me was its size. I counted twenty wasis this side of the Huatanay River, twice as many as in Qomermoya. But a rope bridge spanned the river, and on the opposite side were more wasis. What I did not know, and would not learn until the following morning, was that a second bridge, hidden from me in the growing darkness, spanned the Wilkamayu River, and across it were more wasis still!

I realized it would be impossible to pass through the village unnoticed, even if I waited until everyone was asleep; some sleepless wanderer or a dog would surely hear me and challenge my presence. Of course, the village offered the opportunity to get the information I needed for my journey ahead. Perhaps if I showed a commanding presence, as Chanka had suggested, I could get this information without having to answer too many questions. Unfortunately, I didn't feel like a woman in the service of the Capac Inca, but more like a thief sneaking about in the night.

Chumpi and I made it to the bridge without being challenged, no doubt because anyone who saw us in the fading light would assume we were members of the village. The bridge was well constructed and hardly swayed under our weight. I had just gotten across when a boy ran in front of me and stopped. My heart leapt to my throat. I swallowed and forced myself to speak casually.

"Good evening. It's a lovely evening, is it not?"

The boy turned and called to a figure standing in the shadow of a wasi whose wall leaned precariously outward. "Mother, there's a strange woman here, and she has a big llama with her."

I was glad he had spoken to his mother; I preferred being questioned by a woman rather than a man, especially if that man were a chieftain.

But the woman who approached had an appearance I did not like. She was about the same age my mother would have been had she lived, but that was the only similarity. My mother's face reflected the kind person she was. This woman looked like she had just bitten into a penka fruit, but forgot to first remove the thorns. She scowled with lips pinched over gums that held few teeth. She fixed one eye firmly upon me while the other, which was clouded over, stared out at an odd angle.

"Who are you, and what are you doing here?" Her voice held no kindness.

I struggled to keep my manner casual, though my mouth was so dry I could barely speak. "Good evening, mother. Could you tell me how far it is to the Jochoc River?"

"You haven't told me who you are!" she snapped.

I was afraid her angry voice would attract others. "Forgive me, mother. My name is Yana Mayu and I–"

"Who gave you permission to come here, and who told you could go to the Jochoc River?"

I swallowed the lump in my throat. I wanted to show the confidence Chanka expected of me, but the woman was so unfriendly and talked so quickly, I was unnerved.

"I'm on the service… I mean, I'm in the service of the Capinca… I mean, the Capac Inca." I struggled to pull the gold medallion from under my lliqlla. My fingers were clumsy, and my two necklaces had gotten tangled together. I gave up trying to untangle them.

The woman spat on the ground. "Well, if you're in the service of the "'Capinca,'" you should stay at a tambo. There's one up the road where all those good-for-nothing chasquis and soldiers stay." She looked me up and down. "Aye, I'm sure they'd like your company very much!"

I fought back tears. "I am sorry, mother, to have troubled you. If you will just be so kind as to show me the way to the–"

"Have you eaten?"

"What? No, I–"

"You're hungry, are you not?"

"No, I… yes, but I–"

"Imayoq!"

From behind the woman came a girl's voice. "Yes, mother?"

"Is there anything left of evening meal, or did you eat it all?"

"There is some locro left."

"Good! Put it in a bowl. We have a visitor. Someone who is in the service of the Capinca." The woman cackled then called her son. "Huchuq Uma!"

The boy been gently running his fingers through the tangles in Chumpi's hair. Hearing his name, he spun about. "Yes, mother!"

"Take those packs off that flea carrier and find a place for him."

Alarmed, I turned to the boy, but sensing my anxiety he whispered, "Don't worry, I will find a safe place for him. I'll put him in–"

"Come!" the woman ordered, pulling me by my arm. "There is good food and drink!"

It was the time of the month when Qillamama had her face hidden, and I could barely see to walk, but the woman gripped me tightly with her bony fingers and kept me from stumbling.

"Sit here," she commanded.

I could see the faint glow from a fire and seated next to it the silhouette of someone very fat, presumably Imayoq, the woman's daughter. I was no sooner seated then the girl, without a word, placed a bowl of locro in my lap. I suddenly I realized how hungry I was. The woman, holding the largest chicha jar I had ever seen, sat down next to me.

She thrust the jar under my nose. "Here, drink."

Inadvertently I drew back, for the chicha smelled sour. "Not now, mother, thank you. Perhaps later." Quickly I added, "This locro is delicious!" In fact, the squash in it was nearly rotten.

The woman did not seem offended by my refusal of the chicha. She took a long pull from the jar then smacked her lips appreciatively. "You married?" she said.

Here it comes, I thought, the interrogation I had been dreading. I shook my head then realized she could not see me in the dark. "No, mother."

"Good! It is a terrible thing to be married. Is that not right, Imayoq?"

The girl groaned then awkwardly then pushed herself up, releasing a fart as long as my arm.

"Atatau!" the woman cried. "Marriage will never be your problem, Imayoq. Who wants a wife who only eats and farts?"

Imayoq waddled away toward the wasi.

"That's right!" the woman called after her. "Go ahead and desert our guest." She took another drink from the jar. "Now what were we talking about? Oh, marriage!" She said 'marriage' like it was something dead and rotting. "Perhaps marriage would not be so bad if it were not to a man. A llama. A llama would make a nice husband. They're quiet. They're useful. A llama would never go off and leave when you needed him the most. That llama of yours looks like a nice llama. Let me give you some advice: when it comes time for you to marry, ask your chieftain if you can marry your llama."

This was so preposterous I did not know how to reply. I decided to make light of it. "For shame, mother. What would your husband say if he heard you?"

She sputtered, spraying sour chicha over me.

"Say? What would he say? What do I care what he'd say? Oh, I wish he were here right now! I'd tell him a thing or two about marriage! That I would, the old weasel!"

I set my half-eaten locro aside. "Mother, I'm sorry, is your husband dead?"

She didn't answer immediately because she had her head in the jar again. She smacked her lips and belched. "Dead? I don't know. I think so. I hope so."

This was a horror to my ears! That a wife should wish her husband dead! I thought of my mother and father and the way they had loved each other.

"Where is your husband?"

She belched again before answering. "'e's doing his service."

The woman's words were becoming slurred and hard to understand. "Pardon, mother?"

"I said, 'e's doing 'is service to the Capac Inca."

"I see. My father is also serving. He's in—"

"How long?"

"Pardon?"

"Pardon! Pardon! Pardon! S' what am I, a jail keeper? You huspan, father—whatever—how long he's been servicing the Capac Inca?"

"He left right after we harvested—"

"Seben years!"

"Par—what, mother?"

"Seben years! That's how longs my weasel's been serving!"

I had never heard of such a thing. The maximum years of required service was five, and never all at once.

"You ever hears zanything likes that?" she said. "Somebody servicing seben years?" She lifted the jar, spilling chicha as she drank. "Jar muss be broken. 'S waste of good chicha!"

"No, mother."

"No, what?"

"No, I have never heard of anyone having to do seven years of service."

"Thass right! Thass what I told the elders. Nobodily services seben years! But wha's the use? They're all weasels! All the elders. All men! Weasels! You sure you doan wan' s'more of thish chicha?"

I was too tired to answer. Besides, I didn't believe she was serious in her offer anyway.

"They should declare him dead. Thass what they should do, little weasels. Zen I be free to marry if I wanted. Find me a good one 'is time. 'S hard. Thass what it is. 'S hard bringing up chidrens an' sno man to helps. 'S hard…"

As she went on like this, I dozed off. I don't know for how long, but I think it was the sudden silence that woke me.

"I'm sorry, mother. I must have—"

"I said, my name. You know what's my name?"

"No, mother."

"Choqñi!" It meant 'blind in one eye.' "Choqñi! You believes 'at? Zay names me Choqñi!"

I detected a change in her voice: less fiery, more sad.

"I always did no' look sis way. Now looks at me! Once, I was beautifilled." I could hear the tears in her voice. "More beautifilled zan even you, whatsever you name is!'"

I dozed off again, only to be jolted awake when Choqñi toppled over, her head landing in my lap. I leaned away, for her breath smelled worse than a buzzard's.

Someone tapped me on the shoulder. It was Imayoq. "This way," she said.

I slipped out from under Choqñi and followed.

"Here's the entrance to the wasi," Imayoq said.

I knelt down and followed after her. Once inside I could see nothing.

"This way," she said.

I crawled across the floor until I felt a chusi.

"This is where you can sleep," she said.

Suddenly I remembered Chumpi. "My llama, I need to go—"

"Don't worry. Huchuq Uma put him in a pen by himself. The two wasis next door are no longer being used because no one wants to live so close to mother."

Despite the bad things Choqñi had said about her daughter, I thought Imayoq considerate, and she had a voice which was pleasant to listen to.

"Thank you." I said. The chusi felt terribly coarse, but I was too tired to care. I lay down and pulled the other half over me. As soon as my head touched the floor, I fell asleep.

Sometime in the middle of the night, I awoke. My legs and arms itched terribly. I knew at once the reason: fleas! There must have been dozens of them. Sitting up, I flung the chusi off me. I scratched my arms and legs until they bled. Atatau! How could anyone live with such vermin? I wondered.

I had to get up! I had to get away from there! I only lay back for a moment to gather my strength. When I woke again, it was because someone was shaking me. I slowly sat up. "What—"

"Shhh!" Imayoq said. "It's time for you to go."

Through the entryway, I could discern the predawn light.

Outside the girl cautioned me again to silence. On the ground, just as I had left her, lay Choqñi with the jar of chicha tipped over on its side. Imayoq's warning seemed unnecessary. Over the rattle of her own snoring, I doubted Choqñi would have heard us had we danced around her beating on drums.

On the road stood Huchuq Uma, holding Chumpi, my packs already on Chumpi's back.

"We can go with you along the road for a way," Imayoq said.

This sounded more like a request than a statement. I nodded, and we proceeded to walk quietly through the village. All but the brightest stars were gone from the sky. In the pale light, I could see the bridge I could not see the night before and the outlines of many wasis on the far side of the river.

I pointed. "It that the Wilkamayu River?"

"Yes," Imayoq whispered. I sensed her need for us to proceed quietly. But as soon we were out of hearing of the village, the silence ended.

"What are you doing traveling alone?" Imayoq said.

Before I could answer, Huchuq Uma said, "What's your llama's name?"

I answered the easier question first. "I call him Chumpi."

"How did—"

"It's my turn!" Imayoq shouted, shoving her brother hard. She repeated her question.

"It is difficult for me to answer," I said. I looked down the road we were traveling. Though I was nearly certain I was going the right direction, I wanted to be sure. "Is this the way to the Jochoc River?"

Huchuq Uma spoke. "Why do you want to—"

Imayoq shoved him again.

"Stop it!" Huchuq Uma yelled, shoving her back.

"Then shut up so I can ask a question!"

"You just asked a question!" he shouted, punching her.

Atatau! Those two fought worse than cats. I had to shout to be heard. "I'm going there to see someone!" It was true enough. I hoped to find someone who could tell me about the road that followed the Jochoc River. "Do you know how far it is?"

"It will take you three days to reach the Jochoc River," Imayoq said.

"Not true!" Huchuq Uma shouted. "Only two!"

"What do you know about it, you little weasel? Have you ever been there?"

"Don't call me a weasel, you fat guinea pig! Allallanka's father went to Pisac in a day, and Pisac's more than halfway to the Jochoc River."

I interrupted. "So if I make it to Pisac today, I will be over halfway to the Jochoc River?"

"You will have to hurry," Imayoq replied. "Allallanka's father is a fast walker."

"What about the tambo your mother spoke of? Will the soldiers give me any trouble?"

"People travel along this road all the time. Just tell them you're going to Pisac to deliver vegetables."

Inti appeared above the hill, and Imayoq and Huchuq Uma immediately stopped, though I didn't realize this until I had walked a little farther. I turned and looked back. They were both standing in the road looking at me. "What's the matter?"

"We have to go back," Huchuq Uma said.

Both brother and sister looked sad. I led Chumpi back to where they were standing. "Tell your mother I am very grateful for the meal and a place to sleep."

"I hope the fleas didn't eat too much of you," Imayoq said.

I rummaged through one of my packs until I found a ball of yarn used for mending. I held the ball out toward Huchuq Uma. "Here, take this."

"What for?" he said.

"Do you know how to braid?"

He nodded.

"Then braid a halter for your llama."

"I don't have a llama."

"Maybe if you braid a halter, a llama might walk into it."

Huchuq Uma smiled and took the ball of yarn.

To Imayoq I gave the pink feathers which I had found by the lake. "You have a lovely voice, Imayoq. I imagine you sing like a bird. These two feathers are in honor of your voice."

A great smile spread across her face.

I thanked them again for their hospitality then turned Chumpi around and started down the road, setting a pace that I hoped would get me to Pisac before the day ended. In a little while, I looked back. Brother and sister stood where I had left them. Even from a distance, I could read their expressions; they too wished to walk down the road that would take them away from their troubled home.

I waved, then continued on. In a little while, I looked back once more. They were still there. I waved again, and they waved back, their arms golden in the early morning light. I walked on and this time did not look back.

Chapter 26

Despite walking at what I thought a fast pace, I did not make it to Pisac that day. Perhaps it was because I took time to bathe and rid myself of fleas. I passed many people as I travelled, some leading trains of llamas with packs upon their backs. No one asked questions of me. I need not have been worried about the tambo. The soldiers there were too busy unloading supplies from a recently arrived train of llamas to take notice of me.

The road was wide enough to accommodate travelers going both directions. This was true even where the river canyon was so narrow the road had to be carved out of the rock. Such an achievement was another example of the power of the Capac Inca and the capability of those under his command.

Because of the narrowness of the river canyon, I was forced to spend the night on the side of the road. With my chusi wrapped around me, for the air was chill in the bottom of the canyon, I sat cross-legged upon a flat rock and chewed a piece of charqui as I watched darkness fill the canyon. I was too tired to build a fire, and once finished with my meal, I lay upon my side and listened to the chatter of swooping bats and the whistling flight of nighthawks before falling asleep. I woke when it was still dark. As dark as the sky was, the walls of the canyon were darker still, and in contrast to these black walls the stars blazed with a glorious intensity. Intuillapa's river was a bridge of light arching across the canyon. I said a prayer, thanking Intuillapa for his gift of beauty. I also prayed to Urcuchillay, who watched over llamas and whose bright eyes looked down upon me.

By starlight so bright I could see my breath in the cold air, Chumpi and I made our way along the road. We walked perhaps a tupu before the stars began to fade, and I stopped and made a small fire. I enjoyed a cup of tea and a maize cake as I watched Inti chase the darkness from the canyon.

"I think we must not be too far from Pisac," I told Chumpi as I prepared to continue on.

I was right in my thinking, for it was not long before the canyon began to widen, and there was the beginning of a broad valley through which the Wilkamayu River flowed placidly. By mid-morning, I was in Pisac, my first experience of an actual town. Besides row upon row of wasis, I saw many colcas, food storage houses, twice the size of the wasis. Upon a hill was a temple to Inti. Like the one in Tambo Puquio described by Charapa, it was a circular building fashioned of stones.

My arrival in Pisac coincided with the beginning of the Coya Raymi festival, a time when no one was to quarrel, for to do so was to invite a year of discontent and sickness. The air was hazy with the smoke of camasto leaves. Over the smoldering leaves, men held chusis to rid them of parasites. Other men washed the walls of the wasis or patched them, using fresh mud. To ward off sickness, a man I took to be the camasca went from wasi to wasi smearing sanco, a porridge made of ground maize, over the entryways.

While the men cleaned, the women prepared morning meal in the shade of a large molle tree. As I approached, I could hear their good-natured comments concerning their men folks' awkward attempts at housecleaning. A woman, soon to give birth, came forward to greet me.

"Good morning. There will be no trading today, for as you can see, it is the beginning of the Coya Raymi festival."

I moved closer so my voice would not be heard by others. "Good morning. I've only come to trade for information, though I have little to offer in exchange for it."

She raised an eyebrow. "What kind of information?"

"I just wish to know how far it is to the Jochoc River, and if I might find a village there."

"Why is it you wish to go to the Jochoc River?"

I had already decided to offer a less pretentious reason for my traveling than being in the service of the Capac Inca. "I am on a type of pilgrimage."

The woman laughed loudly, attracting the attention of the others. "When you come to where the Wilkamayu and Jochoc Rivers join, you will find Calca, a scruffy, little town where, I assure you, there is nothing a pilgrim would find sacred!"

Atatau! How was I to gather information without telling the whole truth? Anything less always led to a misunderstanding. Yet I hadn't time to fully explain my reasons for going to Calca, especially since such an explanation would only raise even more questions and delay me further.

The woman placed her hand on my arm. "You are not in trouble, are you?"

I shook my head. "It is just important that I get to Calca as soon as possible."

She released my arm. "Well, unless you have wings, you will not get there today. We were just about to have morning meal. Come join us. Some hot food will give you strength to travel."

Turning in the direction of the other women, she called, "Sumaq Uya!"

A small girl ran toward us, her hands covered with the dust of ground maize. "Yes, mother?"

"Find some vegetable scraps and feed them to our visitor's llama."

The woman took me by the hand and led me to the shade of the molle tree. "What is your name?"

"Yana Mayu."

Before I could ask hers, she announced, "Everyone, this is Yana Mayu, and I've invited her to join us for morning meal."

The women welcomed me with smiles. I smiled in return though I was not prepared to socialize. Besides my reluctance to converse, I was dirty from walking on the dusty highway. I excused myself, explaining my need to wash. At the river, I was joined by Chumpi and Sumaq Uya whose name, meaning "pretty face," though very common, was appropriate nonetheless, for she was pretty enough to be an aclla, one of the chosen women.

As I splashed water on my face, Sumaq Uya said, "Senqa Qilli is pregnant."

I thought it odd for her to remark upon her mother's obvious condition. And what an inappropriate name! Her mother's nose was not big at all.

"When she gives birth, I get to raise the baby."

Startled, I stared at her, but Sumaq Uya acted as if there was nothing strange about a child raising her mother's baby.

"I hope the baby grows up to be as handsome as yours," she said, pointing to Chumpi.

I laughed, relieved that Sumaq Uya was talking about a pregnant llama and not her mother. "I'm sure you will do a wonderful job raising it," I told her. "Tell me, Sumaq Uya, what is your mother's name?"

"Ichuq Maki." This also was a common name for those people who were left-handed.

"What's the name of your llama?" she said.

"Chumpi."

"May I comb Chumpi? I have a nice comb. I won't hurt him, I promise. He looks like he's not been combed in days."

"I'm sure Chumpi would like that very much, especially after you have already befriended him with food."

While Sumaq Uya went to fetch her comb, I returned to the women who were now joined by the men, anxious for morning meal. Never I had seen so many people in one place. This was good, for among so many, I was less likely to be noticed. As the men lined up to receive a bowl of sanco, a traditional dish for Coya Raymi, I listened to their ribbing of a handsome young man.

"You did a good job beating the dust out of those chusis, Pakpaka. You will make someone a good wife someday."

Pakpaka's face reddened.

"Yes, and a very pretty one, too!" another added to general laughter.

After all of the men had been served and gone off to sit by themselves, the women sat down to eat. I was given a bowl of sanco and went to sit with Ichuq Maki who made a place for me next to her.

"I noticed several of the young men talking about that pretty woman they had not seen before," she said.

"All the young men ever talk about is pretty women," another woman said. "Atatau! I liked them better when they were boys, and all they talked about was llamas."

The women laughed.

The food, though simple, was hot and delicious. Such a contrast to that given me by Chogñi!

"There is plenty more when you finish that," Ichuq Maki told me.

"But save room for lucumas," said an old woman.

I looked up expectantly, for I hadn't tasted that delicious fruit since Tambo Toco.

At my reaction, the old woman clapped her hands and laughed.

"Don't pay any attention to Qallo," Ichuq Maki said. "She likes to fool people by tempting them with things we don't have." Then she changed the subject. "So, Yana, where are you from?"

What I told was the truth, sort of. Pointing upriver, I said, "I come from…" It suddenly occurred to me that I'd never asked Choqñi the name of her village. "From up the road a way." It was a feeble response that was met with an uncomfortable silence.

"And why are you going to Calca?" another woman said.

Obviously Ichuq Maki had been talking about me. "Perhaps I'll trade."

But only for information. I was getting good at this telling the truth while not telling the truth, but it was not something I was proud of.

Qallo, the old woman who had fooled me about the lucumas, spat on the ground. "Calca! That place is filled with criminals."

"Now, Qallo, you know that's not true," Ichuq Maki said. She turned to me to explain. "The people of Calca are just as good as people anywhere. But it is the place where criminals are lodged on their way to the coca plantations in the jungle."

Again, there was silence.

"We don't talk about the plantations," Ichuq Maki said, "for we have heard many terrible stories. It is not a pleasant place to be."

"Are you going to Calca to visit a criminal?" Qallo said.

While the others laughed, I shook my head, embarrassed. I wondered what they would have said had I told them my brother was in prison.

Fortunately, I was spared further questioning by the sound of the men returning to work. The women quickly finished eating and began to clean up. I helped wash dishes. I'd never seen so many to wash. But with so many hands to help, the job went quickly. When we were done, I went to Ichuq Maki to thank her and say good-bye. She walked with me as I went to find Chumpi.

"Here," Sumaq Uya said, offering me a large ball of wool she had combed off of Chumpi.

I shook my head. "It is yours in exchange for all your hard work. Chumpi looks very handsome."

"You should take the wool," Ichuq Maki said. "It has value."

"Not nearly the value of the hospitality I have been given."

Ichuq Maki smiled, then suddenly became serious. "Are you sure you're not in trouble? We are rarely visited by young women traveling alone."

I shook my head. "It is difficult to explain, but I have an important reason for going to Calca and need to get there as soon as I can."

"Then you better go. Soon the men will be done working, and then the young men will insist that you stay for the festivities."

I thanked her and Sumaq Uya again, then, taking Chumpi by his halter, quickly left Pisac.

Chapter 27

The next day I reached Calca, a city nestled in the center of a broad valley walled by lofty mountains. The town itself looked much like Pisac—so much so that I became alarmed, momentarily, thinking I had gotten turned around somehow and gone back the way I came. But no, Pisac did not possess the magnificent bridge that spanned the Wilkamayu River. I stood aside and waited as an old man led a string of six llamas by a rope. Whether he pulled upon the rope to urge the llamas forward, or used the rope to support his tired body, I could not tell, but he did not notice when Chumpi and I fell in line behind the last of his llamas and followed along across the bridge.

Upon entering the town, the old man continued toward several large colcas. I had no idea where to go. I needed information, and the best person to provide this information would likely be the one most sympathetic to my reason for seeking it: the camasca who served the town. But how to find him?

I turned down a path that ran between a row of wasis, several of which had llama pens attached. It was very quiet with no one about, a perfect place for me to sit and gather my thoughts. There was a small pool of water for watering the animals. I splashed some water on my face then sat where I could lean against one of the wasis. The wall felt warm against my back and smelled of mud baking. I stretched out my tired legs and rested my chin upon my chest. I only had meant to rest for a moment, but fell asleep. When I awoke, it was mid-afternoon.

At the end of the row of wasis, a boy appeared, herding several llamas ahead of him. I stood up quickly, too quickly, and had to brace myself against the wall until the dizziness passed. The boy took no notice of me, but when he saw Chumpi, he became very excited and quickly ushered his llamas into a nearby pen. Then he approached Chumpi cautiously, holding kernels of maize in his outstretched hand. His caution was, of course, unwarranted.

"Chumpi is a friend to anyone with food," I said. The boy's being friendly with Chumpi provided me the opportunity to ask questions. "Where do I find your camasca?"

The boy did not answer, but giggled as Chumpi prodded his chest, seeking more food.

I spoke more loudly. "Excuse me, boy, do you know where I might find the camasca."

Still ignoring me, the boy took more maize from the bag he carried.

I thought his disregard of me most inconsiderate. "Boy, I asked you a question. Where do I find your camasca?"

Turning his back to me, the boy teased Chumpi by holding the maize just out of reach.

That I should be snubbed while those two enjoyed their merry game infuriated me. "You, boy! Are you deaf?"

"Yes, he is."

Startled, I turned about. Two older boys stood before me. "I'm sorry, I did not know. I was only trying to ask him a question."

The younger of the two boys, pointed at Chumpi. "Atoq, look! It's Qilli Chukcha!" He ran to join Chumpi and the deaf boy.

"Who is Qilli Chukcha?" I said.

Atoq, a somber-looking youth, made no eye contact as he answered. "My youngest brother, Ruwayniyoq, the one who is deaf, once had a llama much like yours. We called him Qilli Chukcha for the off-colored band of hair about his middle."

"What happened to his llama? Did he die?"

Before he could answer, the other boy interrupted. "Can we take the packs off your llama to look at him more closely?"

"Yes, but be very careful. I have a special jar in one of those packs, and I don't want it broken."

As they carefully slid the packs off Chumpi's back, I waited for Atoq to explain what happened to the llama. When he didn't say anything, I had to ask again. "So what happened to Qilli Chukcha?"

Atoq looked at his feet and moved a small rock with his toes. "We don't know. Maybe a puma carried him away. Maybe he was eaten by an escaped prisoner."

"Escaped prisoner?"

He shrugged, "Sometimes prisoners untie themselves and get away. Of course, it is forbidden for anyone to help prisoners, so they have to manage as best as they can by killing animals or stealing food." A small smile appeared on his otherwise solemn face.

"Why are you smiling?" I said.

His smile vanished. It was obvious he did not like it that I had noticed.

"It's just that all the prisoners are caught eventually. That's when the wild animals eat them!"

I shuddered. He was referring to the Uatay Uaci Zancay, the prison where the criminals were thrown in with the wild animals.

Atoq misinterpreted my reaction. "You don't believe me?"

"No! I mean, yes, I believe you. But where I come from there are no prisoners."

For the first time, Atoq looked directly at me. "There's some in town right now. Want to see them?"

I shook my head. "No, I need to find—"

Before I could finish, Atoq grabbed my arm and began to pull me away. "Kumari, you and Ruwayniyoq watch her llama. We're going to look at the prisoners!"

Atoq seemed determined, and though I had urgent matters to attend to, I was also curious, for I had never seen prisoners, and I wondered if they looked different from other men.

He led me to the main thoroughfare, a wide road lined with beautiful trees, their branches heavy with clusters of bright orange flowers. I remembered Charapa telling Ipa and me of similar trees growing in Tambo Puquio. Ipa had called them Pisonay trees.

"There they are!" Atoq said, pointing.

Others were looking also. I had to lean out in the road in order to see around them. Sitting in the shade of the trees were a row of men, each with his hands bound, and each tied to the man seated next to him.

I'm not sure what I had expected to see. Perhaps men with sharp teeth and claws and hair covering their faces. In reality, they were just men, though the most miserable looking men I'd ever seen. Some were emaciated; others had open sores. They sat listlessly, their eyes empty of life. Their sad appearance was made worse by their lack of clothing, for each man wore only a loin cloth, and none had sandals.

My heart went out to these poor creatures. Tears stung my eyes. I thought of Charapa and was filled with a tremendous sense of urgency. I had to get away! I had to find the water at the end of the world and quickly!

Atoq poked my arm. "Look at that one."

Reluctantly I looked where he pointed. Farther along the street sat another prisoner separate from the others. He was a man in the prime of life who sat up tall, his back arrow-straight, his chin lifted. He too had a vacant stare, but it was the look of one who kept his own consequential thoughts and deemed nothing that passed before him worthy of attention. The guards seemed wary of him. One approached him, carrying a cup of water, but kept his eyes averted as he set it at the prisoner's feet. Only after the guard left, did the man casually lift the cup and sip from it.

There was one more aspect I noticed about this prisoner: a stripe of paler skin around his forehead where once there had been a llautu.

"That man is an Inca," I whispered.

Atoq nodded. "I wonder what crime he committed?"

A man standing next to us answered. "Whatever his crime, you can be sure it far worse than the others'. Rarely do Incas punish their own!" The man spat on the ground then strode away.

I pulled at Atoq's sleeve. "I must talk to the camasca at once. Where can I find him?"

Atoq pulled away and started back the way we'd come. I chased after him. "Please, it is very important!"

Over his shoulder, he said. "You can't."

I took him by the arm and roughly spun him around. "Why can't I?"

"Because he's not here. He was ordered to go to Qosqo along with the camascas of other towns. Topa Inca is very sick, don't you know?"

I had not expected this. My distress must have shown.

"Why must you see the camasca?" Atoq said, not unkindly. "Are you sick?"

I shook my head. "I need to ask him some questions. I need to know about the Jochoc River and the road that follows it."

"Then Kaka is the one you should talk to. He knows all about the road."

"Will you take me to him?"

"Yes, but first let me see what my lazy brothers are doing."

We found Ruwayniyoq still with Chumpi, but Kumari was gone.

"Leave it to Kumari to run off when there's work to be done," Atoq said.

I ignored Atoq's irritation and studied the strange scene before me. Somehow Ruwayniyoq had gotten Chumpi to lie down and was rubbing him with his hands. In the eyes of Chumpi was a look of pure bliss.

"What is Ruwayniyoq doing?"

Atoq's look of irritation was replaced by one of pride. "Ruwayniyoq has a great way with the silent brothers. He can sense which muscle of a llama is sore and needs massaging. He knows every itch that wants scratched."

Atoq moved his hands rapidly, rotating one around the other followed by a grabbing motion. Ruwayniyoq watched, frowning, then nodded when Atoq stopped.

"What is that with your hands?" I said.

"It's the way we communicate with Ruwayniyoq, using hand movements in place of words."

"What did you tell him?"

"To quit wasting time and go collect some llama dung. Now I will take you to Kaka's wasi, then I must go and find Kumari."

Atoq gathered my packs, still leaning against the wall.

"Here," I said, "put the packs on Chumpi. They're heavy."

With a wave of his hand, Atoq dismissed my suggestion. I hurried after him as he strode down the path between the wasis. At the end of the row, there was a small clearing, and beyond it another row of blossoming Pisonay trees. Atoq passed beyond the trees to where there was a large colca and next to it, a wasi.

"Kaka, there is someone here to see you!" Atoq shouted. He set my packs next to the wasi's entrance before hurrying away.

I waited for Kaka to reply. When he didn't, I called, "Hello? Kaka?" When there was still no reply, I thought no one inside. Then I heard someone muttering.

"Hello?"

This time I received a response, something between a grunt and a shout. I took this for an invitation and, kneeling, pushed back the curtain to enter. By the light coming through the opening, I could see an old man sitting cross-legged in the center of the floor, fingering a long quipu, a string with knots used to record information. I dropped the curtain behind me and sat very still, knowing I would have to wait, for one never interrupted a quipucamayoc while he was counting his knots. Slowly my eyes adjusted to the dimness. Behind Kaka was a long row of wooden pegs upon which other quipus dangled. To my right lay a chusi rather rumpled. There was nothing else save a chicha jar and a cup both near to Kaka.

As my ability to see increased, I noticed Kaka's facial features. There was something wrong with his eyes. Just a slit of white showed between upper and lower eyelids, and a thick liquid drained out of one of them. I realized Kaka was blind, which surprised me, for I did not know how a blind person could distinguish between the various quipus, which were colored differently depending on what they represented.

Eventually Kaka set his quipu aside. He poured chicha into the cup and took a sip. His voice, when he spoke, was low and gravelly. "I was just reviewing the amount of maize harvested. It has not been a good year. Now, what can I do for you? It is not often I have a pretty young woman visit me."

What made him think me pretty? I wondered.

"Because my nephew Atoq is always uncomfortable around young women, especially pretty ones. He would not have been so brusque had you been less lovely."

"Atakachau! Can you hear my thoughts, Kaka?"

"No more than anyone else. It is only that the blind have different ways of seeing. Now, what brings me the pleasure of your company?"

"Kaka, I have come a great distance, and I fear I have still have far to go. I know nothing of the country I find myself in. I was told there is a road that follows the Jochoc River. Can you tell me something about it?"

Kaka waved his hand as if brushing away a fly. "There is no reason for you to go that way. Beyond Calca, there are no more villages. The road is winding and very steep. It ascends into the mountains, high, high up—so high the peaks are forever covered in ice. Evil spirits inhabit the mountains and blow harsh, icy winds that cut your face. And beyond the mountains…" he sighed, "…beyond the mountains is the jungle, and, believe me, you don't want to go there!"

My stomach began to knot in response to his description. Yet what was I expecting? That little birds would carry me over the mountains? A gentle wind would bear me to the water at the end of the world? I thought of my brother and the hapless prisoners I'd just witnessed and pressed on.

"Kaka, I have no choice. No matter the danger, I must cross over the mountains."

Kaka frowned. "Who are your traveling companions. Why am I not talking to your husband?"

I lowered my head. "I am not married. I travel only with Chumpi, my llama."

Kaka snorted.

I looked up, irritated. "I have made it this far on my own, haven't I?"

"Perhaps I haven't sufficiently impressed upon you the dangers you will encounter. Granted, you may be able to cross the mountains. The road is good; you are young. But beyond the mountains is the jungle, and the jungle is very dangerous, particularly if you are traveling alone. Have you heard of a jaguar?"

I nodded my head, forgetting his blindness.

"I take your silence to mean you have not."

"Excuse me, Kaka. Yes, my aunt told me about the jaguar. He's like a puma, but his fur is mottled black and orange."

"Atatau! A jaguar is nothing like a puma! A puma is like a kitten by comparison. A puma rarely attacks people. A jaguar would think nothing of making a meal of you and your llama.

"But jaguars are not your only worry. In the jungle, there are massive reptiles with needle sharp teeth. They can swallow a child whole. And there are nasty, sharp-fanged, poisonous snakes. If they bite you, you die this fast." He snapped his fingers.

Weighed down by his words, I hung my head.

"But worst are the humans, if you can call them that. Look at me!"

With an effort, I raised my head. Kaka was pointing to his eyes.

"They did this to me. As a soldier in the Capac Inca's army, I, along with the others of our unit, were ordered to enter the jungle, locate the inhabitants, and impress upon them the advantage of their becoming part of Tahuantinsuyu. We were to do this peacefully, if possible, but to use our weapons, if not.

"Atatau! What a horrible place the jungle is! It's wet because it's forever raining. And hot! Unbearably hot! And the insects eat you alive. We covered ourselves with mud to stop their biting, but it did little good.

"You cannot imagine how things grow there! Trees so close together they block out Inti's light. And there are vines as big around as a man's leg that grow on the trees. The ground is thick with vegetation, and you can't see where to step. We had to hack our way through the growth just so we could move forward."

Kaka took a sip of chicha before continuing. "It was while we were hacking away that we were attacked. We never saw our attackers, only their arrows. I was one of the lucky ones. The arrow that hit me did not penetrate deep. We ran as fast as we could, those of us still alive. But soon I became very sick. The arrow that had hit me had been poisoned. Only with the help of my companions was I able to make it back to the main body of the army. There I fell into a sleep much like death. I was told I was unconscious for days. When I finally awoke, I could not see and have been blind ever since.

Now, do you still wish to go into the jungle? Do you think you could possibly survive?"

With head bowed, my tears fell freely into my lap. My head pounded with the effort of holding back my sobs. "Kaka… I still must go!"

Kaka took another sip of chicha before responding. "Good! I'm glad to hear it!"

My head jerked up. Kaka was smiling.

"Forgive me," he said. "It was a cruel joke, but necessary, I think. I wanted to test your resolve. Actually, the jungle is not as bad as all that."

"But why? What have I done that you should frighten me so?" I heard my voice rising, but could not control it. "You do not even know me!"

"You are Yana Mayu, are you not?"

I was stunned. How did he know my name?

Kaka laughed. "Now you're going to ask again whether I can hear your thoughts. I assure you I cannot. So, let me explain how it is I know your name.

"Two days ago, a young man came to our town with a message for our camasca. Though the young man looked like a chasqui, he was not in the service of the Capac Inca. This messenger told our camasca to look for a young woman, named Yana Mayu, traveling with a llama, and to assist this woman if she were still determined to follow the road that leads to the jungle. Since our camasca was just then leaving for Qosqo, as ordered by the Capac Inca, he told the elders of this strange message."

"But who sent this message?" I said.

"A camasca from Tambo Toco named Mana Chanka."

This time, I could not hold back my sobs.

Kaka reached forward and laid his hand upon my arm. "Daughter, why does this message make you so sad?"

It was a while before I could speak. "I'm not sad, Kaka." I tapped my chest. "It's just that I have been holding my loneliness deep inside me. Now, in crying, I am letting some of it go, for the message tells me that, though I am alone, I have a good friend who remembers and looks out for me."

But how did this message precede me? I wondered. The answer came in a flash. By the shortest route, through Qosqo, the way I could not go because of Anka!

Kaka patted my arm then released it. "So why is it you must travel the road that leads to the jungle? What is it that you seek there? Can you tell me?"

"It is a story that would take a long time to tell, Kaka, and I'm sure you have more important responsibilities."

"Time moves very slowly in my world with little of interest other than strings, knots, and memorizing lists. A story would be like a good bowl of locro, a long story would be a feast."

I was actually glad of the chance to tell Kaka my story, for there were puzzling aspects of it–especially Mana Chanka's journey into the spirit world–that I thought he might be able to help with.

So, I told him everything, including my dream so he would understand why I believed the water at the end of the world was underground. The telling took a long time. The little light within the wasi gradually dimmed as Inti neared the end of his journey across the sky. When I finished, Kaka made no immediate reply, and I wondered if he had fallen asleep. Then a woman's voice called from outside.

"Kaka?"

"Yes, Kusisqa," he answered.

The curtain was pulled back, admitting Inti's slanting rays which lit the back wall of the wasi.

"I have brought food for you and your visitor," Kusisqa said.

"We will eat it inside."

"Very well." Kusisqa passed a bowl of locro through the opening, and I hurried to receive it. Another bowl followed then a plate with several maize cakes and what looked to be dried fruit, but of a type I had not seen before; each circular piece was pale yellow in color.

A smiling face followed the food. Obviously, Kusisqa was planning to join us.

"Leave us, Kusisqa," Kaka commanded.

The smile vanished, and the head slowly withdrew.

"And tell Atoq to have Ruwayniyoq take care of my visitor's llama."

I was glad to hear this, for I knew in Ruwayniyoq's hands, Chumpi would be well cared for.

We ate in silence, giving the delicious food our full attention. It was not until I bit into the dried fruit that I spoke. "Kaka, this fruit is wonderful! I have never tasted anything so delicious. It is sweeter than lucumas."

He smiled. "Those fruits only grow in the jungle. The advantages of trade are not lost even upon the savages who live there." He pushed the plate of fruit toward me. "Eat them all. I don't like the way they stick in my teeth."

I took the remaining pieces, but only ate one and saved the rest for another time. Then I gathered the empty bowls and set them outside. I did not wish to take time to wash them, for there were many questions I needed to ask Kaka. I began with the one foremost in my mind. "Kaka, is anything about Chanka's spirit journey familiar to you? Is there a large outcropping of rocks close to the road? Do you know where I might find the tunnel?"

"I have been thinking of just this while I have been eating. I think Chanka is correct. The place you seek is across the mountains. And I think it should cheer you to know you probably will not have to descend all the way into the lowlands of the jungle to find it.

"Before my vision was taken from me, I crossed the mountains many times, serving the Capac Inca. I remember there are many ridges of rocks. In fact, the road winds to circumvent these large outcroppings."

"And the tunnel?" I said.

"The legend of tunnels is familiar to me also: one north, east, south and west. However, in this matter, I cannot help you. During my travels to and from the jungle, I never saw a tunnel like the one you described, though I remember seeing several caves in the rocks. I could make further inquiries, though I doubt anyone could add to what I have told you. And such inquiries would take time which you don't have. It was out of desperation the Capac Inca summoned our camasca to Qosqo, for Topa Inca is dying, and if you are to help him you must do so soon. I am afraid if this tunnel exists, your birds will have to show it to you."

I swallowed my disappointment and tried to gather hope from what he said about the rock outcroppings. "So where is this road into the jungle? I was told it follows the Jochoc River, but I have yet to see this river."

"The river is nearby, just to the north. If you continue upon the road that follows the Wilkamayu River, you will come to the river and the road that follows it. As I said, the road is a good one. The Capac Inca insists it be well maintained so prisoners can be taken to the coca plantations and the coca leaves brought back."

I tried to think of more questions, but the food sat heavily in my stomach, and I was getting sleepy.

"Yana, there are two matters I must speak of concerning your traveling upon this road."

I tried to remain alert, but it was so easy to close my eyes since it was now dark anyway.

"First, it is a lonely road. As I said, there are no villages along it. You will see few people, perhaps none at all. When the coca is being transported, you might briefly see two hundred or more pack llamas and twenty or thirty people, but shipments are infrequent. Prisoners are also driven along this road to the coca plantations, but this also does not happen often."

"Atoq took me to see a group of prisoners," I said.

"Yes, I heard they were in town. Here they are given food and water and allowed to rest. I warn you, stay away from these criminals! If you come upon them while traveling on the road, keep your distance. They often look harmless, but they are very dangerous men. Also, the guards will react aggressively if you should approach the prisoners.

"But my point is this: few people travel upon this road and if something should happen to you, most likely there will be no one there to help.

"The second thing I wish to tell you is that I think you must travel this road alone."

I answered tiredly. "Yes, Chanka told me the same thing, and that is what I have been doing."

"No, Yana, I mean alone."

Suddenly, I was alert. "You don't mean without Chumpi?"

"I take it you are fond of this animal."

The word 'fond' did not come close to describing my affection for Chumpi. My father had given me Chumpi to raise when I was only a child. Since then, we had always been together. To me Chumpi was a member of my family.

"Chumpi is like a brother to me. Wherever I have gone, he has gone with me."

"Then if you care for Chumpi, do not take him with you."

I suddenly felt like striking this blind, old man. I wedged my hands in the pits of my arms to contain myself. "But why? Haven't you been listening to what I've been telling you? It was Chumpi who found me buried under the rocks. He saved my life. What happens if I get hurt while traveling into the jungle? You, yourself, just told me there will be no one to help me."

"Where you are going, he will be a danger to you."

But I wasn't listening. I had just thought of another reason why Chumpi must go with me. "Who will carry my supplies? They are too heavy for me to carry by myself."

"Then take only what you need."

"Everything in my packs, I need!" My whole body shook. I felt as cold as if I were sitting on a bank of snow.

Kaka spoke in a gentle voice. "I can tell you feel very strongly about this. It is difficult to separate yourself from something you have great affection for, and you may not be able to do this. But let me tell you why I think it necessary that you leave your llama in our care while you continue your journey. I have already mentioned to you about the jaguar. I confess I exaggerated. The jaguar rarely attacks humans. However, he would not hesitate to attack your llama. Trust me, if a jaguar sees it, he will kill it, and in the attack, you might also get hurt. In this, I am thinking only of you.

"Yet I know you also wish to consider your llama's well-being. When you find this tunnel you seek, will your llama follow you into the darkness? Will the tunnel even be large enough to accommodate him? Have you thought about this? If your llama cannot or will not follow you, what will you do then? Just leave him to be eaten by some wild animal?"

I wanted to kill his words. "Have you thought about what separating us might do to Chumpi? We've always been together. How will he react if I just leave him here and go on without him?" I hurried on before Kaka could answer. "He'll think I've abandoned him! How can you ask me to do something so cruel?"

Kaka sighed. "Yes, this is not a simple matter. There are many factors you must consider. I offer you suggestions based upon my experience. I only ask that you think about what I have said.

"Now, I know you must be tired, and it is never good to make a decision when tired. In the morning, you can decide. I offer you my wasi as a place to sleep, providing you don't mind an old man's snoring. You are welcome to lay your chusi right where you are sitting. Now, I must relieve my swollen bladder and then go to sleep. Counting knots is more tiring than people think."

Kaka moved past me to the entryway. I crawled outside after him. I noticed the dishes had been taken away. I dragged my packs into the wasi where they would be safe from marauding dogs. As I rolled out my chusi, Kaka returned and, without a word, went to lie down. Then I went outside to relieve myself also. When I returned, Kaka was snoring loudly.

I lay upon half my chusi and pulled the remaining half over me. Though tired, it was a long time before I fell asleep, though it was Kaka's words of advice, and not his snoring, that kept me awake.

Chapter 28

I dreamt I was giving Kusi a bath. He laughed as I sprayed him with water warmed in my mouth. Suddenly icy water drenched us both. Kusi wailed in protest. I turned in the direction the water had come from only to receive another spray full in my face. Kusi wailed piteously, his body quivering.

You make him weak! Ipa screamed at me. How will he ever become strong if you spoil him!

A fire burned within me that could not be extinguished by the water.

What do you know of strength? I screamed back. The people of my village suddenly materialized, alarmed by our shouting. What do any of you know of strength!

A blast of water struck me in the back of the head, knocking me down. I tried to stand, but the force of the water was too strong. I was in the grip of a mighty river. Gone were Kusi, Ipa, the people of Qomermoya. Alone, I struggled to keep from being pulled under. I looked ahead and saw the river rushing into a chasm. Frantically, I battled against the current, but my wild strokes were as nothing, and I felt myself being pulled down as if I were food being sucked into the mouth of some monstrous animal!

I sat up and placed a hand over my hammering heart. It took a moment to remember where I was: inside Kaka's wasi. Chilled, I reached for my chusi, which I had kicked off in my sleep, pulled it over my shoulders and lay back down. Upon closing my eyes, Ipa's face leapt into my mind. I opened my eyes, but her face was there in darkness. You make him weak!

It wasn't so much her words, but the fiendish expression on her face that tormented me. I struggled in vain to replace this image with the face of the kind and loving woman I knew. Never had Ipa scolded me out of malice, but only because she wanted me to be a better and more capable person. If she appeared hard, it was only because she loved me.

Suddenly I felt a brief constriction of my arm as if someone had squeezed it then let go. Then I heard Ipa's voice as clear as if she were lying beside me: "You must understand that sometimes a kindness given now may result in greater suffering later on. Someday, you may have to hurt someone, perhaps someone you love, for their own good."

I turned over onto my other side and pulled my chusi over my head, but could not silence her words "...hurt someone you love for their own good."

I flung off my chusi and rolled over onto my knees. Crawling to the opening of the wasi, I pulled back the curtain and tossed my chusi outside. I then dragged my packs after me as I crawled backwards through the entryway.

Clouds had moved in, obscuring the light of the stars, making it impossible for me to tell how much of the night remained. It did not matter. I was determined that Chumpi and I would leave Calca at once, even if we had to stumble about in the darkness. If Kaka could find his way without seeing, so could we.

But first I had to find Chumpi. I reasoned he must be in one of the pens I saw Ruwayniyoq herding llamas into. I began to feel my way forward toward the remembered line of trees, my arms extended to keep from running face first into one them. I should have also had something out in front of my feet. I tripped over a tree root and fell hard, my chin striking another root, my jaws slamming together. Now I was seeing the stars.

When my dizziness passed, I moved forward again, this time on hands and knees. I crawled over another tree root and continued on until certain I was beyond the line of trees. I stood up and slammed my head into a low branch. Staggering backwards, I tripped over another exposed root, and landed heavily on my rump. Cradling my aching head, I began to cry. I cried for the pain in my head. I cried for all the losses in my life. But mostly I cried because I could not escape the truth of Kaka's words any more than I seemed able to escape Calca that night. And so, I cried for the loss of Chumpi, and my tears were all the more bitter, for in fear of what might lie in the days ahead, I now craved his companionship more than ever.

Eventually I cried myself to sleep. When I awoke, I saw Kaka's wasi, outlined against the growing light in the east. In my flight, I had not managed more than twenty paces.

I stood up and slowly walked back to where I left my packs outside Kaka's wasi. As I opened them, I heard, in the distance, the voices of two children briefly calling to each other. Working quickly, I emptied the packs and began to separate their contents into two piles: one for items I must have, one for those I must do without.

Into the pile of discarded items, I threw the comb for my hair. Fighting sadness, I added the comb I used to brush Chumpi, as well as my paqpa root, an empty gourd, and another ball of yarn I'd been given. Even my cup I discarded.

I kept the rubbing stick, for to have it would save time searching for another stick to use for starting a fire. Of course, I had to take the lantern and the bags of yellow stones. To save space, I poured the stones into the beautiful jar Sumaq had given me.

When I was done, I saw that the pile of items I needed was larger than the pile of discards. I picked up the ocarina Akakllu had given me and transferred it to the smaller pile then changed my mind and put it back. As I debated what else I might sacrifice, Kaka emerged from his wasi.

"Good morning! I hope my snoring didn't keep you awake the entire night." His foot struck one of the piles. "What's this?"

I cleared my throat. "I have sorted out the contents of my packs. I must lighten them if I'm to go on alone without Chumpi."

Kaka bent down and placed his hand upon the pile of items at his feet.

"Those are the things I will not be taking with me," I said. "I was hoping I could give them to Ruwayniyoq in exchange for his taking care of Chumpi while I am gone. I know there are items he can't use, but he could always trade them for things he could."

Kaka straightened up. "There is no need to give away your possessions. Ruwayniyoq will be more than happy to care for your llama. I believe that boy likes llamas more than he does people." He pushed the pile of discarded items with his foot. "Do you have something that will hold all this?"

"I only have my packs which I must take with me."

"No matter. Kusisqa will find something to put these things into. As you saw, I have much empty space inside my wasi. I will keep your possessions until I have the pleasure of returning them to you. Now, let's join Kusisqa and her family and enjoy a cup of hot tea."

"I don't mean to be rude, Kaka, but I'd rather not. You must know how difficult it has been for me to accept the wisdom of your advice. With each passing moment, my resolve weakens. I must go now and say good-bye to Chumpi while I'm still capable."

"I understand. I would take you to Ruwayniyoq myself, only my slow plodding would only frustrate your wish to be gone." He pointed. "Ruwayniyoq and his family sleep in the third wasi across from the clearing, but this time of morning, you will find him and his brothers attending the llamas."

He swung his arm around until it was aimed at me.

I hesitated, then placed my hand in his. "Thank you for your kind hospitality," I said. "Thank you for telling about the road into the jungle."

He slid his hand along my arm until it rested firmly on my shoulder. "By your decision to leave your llama here, you have demonstrated both wisdom and courage. These qualities will serve you on your journey, for the gods favor those who have them."

He patted my shoulder then turned and slowly walked away. I quickly distributed between the two packs the items I would take then slid the packs over my head, one in front, one in back. Even after discarding many items, they were still heavy. Then I removed the packs and leaned them against the wall, for I did not wish Chumpi to see me walking away, shouldering the packs he ordinarily carried.

I found the brothers where Kaka said they would be. Atoq and Kumari were watching Ruwayniyoq as he combed Chumpi. Unseen, I stood for a moment and watched. The brothers looked happy, and it was obvious Chumpi was enjoying the special attention.

Seeing this pleasant scene, I was suddenly filled with anger. I placed one hand against a wall to steady myself as two voices battled in my mind.

Your anger is inappropriate. Be grateful you have someone so caring to look after Chumpi!

But Chumpi is my friend!

Then, go! Go do this thing you must do. Find the water at the end of the world so you can return to your friend.

I willed my feet forward. Hearing my approach, the boys turned. "Good morning," I said, trying to sound cheerful.

Kumari and Ruwayniyoq both greeted me, though not Atoq. I marched straight up to this taciturn boy. "I must continue on my journey, but unfortunately I cannot take Chumpi with me. I have talked with Kaka. He said Ruwayniyoq would be willing to take care of Chumpi until I return."

Kumari answered for Atoq. "We'll be happy to take care of Chumpi for you. It would be like having Qilli Chukcha back again."

I turned and addressed Kumari. "Can you tell Ruwayniyoq what I said?"

Kumari scratched his head. "That's a lot to explain, but I'll try."

Kumari began to move his hands like Atoq had done the day before. After a few movements, he would stop, think, then move his hands briefly again. Ruwayniyoq watched, but looked confused.

"Atatau!" Atoq exclaimed. "Let me." His hand movements were quick and sure. Ruwayniyoq watched, nodding his head. Suddenly Ruwayniyoq began jumping up and down, clapping his hands. A strange laugh came from his throat, more like a howl, yet clearly Ruwayniyoq was delighted with Atoq's communication. His brothers joined in, laughing.

"And tell him…" I tried to make my voice heard over their laughter. "Tell him…" The boys quieted. "Tell him not to let Chumpi be eaten by a puma." Tears I could not stop started down my cheeks. "And tell him… please tell him not to let a prisoner steal Chumpi."

Atoq did not try to translate. I ran forward and threw my arms around Chumpi, rubbing my tear-stained cheeks against his sweet, musk-scented hair.

"You are my friend, and I love you," I whispered. I pulled my face away and looked into his eyes. "Do not worry, Chumpi. I will come back for you, I promise."

Chumpi bleated softly. I buried my face in the thick of his wool to once more partake of his familiar smell.

Leave now, or you never will!

I forced myself to obey the voice in my head. I released Chumpi, determined to walk away as if nothing was amiss. But my feet had a will of their own, and I began to run. Behind me, Chumpi bleated in alarm. I skidded to a stop and looked back. Atoq gripped Chumpi's halter to keep him from running after me while Ruwayniyoq ran his hands across Chumpi's neck and chest, trying to soothe him. This time I commanded my feet to walk slowly. But when I was hidden by the last wasi in the row, I ran again. I tore across the clearing and past the line of trees, but could not outrun the sound of Chumpi's frantic cries. I grabbed my packs and flung them over my shoulders then ran past a long row of colcas. I soon found myself on the road going north. Still I ran. I ran until I was far from Calca and well beyond the range of Chumpi's bleating. Yet his frightened cries continued to sound in my ears.

I covered my ears and ran on.

Part Four

The Tunnel

Chapter 29

I reached a point where I could run no further. Leaning against a huayau tree, I gulped the moist air then released it in body-racking sobs. I was a long time catching my breath; I was longer time crying.

When finally drained of tears, I pushed away from the tree and looked about. There was the Jochoc River, though I hadn't remembered coming upon it in my flight. Far smaller than the Wilkamayu River, it flowed placidly through a wide valley. On each side were cultivated fields and more fields terraced into the surrounding mountains. Upriver, where the valley narrowed, dark clouds hid the mountains. Rain was falling there, and there the road led.

My crying–or perhaps my running, or both–had left me feeling feather light, as if I could float away even with the heavy packs on. Oddly, my heart felt lighter as well. Perhaps this was the work of the spirit of that fertile valley who would not allow grief to linger within her beautiful realm. New plantings of potatoes burst fuzzy green from Pachamama's dark skin, pushing aside dry clods of dirt. The first leaves of maize, like slender spearheads, lay in neat rows and fluttered in the wind that drove the clouds against the mountains. And across the valley, Inti's light pierced the clouds and dappled the slopes of a hillside–now dark, now golden.

I readjusted my packs, which in running had twisted sideways, and marched on with a briskness I planned to maintain, for I was resolved to find the water at the end of the world, or not find it, but either way to be done with the search as soon as possible. By mid-morning, I reached the end of the valley where the mountains to the west and the mountains to the east came together allowing only the little Jochoc River, edged by a narrow strip of bottom land, to pass between them. This flat land was also cultivated, but in less than half a tupu's distance it too was squeezed out, leaving only the river and the road that followed it. As Kaka had said, the road was good, though nothing like the Capac-nan.

After a while, I stopped to rest at a place where a waterfall tumbled over the face of a cliff to enter the river opposite. Shattered drops rained down and cooled my face, and the pounding water drummed against my ears with its hissing and snapping and chest-thumping rumble. I was tempted to take time to feed my spirit with the splendor of the waterfall, but my need to press on overruled my desire for beauty. I contented myself in knowing I would see the waterfall again upon my return. I was reminded once more of just how much my world had broadened, stimulating a taste for new experiences where before I had had no appetite at all.

The canyon became increasingly narrow, and the surrounding mountains ever higher. It was only early afternoon when Inti passed behind the mountains. The rain that I thought to meet earlier finally began to fall. A sharp, down-canyon wind struck my face and brought with it the cold from snowfields high up. I pulled my lliqlla tightly about me, and pushed on against the wind. Soon the road abandoned the river and began to ascend the steep slope. Steps had been dug to provide footing, and as I climbed, I grew hot even with the constant rain. Higher and higher, I climbed until I approached the edge of the clouds, and the road disappeared in the mist. Far below, the Jochoc River was but a slender thread, though occasionally, in the slack of the inconstant wind, I could hear its faint murmuring. Then I entered the clouds and could see but a few paces in front of me.

I found myself leaning toward the mountain, afraid of being blown off the road and becoming lost in the clouds. The cold stung my cheeks and nose. I tucked my icy hands inside my lliqlla.

Suddenly, the sky grew lighter though the opacity of the clouds hadn't diminished. I realized I had climbed so high, Inti was no longer hidden by the mountains. But my hope of soon reaching the top faded as the way only became steeper and the air colder. I had stopped perspiring, and now the moisture beneath my lliqlla felt chill upon my chest. For the first time, I was grateful for my heavy packs as they offered additional protection from the biting wind.

Shortly after Inti passed behind the mountains a second time, the rain turned to snow. This happened so quickly, it was as if the spirit of the mountain had ordered the change with a snap of his fingers. I remembered what Kaka had said about evil spirits who dwelled in the mountains, and I wondered what I might do to placate them. To stop and make an offering of hot tea was out of the question; even if I could have found a place out of the wind, there was no fuel for a fire other than sodden clumps of ichu grass. Instead I broke off a piece of charqui and set it upon a rock, then whispered a prayer asking the spirits to forgive my intrusion.

A sharp bend in the road was followed by a steep climb up steps cut out of rock. Along with the howl of the wind, I now heard the sound of rushing water, and a little later, when a gust of wind parted the swirling snow, I saw immediately to my left the very edge of a great chasm. Summoning my courage, I looked down, but could not see the bottom and was not daring enough to stand at the very lip of the canyon where the ground was slick with snow. I took a good-sized rock and heaved it out into the abyss then instantly regretted having done this, for if evil spirits had not yet turned their attention upon me, the noise of my rock would surely alert them to my presence. I had time to think of this and of possible repercussions before hearing the distant crack of stone striking stone.

The snow which had been but a nuisance was now a danger, for it covered the steps and made the footing treacherous. I considered going back down to wait out the storm, yet was reluctant to give up the distance I had already come. Then again, night was approaching, and I had no way of knowing if I would find shelter ahead. The thought of spending the night bundled in my wet chusi at the edge of that chasm while the wind howled about my head and the snow piled at my feet was more than discomforting; under such conditions, it was possible I could freeze to death.

Deciding to go on a little farther, I pushed away thoughts of the coming darkness and instead concentrated on not slipping on the icy steps. Because I was so focused upon the placement of my feet, I ran into the end of a bridge before I saw it. Made of rope nearly as thick as my leg, the bridge stretched out across the chasm to disappear in the mist.

It was now time for me to decide. There was still time to descend to a level below the snowline before dark. But if I went forward, I might find a tambo or some other man made shelter. For a moment, I studied the bridge which tilted outward under the force of the wind. Then I realized that if I had truly meant to turn back, I would have done so already. I said a silent prayer and stepped upon the bridge, thinking how my bridge of faith was now a bridge in fact. I felt little fear about crossing the chasm, for the sturdy bridge swayed very little even though the wind blew hard. Still I stepped carefully, and my hands never lost contact with the taut ropes that served for handholds. The floor of the bridge consisted of three massive ropes lashed together, and crossways to these a layer of bound twigs, which made a floor the width of my shoulders. Thinner, vertical retention lines connected the floor to the hand lines and fluttered loosely in the wind, for their only purpose was to prevent falling through the gap between the floor and the hand lines. To balance myself on the tilting bridge, I leaned in the direction of the upward slant, and when the wind blew even harder, I leaned further.

Halfway across, the mist parted, allowing me to see down into the canyon. I stepped to the left in order to peer over the hand line. Foolish woman! I was more interested in seeing the bottom than watching where I placed my feet! My foot fell into the gap between the flooring and the main support rope. The pack that rested against my chest fell between the retention lines, its weight causing the bridge to tilt further. I managed to retract my foot, but could find no purchase upon the icy twigs. With a sound like a branch creaking in the wind, the bridge began to tilt even further. I screamed, yet even in my fright, I knew what I had to do: get to the other side of the bridge before I was upended into the canyon below.

Releasing the hand line, I flung myself to the right, my feet slipping on the icy twigs. Just as my fingers touched the hand line opposite, my pack caught upon the retention ropes and yanked me back with a violence that knocked my feet out from underneath me. I managed to snatch one of the retention ropes on the right side, but the rope was so slack, I slid farther down, and my feet slipped off the bridge entirely.

Looking down, I saw my front pack dangling in space. I would have gladly sacrificed both packs had I been able to remove them without releasing my hold, which was all that kept me from falling. Reaching down with my left hand, I grabbed my dangling pack, and pulled it upward until it met the retention lines and caught upon them. I pulled harder, but the pack was stuck. I cried out in frustration and prayed to the gods to give me strength. Out of desperation, I gave the pack a feeble kick. The pack twisted slightly, and I was able to pull it a fraction closer. I kicked the pack again, and this time pulled as I kicked. Kick! Pull! Kick! Pull! In progress measured in finger widths, the pack moved upward. I groaned. I cried. I clamped my jaws until the muscles of my mouth and neck throbbed. I thought my right arm would tear apart under the strain, yet somehow I found the strength to pull even harder.

Then like someone spitting a seed out of his mouth, the pack popped from between the two retention lines and was free. I did not relax for an instant, but lunged upward and with my left hand gripped another retention line on the right side. Then hand over hand, I pulled myself upward. My feet found purchase and the bridge began to right itself.

I gulped air, blinked away tears, and said a prayer of thanksgiving, all in the moment of a heartbeat. Then I willed my arms and legs forward, for I had to cross the bridge before the last of my strength was spent. I didn't even think about rearranging my twisted packs though they dug painfully into the side of my neck. Not even when my feet reached solid ground did I stop, not until well away from the canyon's edge. Then I cast aside my packs, and fell upon the snow-covered ground and thanked the gods for my deliverance. My muscles, taxed beyond endurance, quivered in release. My right arm shook the most, and there were painful knots in the muscles.

Then, for some strange reason, I felt the need to laugh. I laughed until my stomach hurt, and might have continued laughing had it not been for a sobering thought: what if Chumpi had been with me on the bridge? I shuddered to think of the effect of our combined weights. Most likely we would have both fallen to our deaths. Any anger I still harbored toward Kaka for urging me to leave Chumpi behind was now replaced with gratitude.

I forced myself to stand, for I still needed to prepare for the coming of night. Scattered about were rocks left over from the construction of the bridge, enough to construct a makeshift shelter. But a night spent near the edge of that great chasm was not to be considered.

I went to my packs and removed my chusi. It was wet, but even wet llama wool provides some warmth. I wrapped it around me in such a way that my legs were covered then I lifted my packs and placed them on my shoulders. Looking back, I saw the bridge, half-hidden in falling snow, waiting indifferently for the next weary traveler. I turned and strode away. I didn't know how much farther I could go in my exhausted state, but I was determined to put as much distance between myself and the bridge as possible.

Chapter 30

Sometimes I had known the wind to speak with a human voice. Though I had never been able to understand what this voice was trying to say, that did not discourage me from trying. Now the voice of the wind seemed that of an angry man, barking out commands. I stood still and strained to hear the voice cry out once more.

Then through the swirling snow, I saw a man standing with his back to me, a lance in his hand. Beyond him, less visible, were other men nearly naked and tied together. I quickly hid behind a large boulder, for here, high in the mountains, I had come upon the prisoners I had seen in Calca.

Peering around the rock, I saw one of the prisoners lying face down in the snow. The guard stood over him, brandishing his lance. "Get up, you dog! We'll all freeze, waiting on you." He jabbed the prostrate prisoner with the butt of his lance. "Get up! We're almost to the tambo. You can rest there!" The guard jabbed him again. Still the man did not move. I thought the guard stupid, for it was obvious the man was incapable of rising. Perhaps he was dead, for he looked it.

As the guard prepared to strike the man again, another prisoner, the one I had seen in Calca sitting away from the others, the Inca, roughly elbowed the guard in the stomach then knocked the lance out of the guard's hand. Gasping, the guard slowly unbent, and as he did, he unsheathed a knife. Though his hands were bound, the Inca struck the guard's wrist with an upward sweep. The movement was so quick, it caught the guard unprepared. The knife spun into the air. Casually the Inca reached up and caught it.

The prisoner now possessed a knife! I truly did not wish to be near when the guards fought to take it away from him, yet could not bring myself to look away. As it turned out the guards did nothing but watch as the Inca cut the ropes that tied the man lying in the snow to the other prisoners. When finished, he tossed the knife aside then lifted the man from the ground and slung him over his shoulder. Then without a word to the guards, without so much as a glance at them, he marched off with the remainder of the prisoners stumbling after him. The guards hurried to catch up. Only the guard who had fought with the Inca remained behind. He picked up his knife out of the snow. As he slipped it back into its sheath, he looked behind him as if he sensed someone watching him. I held my breath, though I was certain he could not see me in the near darkness. Finally, he turned and followed after the others.

I released my breath. Thanks to the gods, I had escaped detection, but in the meantime, night had come, and I had yet to either find or make a shelter. Then I recalled the guard's words about a nearby tambo, which brought to mind the tambo I had passed on the way to Pisac. I remembered its tall colcas for storing food and the many wasis for travelers to sleep in. I ran forward, following the men's footsteps in the snow. Prisoners or no, I would not sleep in a makeshift shelter if I could help it.

In a very short time I heard one of the guards ordering a halt. Ahead I saw the outline of a shelter hardly bigger than a llama herder's hut. I looked for other buildings, but there was just the one that the guards were now herding the prisoners into. My heart fell, for I had been hoping for the offer of food and a snug wasi to sleep in.

When the last of the men disappeared, I went forward to stand out of the wind in the lee of the shelter. I slipped off my packs then rearranged my chusi to cover my head. Then I began to gather rocks for a makeshift shelter. The work went slowly, for my hands were numb with cold, which is why I dropped a large rock on my foot. It was all I could do to keep from crying out. I sat down in the snow to rub my aching toes.

It was then I smelled wood smoke. I released my foot and stared at the shelter, imagining the men inside. Not only were they safely out of the wind, but they also had a fire to keep them warm. It was reckless of me, but, prisoners or no prisoners, I was determined to sleep where it was warm.

I knelt at the entrance to the shelter, took a deep breath then lifted the curtain and passed through, dragging my packs after me. I was expecting my appearance to cause a commotion, but instead found the exhausted prisoners fast asleep along with two of the guards. The other two guards sat with their backs to the wall, chewing on charqui. Upon seeing me, the older of the two shook his charqui at me. "Get out!" he yelled.

With more courage than I knew I possessed, I shook my head. If only I could stay but a little while, just long enough to get warm, I think I could have faced the night in a makeshift shelter. But the guard was having none of it. He stood and began to pick his way toward me over the prostrate bodies. With a shaking hand, I fumbled beneath my lliqlla for the necklace Anka had given me. I pulled out the golden medallion and turned it back and forth to catch the firelight.

The sight of the medallion caused the guard to hesitate. He rubbed one hand across his chin, then pointed at the medallion. "Where did you get that?"

I squeezed the medallion as if to draw strength from it, then willed my teeth to stop chattering. "That is none of your business."

The guard stared at me, uncertain. Then a nasty grin spread across his face. "You're not an Inca. What would an Inca woman be doing here? Where are your servants? Where are your guards? Come on, little girl, tell me where you stole the shiny metal."

He started toward me again. I knew it likely he'd pitch me out into the snow, if not worse, but I couldn't make my feet move. Unknowingly I had released the medallion and was fingering the yellow feather of my other necklace.

"Stop!" cried a voice from the shadows.

Turning, I recognized the Inca prisoner. With the firelight reflecting in his dark eyes, he glared at the guard.

"Leave her alone!" he commanded.

I could see the muscles in the guard's cheeks tighten as he ground his teeth. Then he shrugged and turned back to his companion.

"You!" the Inca barked, first pointing to me then to the spot next to him. His voice was as hard-edged as his cheekbones, yet for some reason I did not fear him as I feared the guard. I picked up my packs, and stepped carefully over the sleeping prisoners.

No greeting passed between us. It was as if I were of no importance, but only the necklaces I wore. Though his hands were bound, the Inca reached out and took the medallion in one hand. He rubbed the image of Inti with a calloused thumb. A small smile appeared on his face. "So, you are a scholar?"

It was not a question needing a reply. He pushed the medallion aside to examine the feathered necklace. "Would you mind taking it off so I can examine it more closely?"

I was surprised he made this a request and not a command. I took off both necklaces, separated them, and handed him the one with the yellow feather. He held it almost reverentially, stroking it with a finger, straightening the tiny barbs.

"A drop or two of oil will keep it shiny and prevent it from drying out," he said. "How did you come by it?"

I answered loud enough for the guards to hear. "It was a gift from Topa Inca."

To my surprise the Inca did not press me for more details. "In my time," he said, "I have seen many such feathers not only in the vestments of the mighty, but on the beautiful birds that Wiraqocha, the maker of all things, intended them for."

"Pardon me, Father, but you have seen the birds these feathers come from?"

"Yes, many times."

"I am looking for such birds. It is the reason I am here. I'm going to the jungle to find them. I believe..." How could I say this? "I believe they have something to show me." This sounded preposterous even to my ears. Still, he didn't question me.

"I'm sorry, little one," he said, handing the necklace back to me, "I cannot help you. Though I've marched the length and breadth of Tahuantinsuyu, I have yet to travel upon this road."

My disappointment must have sounded in my voice. "I understand, Father. Thank you, anyway."

The Inca regarded me for a while before turning to address the guard who had accosted me. "You have been on this road before. Have you seen birds with feathers such as these?"

The guard nodded.

"Well, speak up! Where exactly can she find them?"

"There are many places throughout the jungle, but one place in particular where birds congregate to lick the minerals that seep from the rocks."

My heart began to pound. Ipa had told me of such a place!

"You must be more specific. Tell her exactly where this place is."

"Once you cross the mountains, you will start down into the jungle, which is usually covered with clouds. Near the place where the road meets the clouds there is large stream followed by a small one. Both streams flow out of a large rock outcropping. If you follow along the small stream, you will eventually come to where the birds feed upon the rocks."

A large rock outcropping! Perhaps it was the one in Chanka's spirit journey!

"We will get there in two days' time," he continued. "You can tag along with us, if you like, and I will show you where the small stream joins the road."

I thanked the guard for his offer, but silently rejected it, for I did not trust him. He reminded me of Anka's brother, Kacha. Perhaps the guard had been among criminals so long, some of their evil ways had rubbed off on him.

"There, now you have the answer to your question," the Inca said. He looked tired. He lifted his arms to stretch, but, finding them tied at the wrists, dropped them back into his lap.

"There is charqui there, if you're hungry," he said, motioning to a large jar in one corner of the shelter.

"Thank you, Father, but I have my own food."

He did not reply, but lay down upon the floor and wiggled until he had formed a depression in the dirt. Satisfied, the Inca closed his eyes, but then immediately opened them again. "Spread your chusi on the floor where you're sitting," he said.

I looked at the guard, who sat staring at me, and thought it might be prudent to sleep near the entryway where I could make a quick escape.

"Don't worry. You'll be safe," the Inca added.

I took a piece of charqui from my pack and chewed on it. When I was done eating, I took my chusi and folded it to use as a pillow, for it was quite warm within the shelter; almost too warm.

Then I had another idea. Ever so gently, so as not to wake him, I lifted the Inca's head and placed the chusi beneath it. Then I lay down and closed my eyes. Immediately I thought of the man I had seen earlier, the one lying in the snow. I raised up on one elbow and looked about.

"What are you looking for?"

I turned to see the Inca staring at me. "I am looking for the man lying in the snow. What happened to him?"

"He was dead before I cut his ropes."

"Then why did you bother to defend him?"

Without bothering to lower his voice, the Inca said, "Because I couldn't wait around for a stupid guard to beat a dead man while we all froze to death."

Chapter 31

I thought the dragon had returned, but it was someone shaking me hard by the shoulder. "Get up!"

In the darkness, I recognized the voice of the Inca prisoner. I sat up, rolled onto my knees, then pushed onto my feet.

With a force that drove air from me, the Inca shoved my packs into my stomach. "Follow me!"

Somehow I managed not to stumble over the sleeping bodies as I followed the Inca outside into the still night. The storm had passed, and before me, black against the water-blue mantle of the sky, mountain peaks rose impossibly high. To the west, stars shimmered above another range of towering peaks, these silver in the starlight. Powdery snow crunched beneath the soles of my sandals as the Inca prisoner led me past two guards talking quietly to each other. They did not seem to care that one of their prisoners was walking about free.

The Inca suddenly turned, and I nearly bumped into him. Quickly, I stepped back.

"It is time for you to go," he said. "That thing you wear, the gold, I don't know how you got it, but it's not safe to have, at least, not around this bunch." He motioned toward the guards.

"But Father," I said in a whisper, so as not to be heard by the guards, "why would they want it? Hatunruna are not allowed to possess gold."

The Inca snorted. I could smell his sour breath. "Do you think that would keep them from stealing it and using it for barter?"

"I do not understand."

He snorted again. "I knew you were not an Inca the first time I saw you slinking up behind us. If you were an Inca, you would not be so stupid. Do you believe all those who rule are good? I know many a supposed nobleman who'd love that trinket of yours if for no other reason than to melt it into a fashionable ear plug.

"So, I'm giving you a warning. Stay away from this bunch. They're dog-eaters, and I'm talking about the guards not the prisoners."

Dog-eater! It was the worst of insults. The guards stopped talking when they heard this, but the Inca did not bother to lower his voice.

"Only the worst kind of soldiers would be assigned this duty. That's why I got you up so early. I want you to go on ahead and stay well clear of them. That should not be difficult even for a short-legged person like yourself." He spat into the snow. "The guards move like old women."

I laid down my packs and pulled my lliqlla tight around me for the air was icy cold. Then I slipped the packs on over my head. As I adjusted them, I looked at the Inca. He was facing east, his eyes bright in the starlight. I felt very sorry for him. I did not know what crime he had committed, but I was certain he was not a bad man; in fact, I believed him a very good one.

"Father," I said, "what is your name?"

He quickly turned. "What is that any business of yours?"

I looked down at my feet. "I'm sorry, I did not mean to offend. I only wanted to know so that one day, if it's in my power, I could repay the kindness you have shown me."

Laughter welled up from deep inside him. It swelled until he could no longer contain it. Then he threw his head back and roared. I did not know what I could have said to make him react this way. Maybe I did not understand him at all. Maybe he was actually a madman.

When his laughter subsided, he ran a finger under his eye to wipe away the tears. "Ah, little mouse, you have just repaid me. It's seems I have not laughed so well in a very long time. Since you ask so politely, I will tell you. I am General Kuntur. Does that satisfy you? But tell me, what could a mouse, such as yourself, offer to a general that he could possibly want? You are too small for me to eat."

A general! I had no idea. "But General Kuntur, how can it be you're a prisoner?" Stupid woman! Always saying whatever came into my head without first thinking.

But in his answer, I heard no reproof. "For winning too many victories, little mouse, far too many victories. And…" he cleared his throat, "…and because my men liked me." He lifted his bound hands and pointed toward the northwest. "Do you see those two distant peaks beneath that bright star? The road passes between them. When Inti rises, the snow will quickly melt, and you'll see the road again. In the meantime, just walk toward those peaks and you cannot possibly get lost. Now, go, little mouse. I don't ever wish to see you again."

As I walked in the direction he indicated, I tried to make sense of what the general had said. Why would a general be punished for being victorious?

It is a general's duty to win battles. Only if he didn't win, could I imagine him being punished.

Then it came to me. Maybe the guards were not the only ones afraid of General Kuntur. Maybe the men the general served also feared him. But who was powerful enough to order a general to be sent off to a coca plantation like a common criminal? Only the Capac Inca had such power.

I recalled the Capac Inca's visit to Qomermoya, and how we had all loved and admired him. The Capac Inca was our wise Father, the descendant of Inti. Could one so god-like be capable of treating a general ignobly? There must be something else about the General I did not know, something he did not tell me.

I recalled the question General Kuntur had put to me: Do you believe all those who rule are good? This led to another thought: if it were possible for the Capac Inca to treat a victorious general unfairly, how might he treat an insignificant Hatunruna like Charapa?

The pleasure I felt at being so early upon the road vanished as I remembered why I was here. The immensity of my responsibility bore down upon me, and I reacted the only way I knew, by increasing my pace, a near run across the slope of the mountain. And as I hastened, Inti rose above the mountains. Suddenly I was no longer moving across a slope of unvaried white, for each icy grain caught Inti's light and threw it back in all the colors of the rainbow.

I smiled in spite of my cares. I playfully kicked up the snow and sent a shower of gemstones skyward. Perhaps I was but a mouse. For certain, I did not understand the ways of the Incas. But these things did not matter. Let the Incas have their gold ear plugs, their fine vicuña clothing, their cloaks made of ten thousand scarlet feathers. Here at my feet I had countless jewels, and that was more than enough.

Chapter 32

General Kuntur had spoken truly, for not long after Inti crested the mountains, the snow began to melt. The gemstones dissolved into slush, into mud that sucked annoyingly at my sandals until I found it easier to walk barefoot. I was soon lamenting the vanishing snow, for Inti's rays were warm and beneath the weight of my packs, I grew hot. But it was not just the heat that troubled me, for I was unable to maintain my brisk pace. Even at a normal walk, I panted like an old dog. Suddenly overcome by nausea, I threw off my packs and sat upon a flat rock. No sooner was I seated then I vomited the contents of my stomach, which were little, for I had eaten only a few bites of charqui the night before. As I wiped my mouth with the back of my hand, I squinted at the still distant peaks bordering the pass. They squiggled in my vision as when looking at running water for a long time turns anything stationary into writhing snakes.

I had a sense of panic, fearing it was my recent head injury causing my suffering. Then I realized my illness was likely due to the altitude, for never before had I been in a place so high up. I reached into my packs and found the coca leaves Chanka had given me along with the llipta, the resinous ball made with ashes. Its taste was not much better than that of the coca, but at least it masked the coca's bitterness.

I pulled my knees to my chest and rested my head on my forearms. Yet even sitting motionless, I felt as if I were on a swaying bridge. I closed my eyes and tried to imagine the land around Tambo Toco: flat, sparsely treed, far from any river canyons, far from swaying bridges. I had never had altitude sickness before, though I had heard others tell of it. I prayed the sickness would soon pass, for I could not afford to linger.

True, I needed to press on, but instead I fell asleep. I did not sleep long–Inti had not traveled far across the sky–and, to my great relief, I awoke to find that not only my nausea had passed, but I was very hungry. I selected the two biggest maize cakes from my supply and ate them greedily along with the half-eaten piece of charqui from the night before.

Thanks to the coca leaves, the rest, and the food, I felt restored. Indeed, I felt wonderful. I wanted to jump up and dance about. Instead I said a prayer of thanks to the gods and offered a coca leaf to Pachamama to thank her for her miraculous gifts of healing.

I had the sense not to attempt my earlier pace and allowed myself to rest whenever I felt the need, for the insubstantial air never allowed me to completely clear my head. Maybe it was due to the mild euphoria caused by my lightheadedness, but truly the world never looked so wondrous to my eyes. The sky was a deep, azure pool unmarred by clouds save one like a feather wafting upward from the taller of the two peaks, my solemn guides. At the end of a particularly steep section of road, I stopped to rest. To the west, I saw a marvel I had heard tell of, but never before seen: a frozen river, its surface buckled in even ridges like ripples upon a lake. The frozen river wound steeply down a valley bounded by sharp ridges before plunging over a cliff and hanging upon the rock as a frozen waterfall. It ended in a jumble of gigantic chunks of ice, cracked and creviced and glowing with a blue as soft as a bird's egg.

I tore my eyes from this grandeur and slowly turned about, taking in all I could see: the sky, the small red flowers clinging to the rocks, the soaring peaks, the laughing trickles of snowmelt glistening golden in Inti's light, and—coming full circle—the frozen river again. Never had I beheld such beauty, felt such beauty, like a piercing of the skin, at once both blissful and painful. I could not explain this feeling. Perhaps it was the work of evil spirits, yet I sensed no malevolence here, though my chest tightened with a pain unrelated to the steepness of the climb or the altitude. It was the pain of yearning, though I knew not its object. I thought of those who travel the underground road to emerge reborn upon the highest mountains. Perhaps it was something of their pain I felt, the pain of rebirth accompanied with the loss of all knowledge of what went before. Yet might there be a moment, when one passes from death to life, when all is made clear; not only the past, but the reason for the future? A moment when one is truly whole with all of Wiracocha's creation?

As I stood in awe of all before me, I too felt whole. Perhaps it was as I said: the effect of the air, delicious yet never enough to clear my head. Then again, coca leaves have a mild, stimulating effect upon the mind. Whatever the cause, I ceased to be troubled by the steepness of the climb or to feel the weight of my packs. I was unaware how far across the sky Inti traveled, or if he traveled at all. I was borne upward by the beauty of the mountains, and I rose like the spirit of the newborn. And when in time not felt I reached the pass, I was not surprised to find many apachetas, little shrines of stacked rocks. I removed the coca from my mouth and left it there as an offering along with a rock I placed atop the others. Then I said a prayer, thanking the gods for the miraculous gift of beauty, and walked on.

Chapter 33

The elation that bore me upward vanished not long after I made it through the pass, leaving me feeling weary. I looked to Inti and realized it would be at least twice the time needed to cook potatoes before he passed beyond the mountains and longer before darkness came. I could not afford to make camp while Inti's light remained, especially since I needed to stay well ahead of the prisoners. Still I longed to do nothing more than to lie down and sleep.

I did, however, take time to make tea, for I had not anything warm in me since Calca and my meal with Kaka. When reaching into my packs, I had a pleasant surprise, for I discovered an exquisite red feather like those I had seen woven into the curtains of the Capac Inca's litter. I knew it was a gift from General Kuntur, though I did not remember seeing him wearing any feathers. I snapped off a loose thread from my chusi, wrapped it around the feather's shaft then tied it next to the yellow feather on my necklace. Together they were a delight to my eyes, and I admired them while I sipped my tea.

I had hoped that, once beyond the pass, I might look down upon the jungle, but another range of mountains blocked my view. The road did not approach this mountain range but went parallel to it, moving in and out of ravines where small streams watered a profusion of short, yellow-flowered bushes new to me. After perhaps the distance of two tupus, the road turned sharply northward and climbed to another pass marked by two massive boulders, or rather one boulder which had split apart, leaving a gap the width of my arms outstretched. As I brushed the smooth surfaces of the rocks with my fingertips, I saw in the distance something that made me gasp. I quickly clambered atop one of the boulders to get a better view.

It was just as Ipa had described it, a great ocean, only green instead of blue. Though I knew it was the jungle I was looking upon and the green a sea of trees, yet the impression of it being water was difficult to dispel. For a long time, I just stood and stared. I think if the god of that place had made me a part of the rock, I would have been content, provided I could face the splendid vision before me. Only Inti was able to force me down from my perch, for he passed beyond mountains to the west, and the jungle soon faded into darkness. I came down from the rock and began to search for a suitable place to spend the night. The road cut across another ravine and I scrambled up the slope until I came to a pool of water so shallow, I had to lie on my stomach to drink from it. Beside the pool was flat rock, covered in moss. I pulled my chusi from my packs and wrapped it about me, using some of it to cover my head, for I knew the night would be very cold. Then I lay upon the moss and looked up at the emerging stars. Their shimmering reminded me of the sparkling snow I had seen that morning. Other pleasant memories of the day crowded in: the frozen river, the twin peaks, the azure sky, and, of course, the jungle. Yet for all their pleasure, these memories were also disturbing, for I wondered whether I would be content to return to Qomermoya after having seen such beauty. Disgusted with myself for spoiling pleasant memories with senseless speculation, I closed my eyes and said a prayer for those I left behind.

I awoke to darkness. Thin clouds hid all but the brightest stars. I felt rested and would have been on my way had it not been too dark to see my way. Lacking anything else to do, I got out the ocarina Akakllu had given me, with the intention of improvising an ode to the jungle, which only awaited Inti's light to be seen again. I played using just enough breath to sound my ocarina. My quiet notes quickly died, for the ravine was open with nothing to echo back my notes. Their quick death seemed to emphasize my loneliness. Taking bigger breaths, I blew longer and longer phrases to minimize the silence between them. Breathing deeply of the chilly air made me sleepy. I set my ocarina aside and dozed. When I awoke, the sky was growing light. I quickly packed my things then picked my way back down to the road. To my disappointment, the jungle was hidden by dense clouds that pushed up against the mountain slopes, like waves breaking upon a shore. My disappointment gave way to a funny thought: perhaps my ode to the jungle had sounded so shrill, the jungle sought to shut out my notes using the clouds.

Recalling what the guard had said about the juncture of road and clouds, I reasoned it could not be far to the streams he had mentioned. In this I was disappointed, for the road before me went as much uphill as down. At times, I felt like a bug floating upon the surface of a stream while the clouds, being the stream bottom, always stayed the same distance below me. It wasn't until late afternoon that the road started to go steeply downhill. Soon I sensed a difference in the air: more moist and not as cool. There was more vegetation also, especially small bushes whose pointy leaves resembled the head of a mace.

A few trees appeared, and as I walked on, they grew in more thickly, eventually blocking out much of Inti's light except in places where a fallen tree opened a pathway to the sky. Despite the shade they provided, the air was growing warmer. The moisture-laden air affected my breathing. I wiped the sweat off my face, yet in a very short time was covered with sweat once more.

Looking about, I recalled Kaka's words: how the jungle was dangerous and to be avoided if at all possible. Yet it did not look as frightening as I had anticipated. I was excited by this new experience of lofty trees and moist, warm air. My excitement only increased as I encountered even taller trees with broader trunks. Leafy branches formed a translucent ceiling, but one riddled with myriad holes through which Inti's light descended in thin columns, illuminating tiny flying insects and dancing motes of dust. Within this dusky twilight, diverse flowers grew, every one new to me. Clusters of brilliant orange-red blossoms dripped from arching stems. Beneath these delicate arches, grew waxy-petalled blossoms—both pink and orange—floating on cloud-shaped leaves. And near to the ground were yellow-orange flowers shaped like tiny jars for holding water. When I tipped one over to empty it, out spilled a tiny yellow and black wasp.

Among these flowers grew ferns larger and more luxuriant than any I had ever seen. Some were so tall that, had I not recognized them by their long, lacy fronds, I might have thought them some strange new tree.

Yet it wasn't only the beauty of the plants that amazed me, but their astonishing profusion, for there was not a speck of ground where some plant was not threatening to overgrow its neighbor. Mats of flowers were amassed around spiky shrubs, which in turn were shaded by the tree-like ferns, and overshadowing them all were the broad-leafed trees. Even the trees themselves had plants growing out of them: small, spiny growths with pale lavender blossoms.

Though I saw no animals, save occasional glimpses of small, bright birds, I nevertheless heard rustling beneath the foliage. I recalled Kaka's warning concerning poisonous snakes, but snakes did not frighten me nearly as much as the thought of the puma's fiercer cousin, the jaguar. Perhaps one was watching me right now from his hiding place behind a large fern. The thought made me wish I had brought a weapon with me: a lance, or a mace. Even a stout club would have given me some reassurance. I spotted a fallen branch, but when I went to pick it up, it crumbled into a thousand pieces.

The thought of jaguars reminded me of the approaching night and the need to find a protective shelter. I studied the tall trees with the thought of spending the night in one. I didn't know if jaguars could climb trees, but thought it likely since pumas could. Yet had I been able to climb out of reach to the very top of a tree, I would not have been able to sleep for fear I might topple over.

I needed to find a small cave wherein I could light a fire. Remembering the outcropping of rocks the guard had mentioned, I hurried forward. Of a sudden, it got darker. Alarmed, I looked up and saw shadows moving across the ceiling of leaves. I had either reached the line of clouds, or, more likely, the clouds were breaking up and rising as they were known to do late in the day in Qomermoya. The shadows further motivated me to locate a safe place to sleep.

As it turned out, I never did come across a cave. Fortunately, I found something better, a man-made shelter, though I nearly passed without seeing it, hidden as it was by ferns. At first, I thought it a type of huaca, a man-made shrine, because of its small size, but when I knelt and looked through the entryway, I saw firewood stacked to one side, and also three large jars which I assumed held food. The entryway did not have a curtain, but a grid work of short, stout poles tied together with thick rope. It was obviously meant to prevent any animal from entering the shelter, and I was grateful for it, though troubled that it might prove necessary.

Though Inti had yet to begin his underground journey, I thought it wise to take advantage of the shelter, for I did not know how far I would have to go before finding another. I confess I was also glad for a chance to perhaps bathe, for I felt hot and sticky. I placed my packs within the shelter. Released from their weight, I sprang lightly upon a large moss-covered rock to have a look about. There were no streams visible, but I could hear water trickling beneath the vegetation. I started up a slope, careful of where I stepped. Before long I discovered a narrow trail, which led to a large, circular pool fed by a tiny waterfall. Yellow, gourd-shaped blossoms overhung the pool and were reflected in the clear water. A flat, moss-covered rock provided access to the water's edge.

I decided against washing my lliqlla as I doubted it would dry in the moist air. Instead I shook the dust from it then laid it over a large fern. As I stepped into the pool, I found the rocks beneath my feet slippery with algae. Stepping carefully, I walked to the middle of the pool where the water was deep, nearly up to my head. The water, cool, not but cold, felt delightful. I ducked under and, looking up, watched as my hair floated across the water's surface amid fallen blossoms. I emerged, pushed my hair out of my face, and spat a stream of water. On the opposite side of the pool, ferns overhung a higher bank creating a hiding place beneath arching fronds. I reached it in three quick strokes of my arms. Turning, I rested my head against the bank, and as I did, something—most likely a small frog—leaped over my head and into the water.

From my hiding place, I looked out upon the rest of the pool and the forest beyond. This scene before me was so lovely and peaceful, I felt little fear. Since leaving Tambo Toco, I had followed Chanka's advice, taking my fear in daily doses, and discovered I could stomach that much. My reward had been seeing beauty beyond imagining: the pink birds at the marsh, the river of ice, the perfect pool of water in which I now floated. I believed these experiences emboldened me. It wasn't that I doubted danger existed, or that I was growing careless, but I was becoming aware that the gods rewarded courage, and I wasn't going to refuse their gifts, such as a bath in an enchanting pool in a magical forest, even if it meant I might be exposing myself to danger.

A large bird suddenly swept over me to land atop a fern. Spellbound, I watched as he slowly, cautiously, made his way from fern to bush to low-growing plants, finally to the edge of the pool. He was a large bird, nearly the length of my forearm, and colored a vivid scarlet save for his wings and tail feathers which were glossy-black like raven feathers. But most amazing was his headdress, a thick plume of scarlet feathers that jutted from the top of his head and reminded me of the headdress worn by the Capac Inca. The red bird dipped his beak, then tilted back his head to down the water in tiny gulps I could see in his throat. He did this several times, preceding each drink with a cautious looking about. Then in a flash of red and black, he was gone.

Taking a lesson from his cautiousness, I decided to return to the shelter. As I stood at the edge of the pool, wringing the water from my hair, I studied a tree. Though dead, it seemed alive because of its thick coat of moss. Only at the top was dead wood exposed. Yet something about the color of the wood was not right, the top less dark than the wood just beneath it. As I crept forward to get a better look, the top of the tree burst into a flurry of feathers and flew away with a mournful cry. A master of disguise, the bird had nearly fooled me into believing he was a part of the tree. I saw a feather floating downward and caught it. It was mottled brown and tan with soft gray edges. I quickly dressed and took the feather with me back to the shelter. There I again robbed my chusi of another thread which I wrapped around the shaft of the feather then added it to my necklace. Though not as striking as the other feathers, its humble beauty appealed to me. The feathers together made me think of three people: myself in the presence of the Capac Inca and Topa Inca.

I shoved the grid of poles in place and braced it with large rocks set nearby for that purpose. Secure from predators, I suddenly realized how hungry I was. I resisted looking in the jars, for I knew the food they contained was not intended for me. Instead, I took two sweet cakes from a pouch, but on seeing my diminishing supply put one back. I did, however, break off a large piece of charqui, of which I still had plenty.

As I slowly ate my meal, Inti's light faded and darkness quickly followed. And with the darkness the forest came alive with sound: hoots, whoops, rattles and squeaks; sad whistles and shrieks. I closed my eyes and delighted in this strange music. I wondered if any of the musicians were dangerous. I did not hear anything alarming in their songs, but was glad, nevertheless, for my sturdy shelter.

I sat and listened for as long as I could, but when I nearly toppled over a second time, I decided it was time to go to sleep. I arranged my chusi so my wet hair would not lie in the dirt, but did not bother to pull the rest of it over me, for the air within the shelter was warm. I smiled, thinking that, even had it been cold, I still would have slept comfortably, warmed by all the beauty I had partaken of that day.

Chapter 34

A light rain was falling when I awoke. I had slept longer than intended, but perhaps this was for the best, for I had been warned jaguars hunted at night, and it would have been unwise to have been upon the road before Inti's return. I studied the area outside the shelter. Nothing threatened. I removed the grid work, and slowly crawled out, alert for any troubling sights or sounds. I was startled by a rush of wings, but it was only a flock of small birds, alarmed by my sudden appearance. I apologized to the birds as I lifted my packs onto my shoulders, then set out upon the road, still warm from sleep.

I walked nearly a tupu before I came to the stream I thought was the one the guard had described. The stream was larger than I had envisioned. I knelt to drink and say a prayer. But when I went to grab a branch to help pull myself up, I almost put my hand on an enormous spider. Recovering from my scare, I approached the spider only to discover I had been frightened by a strange flower whose long stamens I mistook for spider legs.

It was not much farther to the second, much smaller stream, flowing between high, fern-covered banks. Tree branches overhung the stream, blocking the light. To add to the gloom were the thick mosses which dripped from the branches and sent water raining upon my head each time I was forced to push one out of my way. I moved as quickly as I could through this dark underworld and rejoiced when I came to the base of a high cliff where I had a narrow view of the overcast sky. Upon a ledge, swallows perched, all blue-black except for white breasts. A few flew off at my approach, but most just huddled closer together. Opposite the stream, vines tumbled down the bank. Though none of the vines were as big around as those Kaka had described, they were thickly interwoven, much like a fisherman's net. With the cliff forming a wall on one side and the vine-covered bank on the other, I felt as if I had fallen into a pit dug to trap a large animal. I could not have imagined a worse place to suddenly hear the footsteps of something big stealing up behind me.

To my shame, I panicked. I grabbed a vine and used it as a climbing rope to pull myself up the bank. I do not know what exactly I was thinking, perhaps to hide in the surrounding forest or climb to the top of a tree; I just knew I had to get out of the trap. The vine, however, could not bear my weight, and I skidded back down the bank. I picked myself up and ran along the stream, heedless of obstacles, which is why I stubbed my toe on a rock. The pain forced me to stop and think, and the first thing that came to mind was the bird I had seen the night before who used disguise to hide himself. Before me was a great rock which had fallen from the face of the cliff. The rock offered no footholds, but being close to the cliff, I was able to climb like a spider in the gap between it and the cliff. I doubted a jaguar could have done the same. When I reached the top, I covered myself with my chusi, whose color nearly matched that of the rock.

It was not long before I heard a snuffling. Cautiously I lifted the edge of my chusi and peeked out. Waddling toward me was a bear. Every few paces he would stop and sniff. As he grew nearer, his pace slowed. I dropped the edge of my chusi and listened to his footsteps, heavy even in the sand of the streambed. The footsteps stopped. Afraid to peek out, but more afraid not to, I slowly lifted one edge of my chusi. The bear stood upon hind legs directly below me, his front paws resting on the rock as he moved his head side-to-side, sniffing the air. I am certain the bear was just curious about a strange smell. That said, I would not have minded a pair of wings to fly away like the little birds I had scared that morning. Eventually the bear lumbered away, and as I waited for him to put some distance between us, I fingered the brown feather I had been given the day before. I doubt my deception had fooled the bear, but better a silly trick of disguise than running about in panic.

I did not see or hear the bear again. What I heard was the sound of distant thunder. Expecting a drenching, I hurried along until I reached a small lake, the source of the stream I had been following. I also discovered the source of what I mistook for thunder: a great waterfall visible above the trees on the opposite shore. As I skirted the lake, I startled a pair of torrent ducks who, with a flurry of wings, skimmed across the water to settle upon the far side. Once past the lake, I entered a grove of trees. Most of the trees were devoid of branches save at the very top where they grew thickly. The trees made me think of tall women with baskets upon their heads. Perhaps a fire had raged through the grove at some time not too distant, for the understory lacked the variety of vegetation I had grown accustomed to seeing. Only knee-high ferns grew, and as I waded through the tangle of fronds, my legs and the hem of my lliqlla soon were dusted with yellow spores.

The roar of the waterfall grew louder and I knew I must be nearing it, though I could see nothing through the tops of the trees. Then I became aware of a competing sound: the squawks and shrill whistles of birds!

I ran, heedless of anything that might be hiding beneath the ferns, only to burst into the open and nearly tumble off the edge of a steep ravine. Skidding to a stop, I came crashing down on my rump. The pain went unnoticed in my excitement, for now I could see the full extent of the waterfall. What I had seen earlier was only the upper of two waterfalls separated by a short, but raging cascade.

But more magnificent still was seeing Birds! More birds than even Charapa could have counted! Myriads of birds in rainbow colors! They hung upon the face of a cliff like bright fruit. Scarlet birds. Emerald birds. Birds azure and vermilion and golden. I thrilled to recognize the birds I'd seen—or thought I'd seen—the morning of the Capac Inca's visit to Qomermoya. They were as I remembered: all adorned in yellow feathers, save for their wings, which sported feathers a blue to shame the sky. These splendid birds had cousins exactly alike in shape and size, except their feathers were scarlet, the same scarlet I had seen in the curtains of the Capac Inca's litter. My memory only failed as to their size, for being so close, they appeared much larger than I remembered.

Yet the smaller birds were no less dazzling. I saw birds of a green more vivid than moss after a storm. Others had added to their green cloaks splashes of red and bright blue.

If the birds were disturbed by my presence, they did not show it. They were too busy pecking away at the crusty minerals on the face of the cliff. None appeared content to linger in one spot, and being so numerous, there was always a swirling of birds in flight, like bright leaves caught in a whirlwind. The sounds of their cries were hardly less thrilling than their colors, their raucous squawkings and ear-piercing shrieks providing a counter melody to the waterfalls' rumbling bass.

Sitting at the edge of the ravine, I realized I had stumbled upon a world of unimaginable splendor and I gave thanks to the gods for allowing me to witness it. I then recalled Chanka's prediction, that birds would lead me to the water at the end of the world. His words produced no anxiety, only elation. Let the birds lead me; it was what I had come for!

A trio of the yellow and blue birds flew directly over me, their sharp beaks pointing like arrowheads, their long tails the arrows' shafts. I thought it a sign. I flung aside my packs and raced after them. I quickly lost sight of

Michael Easterling

the birds, for I could not see them as they flew above the tree tops. No matter. I ran in the direction they had flown, carving a trail through the ferns. I ran until my lungs were afire, yet did not stop. Finally, when my chest felt like to burst, I collapsed upon a mossy rock and drew in great gulps of air.

My running had taken me far from the mineral deposit, yet I saw nothing of the water at the end of the world, nor an entrance to a tunnel wherein the magic water might be. All around me was just the jungle forest as I had come to know it: warm, silent, and green. Wiping the sweat off my forehead, I decided that I must have followed the wrong birds. Well, there were plenty more. I began to lope back to the cliff, following the trail of flattened ferns. This time I saw two scarlet birds winging toward the lake, and once again I chased after my feathered guides.

I went on like this for the remainder of the afternoon. I chased after birds flying north, east, west and south and every point in between. After many fruitless excursions into the forest, I began to use what little intelligence I still possessed, and reasoned that if the water at the end of the world was to be found underground, then the entrance to that underground world most likely was to be found somewhere along the cliff, only a portion of which the waterfall spilled over. Consequently, I began to follow birds that only flew toward some part of the cliff. I explored on both sides of the waterfalls, all the way to where the cliff sloped off to become level with the forest floor. I climbed upon the face of the cliff as high as I dared. I peered behind countless bushes. I even managed to climb one of the highest trees and scanned the surrounding area. Yet nowhere did I find an entrance to a tunnel, nor so much as a cavity big enough to stick my empty head into.

Late in the afternoon, I returned, exhausted and despondent, to sit where I had first come upon the birds. It was here that General Kuntur stole upon me as silently as a puma stalking a deer. My energy spent, I could only muster a small, startled cry when he touched the back of my shoulder. Upon seeing him, something broke within me, and I began to cry. I could not help it; nor could I stop. He moved a little way off and stared at the birds until I finally got control of my emotions. Then he spoke.

"In all my travels, I have never seen a place such as this. Look at the magnificent feathers of the birds!"

This reminded me of the feather he had given me. I wiped my runny nose, then found my voice. "Thank you for the gift of the red feather."

He laughed, pointing to the ground beneath the mineral deposit. "Here, you can gather them by the armful."

I pulled my feathered necklace from beneath my lliqlla and held the feathers in my hand. "To have an armful would not make my gifts less treasured. I value them for the people who gave them to me and for the lessons they have taught me."

The general turned and looked directly at me. "Ah, the crazy girl has some wisdom after all."

Crazy? The epithet surprised me, for I thought as crazy only those old people who sometimes talked to people who weren't there. Surely I was not like them. Then I recalled my wasted afternoon spent racing after birds and had to smile. Perhaps I was a little crazy after all.

"How much better a smile looks on your face than tears!"

My smile faded as I suddenly remembered the troublesome guard. "General, where are the others?"

His pointed with a thumb. "I left them back by the road. It was just as I thought! The head guard, that dog-eater, was planning to follow you here and steal your medallion!" He smiled as he rubbed together hands no longer bound. "I seized his lance and cut my bonds. Then I gave him a drubbing he'll not forget!" He bunched his fingers. "Atakachau! It felt good to use my fists again!"

He turned to face the birds. With arms outstretched he sang out in a deep, gravelly voice:

> Kuntur, hear me, I am your son!
> Like you, I search the world.
> I soar above the mountains.
> On mighty wings, I have crossed the desert.
>
> Kuntur, hear me, I am your eyes.
> I see the battle below me.
> I know where the enemy hides.
> He cannot escape!
>
> Kuntur, hear me, I am your heart.
> Where the wind blasts the mountains,
> I am beating.
> Where the puma crouches, waiting,

I am beating.
Where armies clash
I am beating.

In battle, in victory, and in peace,
I am beating.

His words reverberated off the walls of the cliff, silencing the birds. Only the falls rumbled on. The general dropped his arms and turned toward me.

"I didn't actually expect to see you here. I thought you would have found what you were after and moved on. I only came because I was curious about this place. Now I must return. The idiots will be standing around scratching their butts, not knowing what to do. How can they show up at the coca plantation without their prize prisoner?"

"But, General Kuntur, why go back? You're free!"

"Atatau! I have given my allegiance to the Capac Inca. I will never be free of it."

He reached down and placed three calloused fingers upon my head. "The gods have touched you and made you a little crazy. I have seen it before. A word of advice: do not despair. If you cannot find what you seek, wait. It will find you."

Leaving me with these words, he stole away as soundlessly as he came. I hated to see him go. The sadness I felt at failing to find the water at the end of the world was harder to bear alone. Still, I was grateful for his visit, and thinking about his advice, I realized I had no choice now but to wait, for now I no longer knew where to look for the water at the end of the world. The question was, where to wait?

I looked about. What better place than this? Worn out from an afternoon of mad scampering, I sat and waited as night approached. In small flocks, the magnificent birds began to fly away to their roosts. When most were gone, I took my packs and walked to the pool at the base of the falls, planning to wash away the sweat and dirt from my body. Standing at the edge of the pool, I could feel the pounding of the waterfalls through the soles of my feet. Its roaring drowned out all but the most piercing cry of the birds.

I removed my lliqlla and sandals then decided not to go into the pool. Instead I approached the lower falls until I came to stand in the path of its spray. Never had I had such a bath! Like General Kuntur, I stood with arms outstretched and slowly turned while the spray drenched my body. It felt wonderful! How many could boast of ever having such a bath? Wait until I told the people of my village about it!

The thought of my village drove away the pleasure of my bath, for what would it be like to return to Qomermoya without having found the water at the end of the world, without having found a way to free Charapa from prison? With a sad heart, I walked from under the spray to sit and think while I let the air dry me.

Later, as I was wrapping my lliqlla around me, I again heard the cries of birds, only these were different: not shrieks and squawks, but short whistles like high notes played on a flute. Looking up, I saw countless swifts, a type of bird common to the mountains above Qomermoya. Many times, when guarding llamas, I had sat and watched as these agile fliers swooped and soared and spun in the air and rarely landed except when feeding their chicks nestled in the crevices of nearby cliffs.

In a couple of ways, the swifts I was watching now differed from the swifts back home. For one, their color was darker. And never had I seen so many swifts flying so close together. I was astounded they did not fly into each other. Then to amaze me further, they flew even closer together as they circled around each other.

Seeing them swirl caused a chill to run from the base of my spine to my neck. Tighter and tighter became their orbits until I could no longer distinguish individual birds, only a blur of black specks. A whirlwind of birds!

I leapt to my feet and ran to get a closer look. The swifts had formed a funnel that appeared to empty directly into the top of the upper falls. Such a thing did not seem possible. I scrambled up to the top of a boulder, and from there could see the funnel of birds disappearing not into the actual falls, but directly behind it!

Behind the falls! The one place in all my searching that I had never imagined looking! Behind the waterfall must be the entrance to the tunnel wherein was the water at the end of the world. And just as in Chanka's journey into the spirit world, birds had led me to it!

I stood upon the rock, laughing at the memory of General Kuntur's parting words: "If you cannot find what you seek, wait. It will find you."

The entrance to the tunnel had found me!

Chapter 35

As it was nearly dark, I could do no more exploring that day. From my place atop the rock, I could see the slender edge of Qillamama's face, and by her small light I made my way back down to where I had left my packs. I elected to spend the night beside the ravine, and I made a fire to discourage predators. Most of the wood I gathered was damp and my fire produced more smoke than heat. Even so, I welcomed the firelight, and used it to again reorganize my packs, this time in preparation for my journey underground.

First, I inventoried my supply of food. I had but a handful of maize cakes left, but sheet after sheet of charqui—enough to last a week at least. A week within the tunnel? I shivered at the thought.

I might have food to last a week, but did I have the means of carrying a week's supply of water? Chanka had given me a watertight gourd, which I had used only once, since water had been everywhere available. I estimated the gourd could hold enough water to last me for two days, maybe three if I was sparing. There was also the beautiful jar Sumaq had made for me, which now held the burning stones. It was larger than the gourd and could probably hold enough water to last three days. By filling both jar and gourd, I would have water for at least five days' travel, five days in which to find the water at the end of the world. Yet I realized that once I filled Sumaq's jar with the curative water, I would no longer be able to drink from it, since the water had to be saved for Topa Inca. Thus, I would have a five-day water supply going into the tunnel, but much less coming out. I thought of my bridge and told myself to take one step at a time. Perhaps there would be other sources of water within the tunnel.

I transferred the remaining maize cakes from the gourd that held them to the one containing the charqui. The now empty gourd I filled with the burning stones from Sumaq's jar. Still the jar remained half full. Having, no other containers, save a gourd which protected wood shavings I would need to start fires, I poured the stones loose into the bottom of my packs, dividing them equally in case one pack should tear.

Next I took off my sandals, the same ones I wore when I left Qomermoya. Tattered and torn, they had served me well, but now it was time to replace them with the ones Chanka had made for me. The making of sandals is the work of men; my old ones had been made by Charapa. I wondered where he was now and said a prayer for his safekeeping. Then I thanked my old sandals for their service and, on impulse, hurled them over the edge of the ravine to land with a splash in the stream below.

There remained two items for me to decide whether or not to take: the jar I used to heat water, and the ocarina Akakllu had given me. The jar had its uses: for one, it could hold a day's supply of water. Then again, it had no lid, and I would be forced to carry it by hand to keep the water from spilling. Since I would be holding the lantern with the burning stones in one hand, I chose to discard the jar lest I not have a free hand as I made my way through the tunnel.

Whether to keep the ocarina was a harder decision. It was a gift from Akakllu, and though I didn't wish to carry anything in the tunnel I didn't absolutely need, I was reluctant to part with it. I blew a few notes, then tucked it away in one of my packs. I could always discard it later.

My packs were hardly lighter for all my sorting. Still, any lightening was beneficial, for I hoped to minimize my time in the tunnel by traveling swiftly.

With nothing to do now but await Inti's light, I spread my chusi over a bed of soft moss, though I doubted I would be able to sleep. My skin tingled, but whether from excitement or fear, I was uncertain—perhaps both. I put more pieces of wood upon the fire then lay and stared at the growing flame. In a little while, despite my doubts, I fell asleep.

For the second morning in a row, I awoke to a gentle rain. I rose, shook the damp from my chusi, then carefully packed it away. Everything was now prepared for my journey underground. Yet before I could go into the tunnel, I needed to prepare my spirit also. As I had done the night before, I went to the pool by the lower falls and removed my lliqlla and sandals. This time I walked directly into the pool. I used handfuls of moss to scrub my body then held my head underwater and rubbed my scalp until it hurt. When I judged myself as clean as I would get without paqpa root, I waded out of the pool and sat cross-legged upon a rock. The rain had stopped, though the sky remained overcast. The birds were already pecking away at the mineral deposit, but I did not allow their beauty to distract me. I closed my eyes and focused upon the sound of the waterfalls. Only when I had stilled my thoughts, did I allow myself to think about the journey now before me.

By lonely roads and unfamiliar trails, I had come to the place where I now sat. Often I had wanted to turn back, yet heeding Chanka's advice, I had continued on, managing my fears one step at a time. Admittedly, there had been the possibility that I would not find the tunnel which held the water at the end of the world. There was even the possibility that the tunnel did not exist. A part of me had wanted this to be true. Then no one would have blamed me for not finding the water at the end of the world. I could have gone home, knowing I had done my best, but was thwarted by matters beyond my control. But now that possibility was no more, for I knew, as surely as I knew the gods existed, that the entrance to the tunnel awaited me behind the waterfall; my dreams, Chanka's spirit journey, and everything that had happened to bring me to this place confirmed this.

I directed my thought upon the tunnel and the possibility of having to walk for days with only a burning stone to hold back the darkness. I recalled the dream that had driven me to leave my village: the beautiful crystals, the life-giving water. These images were reassuring and instilled me with hope. But I also remembered the thing that had moved toward me in the darkness, and I began to shiver even though the day was growing warm.

I pushed aside this thought and again focused upon the sound of the waterfalls. Yet my frightened reaction served to show how quick my fears were wont to surface. They were embers that flared at the slightest breeze. I would need a greater and more constant courage if I were to overcome the challenge of the tunnel. I prayed to the gods that they grant me this courage and they, in turn, placed in my mind another disturbing thought: perhaps I would not be so easily frightened if I accepted the inevitability of my own death.

My heart rebelled, for surely the gods had not brought me so far only to have me perish underground. But what did I truly know of the gods? Though I was fairly certain they had chosen me to find the water at the end of the world, the extent of their plans was, and perhaps always would be, a mystery. They never acted as I thought they would. Even as I struggled to do their bidding, they always demanded more of me. Why? What did they want? Surely not my death.

I felt a sudden need to wash away my troubled thoughts in the clear, cold pool, or soothe them by watching the beautiful birds. Yet I fought these urges, for if I had been led to consider my death, I dare not abandon this consideration without some resolution. I breathed deeply and concentrated.

It is inevitable that all things die, yet I always believed I would die an old woman, long after I had married and had seen my children, and their children, grown. Had my mother thought the same thing? What purpose had it served for her to die so young? Perhaps there had been none.

Anger stirred in my heart. Surely there had been a reason for her death, as well as for her life; it was unthinkable for it to be otherwise. But if it was unthinkable, what had I to fear, for Ipa had assured me the gods always acted for the best? Surely they had acted for the best when they had taken my mother's life, and the same would be true when they took mine. What more could I ask for but that my death, when it came, would be for the best?

My mind was satisfied with this, but in my heart, I was still afraid to die. Then I reflected upon fear itself. Why did it exist? How much easier my life would be without it. Yet I had never met anyone completely free of fear, not my father, not Weqo Churu. Though I did not understand why, I knew there had be a reason for fear and, like all things, that reason was for the best.

I breathed in the moist air and slowly released it. I felt I had now given fear and death enough consideration, so I redirected my thoughts to something more pleasant. I thought of those I loved, envisioning their faces each in turn: my father, Kusi, Charapa, Ipa. I prayed for the safekeeping of each. Unbidden, the faces of Anka and Chanka came into my mind, and I prayed for them also.

Lastly I pictured myself sitting beside the stream that ran near our village, holding Kusi in my lap. Though Kusi was but an image in my mind, I could almost feel his small arms around my neck. How I loved him! How I loved them all! And in turn, I knew they loved me, and though separated from them by distance, I nevertheless felt upheld by their love.

And then it came to me, the resolution I had been seeking, that for fear and death there was an antidote, and that antidote was love. I had come to this strange place because of love, and I knew this love could not be taken from me because of darkness or fear or even death. It was a part of my sonqo, my life spirit, and I believed it would sustain me no matter what the future bore.

Slowly I opened my eyes. The sky was bright, for the clouds were starting to lift. I turned so I could watch the birds pecking away upon the rocks or circling through the morning air. They appeared more wondrous to my eyes than ever before. Perhaps this was due to the peace I now felt.

I stood up, put on my lliqlla and went to gather my packs, which lay beside last night's fire. I had no thought of restarting the fire or brewing tea or making an offering to the gods. My life was now the offering.

I shouldered my packs then studied the upper waterfall, behind which the swifts had disappeared. The approach from the right side required a near vertical climb over wet rock, but the left side was just a steep slope, though choked with vegetation and drenched by spray.

I filled both water containers before starting up the left side. Each step brought me more within the spray of the falls, and soon I was soaked to my skin. Besides the drenching was the blast of wind generated by the impact of the falls upon the ledge. It whipped the stunted trees that clung to the slope, bending them nearly sideways. They partially righted themselves only when some freakish change in the direction of the wind momentarily pushed the spray in the opposite direction. Despite this battering of wind and water, the stunted trees grew close together, and twice I had to remove my packs to order to squirm through narrow spaces between them.

As I neared the top of the slope, my way was blocked by a wall of rock higher than I was tall. A gnarled, wind-whipped tree grew atop it. I caught a toehold in a crevice, stepped up, and lunged for a tree branch. With a sound like the snap of a whip, the branch broke off, and I scraped both arms as I went sliding down the slope until other trees arrested my fall. Pushing onto my feet, I examined my arms. The lacerations were superficial, and the spray instantly washed the blood away. Looking up, I saw that much vegetation had been uprooted by my fall. I moved to one side to avoid climbing over this slippery scar, then struggled upwards until, once again, I reached the wall of rock. This time I searched for good foot and hand holds. When my head rose above the top of the wall, I received the full force of the spray. It was like looking into the face of a gale. I reached toward the stunted tree and this time clutched a thicker branch. It took my weight, and I dragged by body atop the rock.

I dared not try to stand before the blast of the spray. Fortunately, the way ahead was less steep, and I was able to crawl. The spray was so heavy and the wind so forceful, I could barely keep my eyes open. Not surprising, my head hit against the base of the cliff before I saw it. Using handholds in the rock, I pulled myself upright then began to creep closer to the falls. Suddenly the wind shifted, and I was hammered by the force of the water. Somehow I managed to hold on until the wind shifted again, yet it was obvious I could get no closer to the falls. So how was I to get to the entrance to the tunnel? There was no space between the waterfall and the cliff to crawl through, and neither could I hope to push through that mighty wall of water into the cavity that lay behind it. With a sinking feeling in my stomach, I realized I would have to go back down and try to approach the base of the falls from the other side, though I did not know if I could scale the vertical rock.

Then the capricious wind shifted again, this time pushing the falls away from me. It was as if a great, invisible hand had drawn back a curtain to reveal a passageway between the falls and the cliff. As if only to tease me, the hand quickly lowered the curtain.

I clung to the rock and bent my knees a little so that the next time the curtain opened, I would be set to spring forward. The wait seemed interminable; my teeth chattered uncontrollably; the muscles in my legs cramped; and when the wind finally shifted, it was in the wrong direction. Once again I was pummeled by the water. I could not breathe. It was like being held underwater. Just when I thought I would drown, the wind shifted once more and, suddenly the passageway was again revealed. I lunged forward, headfirst just before the curtain closed.

I landed facedown upon slick rock, coughing and retching, the falls buffeting me with stinging spray. The very rock shuddered beneath my body. Blinded by the spray, I tried to slither forward, but it was like wiggling uphill on ice. I pulled both legs up under my body then lurched forward. I used the momentum to tuck my legs and lurched forward again. Like a small caterpillar, and not much faster, I wormed my way across the slippery rock. My hand brushed a raised knob on the rock's surface, and I said a prayer of thanks, for I was able to cling to it and rest.

I was now far enough out of the spray that I could open my eyes. The rock before me was a series of thin ledges each no wider than a hand width. Gripping the knob of rock, I pulled myself onto my hands and knees and began to crawl forward. Compared to what I had just undergone, it was surprisingly easy. One hand sunk into what felt like mud. Touching it released a pungent odor, and I realized it was not mud, but an accumulation of bird droppings. Looking up, I saw a white-washed crevice in the side of the cliff, the roost of the swifts.

I managed to stand and step over the line of droppings. A few more steps brought me to the side of the cliff upon which I leaned and said a prayer of thanks for my deliverance. When my heart ceased pounding, my eyes immediately sought for the tunnel entrance. The base of the cliff was a rough half-circle. I scanned the wall from one side to the other, but saw nothing that looked like an entrance to a tunnel. Alarmed, I began to move to the right, clinging, as best as I could, to the face of the cliff, to keep from slipping on the wet stone. My progress was stopped by a great slab of fallen rock leaning against the cliff. It took a moment for my eyes to adjust to the darkness made by the rock's shadow. Then I saw, hidden behind the slab of rock, an opening in the cliff hardly bigger than the entrance to a wasi. I squeezed my way between the slab and the cliff, and knelt before the opening. I felt cool air coming out of it. For some reason, the cool air made me think of the mountains above Qomermoya. I took this as a good sign.

From one of my packs, I took the lantern Chanka had given me and placed one of the burning stones into it. I used my rubbing stick and a few wood shavings to light the stone. I had forgotten how bad the burning stones smelled. Coughing, I fanned the air with my hand. Inside the lantern, the fire burned in a tiny pool of melted stone with a color more blue than yellow.

I put the bag of stones back into my pack along with everything I had taken out to access the lantern—everything except the ocarina Akakllu had given me. This I left before the opening, as an offering to the gods, to the swifts, to the unknown builders of the tunnel before me. Then I took a big breath, said a silent prayer, and with my lantern before me, I crawled inside.

Chapter 36

According to legend, Manka and Kachi, after traveling many days underground, found themselves in a cavern with a small opening through which Inti's light entered. Many times, I had imagined this cavern: large and mysterious, a cavern like the one at Tambo Toco only without the bodies of ancestors. Thus, it was a disappointment to crawl through the opening and to find myself in cave so small, I could not stand upright. Stumbling along in a half crouch, I nearly drowned the flame in the lantern and had an anxious moment before it caught again. I had learned my first lesson concerning the lantern's use: always keep it level!

I moved forward with one hand against the wall to steady myself. Suddenly the floor disappeared. With trembling hand, I held my lantern before me and peered down. Below was a stairway so skillfully constructed, each step appeared to be exactly equal in height and depth. I longed to know who had carved them, how long ago, and, of course, for what reason.

The air grew cooler with each step downward. The stairs ended on a level floor within a large tunnel. I held the lantern above my head, and the small flame cast a surprisingly broad light, illuminating the tall ceiling, which I could not have reached had I jumped. The tunnel appeared to have been carved out of solid rock. I looked for scratch marks made by the diggers, but could detect none; the rock was all a uniform gray-black.

The tunnel was wide enough for two people to walk side-by-side, and appeared to go in a straight line. The floor was smooth and equaled the best roads I had journeyed upon, though how it could have been leveled so smooth I did not know. The floor was also surprisingly clear of debris, so much so that it came as a surprise to have to stop at a place where rock had fallen from the ceiling. Once stopped, I was immediately aware of the silence. Except for my breathing, the quiet was absolute and seemed to have substance, a weight pressing heavily upon my ears. Quickly I stepped over the rocks and continued on, glad for the slap of my sandals upon the floor.

The ease of walking through the tunnel did much to assuage my fear, though it felt strange to be wrapped in darkness when I knew that above me Inti traveled the sky. I estimated I had walked a half a tupu when I saw ahead a pinhole of light. At first, I thought it a trick of the lantern light upon my eyes. But the pinhole grew to the size of a large seed then to the size of a small pebble. Joy filled my heart, for I realized I was seeing the end of the tunnel and would be spared having to walk days in darkness. This also meant the water at the end of the world must be nearby. I could fill Sumaq's jar and exit the tunnel before the day was even over!

How foolish I was to think it would be so easy. The light, when I finally reached it, was due to a collapsed section of the tunnel's ceiling, which allowed Inti's light to enter indirectly. I yearned to climb out of the tunnel, and stand directly beneath Inti's light, but I was not tall enough to reach the opening, not even when I stood upon the rubble pile directly beneath it. Still, I had the pleasure of looking upon things green, for everything touched by Inti's light—the floor of the tunnel, the walls, even the undersurface of the ceiling—sprouted some greenery. Atop the rubble pile, a moss-covered rock formed a natural catch basin for rainwater, which I half emptied in my thirst. I tore off a piece of wet moss, redolent of moist earth and decaying vegetation, and dabbed my face with it.

Beyond the opening, the tunnel continued, but as soon as the darkness again enclosed me, I realized my lantern had gone out. Lesson number two: always keep the lantern supplied with stones! I retraced my steps and by the light of the opening, relit my lantern before again continuing on. Occasionally I would look back, drawing comfort from the light which, of course, diminished as I walked on: a pebble, a bean, a pinhole. Not wanting to see the light disappear altogether, I did not look back again, but walked as fast as I could. Yet if I walked too fast the lantern light would flicker and dim. This was frustrating, for I was in a hurry to discover the water at the end of the world.

By the time I had walked what seemed like many tupus, all I had discovered was that the tunnel did not always go in a straight line, but sometimes curved. Also, the floor slanted uphill, though this may have been an illusion caused by my growing fatigue. I realized that without being able to see Inti's position in the sky, I would not know when it was time to sleep. Not wishing to be in the tunnel a moment longer than necessary, I thought to walk until exhausted, rest, perhaps sleep, then continue on. Fortunately, I recognized the foolishness of this, for fatigue is the enemy of reason, and if I wanted to be able to think clearly, I would need to sleep and eat regularly.

The thought of eating made me realize I had taken no nourishment that day. I stopped, set down my lantern, and removed my packs. It felt good to be free of their weight. My back had aches which I had never felt until walking in the tunnel, which made me realize that I was also carrying the weight of my fears.

As I sat upon the floor and nibbled a maize cake along with a piece of charqui, I debated whether or not to extinguish the flame to save on the burning stones, for eating certainly did not require light. I justified the light as time saved having to relight the stones. Nevertheless, I ate quickly, for I estimated that above ground it was likely time for evening meal, which meant I could walk at least another tupu before it was time for sleep.

Before I put on my packs, I added another stone to the lantern, an act which made me realize I had a way of measuring time. I quickly emptied my packs of the yellow stones and counted them. There were one hundred and twenty-three stones remaining. I had burned ten since entering the tunnel and would probably burn one or two more before I stopped to sleep. Considering that I had not entered the tunnel until mid-morning, I estimated I would burn fifteen stones for each "day" spent in the tunnel. At fifteen stones per day, I would have enough to last for eight more days, the same number of days my water supply would last, though, if necessary, I could walk for an additional day, perhaps two, without water. Could I walk without light? I prayed I would never have to find out.

I put away my stones then shouldered my packs. In the brief time I had stopped, I had grown chill, for the air within the tunnel was always cool. This did not greatly trouble me, for I had lived my whole life in a village where frost edged the stream in the mornings and where cold winds regularly swept down from the surrounding mountains. Still I would have liked to have sat for a while, weaving upon my loom beneath Inti's warm light.

After a while, I added a burning stone to the lantern, then later, another. I was becoming weary. Was it time to sleep? I hated not being able to see Inti or Qillamama. Now I knew how Manka and Kachi felt on their journey in the darkness. What joy they must have felt upon entering the cavern and seeing Inti's light pouring into it. I ached to know that joy myself, for people were meant to live in the light, not darkness. Without Inti's light, nothing would grow, nothing would live, and all would return to the time when Wiraqocha, the great creator, sat alone in the darkness, and light and life were but an image in his mind.

I should not have been thinking these thoughts, but instead watching where I was going. I stumbled over a bump in the floor; the stone spilled from my lantern and the light went out. I was stunned, mostly because it had happened so quickly. I told myself it did not matter; it was time to stop and rest anyway. I would not have stumbled had I not been so weary.

But it did matter. There within the tunnel, I was always at a loss. I didn't know whether it was night or day; I didn't know which direction I was going; I didn't know how far I would have to travel before I found the water at the end of the world; I didn't even know when it was time to eat or sleep. But at least I could decide when to extinguish the light. It was as if some unseen hand had reached out and snuffed the light before I was ready.

I took off my packs and sat upon the floor, feeling very frightened. I reasoned it was my fatigue and the utter darkness that made me so afraid, for I had encountered nothing in the tunnel to warrant my fears. Walking had been actually easy, for there were no mountain slopes to climb, no streams to ford, no boulders to climb over. Within the tunnel, nothing seemed to change.

Yet this lack of change was the problem. I had walked for tupu after tupu and the tunnel appeared no different than when I first entered it. I craved even some tiny change, if for no other reason than to assure myself I had not spent the day walking in a great circle.

Day? How did I know I had not walked through the night as well, for surely I felt as tired as if I had?

I told myself I mustn't become upset about matters I could do nothing about. This was only the first day in the tunnel, and my fears would only worsen if I did not exercise discipline over that which I did have control: my emotions. With this in mind, I said a prayer of thanks for having come so far and not having encountered danger. Then I felt about in my packs until I found my chusi. The llama wool had a smell that was comforting, for it reminded me of Chumpi. A lump suddenly came to my throat and despite my resolve to discipline my emotions, I pulled my chusi over my head and cried myself to sleep.

When I again opened my eyes, it was pitch black. Were my eyes truly open? I blinked several times. No difference. As I slowly sat up, my chusi slipped from my shoulder, exposing me to the chill air. I reached for my packs. They were gone! My heart began to pound. I groped about in the darkness, searching. I found them on the other side of me. The darkness was so disorienting, I had forgotten on which side I had placed the packs.

By touch, I found my rubbing stick and the wood shavings, then started a small fire. I held a burning stone to the flame until it caught then placed it in the lantern. With the light, my apprehension diminished and a feeling of excitement grew, for perhaps this very day I would find the water at the end of the world. I shouldered the packs, lifted the lantern, and started to walk forward. Suddenly I stopped. Turning, I held my lantern high to see that I had left nothing behind. I congratulated myself on my presence of mind, for everything I now carried was of importance.

Walking soon took the chill from my body, but didn't lessen the tiredness I felt. Perhaps I had not slept long. There was no way to tell, but since I was able to walk, I walked.

"What I can do, I will do," I said. My voice sounded very loud within the confines of the tunnel, yet what I spoke was the type of practical advice Ipa would have given me: "When you can walk, walk. When you get tired, sleep. When you're hungry, eat. You may not know whether it's night or day, but you know what your body needs!"

I smiled to hear her voice if only in my mind. I recalled pleasant times we spent together, special experiences we shared. I listened as she told stories at night around a fire with the people of Qomermoya captivated by her voice. By listening to her, the time passed quickly, and I traveled a great distance without seeming to notice.

It was after I'd resumed walking following a rest and a bite to eat that I noticed a speck of light similar to the one I had seen the day before, and like it, it grew in size as I continued on. This time, I governed my emotions; I dared not imagine I had reached the end of the tunnel. It was probably just another section of collapsed ceiling. Even so, the thought of standing beneath Inti's light drove me to quicken my steps and, in my haste, my lantern swayed wildly side-to-side, and the light went out. Fortunately, the distant light cast a path upon the floor for me to follow.

As I suspected, the source of the light was not the end of the tunnel, but only another place where the ceiling of the tunnel had fallen in. Still I was heartened to see Inti's light and felt like a captive animal suddenly released from its cage. Though the sky was overcast, Inti's light felt delicious upon my face. I spun in slow circles so the light would touch every part of my body. I did this until dizziness forced me to stop. Like the other section of collapsed tunnel, this one was also filled with plant life. What a joy to see things green and growing after all the darkness! And just like the other section of collapsed tunnel there was a small pool of water in the recess of a rock atop the rubble pile.

All the joy suddenly drained from my body. Horrified, I stumbled forward. Within the catch basin was an exposed area where a piece of moss had recently been torn away.

"No! No! No!" I cried out. Impossible! It couldn't be!

But I knew it was. I had returned to the same place I had been the day before!

In anger, I shoved the basin from its perch, and it spilled its precious liquid. Oh, how foolish to compound my anger with stupidity! Yet I was too distraught to care. In anger, I ripped the poor plants from their shallow beds. I threw rocks which banged loudly off the walls of the tunnel until, tired, I dropped to the floor and my anger gave way to tears. Holding my head in my hands, I asked myself how I could have been so stupid! Yet my error was understandable, for that morning, in my waking confusion, I had not thought to determine which direction I should head.

I blamed my carelessness; I blamed the gods for being so silent; I even blamed my brother for his selfishness, and Ipa and Chanka just because they had encouraged me to find the water at the end of the world. Yet none of my accusations changed the fact that I was where I was. Nor did it lessen the pain of knowing the consequences of my folly were not over, for I had many tupus to walk just to return to the place where I had slept the night before. I believe this last was the most dispiriting aspect of my folly, and I cried some more.

I should not have wasted my tears. Water is always precious, yet even more so when scarce. I realized this when, overcome by thirst, I stood up and saw what I had done. The catch basin lay on its side, all its precious contents having dribbled away. Feeling contrite, I wrestled the rock back atop the rock pile so that when next it rained, the basin would fill once more.

It was then that I almost gave up. Never in my search had I felt such an absence of hope, not even when I learned the caves of Tambo Toco did not contain the water at the end of the world. I lifted my head to the light, and prayed to Inti to give me the strength I no longer had.

And in response, he sent me rain. It fell hard upon my forehead, streamed down my tear-stained cheeks and ran cold beneath the collar of my lliqlla. Shivering, I stepped back into the shelter of the tunnel and watched as the catch basin began to fill. As soon as it collected a little water, I came forward and greedily sucked up the cool liquid then waited until it was nearly full before filling my half-empty gourd by tilting the basin to channel the water into it. I then drank again, not out of thirst, but to delay the time when I would need to drink again.

And still the rain fell. The basin overran. I watched the water pour over and splash upon the rocks below. Then as quickly as it came, the rain stopped.

Of course, I knew what it all meant. I had asked for strength, and the gods had sent water to restore me. I had sought hope, and they had shown me that that which was empty can be filled again. I took from my pack a sheet of charqui and set it alongside the basin as an offering. It was more than I could spare, but far less than I owed.

I then took up my packs and began to retrace my steps. At some point, I must have passed the place where I had slept. Still I walked on. I walked until my legs grew stiff and my back cried out in pain, yet when I finally stopped, it was not so much from my aches, but because I feared that, in my weariness, I might stumble and break the lantern.

But before going to sleep, I arranged small rocks in the shape of an arrow, so that when I awoke I would know the direction I must go.

Chapter 37

I awoke suddenly, fear clutching my heart as it had that night I ran to escape Anka's brother Kacha. Wide awake, I listened, but heard nothing but my own rapid breathing.

I flung off my chusi and reached for my packs. With trembling hands, I got the lantern lit. Then with my chusi wrapped around me, I sat and swayed side-to-side, remembering when as a child my father had comforted me by rocking me in his lap. I said a prayer for him and each member of my family. I realized once again the value of prayer, for it connected me to the world outside of the darkness. And because I knew the members of my family were praying for me in turn, I was heartened and my fear lessened. Then I packed away my chusi, shouldered my packs, and held my lantern high to see that I was leaving nothing behind.

But as I started to walk in the direction indicated by my row of rocks, I was again gripped by a fear of being pursued. I tried to reason against this fear, telling myself that with all I had to endure—loneliness, darkness, disorientation—it would not have been surprising if I were beginning to imagine things. Moreover, how could anyone be following me when no one knew where I was? Yet my pursuer might be someone I did not know: an evil spirit of that dreadful place, or one of the dead traveling the underground road to be reborn atop the mountain.

My response was to walk faster in order to distance myself from any pursuer. When I had gone half a tupu, I began to notice changes. The first was in the color of the rock of the tunnel, no longer black, but gray with tiny flecks of something which reflected more of the lantern's light, brightening the passageway. The second change was not as welcome: the air was growing colder, my breath coming out in visible wisps of moisture. I stopped, removed my chusi from my pack, and wrapped it around me. But as I slipped my packs over my head, again came the feeling of someone there in the tunnel with me. I held my breath, listening. It was so quiet, I thought I could hear the blood rushing through my veins.

I hurried on, still not wanting to give credence to my feeling. To occupy my mind, I began to sing.

Two doves,
Two snow-white doves,
Winging the skies as one;
Two doves,
Two–

The sound of my own voice, echoing through the tunnel, was worse than the silence! Oh, how I yearned to be where birds sang and people laughed and waters gurgled over stony shallows! Suddenly I wanted to attack the rock with my bare hands! Scrape it! Scratch it! Burrow right through to the surface where, beneath Inti's glorious light, I might again stroll among things green and living!

I redirected my fury by going even faster. Even in this, I was frustrated for, too fast, and my light started to flicker. I swallowed the urge to scream. I was an arrow cocked in the bow, never to be released!

I pulled my chusi over my head to cover my cold ears then immediately flung it back, for if there was someone in the tunnel with me, I wanted to be able to hear him coming. Later, when I stopped briefly to eat and rest, it seemed even colder. My teeth chattered so, I gave up trying to eat my charqui.

Then as I was putting my food away, I thought I heard something. I clamped my jaws to keep them from chattering.

Nothing, just silence.

Despite everything, I had to smile to think of mistaking the sound of my chattering teeth for someone's footsteps. I shouldered my packs and moved on. To distract myself from the cold, I imagined Ipa telling a story, the one in which Manka stood upon the mountain called Huanacauri and dazzled the residents of Qosqo with his magnificent coat made of gold, a gift from Inti. Surely, it must have shone as brightly as Inti himself.

For a moment, I thought I had become a part of Ipa's story, for one side of the tunnel wall sparkled in the lantern's light. I ran hand across it and came away with wet fingers. Pressing my mouth against the wet rock did little more than moisten my lips, so I hurried forward, hoping to find water in greater abundance. I was soon rewarded with the discovery of a tiny pool in a crack in the floor.

Kneeling, I slurped the water much like a dog. The water was ice cold, pure, and delicious. I took off my packs and found my gourd then used my hand as a ladle to fill it. This was slow going, but eventually I managed to fill my gourd to the brim. I drank again then said a prayer, thanking the gods for this precious gift.

But as I pushed up from my kneeling position, I heard a sound and knew this time it was not my imagination. I froze, half-standing, straining to hear the sound again, though that hardly seemed possible over the roar of blood surging through my ears. Then I heard it.

Klak-klak!

Even small noises reverberated a great distance through the tunnel, making it impossible to judge how far away the source of the sound. But, undeniably, someone was in the tunnel with me. But who? Or perhaps what? The sound did not resemble human footsteps, more like someone striking stone against stone. I feared the noise was not of human origin, but made by an evil spirit. Or perhaps it was one of the dangerous animals Kaka had warned me of.

Klak-klak! Klak-klak!

It sounded like claws rapping upon the rock floor.

Klak-klak! Klak-klak! Klak-klak!

What was I to do? I grabbed my packs and hurried on through the tunnel. But the floor was wet and slick and in my haste, I slipped and fell hard, dropping the lantern. The light went out, and I was instantly enveloped in darkness. Frantically I groped about, but could not find the lantern. On hands and knees, I widened my search. Finally, I found it, up against the wall of the tunnel. Thank the gods, it was not broken!

Klak-klak! Klak-klak!

The sound was getting closer. How doubly frightful to have to face this thing in the darkness! I sat upon my heels, fumbling in my packs, trying to find my rubbing stick.

Klak-klak! Klak-klak!

I grabbed a handful of shavings heedless of the waste. But where to make my fire? Impossible on wet stone. I crawled on hands and knees, searching, but everywhere was slick.

Klak-klak! Klak-klak!

The thing seemed right on top of me. Still on my knees, I faced the direction it was coming from. Should I stand up? Should I remain kneeling or perhaps curl up next to the wall and hope it would pass me in the dark?

Suddenly, in my mind, I saw Ipa hurling icy water upon me.

You're weak! Is this the way you wish to face death?

I didn't wish to face death at all, but if I must...

Using the wall for support, I pushed up onto my feet. Though my legs trembled and were like to buckle under me, I released the wall and stood on my own. My mind spoke a thousand wordless prayers. To my dismay, I realized I had nothing to say at the moment of my death.

Klak! Klak! Klak! Klak!

I did the best I could, I sang.

> Two doves,
> Two snow-white doves,
> Winging the skies as one;

My voice was little more than a croak, but I could not sing any louder.

> Two doves,
> Two snow-white doves,
> Joined together in love.

Tears streamed down my cheeks. In my mind, I wanted to hold the image of each member of my family, but all I could see was Anka's face.

The creature, hearing my voice, must have halted, for I no longer heard his footsteps. Yet I feared he was near and preparing to strike. Now I knew how the soldier felt when, having lost his shield in battle, he was defenseless against the enemy's spear.

Time seemed to stretch out before me, and within that time within time, my terror vanished, and I grew strangely calm, leaving me as prepared as I ever would be for what was to come.

And what came I could not have possibly imagined: the call of an animal in distress.

"Maaaaa!"

At first, I recoiled at the sound.

"Maaaaa! Maaaaa!"

I drew in a breath. No! It could not be! Impossible!

"Maaaaa!"

Yet I knew that voice as well as my own.

It was Chumpi!

Chapter 38

Not caring if I should slip on the wet floor, I ran forward and crashed into Chumpi. I wrapped my arms around his familiar neck and buried my face in his rough wool.

"Oh, Chumpi! Chumpi! How did you ever find me?"

Chumpi, in turn, hummed ecstatically. I rubbed my chin against the side of his face then once again sank my tear-stained face into his thick wool. Back in Calca, likely there were three very distraught boys, but I cared not a whit, for here in the darkness, Inti was pouring his light upon me, and I cried with the joy of it.

"Thank you, my friend, for finding me! Thank you! Thank you!" I spread my arms wide to take in as much of Chumpi as I could. Pressing my nose into his wool, I drank of his delicious smell. I do not know how long I stood there, holding on to him. I wanted to hold him forever, but the cold finally recalled me to our situation there in the dark.

"I need to find my lantern. It shouldn't take long."

On hands and knees, I crawled back the way I had come, sweeping one arm in front of the other.

"Maaaaa!"

"Don't worry, my friend, I'm right here. Just as soon as I—"

My hand brushed my rubbing stick and a pile of wood shavings now damp. I tucked them into my pack.

"I found my rubbing stick, now I only have to find my lantern." How wonderful to be able to talk to someone! "It should be right here! No, wait. I left it resting against the wall. It must be to my right and back a little way." I babbled, not caring. "Here it is!"

I stood, holding the now cold lantern. "Now, where are you my friend? Have you ever imagined such darkness? Ah, here you are. Let's see if we can find a dry spot so I can light the lantern."

I gave his halter a little tug, but Chumpi stepped back, taking my arm with him. "Sorry, Chumpi, but that is not the way. I've already made that mistake once."

I tugged harder, but Chumpi resisted.

I felt a knot in my stomach. I released Chumpi's halter then gently rubbed the hard ridge above his nose. "I cannot go that way my friend, not yet. First I must find the water at the end of the world, and it lies somewhere in the darkness ahead."

"Maaaaa!"

"Yes, I know you understand me." I gave his halter a gentle tug, but still he resisted. I released his halter, but when I reached to scratch his nose, he turned away from my touch. It hurt, this rebuff, but I understood the reason for it.

"I know, it's miserable being here in this tunnel, and I can't blame you for wanting to go back. I feel the same way, only I've come too far to turn back now."

This time he did not turn away as I lay my hand upon him. And when I again tugged on his halter, he did not resist, but let me lead him forward. I quickly realized I needed a free a hand to feel my way along the wall, so I stopped and placed the lantern inside my pack. Then I led Chumpi forward until the floor no longer felt slick beneath my sandals. I knelt down and began the process of lighting my lantern. This was very difficult in the dark, and it did not help that my fingers were stiff with cold. While I struggled, I assailed Chumpi with mindless chatter. When the lantern was finally lit, I held it high. Chumpi, curious, raised his head toward it, but when he got a whiff of the smoke, he stepped back, snorting.

"The burning stones stink, but make a good light." I started forward, but Chumpi again held back. I tried to keep the gentleness in my voice, but I was feeling increasingly anxious. "Chumpi, I cannot go back until I've found the water at the end of the world."

In response, Chumpi took my pack in his teeth and tugged.

"Atatau! How stupid of me! I've carried these packs so long that I had forgotten whose job it is."

Quickly I transferred the packs from my shoulders to his broad back. It was a relief be free of their weight, but much greater was the lightness I felt with having Chumpi for company. I wanted to sing, but still did not like the way my voice echoed in the empty darkness, almost as if the tunnel was laughing at me.

"I will just have to talk to you instead of singing, Chumpi. There's much to catch up on. Did you see all those beautiful birds? And how did you ever make it past the waterfall?"

For what seemed a very long time, we walked steadily on. I had given up trying to figure out whether it was day or night outside. The problem was I never knew how long I slept. As a result, I had settled upon thinking day was when I walked and night when I slept, and this, along with counting the number of stones I had left, ordered my time within the tunnel.

Finally, too weary to continue, I stopped to eat then sleep. I had two maize cakes left and gave one to Chumpi. Though a llama could travel many days without food or water, I could not deny my friend this treat.

"Enjoy it, because it's the last one you'll be getting for a while." Which was not exactly true, for when he had eaten his cake, I gave him the remainder of mine. It seemed the tunnel had stolen my appetite.

I couldn't find stones to make my pointer—it was as if someone had swept the floor clean. Instead, I set my rubbing stick next to the wall with its charred end pointing the right direction. Then I spread my chusi next to Chumpi so I might share his warmth. The relentless cold was beginning to trouble me, for I felt chill even when walking with my chusi wrapped around me. I was glad for Chumpi's thick hair to snuggle my back against.

I was reluctant to extinguish the light, afraid of Chumpi's reaction. "I have to blow out the flame now, Chumpi. We cannot afford to waste the burning stones." He must have understood, for when the darkness enveloped us, he did not stir.

"Goodnight, my friend. At least I think it's night."

I awoke when Chumpi stood up and walked away. Groggily I sat up and felt about in my packs for my rubbing stick. Then I remembered I had used it for a pointer. This created a dilemma, one that my fuzzy brain seemed incapable of solving: if I used my stick to start a fire, I might forget in which direction it had been pointing. I finally decided to replace the stick with the necklace Anka had given me, aligning the cord along the stick's length and letting the medallion act as pointer. When my lantern was lit, I repacked everything but my chusi, which I wrapped about me. As I placed the packs on Chumpi's back, he explored the creases in the chusi, searching for sweet maize cakes.

"I told you, they're gone. I'd offer you some charqui, but likely you'd be eating one of your cousins."

I picked up my lantern then checked that I'd left nothing behind. There was only Anka's necklace, which I slipped over my head.

"We go this way, Chumpi. Perhaps today we will find the water at the end of the world."

We walked until my stomach's grumbling could no longer be ignored. Outside of a few bites of maize cake, I had not eaten since Chumpi's arrival. I sat, leaning against the wall of the tunnel and chewed a piece of charqui. Chumpi nosed my ear. Smiling, I pushed him away. "I told you, all the maize cakes are gone."

He sniffed my hand, and I pulled the charqui away. "Trust me, you wouldn't like it. Your problem is you're spoilt. I have a feeling those boys fed you too much, and you were already too fat to begin with." Yet I was grateful for the extra pounds Chumpi carried, for he might need those reserves before we emerged from the tunnel.

When the charqui was gone, I continued to sit, reluctant to continue on. It took a great strength of will to force myself onto my feet. I hobbled about a little, for the joints of my knees ached. The pain might have been the result of walking so long upon the hard surface, or perhaps it was due to the cold.

I teased Chumpi. "If my knees hurt too much, you'll have to carry me." I had never attempted a ride on Chumpi's back, for even as a young girl, I was too heavy. But once I tried to ride a llama whose great size made me think he could support my weight. The llama had quickly flung me off. I remembered the exhilaration of flying through the air followed by the pain of landing upon a sharp rock. That landing had cured me of any desire to travel other than by my own two legs.

I ran my hand through the hair at the base of Chumpi's neck. "I suppose I'm still too heavy, even though I must have become quite thin."

I struggled for something else to say: a word or two to cheer my spirits. Yesterday, following our reunion, I had been quite chatty, but my appetite for talking had since diminished, dulled by the oppressiveness of the tunnel. Yet if my speech had diminished, my hearing remained acute, for I was always alert for the sound of moving water. Unfortunately, all I heard were our footsteps. The klak-klak and slap-slap were so unvaryingly repetitious, they brought to mind musicians beating upon drums. Sometimes I imagined a counter-rhythm and above that the sound of a woman singing. Of course, these imaginings were only to take my mind off the dreariness of endlessly placing one foot in front of the other.

After another day of fruitless travel, we stopped. I spread my chusi on the hard floor and fell asleep immediately. Yet I slept fitfully, bothered by a nervous tingling in both my arms and legs. I woke with a tremendous thirst and drank all the water left in the gourd. Perhaps I had been too sparing of my water. I vowed to drink more, for I still had Sumaq's jar, which was full.

My water supply got me to thinking about my supply of burning stones. I poured them out upon my chusi and counted the number remaining: sixty, less than half of what I started with. Where had they gone? I sat cross-legged and rubbed my face with my hands. I realized that, from now on, each step deeper into the tunnel meant a step taken in darkness later on. How much farther dare I go? Must I continue until all the stones were gone? I prayed to the gods for guidance, but the only response I got was the sound of Chumpi urinating. Angrily, I shoved the stones back in my packs. The gods seemed to speak when it pleased them, but I had not the luxury of waiting on them. My burning stones were over half gone; my gourd was empty of water; and it seemed I would go mad if I spent one more day in that dreadful tunnel!

I stood up. Involuntarily I cried out from the pain in my knees and Chumpi came to stand by me. It was then I reached a decision. "I know you hate this place as much as I do, Chumpi, so you'll be happy to know I've decided that after today if we have not found the water at the end of the world, we will turn back. Surely, the gods cannot ask any more of us than that."

Yet having set this limit, I drew no comfort from it, for I knew I must make the most of the time remaining. But to my consternation, my pace was slowed by the pain in my knees, particularly my right knee. I shortened the stride on my right side, which reduced my speed, but eased the pressure upon that knee. Though I had worried about running out of provisions, I had never factored in the possibility of being slowed by pain. This realization added to my gloom, which only deepened as the day wore on.

To combat my despondency, I made a game of the rhythms our footsteps made. Chumpi, who appeared none the worse for his travels other than for tangles in his hair, provided his steady klak-klak, klak-klak. Over this was my off-balanced stride: slap-slap, slap-slap, slap-slap. I played with other rhythms, some of which seemed to ease the pain in my knees, and some which did not. I was reminded of the time when Akakllu and I first played music together, only now it was Chumpi who provided the steady beat while I limped in improvised rhythms.

I soon tired of my game. I was tired of everything: the pain in my legs, my worries, the cold. Given the choice between finding the water at the end of the world or sleeping upon grass under Inti's light, I would not have hesitated to choose the latter. I wondered if the gods now regretted choosing me as their servant.

Thinking about the gods made me think once again about the limit I had set. I believed I could not go much further because of the pain in my knees and my diminishing supply of burning stones. Yet perhaps it was neither pain nor burning stones I should be concerned with. What mattered most was that I find the water at the end of the world. Thinking this way, I realized it was my food and water supply, not the number of burning stones, that were the determining factors in my setting a limit. Though I hated to think of doing so, I could return to the tunnel entrance in the dark, for I was now familiar with the tunnel and knew the floor was almost entirely free of anything I might stumble over. Provided I marked my direction of travel before I slept, I could find my way out.

As to my food needs, they worried me the least, for I still had enough charqui for several days and knew that, if I had to, I could travel for two, maybe even three days without food.

So that left only my water supply I had to consider. It had been two days since I had filled my gourd at the spring within the tunnel. Subsequently, I had used up that water. This meant a two-day supply was its capacity. Yet, if necessary, I could go a third day without water. So, once I found the water at the end of the world, I would have three days to return to the spring where I had filled the gourd. Thus, I dare not travel more than three days from the spring, and this was my third day.

I felt an unseen weight lift from my shoulders. My reasoning had only confirmed the decision I had made that morning. If by day's end I had not found the water at the end of the world, I would turn back.

Still, something niggled in the back of my mind. Had I thought of everything? Maybe I could go more than one day without water; maybe another half-day.

No! The pain in my legs was slowing me, and I would not risk killing myself. I truly did not believe the gods wanted my death. What would it profit them? Yet who knew what the gods wanted exactly?

I stopped to eat and drink. I did not sit down, but leaned against the wall to avoid the pain of getting back onto my feet. In contrast, Chumpi lay down with the packs on. I worried that he might refuse to rise then realized that might be for the best. Maybe it was time to go back. Then I thought about what my turning back would mean for my brother, for Topa Inca.

I sighed. "Let's see how far we can go, Chumpi. We'll not stop until one of us can go no further. Then if we haven't found the water at the end of the world, we'll at least know we did our best."

Having reached this decision, it was surprising just how far I could push myself. We walked for tupu upon tupu upon tupu, and when I felt I could go no further, I rested, leaning against the wall, then continued on. Three times I did this: walk-rest; walk-rest; walk-rest. And when I stopped to rest for the third time, I knew I had truly reached the limit of my strength. I lifted my lantern high, but it was as before. Though the tiny, black flecks in the rock sparkled with the same absurd cheerfulness, there was no water at the end of the world.

I had failed. I felt very sorry, but what more could I do? I absolutely could not go one step further. I couldn't even start back unless I slept first. I hobbled toward Chumpi to remove the backs from his back. But as I began to lift them, a voice spoke in my mind.

Not yet!

The words, spoken like a command, frightened me. Why, not yet? Why not stop right where I was? What difference would it make if I continued on?

"Nothing changes here!" I shouted. Yet I staggered on and on. Once I thought there was something the matter with my lantern, before realizing a film obscured my vision. Not long afterwards my legs buckled, and I fell to the floor, only just saving the light in the lantern. I set the lantern down and rested with my head upon the stone. Chumpi came to stand over me and nudged me in the small of my back. I pushed back onto the balls of my feet.

"This is it, Chumpi. This is where we stop. I don't care what any voice says." Taking up the lantern, I held it above my head. It was as I had said before: nothing changes here. Black flecks sparkled in rock the color of ash. But there was no water at the end of the world.

I set the lantern down, and not caring about the cold, lay face down upon the stone floor and cried myself to sleep. Being so very weary, I was not long crying.

Chapter 39

I do not now believe it was long before I awoke, shivering. I reached out and touched Chumpi, who was lying with the packs still on him. I pulled the packs free then found my chusi. With my chusi wrapped around me, I nestled up against Chumpi, using his flank to rest my head upon. Warmed by his body, I fell back to sleep. And in sleeping, I dreamt the dragon had returned.

But it was no dream. Funneled through the narrow tunnel, the dragon's roar was that of a hundred dragons. My head hit the stone as Chumpi scrambled to his feet. I tried to follow, but a rock fell hard upon my shoulder. Another glanced off my head. I curled up into a ball and prayed for deliverance. Yet even when Pachamama stopped shaking, rocks continued to rain down around me, and the dragon raged on in a voice of a thousand storms united. I had known what it was like to be crushed by a river of rocks; now I was being crushed by wave of sound. I could do nothing but cover my ears while thunderous echoes pounded my body and quashed my every attempt to draw breath.

When at last released to breathe, I drew in a lungful of dust. Gagging, I pressed my face to the floor. Then I remembered Chumpi. Given the darkness and the rocks that likely littered the floor, I knew it would be madness to go chasing after him, though that is exactly what I wanted to do. Instead, I knelt and reached out like a child for her mother.

"Chumpi!" My cry was but a croak. I spat dirt, tried again. "Chumpi!"

I heard him sneeze. On shaking legs, I managed to stand. Something told me not to move from where I stood. "I'm here, Chumpi. I'm right here."

I heard cautious footsteps then felt his leg brush against mine.

"Chumpi, you're alive!"

I explored his body, feeling for injuries. He had a fit of sneezing. I waited until it passed before feeling along each leg and across his back. At the base of his neck, I felt something wet. It tasted of blood mixed with dust. As I probed more deeply, Chumpi bleated and tried to pull away.

"Hush," I whispered, "it's all right." Chumpi had a long cut at the base of his neck, but, thanks to the gods, it was not deep. As I ran my hands up his neck, searching for other possible wounds, Chumpi sneezed right into my face.

"Atatau!" I cried, wiping my face with a forearm. "I'll do my own bathing if you don't mind." Considering the situation, I was surprised at the cheerfulness in my voice. Yet I knew the reason: Chumpi and I were alive and uninjured, save for my bruised shoulder and the shallow cut at the base of his neck.

"Once again, the gods have delivered us from the dragon," I told Chumpi. "Let's hope they have also spared my provisions." I was glad I had had the sense to not move about, for I soon found my packs. I shook them gently. Nothing sounded broken. I found my rubbing stick, and eventually was able to light my lantern. It cast a dirty-yellow light, for the air was filled with dust. The floor of the tunnel was peppered with rocks fallen from the ceiling. I suddenly remembered I had not made my little arrow of stones before falling asleep. No matter. I knew for certain the direction we had come.

"Stay here, Chumpi. I'll not be long."

Holding the lantern before me, I cautiously picked my way back through the rubble. I did not have to go far before finding the tunnel completely blocked. Now I understood why the words "not yet" had entered my mind the night before. Had I not somehow managed to struggle onward, Chumpi and I would surely have been buried under the rocks I saw before me.

I recalled my anger when I had asked the gods for guidance and gotten no reply. At the time, I may have even questioned the gods' ability to protect those beneath the ground. Now I knew they were everywhere powerful, and from this, I drew strength.

"Maaaaa!"

"I'm coming!" I cried, turning away from the blocked tunnel.

I had never seen Chumpi look so dirty. I set down the lantern and began to brush him with my hands. "As soon as we're out of this horrible tunnel, I'm going to find a river and push you in, and I don't care how cold it is!" I must have looked equally as dirty. I took off my chusi and shook it out. Oh, how I longed for a stream where I could bathe and wash out my clothes. And for paqpa root!

I took Sumaq's jar from one of the packs and drank from it. What a relief to finally clear my throat! Though I should have saved the water, I let Chumpi drink a little as well, for I knew his throat felt like mine. Then I took a dried hanca leaf from my supply of medicines, crushed it, and mixed it with a little water to make a paste, which I smeared over Chumpi's cut. Though the cut had already stopped bleeding, the paste would make it heal faster.

As I repacked my supplies, I explained to Chumpi our predicament. "Chumpi, the gods have decided we are not to go back the way we came."

I recalled worrying over whether I had enough provisions to sustain me on my way back out of the tunnel. Like all worry, it had been fruitless, for now returning was no longer possible. Yet knowing the futility of worrying did not keep me from worrying still. How far would we have to walk now before returning to Inti's light? And where would we be once we emerged from the darkness? What if the dragon had blocked both ends of the tunnel? Yet surely the gods had proved they had not abandoned us. When would I ever have the courage that came with faith?

Mindful of his wound, I placed the packs upon Chumpi's back. Though my knees still ached, compared to all we had just endured, the pain seemed insignificant. I even felt an energy in my limbs I had not felt in days. Chumpi also appeared reinvigorated, and as we picked our way over the debris, he moved ahead and seemed frustrated the light did not accompany him.

"Chumpi, you seem to forget my short legs are not as fast as your long ones."

In response, he stopped and stood with ears erect.

"What is it? Did you hear something?" I felt certain something had aroused him, yet when we walked forward again, he seemed content to stay beside me.

After a while, I stopped to rest and eat. Rather than pester me for food, Chumpi stood, looking down the tunnel, occasionally stamping his feet, as if anxious to be going. I tucked away my half-eaten piece of charqui and got to my feet. We had not gone far when Chumpi again stopped and stood with ears erect. I listened, but could hear nothing.

"Chumpi, you're starting to worry me. What is it you're hearing?"

Chumpi shook his head then used his teeth to scratch an itch on his left shoulder. But as I started to scratch it for him, he suddenly ran from under my hand.

"Chumpi! Wait!" But he was gone, swallowed up by the darkness ahead. As I hurried to catch up, I heard a sound I would have known anywhere: the singular ping of a drop of water falling into a pool. My body tingled with excitement. What lay ahead? A small spring like the one I had encountered before or something more? I walked as fast as I could without spilling my light. The tunnel began to widen, making my circle of light seem small. I lifted the lantern high. Still the light died within the emptiness of space.

"Chumpi!"

My voice echoed off unseen walls and returned to me from every direction. I heard a snort followed by the sound of dribbling water. As I walked toward the sound, two eyes appeared reflecting the lantern's light.

"Chumpi, why did you run off like that?"

Ignoring my scolding, he turned away and the points of light disappeared.

I reached a small ledge beyond which the floor gradually dropped away in layers of polished rock, white in color. Careful not to slip on this polished surface, I crept forward sideways and landed calf-deep in ice-cold water. I stepped back and held the lantern out before me. The water was so clear I would not have known it was there had not my dirty leg discolored it. Yet there must have been some current within the pool, for as I watched, the water began to clear.

I closed my eyes and tried to visualize the water I had seen in my dream: so clear as to be invisible. I opened my eyes and looked down at the water. It was the same!

I knelt down at the water's edge. Slowly, I slid one hand down along the white stone and into the water. The rock beneath the water was even smoother than the rock above; as smooth as the cheek of an infant. I lowered my head and cautiously sipped. In two ways, this also was as I remembered in my dream, for the water was ice-cold, and so pure as to be without taste. But drinking it was not exactly like drinking air. And yet… Had I drunk of the water? The coldness in my stomach, and the wetness on my lips assured me I had, but there was nothing for my sense of taste to confirm. I drank again, drank until the icy water brought daggers to my head. The water was wonderfully refreshing though I could not say, because of its lack of taste, that it was delicious. I only knew I had never drunk any water like it.

I sat back upon my heels. Chumpi came to stand over me, water dripping from his muzzle down my neck. I reached up and stroked the side of his head.

"Chumpi, I believe we've found it! The water at the end of the world!"

Though I knew this was what the gods had been leading me to all along, I found the reality difficult to credit. I prayed, thanking the gods for their guidance, for making it possible for me to find this miraculous water by revealing to me strength I did not know I possessed. A feeling of joy swept over me, all the more wonderful because it seemed forever since I had felt joy in any small measure. Now I could save Topa Inca! Now I could free Charapa from prison!

I took the packs off Chumpi and found the special jar Sumaq had given me. I wasn't sure what to do with the water it still held. I certainly did not want to mix it with the water at the end of the world. I walked back into the tunnel and sprinkled the water onto the floor where it was quickly absorbed by the dust. Returning to kneel beside the water at the end of the world, I submerged the jar then pulled it heavy from the pool. Setting it upon a level rock, I bound the lid to the jar, using the strips of cloth Sumaq had given me. The pitch she had supplied me with to smear over the cloth had hardened, so I warmed it above the lantern before spreading it thickly over the cloth. Finally, I wrapped the remaining cloth strips over the pitch and set the jar aside until the pitch again hardened.

Next I filled my empty gourd then carefully put it back into my pack. With Sumaq's jar now sealed, the gourd of water was all I had to drink. I prayed I would find more water before I emptied the gourd. Better still, I would first reach the end of the tunnel.

Though I needed to continue on, I remembered the sparkling crystals from my dream and wanted to see if I could find them. I went along the edge of the pool, which I found not to be a pool, but a slow-moving stream about two paces in width. I came to a pair of large rocks that looked as if white mud had been poured over them and left to harden. They served as sentinels to a smaller cavern, which I entered and found myself face to face with the dragon!

I don't know by what courage I stood there and did not run. Perhaps I was just too frightened to move. What I saw before me was the dragon's open mouth revealing a mass of crooked teeth jammed in every which way. The dragon's upper teeth displayed sharp, short teeth next to long ones; clumps of wicked fangs adjoined jagged molars. Though smaller, the lower teeth were equally as repulsive, even more so because half-masticated matter oozed out of them. A few of the lower teeth even closed with the upper ones with viscous streams of what looked like saliva dripping from top to bottom.

One particularly sharp fang drew my eye upward, for it glistened more than the others. A tiny drop of water was suddenly released from its tip and, with a ping, landed in a small pool of water within the cavity of a molar. Here was the source of the sound I heard earlier.

Though I feared to linger so close to the dragon's mouth, I yearned to know what one of his teeth felt like. I selected the nearest tooth and cautiously crept toward it never taking my eyes from the teeth above me, lest the mouth spring shut and a tooth skewer me like spear through a fish. Like a child stealing a sweet maize cake, I cautiously reached out until my fingertips brushed across the tooth's surface. It felt coarse and bumpy. Risking being impaled, I sneaked a look at what I had fingered. The surface of the tooth was coated with translucent grains of sand in clusters that looked like the emerging buds of the chilca bush. The grains glimmered as if wet but were dry to the touch.

Satisfied, I quickly stepped back. The mouth was terrible, yet fascinating, and the more I looked at it, the more I wondered whether it was actually the dragon's mouth, for twice I had heard the horrible gnashing of the dragon's teeth, and this mouth seemed petrified and incapable of closing. Rather it appeared to be something from an ancient story, lost and forgotten. Perhaps, like Kachi, this monster had once terrorized lesser creatures until the gods had been forced to turn it to stone. And here before me was its hideous mouth, frozen in a scream of rage.

I turned away, done with exploring. Perhaps there were other mysteries to be discovered within the cavern, but one monster's grotesque mouth was enough. I retraced my steps and found Chumpi standing by the water's edge drinking once more. I knelt beside him and did likewise, only slowly so as not to pain my head. Then I packed away Sumaq's jar and put the packs atop Chumpi.

"Come, Chumpi, let's see if we can find a way out of this cavern."

Yet I lingered by the water's edge, knowing I would never again see its like. And because I had been careless in attending to my lantern, the flame suddenly went out, taking away the light.

Yet not quite all the light. Perhaps it was a trick of the eyes, but for a moment the white stone beneath my feet seemed to glow. Not so the water at the end of the world. It was a black river winding darkly into the unknown.

Chapter 40

I was getting used to lighting the lantern in the dark. Taking it up, I led Chumpi through the cavern and into another tunnel, outlined with gray-white rock, the color of dirty snow. Yet once within the tunnel, it was as before: the rough ceiling, the dark floor lightly covered with dust, the walls set just far enough apart to allow Chumpi and me to walk side-by-side. It felt oddly reassuring to return to that familiar space after the great emptiness of the cavern, though I would have gladly traded either place to be above ground, even if it were on a mountain top in a blizzard.

To occupy my mind and help divert it from the chronic pain in my knees, I imagined the Capac Inca's reaction to my presenting him with the water at the end of the world. I played out various scenes in which Charapa was released from prison at the command of a grateful Capac Inca. These airy thoughts carried me several tupus, but would not leave off when, weary after another inconclusive day of walking, I lay upon my chusi and tried to sleep. If anything, they became more fanciful. I saw the Capac Inca, surrounded by his retainers, standing over Topa Inca, who lay as still as death. The silent crowd watched as I approached the boy's body, holding Sumaq's jar containing the water at the end of the world. Carefully I dribbled some of the water onto Topa Inca's lips and in response, he sat up, smiling. Then, throwing off his fine vicuña chusi, Topa Inca leapt to his feet, grabbed me by the hands and began to dance. Suddenly everyone was dancing. Laughter filled the air because the young leader was cured. In my mind, I might have even danced once or twice with the Capac Inca himself!

Atatau! It was the stuff of children's games, as real as llama eggs. Still I could not keep these fantasies from endlessly repeating. Eventually, I managed to sleep, though when I awoke, I felt I as if I had not. Furthermore, I was feverish, and though the tunnel was as cold as ever, my lliqlla was damp with sweat. Slowly I sat up, my head spinning. Reaching out in the darkness, I found my packs, but before pulling out my rubbing stick, I first located my gourd, for I had a terrible thirst.

I was slow in getting the lantern lit. If I had had any sense, I would have gone back to sleep and given my body the rest it needed. I told myself I would rest after I'd given the Capac Inca the water at the end of the world. On shaky legs, I lifted the packs onto Chumpi's back. Together we managed to walk a fair distance before I stopped to eat some charqui and drink some more water. The water at the end of the world was truly miraculous, for as I resumed walking I felt reinvigorated, my ailments gone. I voiced my astonishment to Chumpi. "Atakachau! Wait until the Capac Inca sees what this water does for his son." I smiled at this, but shut my mind to the fantasies I had indulged in the day before; I could not afford another restless night.

Around the time I thought of as midday, Chumpi and I entered another cavern. Even though I had carefully laid my little arrow of stones the night before, my first reaction was that I again had made the mistake of retracing my steps. I quickly saw, however, this cavern was considerably smaller than the one in which flowed the water at the end of the world.

But my relief at having not retraced my steps was short-lived, for it appeared I had come to a crossroads beneath the ground. Looking directly across the cavern, I saw an opening where the tunnel continued on. But to my left and right, directly opposite each other, were two other tunnel entrances. Previously my only choice had been whether to go forward or back. Now I had to choose between three different directions.

My initial instinct was to cross the cavern directly and continue on. But what if that took me in a direction I did not want to go? I recalled what Chanka had said about the tunnels that intersected beneath Qosqo. In one direction, a traveler could walk all the way to the ocean. Atatau! What if the tunnel opposite was like that? I would never have enough provisions to make it so far.

My ability to make a decision was frustrated by not knowing which way was east or west. I decided to explore each tunnel a little way in hope of discovering something that would help me make the correct decision. But before I started, I piled rocks before the tunnel I had entered the cavern from, for I knew from experience how easy it was to become disoriented underground. As an extra precaution, I started my exploration with the tunnel to my left and continued in that direction.

I burned two of the precious stones in this endeavor, yet discovered nothing to help me reach a decision. Each tunnel seemed so alike as to be indistinguishable. Chumpi, who had accompanied me dutifully, stood motionless beside me at the place where we began our explorations. "Well, my friend, can you tell me which tunnel we should take?" In response, he nuzzled my chusi, looking for maize cakes. I gently pushed him away, then closed my eyes and asked the gods for guidance. As I waited their reply, I examined my feelings. There was something about the tunnel to my left that I did not like. Though it was only a feeling, more and more I had come to rely upon my feelings. The choice then was between the tunnel directly opposite us or the one to the right, and about these two, my feelings told me nothing.

Having wasted much time in exploring the tunnels, I quickly reached a decision based on my initial intuition. "I think first instincts are best, Chumpi. Let's continue in the direction we've been going." But looking as we passed the tunnel to the right, I wondered if that were the best way to go. And then a hopeful thought entered my mind. Perhaps choosing either tunnel, or any of the three, would quickly bring us to Inti's light.

As we made our way along, I felt the return of the sickness I had experienced that morning. I started to sweat and was forced to stop and take off my chusi. I wanted to drink more of the water at the end of the world, but refrained out of fear I might run out. Feeling very sleepy, I began to walk short distances with my eyes closed. I had no fear of stumbling, for we had come across no debris left by Pachamama's shaking in the last two or so tupus. It felt good to walk with my eyes closed, almost like walking in a pleasant dream. I imagined myself crossing a high, empty plain warmed by Inti's light.

And it was while walking half-asleep that I ran smack into a giant sitting in the middle of the tunnel! I jumped back, screaming, and he responded to my terror with a hideous grin.

Then I saw, and would have seen at once had I not been walking half-asleep, that the giant was dead, and that his hideous grin the result of shrunken flesh that exposed yellow teeth. His body was like those I had seen in the cave at Tambo Toco only with two differences. First, the bodies at Tambo Toco had been positioned with their knees drawn up to their chests; this dead person sat cross-legged. Second, was the matter of size. Standing, I looked directly into the hollows which once contained his eyes. And despite shriveled muscles and exposed bones, the width of his shoulders was twice that of any man I had ever known. When living, he must have towered above all others and had been fearsome to behold.

Yet there was something, even in death, that suggested this giant was not a ferocious creature. Perhaps it was the way his back, impossibly straight, suggested pride, dignity, even wisdom. A dust-covered mantle dangled from his clavicles and hid his ribs. Curious, I pushed it apart to expose a disc of gold hanging from his neck by a desiccated thong of llama leather. The disc, hammered round and thin, bore no image, yet the existence of gold upon his body proved that the giant had been, if not an Inca, then someone of importance.

But why was he here and how did he come to die? I tried to answer the second question first. I could detect no evidence that he died by violence, for I saw no weapon about him save a knife still sheathed within a frayed belt. Neither did I believe his body had been placed there by others, for they would have positioned him with knees against his chest to signify the return of the body to the womb of Pachamama. I concluded that the man had probably died alone, and in realizing death was near, had met it with peace and dignity.

A cold shiver rippled down my spine despite my fever. Suddenly I was certain of how the giant had come to die. Like me, he had been a wanderer in the tunnels, only he had perished before he could find a way back to Inti's light. And if I did not find a way out soon, before my provisions were gone, I too would be a desiccated corpse waiting for some other lost traveler to stumble upon.

I took a small piece of charqui and placed it in the shriveled hand of the giant. Then I sprinkled a few drops of the precious water upon the giant's face. I'm not sure why I felt the need to do this. The man was not a god, though god-like in size. I believe I was moved by the loneliness of his death. Also, it was the only way I knew to thank him, for I believed he sat in the center of the tunnel for one reason: to warn others of the futility of continuing any farther in that direction.

I turned Chumpi back the way we had come. I was feverish in body and mind: feverish in body because of sickness; feverish in mind because of my burning need to erase the distance we had traveled down a false path. Though I had ceased counting the remaining burning stones, I knew my supply was running low. I considered walking in the dark as I had done once before when retracing my steps, but I rejected this idea, for now I was more anxious than ever to go as quickly as possible.

When we finally returned to the cavern, I immediately entered the tunnel to my left. I was exhausted and ill, and it would have been better had I slept awhile, but the memory of the dead giant and the fear of sharing his lonely fate drove me, if not wisely, then determinedly onward. Chumpi, good companion that he was, made no complaint, but kept pace beside me. I suddenly realized it had been four days, by my underground calculations, since he had eaten anything, and then only a maize cake. The thought of him starving to death was a further goad, and I vowed to offer him some charqui when I next stopped to rest.

But it was a long time before I rested. I drew upon my fear to cover as much distance as possible. And I also drew upon hope, or perhaps desperation, that soon I would come to the end of the tunnel. Nothing else seemed to matter. Gone was the controlled reason that parceled out my energies in finite periods of walking followed by periods of rest. Now I felt I was in a race with death. My greatest fear continued to be that I would run out of burning stones before I returned to Inti's light, even though I had told myself repeatedly I could continue on without the use of the lantern. Yet having once been forced to choose among different tunnels, I quailed at the thought that I might have do to so again in utter darkness.

Tunnels, burning stones, Inti's light, miraculous water, a dead giant, pain, fever, cold, darkness—all these were themes that played over and over in my mind. There was no beauty in this music only a jumble of discordant melodies wherein one would rise up shrilly to be drowned out by another. I did not bother to fight this mad music, but instead concentrated on placing one foot in front of the other. I found myself again walking with my eyes closed, one hand resting upon Chumpi, who was now my guide. Once again, I thought to save my precious burning stones by walking in darkness. My whole being rebelled against this. Without my small light, the tunnel was a night with no stars; it was the black depths of an icy lake. Worse! It was death and the underground road. To escape my dark thoughts, I drew comfort from Chumpi by leaning upon him.

Poor Chumpi, four days and no food. Had I shared my charqui with him? No, I could not have, for that would have required stopping, and I had told myself I would not stop until once again I was standing in Inti's light.

But I must have stopped, for I found myself upon the cold, hard floor of the tunnel, shivering.

Where was my chusi? Where was Chumpi? Why, I wondered, was it dark? Had I used up all the stones? No matter. Nothing mattered except Chumpi. Where was he? I was so sleepy. I had to sleep. Not like the giant. Not cross-legged, back straight—too difficult. But I had to sleep.

When I awoke, I found myself nestled against Chumpi, my head upon something hard in one of the packs. Madly, I fumbled about until I found

the water gourd. Overwhelmed with thirst, I drank deeply. I pushed the gourd
into Chumpi's face, then poured water into my palm and let him lap it. Some
spilled between my fingers and was wasted. No matter. Nothing seemed to
matter. I poured him some more and listened to him slurping. Then I drank
deeply again. The water at the end of the world, it had to be magical, for I
was on my feet again, leaning upon Chumpi.

Something was not right! Where was my arrow of stones? No matter. I
would let Chumpi lead me. But why was it so dark? I must have some stones
remaining, at least a handful.

My stiff fingers searched in the packs even as I walked. I found a few.

But where was the lantern I always carried?

I knelt upon the floor, sweeping my arms out in the darkness. I heard
Chumpi's footsteps fade in the distance.

"Chumpi!" I yelled. Tears flowed down my cheeks. Water wasted.
"Chumpi!"

I was on my feet, stumbling after him in the dark.

I was Kaka, a blind man feeling his way along the wall of the tunnel.
Suddenly the wall was gone. Another cavern? Another crossroads?

Instinctively, I moved to the left. Always to the left! The wall turned
sharply. There was another tunnel! No, not that direction! A bad feeling.

"Chumpi!"

I heard him off to my right.

"Chumpi! No! Stay with me! Stay to the left! Don't get lost!"

But we were lost. I crossed empty space. Two paces, three, four, more
than the width of a tunnel. My hands brushed against stone. Sliding one hand
along the wall, I walked until the wall took another sharp bend.

Another tunnel, but this one different! The air fresher, warmer. I had
forgotten what fresh air smelled like!

"Chumpi!"

Again, I heard him moving off to the right.

"Chumpi, come back! I've found it! Fresh air! The end of the tunnel!"
Silence.

"Chumpi!"

There was the sound of his hooves, slowly moving away.

"No!" I screamed. Anger and fear were two rocks in my belly. I moved
across empty space, abandoning the warm, sweet air. I came to another wall
which turned sharply once again. It was another tunnel and within it the

clatter of hooves.

"No, Chumpi! Not that way!"

I took a few steps within this other tunnel and hit my head hard upon a rock. The tunnel was smaller, cramped. It smelled like nothing.

"Chumpi!"

His footsteps seemed far ahead. I moved forward, fighting the urge to go back to the other passage, the one with the fresh air. Suddenly I tripped over a large rock, and fell hard upon the stone floor of the tunnel.

Lying with my head upon the cold stone, I could go no further. I felt death must be near, yet death was not as I imagined. There was darkness, yes, but a darkness unlike the tunnel's. It was comforting, like being wrapped in a warm chusi, like being held in Pachamama's arms. She smelled of dried ichu grass! Of maize cakes baking!

How should I meet this death? I was neither an Inca, nor a giant. I was just a foolish young woman, as yet unmarried.

I used my list bit of energy to sit up and wrap my arms around my knees. But before passing from this world, I reached beneath my lliqlla and took hold of Anka's necklace.

Part Five

Qosqo

Chapter 41

Once more I was walking within the tunnel, this time little caring where it led. Though I could not see in the darkness, I felt certain nothing lay in my path to trip me, nor projected from the ceiling to surprise my unsuspecting head. The floor of the tunnel angled up sharply, but this did not trouble me either. In fact, I could have run up the steep slope and never tired. But running was not a consideration, for that would have brought me too soon to my destination, and I savored my leisurely climb. With each step, the air became fresher, sweeter, sometimes delightfully cool upon my face, other times seductively warm.

For days, I walked–weeks, months. I knew not how long nor thought it important. Neither did I hunger nor sought to satisfy my thirst. Yet with each step, I grew stronger, healthier, more alive, until there came a point where such vitality could no longer be contained within one body, and I became one with all of life itself: plants, animals, people, Pachamama, Qillamama, Inti–all the same.

And in that instant, when I was made whole and knew it, I was cast into the light, a seed from its shell, and reborn upon the mountain. I cried for the loss of something I knew not, but Inti comforted me with his healing light. I ran through fields of flowers watered by melting snow, and, to my surprise, grew weary and found shade beneath a tall Pisonay tree, dripping with clusters of red-orange blossoms. The slender leaves filtered Inti's light, and it rained down as golden motes. I fell asleep. But it was not upon the mountain that I awoke.

A fly buzzed annoyingly about my head. I brushed him away, but he was persistent. I swatted at him again, and hit upon something soft that carried with it the smell of half-digested ichu grass. I opened my eyes and found myself looking directly up into Chumpi's face. With an arm nearly numb from lying awkwardly upon it, I reached up and scratched above Chumpi's nose. He leaned in closer and blew his sweet breath into my face then hummed in my ear. I smiled and closed my eyes. I had never felt so relaxed, so rested. I wanted to sleep longer and not yet live again.

But life called to me. The fly buzzed me once more, and overhead dry leaves rattled in a wind I could not feel. I opened my eyes and stared up at tear-shaped leaves, dancing beneath Inti's light.

Inti's light!

I sat up quickly, too quickly, and had to lean upon trembling arms until the dizziness passed.

I was alive! But more than that: I was free! Free from darkness! Free from endless walls! Alive to Inti's light, to things living!

But how?

I remembered that, in following Chumpi, I had hit my head upon an unseen rock. Perhaps it had not been a rock after all, but one of the branches above me. Why then had not I seen the branch as I did now? The reason was obvious even to one still half asleep; it must have been dark when I escaped from the tunnel. With shame, I recalled the anger I had felt toward Chumpi, believing he was leading us down the wrong tunnel. I pushed up on wobbly legs, clung to a sturdy branch until my dizziness passed then stepped next to Chumpi and put one arm around his neck.

"I am a fool who does not deserve to be called your friend. Can you forgive my anger? Can you forgive me for not trusting your instincts?"

His contented hum told me he bore no hard feelings.

I ran one hand along his back. To my horror, I realized the packs were gone. "The packs! Chumpi, did we leave them behind in the tunnel?"

I looked back at the tunnel entrance, and shuddered at the thought of having to return to the darkness. When I turned back around, Chumpi was gone.

"Chumpi!" I yelled and stumbled after him through the brush. I had not gone far before I came upon the packs dangling from a branch that must have snagged them when Chumpi passed that way earlier.

Carefully, I slid the packs off the branch and examined its few remaining contents. To my great relief, Sumaq's jar was undamaged and still heavy with the water at the end of the world. I carried the packs over one arm and used the other to push aside branches as I followed Chumpi. The brush came to an abrupt end at the edge of a dry wash, beyond which was open land with sparse vegetation. I thought I still must be still asleep and dreaming. I had entered the tunnel, leaving behind the luxuriant plant life of the jungle, and had emerged into a broad valley not unlike that in which Qomermoya was situated. In the middle distance, a band of bright green suggested the presence of water, though I could see no stream from where I stood. Beyond was a steep, treeless slope dotted with spiky paqpa plants, some with tall flower stalks heavy with blossoms. One of my worries had been that I would emerge from the tunnel and find myself deep in the jungle with no idea of where I was. I still did not know, yet took comfort from the fact that this country had the look of home.

Chumpi returned and stood stamping his feet, anxious for me to follow. I thought of the hidden stream and realized how thirsty I was. Yet even greater than my thirst was my desire to bathe. But before I could satisfy either desire, there was something I had to do first.

"You go on ahead, Chumpi," I said, waving him on. "I will join you shortly."

I searched through my packs until I found the last of my burning stones. There were only three. I recalled that day when Chanka had shown me the stones and my amazement of how they burned. Without Chanka's thoughtful planning, I would not have had light within the tunnel, and without light, I would have never found the water at the end of the world. I did not know which way was Tambo Toco, but I made a guess and whispered my thanks to Chanka. Then I took my rubbing stick and started a fire using a handful of dried leaves. When the fire was going well, I placed the burning stones upon it as an offering to the gods, thanking them for leading me safely out of the tunnel. It was a small offering, yet had I been able to sacrifice a thousand guinea pigs, it would not have been enough. The realization was humbling. So great the gods, so small Yana Mayu.

It was strange to hear my name even if only in my mind. I am a small dark river, I thought, flowing from an infinite sea that is Wiraqocha. Yet small as I was, the gods had chosen me to find the water at the end of the world, and, thanks to them, I had succeeded. I felt both elated and relieved, though my task was still far from over. In my mind, I again saw myself presenting the water to the Capac Inca. Then I laughed. I could not imagine him receiving me unless I first had a bath.

Because of its shallowness, the stream was not very cold. I knelt and drank deeply then went in search of deeper water in which to bathe. The best I could find was a place where I could immerse my body if I lay down. I set down my packs then quickly shed my lliqlla and washed it as best as I could. Then I lay with my back on the sandy bottom of the stream and pushed my fingers through the tangles in my hair before rubbing myself all over with soft sand. I was startled by how thin I had become. I imagined I must look as gaunt as the giant I had met in the tunnel.

That memory was too painfully fresh, so I rolled over onto my stomach and watched the bees buzzing around the blossoms of a paqpa plant. Seeing the paqpa plant made me wish for a piece of its root to use as soap, but, unfortunately, I had nothing to dig in the hard soil with.

When I was as clean as I was going to get, I sat upon a rock to dry. The simple act of washing had left me feeling as tired as if I had spent the day walking. From one of my packs, I took one of the few remaining pieces of charqui. I was not hungry until I started to eat, then could not stop. I devoured a second piece as quickly as the first and had to keep myself from eating a third, for now there were only two left.

My meal over, and with the luxury of nothing to do until my lliqlla dried, I lay upon grass beneath Inti's warm light and slept. When I awoke, Inti had already passed behind a ridge to the west. To my delight, Qillamama floated lovely in the cloudless sky. When I had entered the tunnel, she had only begun to reveal her face. Now, more than half her face shone out, which meant I had been in the tunnel at least seven days.

Seven days! I shivered at the thought of all that time spent in darkness, and I prayed I would never have to go underground again. Yet even as I made this request, I remembered my recent dream, and how I had ascended through darkness to the mountain top and felt no fear, but only a sense of peace and of being connected with all things. I realized the gods had granted me a vision of the underground road upon which all people must travel one day. The serenity I had felt made me aware I now had little reason to fear death. That said, I still hoped I would never have to travel underground again, at least not in this life.

I stood up without experiencing the dizziness I had felt earlier. I quickly dressed then slipped the packs over my head. I decided I would carry them from now on, for I felt better having Sumaq's jar safely against me. Besides, the packs were now but a small weight to carry, the burning stones having been consumed, and the water gourd lost in the tunnel.

I called to Chumpi. "With Qillamama to light our way, let's see where this stream leads." I needed to know where I was, and my best chance of finding out was to follow the stream, for, sooner or later, all streams led to a village.

It was pleasant to walk now that I was rested. The way was open, and the trail was easy. Dry grass gave off the smell of something good baking, and cicadas sang from clumps of bushes. I came upon a short stone wall built to enclose a spring. Overhanging the spring was a huaranhuay bush, bright with yellow blossoms. I broke off a sprig and placed it behind my ear, but as it would not stay, I slipped it under Chumpi's halter then added another on the opposite side.

"Now you're ready for a festival." Dust rose as I patted his back. "Atatau! I said I was going to push you into a stream. Well, just don't think you're going to get out of taking a bath!"

A little farther on, the stream joined a larger one. I was glad to see a trail edged this larger stream, though sections were now in shadow.

"As long as we can see where we're going, we'll continue on, Chumpi. But if it gets too dark, we'll stop. You and I have gone through too much to risk breaking Sumaq's jar."

Chumpi wasn't listening. With head thrust forward, he was sniffing the air.

"What do you smell? It can't be water. I just hope you won't desert me like the last time."

But that's exactly what he did.

"Chumpi, come back!" I quickly followed, more curious than alarmed. Rounding a bend in the stream, I saw a llama herders' shelter then heard several people shouting at once. I rushed in upon a group of young men laughing as one of their number was trying to shoo Chumpi away from an oven on which maize cakes were baking.

"Chumpi!" I yelled, grabbing him by his halter. "I'm so sorry," I said to the young man who had been trying to shoo Chumpi away. "I'm afraid Chumpi has forgotten his manners. He wouldn't have dared act so rudely at home."

The young man looked at me then at Chumpi then back to me. "You have a strange way of treating llamas. Around here, we put the flowers on the women and the packs on the llamas."

This bit of wit drew more laughter from the other herders.

Smiling, I pulled the flowers from Chumpi's halter. Against my will, my eyes were drawn to the oven on which a pot of locro was cooking alongside the neat rows of maize cakes.

The young man followed the direction of my gaze. "It seems the llama isn't the only one who wants some of our food." Again, the other young men laughed.

Embarrassed, I quickly looked away. "I'm sorry. We didn't mean to interrupt your meal." But as I started to lead Chumpi away, the young man leapt in front of us.

"But you did interrupt," he said, "and I'm glad of it!" He pointed toward his comrades. "You see I have been with these sorry excuses for llama herders for five days now. Five days without any intelligent conversation!"

This remark was met with boos and hisses.

I responded as I would if he had been one of the young men of Qomermoya. "Perhaps it is because they take after their leader."

The others laughed at this rejoinder, but the young man was not to be outdone. "You see? You see? It is just as I thought. She's far more intelligent than you louts. She recognizes who the leader is!"

"But Tuku," one of the others said, "how can you lead when your butt is always where your head should be?"

Tuku shook his head. "Now you see the level of conversation I have to put up with. But please, come! We would be glad for you to share our meal. Piki, raise your lazy carcass up so our guest can have a place next to the fire!"

A young man, smaller than the others, stood up and motioned for me to take his place. The warmth of the fire felt good, but just as I was getting settled, Chumpi bleated anxiously.

"Are you still here?" Tuku said, addressing Chumpi. I was afraid he was going to chase Chumpi away, but instead Tuku took one of the maize cakes off the oven. "Now, if I give this to you, will you leave us alone?"

As Tuku broke the hot maize cake into smaller pieces, the others began to serve themselves from the pot of locro. A bowl of locro, smelling delightfully of guinea pig and peppers, was given me along with a maize cake. Fortunately, the locro was very hot, otherwise I would have embarrassed myself by gobbling it down like a starving dog. Tuku, having finished giving Chumpi the maize cake, dished himself a bowl of locro and sat down opposite me.

"Thank you for giving some of your good food to Chumpi," I said. "I'm afraid I spoil him."

Tuku shrugged. "It is easy to spoil our silent brothers." He raised his voice. "Sometimes I prefer the company of llamas to that of some people I know!"

This jibe went unanswered, as the other herders were intent upon their meal.

"This food is delicious!" I said. I raised my voice so that everyone could hear me. "Thank you for sharing your meal with me."

The young men nodded in reply, but none spoke. Now that the excitement of our arrival had passed, the herders succumbed to their obvious fatigue. I finished my locro then broke apart the maize cake and saved half to give to Chumpi later.

"Would you like more locro?" Tuku said.

I shook my head. "It was delicious, but I'm full." On meager rations, my stomach had shrunk.

One by one, the others returned to the pot to refill their bowls. The last person scraped the pot with a long-handled spoon. Piki, I noticed, had fallen asleep with a half-eaten bowl of locro in his lap.

"In exchange for this excellent meal," I told Tuku, "I insist on cleaning up."

He shook his head. "We just rinse the bowls in the stream. It only takes a moment. Though if you insist, you can wash out the empty pot, which is all that will be left to clean. We're traveling pretty light these days."

"You all seem very tired," I said.

"The wilka camayocs have sent us to scour the countryside in search of more white llamas," Tuku said. "Ordinarily, they don't need so many, but... well, you know."

I shook my head. I did not know.

"With Topa Inca getting sicker and sicker, there's been a greater need for more llamas to sacrifice."

"I heard Topa Inca is dead," one of the others said.

My heart stopped beating.

"Shhh! Don't say that!" Tuku scolded. "You know that's not true."

"You don't know it isn't."

"If Topa Inca is dead, why are the wilka camayocs still sending us out in search of llamas?"

"Well, everyone in Qosqo is acting like he is."

At the mention of the word Qosqo I jumped to my feet. "Did you say Qosqo? Do you know where it is?"

Everyone stared at me. "Where did you come from?" Tuku said, pointing upward. "Someplace up there with Qillamama?"

They all laughed save Piki who was still asleep.

"I'm sorry, but I live in a small village far from here, and I have gotten lost. But I need to get to Qosqo. Can you tell me how to get there?"

The man seated next to Tuku answered. "Just follow this stream."

"Or any stream," someone else said.

Hearing this, I was anxious to be going, especially after all the gloomy talk about Topa Inca. "I know it's very rude to leave so quickly after eating, but I must get to Qosqo as quickly as possible." As I moved toward Chumpi, I added, "Thank you again for sharing your meal with me."

Piki, who had not been asleep after all, said, "What about cleaning the pot?"

I turned back and lifted the empty pot off the oven. Tuku quickly took the pot from me and set it back down. "Come! I'll walk with you and show you a shortcut."

"No! No! You're too tired, Tuku," said a sturdy young man who reminded me of Charapa. "Let me show her!"

Grinning, Tuku dismissed him with a wave of his hand. Stepping quickly, he led Chumpi and me along the trail that bordered the stream. Qillamama's light shone brightly, and occasionally I saw her face reflected in the water. After we had gone about half a tupu, we came to a crossing made using flat rocks. Instead of following Tuku as he stepped from rock to rock, I slipped out of my sandals and waded into the sluggish current. Stopping midstream, I waited until Chumpi drew alongside, then I flung sheets of water upon his unsuspecting back. Startled, he bleated piteously and sought to escape, but I grabbed him by his halter, turned him around, and soaked his other side as well. I didn't stop until I had succeeded in rinsing most of the dirt off him.

Looking thoroughly miserable, Chumpi dragged himself from the stream and began to shake himself. Tuku, who had stood the whole time, watching us, jumped back to avoid a shower.

"Why did you do that?" he said.

Nearly soaked myself, I walked out of the stream, laughing. "I'm just keeping a promise I made earlier to give Chumpi a bath." But into Chumpi's ear, I whispered, "Just be glad I didn't push you in all the way."

Tuku pointed to a lesser trail which ascended to the top of a ridge in the near distance. "This trail is a shortcut to Qosqo." His longer stride got him to the ridge top well ahead of me, and I could see him silhouetted against the sky as he waited for me to join him.

"There!" he pointed, as I came up alongside.

As children, we often played games on festival nights, and I remembered that sometimes our games took us up the mountain slopes. When tired of playing, we would sit and look down upon the fire around which our parents sat. That was a magical sight: the orange-red glow of the fire whose light was reflected in the faces of our parents. Now, looking where Tuku pointed, I saw in the distance not what looked like one fire, but hundreds, almost as if the whole plain before us was afire. In the center, one fire blazed up far brighter than the others.

"What am I looking at?" I said.

"What do you mean? You're looking at Qosqo!"

I shook my head. "No! That's not possible! Qosqo must be far from here!"

"Excuse me, but having been born and raised in Qosqo, I think I have a better idea of its location than someone who comes from nowhere and is obviously lost."

I rushed to apologize. "I'm sorry. I didn't mean to doubt you, it's just…" How could I explain? I could not believe it myself. The city I had longed to see, the city where the Capac Inca and Topa Inca lived was right before me. For seven days, I had journeyed through darkness, never imagining that in my traveling I had actually passed beneath the mountains and emerged near to my destination.

"That's Qosqo?" I said, still not believing it.

"Chumpi, come here," Tuku said. "Let me talk to you. This other one doesn't seem to hear so well."

"Atakachau!" I whispered, "Truly, the gods are amazing!" I tore my eyes from the glowing city and looked at Tuku. "I have heard the buildings of Qosqo are made of gold. From here, it looks as if they're made of light."

Tuku answered with obvious pride in his voice. "Not all the buildings are of gold. The wasis of the Hatunruna are the same as anywhere, I suppose." With a wave of his hand, he dismissed this as being of no importance. "But the walls of Inti's temple, the Coricancha, are indeed covered in gold, as well as those of the Cora Cora where the Capac Inca lives."

I wanted to hear more about the Cora Cora, but first sought to satisfy my immediate curiosity "Why is that one fire bigger than the others?"

"The big fire you see is the great pyre on which the llamas are sacrificed to Inti. It's located in the Huacaypata, which is the great square where all the important ceremonies take place. Since Topa Inca became ill, the fire has been burning continuously."

"Where is the Cora Cora in relationship to the Huacaypata?"

"Not far, just to the north and a little east."

"So, if I went across the Huacaypata, I would come to the Cora Cora?"

"Cross the Huacaypata? Not likely! Not unless you're an Inca."

I looked at Tuku, not understanding.

"Only Incas are allowed in the Huacaypata. But you can see everything that goes on there from the Kusipata, which is the park where all the Hatunruna gather during celebrations. It's actually much larger than the Huacaypata."

Since Tuku obviously enjoyed imparting his knowledge, I continued to draw him out. "Where is the Yachawasi?"

"Atatau! Are you planning to enter the school for the sons of Incas? A woman of your beauty should be in the Acllawasi."

"I'm not nearly pretty enough to be an aclla, though it would be nice to be in the Acllawasi, where I would not have to listen to the remarks of a certain conceited young man."

Tuku took hold of Chumpi's halter. "Did you hear that, Chumpi? 'A conceited young man.' Now who do you think she's talking about? I'd better hurry and answer her questions so I can return to my friends, for I think I prefer dull wits to sharp tongues!" He pointed again toward Qosqo. "You see the dark area to the left of the Huacaypata? The Yachawasi is there, though I don't know why you..."

I turned to see why he had stopped talking.

"I realized I have been talking to you and I don't even know your name," he said.

"My name is Yana Mayu."

"Well, Yana Mayu, no one seeing Qosqo for the first time should see it alone. She should be accompanied by someone who knows the city intimately, even if that person is a conceited young man. Qosqo is the most beautiful city in all Tahuantinsuyu. I could not imagine living anywhere else." He sighed. "I wish you would delay your visit for another time."

"I cannot wait until you are available to show me about the city. I must get to Qosqo at once. Even tonight, I plan to walk as far as I can while Qillamama lends her light."

"You misunderstand me. It's just that now Qosqo is not a happy city. Everyone has a long face because Topa Inca is dying. All the festivals have been cancelled. There's no music, no dancing, no drinking." He shook his head. "I don't want you to see Qosqo when it's like that."

"Yet to someone like myself, who has spent her whole life in a small village, Qosqo will appear magnificent." I wish I could have told him I knew the cure for his sad city, but I realized it would be very unwise to let anyone know I carried the water at the end of the world. "So, will this trail lead me to Qosqo?"

"It connects with the Capac-nan, which is a main highway into Qosqo." Tuku looked up to see the position of Qillamama. "You will not be able to reach the Capac-nan before Qillamama passes beyond the mountains. There is a small lake about half a tupu farther on, and I suggest you sleep there tonight, for the trail beyond the lake passes through thick brush and is difficult to see in places, even in Inti's light. Also, there is no water beyond the lake until you reach the Capac-nan. Tomorrow, if you get an early start, you should come to the Capac-nan by midmorning. Then just follow the crowds of people and pack trains of llamas bringing goods to the city."

I searched in my packs for something to give Tuku in exchange for his help. All I had was a dried gourd which contained the two sheets of charqui. I removed the charqui and held the gourd out to him. "It is a poor gift for all your kindness, but it is all I have."

He shook his head. "A gift for an undercooked bowl of locro?"

"The locro was excellent, and you went out of your way to show me this shortcut."

"As for that, your company had been reward enough." He stepped closer. "Come to Qosqo sometime when I'm not chasing after llamas, and I will show you its splendors."

I thanked Tuku for his offer then said goodbye. Chumpi and I had not gotten ten paces down the trail before Tuku called out.

"If you want to find me in Qosqo," he said, with laughter in his voice, "just ask for the conceited young man!"

Chapter 42

"Atatau!" I exclaimed, not for the first time that morning. "I'm getting poked to death!" Tuku had said the trail beyond the lake passed through thick brush, but he failed to mention the brush was mostly prickly checche bushes.

Chumpi, who was walking in front of me, released a branch that, snapping back, bit into my leg. "Atatau, it's no fair! You have that thick coat of hair to protect you. Look at my legs! It's like someone lashed them with frayed rope!"

Yet despite complaining of scrapes and scratches, I felt well indeed, for both Chumpi and I were rested after an uneventful night spent by the small lake. Now Inti's light shone brightly, and though it was growing hot along the trail, compared to being in the tunnel, this was bliss.

I thought about the fires of Qosqo seen from the ridge the night before. It was difficult to judge distances at night, yet they had seemed not far off, certainly within a day's travel. That meant I would probably be in Qosqo before the day was over. Then it would not take long to find the Cora Cora, where I could present the Capac Inca with the water at the end of the world. And once he received the miraculous water, he would release Charapa from prison. Atakachau! This very day I might be reunited with my brother!

Suddenly, I thought I heard voices. "Chumpi, did you hear that?"

Chumpi, ignoring me, walked on. I stopped to listen, but heard nothing other than the buzzing of flies. I hurried to catch up with Chumpi and had just caught a glimpse of him when he disappeared as if swallowed up by Pachamama. I followed cautiously until brought to a halt at the edge of a short, but very steep bank. Below was a wide road, undoubtedly the Capac-nan. I slid down the bank on the soles of my sandals. Once on the road, I looked for the people whose voices I thought I heard, but saw no one.

Though not paved with stone, the surface of the Capac-nan was as smooth as if people had swept it clean, which perhaps they did. As Chumpi and I hurried along, I thought of the circuitous route which had brought us back to the great highland road which Akakllu's uncle had helped to build. It seemed forever since I had last seen Akakllu, and I wondered if the young musician had managed to return to Tambo Toco in time for the Coya Raymi festival.

The trimmed checche bushes which lined the road gave way to open country dotted with clumps of ichu grass. I spotted a nearby stream and, of one mind, Chumpi and I stepped off the Capac-nan to satisfy our thirst. The water was clear and refreshing, and when I had drunk my fill, I sat and splashed cold water over my scratched legs. Then I heard voices again, and looking back, saw two men leading a train of llamas bearing loads of firewood. Seeing the men brought back my old worry about having to answer questions. I jumped up and led Chumpi back onto the Capac-nan where we hurried to outdistance the laden animals. Our rapid pace, however, caused us to overtake another llama train, also hauling wood. Atatau! Tuku was right: the road to Qosqo was crowded!

Despite my worries, I was too anxious to get to Qosqo to tarry behind the toiling llamas. "Good morning," I said, as I quickly strode past. The man leading the llamas did not reply, but swatted at the flies that buzzed around his head. We passed several more llama trains in this manner along with two coming the opposite direction. I soon realized a greeting was not required; most travelers neither gave one nor expected one in return. Unable to pass a llama train because of two others coming the opposite direction, I decided to rest and eat one of my two remaining pieces of charqui. I was sitting in the meager shade of a queuña tree when a group of six soldiers came tramping along. Seeing the soldiers started my heart to racing, but they took no more notice of Chumpi and me than if we had been rocks—that is until they were past. Then one of the young soldiers looked back and smiled. This prompted the soldier marching behind, perhaps the smiling soldier's superior, to shove him roughly in the back. The young soldier stumbled and barely managed to avoid running into the soldier in front of him. The man who shoved him spoke a few words I could not hear, but which drew laughter from the others.

By mid-afternoon, traffic upon the road was so heavy, I could no longer pass by anyone. I saw several women my age. A few also led llamas, though most bore their goods upon their backs. The presence of these young women should have lessened my fear, but I still felt an uneasiness I could not explain until I realized it was a reaction to the sheer number of people. Already I had seen countless more people than all those who lived in Qomermoya. I wondered how I was going to feel once I reached the city of Qosqo?

There was a shrill blare of a quepa, a trumpet made from a gourd, and everyone scurried to the side of the road. This was not easy, for the llamas did not move quickly. I helped the woman ahead of me push her llamas to one side, and as a result just managed to pull Chumpi from the road before the appearance of a litter born by eight men. The litter was little more than a seat upon two poles. There were no curtains of red feathers or panels of gold as on the litter that bore the Capac Inca. Though the occupant wore a yacolla dyed with many colors, he sported no mantle made of exotic bird feathers. Neither was he accompanied by soldiers, but only the men who carried the litter. My guess was he was a minor government official.

After the litter passed, I moved back into the road ahead of the others and got a clear view ahead. I saw row upon row of colcas, so many I could not count them all. I could not fathom the amount of goods necessary to fill them all.

As we approached the outskirts of Qosqo, I saw row upon row of wasis. These amazed me also, but only because of how closely they were crowded together. A family could not have eaten a meal without having to listen to their neighbors' conversations. Atatau! How could people live like that? I remember Tuku saying he could not imagine living anywhere else but Qosqo, which made me wonder if he was not only conceited, but crazy.

The ground around each wasi was so trampled, nothing grew. Only Pisonay trees, which now lined the Capac-nan, relieved the starkness of the landscape. Like those in Calca, these trees were heavy with clusters of red-orange blossoms. Bright flowers rained down upon the road, and dry petals were stirred up by the passing of feet.

Yet the beauty of the trees seemed to go unnoticed by the travelers. Studying the faces of those I passed, I recalled Tuku's comment concerning the general sadness caused by Topa Inca's illness. Rather than sad, I thought the people looked preoccupied. Everyone was so busy trying to get somewhere, I felt out of place and thus unwilling to ask for directions.

Suddenly the road opened upon a park filled with plants to delight the eyes. At first, I thought I had come upon the Huacaypata, where the sacrifices took place, for the park showed great care in its planning. But when I saw others like myself walking amid the splendid greenery, I realized this park must be the Kusipata. How appropriate its name: the place of joy! It was in the Kusipata that I saw, for the first time, people markedly different than myself. A group of men wore unkas so short, they barely covered their breechcloths. And the material they saved by this design was wasted upon long sleeves that concealed most of their arms. But more startling was their hair. They had shaved it all off save for a spiky tuft on the very top that made them look like exotic birds.

But stranger by far was the appearance of a group of women who sat in a circle, talking animatedly in a language I could not understand. At first, I thought they were wearing cone-shaped hats, but upon closer inspection, I saw their heads had somehow been formed into this bizarre shape! I did not realize I had stopped to stare until one of the women pointed me out to the others. Then they all turned to stare back. Embarrassed, I took Chumpi by his halter and hurried toward a thick column of smoke, which I assumed emanated from the great sacrificial pyre within the Huacaypata. Yet there was much more smoke in the air than could have been produced by that one source. I wondered how the residents of Qosqo could stand to breathe such foul air or tolerated a sky the color of dull metal.

At the edge of the Kusipata was a narrow river, channeled to run arrow-straight. Beyond the river, I saw a great stone altar upon which a fire burned brightly. I watched as a young man added wood to the flame, pieces that had been elaborately carved with the figures of animals. Near to the altar stood two men, each attired in long red yacollas tied with sashes whose excess length dropped nearly to their feet. Necklaces of seashells hung about their necks, and each wore a headdress with more bright and beautiful feathers than that of the Capac Inca. The men were undoubtedly high-ranking wilka camayocs. I watched as these priests lifted a bleeding llama and carefully laid it upon the fire.

Then came a procession of young women. Even from a distance, I could see their beauty was beyond compare. They wore lliqllas of the purest white, and each carried a stack of woven cloth of various vivid hues. Either the women were very strong, or the material light, for they bore the weight of the cloth effortlessly.

The procession came to a stop before the altar where the first two women reverently offered their magnificent bundles to the wilka camayocs who spoke a few words over the bundles before committing them to the fire.

Atakachau! To think I saw such a wondrous thing! It shamed me to think of my unfulfilled promise to offer the gods a trifling guinea pig when before my eyes they received gifts of such incalculable value. Yet greater than awe was the fear I felt. If these magnificent gifts were insufficient to restore Topa Inca's health, what of the water at the end of the world? Could it do what these offerings could not? What was it I carried upon my back? A treasure greater than all the offerings I was witnessing?

Sumaq's jar now seemed an unbearable burden, and I was determined to find the Cora Cora at once. Yet even as I turned away from the Huacaypata, more bundles of cloth were given to the flames.

Following Tuku's directions, I went northward and found a wooden bridge that spanned the river. I stood a moment upon the bridge where the light of the pyre reflected blood-red in the sluggish current. The road beyond was surprisingly empty, though I could not see far because of the trees that lined each side. In the opposite direction, Inti stood low in the sky, his color also blood-red due to the thick smoke. With darkness approaching, my resolve began to waver. Maybe it would be better to go see Anka first, so he could use his influence, or that of his father, to gain me an audience with the Capac Inca.

I chastised myself for my lack of courage. Topa Inca was close to death. For his sake, as well as my brother's, I had to get the water at the end of the world to the Capac Inca without delay.

I took hold of Chumpi's halter and walked off the bridge. We did not have to go far upon the road before it opened upon a great square formed by walls more than three body-lengths in height. Though I could see no openings in the wall, I suspected they served to enclose the Cora Cora. The walls were not made of gold as I had envisioned from Tuku's description. However, the stones, of which the wall was built, were outlined in silver. Yet the silver was but a shiny decoration; the real beauty of the wall was in the unmatched craftsmanship that had so skillfully joined the massive stones that a strand of hair could not have fit between them.

So engrossed was I in examining the walls, I failed, at first, to notice a group of boys coming toward me. I grabbed Chumpi and pulled him back around a corner of the wall, praying we had not been seen. With my back to the stones, I waited for the boys to go past. Judging from their multi-colored unkas and well-crafted sandals, they were Incas, yet they behaved like boys anywhere when not under the direct eyes of an elder: laughing, making faces, playing at fighting. I stopped breathing when one of the boys turned and pointed at us, but a taller boy slapped his hand down, and they moved on.

Leading Chumpi, I quickly walked to the next corner and peered around. There was a wide stairway leading to an opening in the wall. Burning torches had been placed at the ends of each step save the lowest where stood a row of grim-faced soldiers holding spears longer than they were tall. The soldiers stood motionless, but two older men, wearing beautiful yacollas, stood in the road, talking with the aid of gestures.

I rubbed my chest to loosen the sudden tightness. Of course, I knew the entrance to the Cora Cora would be guarded. Yet the soldiers looked so fierce, and there were so many of them! Recalling how fiercely they had guarded the Capac Inca during his visit to Qomermoya, I now wished I had gone to see Anka first.

Then I remembered I was not just an insignificant Hatunruna coming with the offering of a washcloth for a boy who had vomited. The gods had entrusted me with a miraculous gift, the water at the end of the world, and charged me to bring it to the Capac Inca so his son might be restored to health.

I took several deep breaths then took Chumpi by his halter and approached the nearest guard, stopping well out of the reach of his spear should he decide to swing it at me.

"Please, sir." My words came out barely above a whisper. I wet my lips and tried again. "Please, sir, I have—" Something shiny caught my eye. At the top of the stairs was a magnificent door upon which Inti's face had been recreated in gold. His hair and beard, sweeping outward, were of silver. The light of the torches reflecting in this image was almost as bright as Inti himself. I stood transfixed by the door's splendor, unable to utter another word.

"You, there!"

The sharp words were like a lash, startling me awake. I spun about to see one of the two men who had been talking in the road coming toward me, anger clearly on his face.

"What do you think you're doing here?"

"Please, I've come to—"

"Shut your mouth, and be off! And take your filthy llama with you, before I have him cut up and served as a meal for the guards!"

Confusion, fear, anger, reigned in my mind. Without thinking, I began to ask directions to the Yachawasi. "Where—"

"You know where!" He raised a stick I had not seen. I brought my arms up to shield my unprotected head, but rather than strike me, the man used the stick as a pointer. "Go back to the Chinchaysuyu, that quarter of the city where all your type belongs!"

I ran away as fast as I could pull Chumpi along. I don't believe that even in the tunnel, with Pachamama shaking, I had been so frightened. We did not stop running until once again in the Kusipata where, beside a tall molle tree, I released Chumpi and dropped to the ground. My lungs were afire, and my throat burned from all the smoky air. Added to this was my disbelief at having once dreamed of coming to Qosqo. Atatau! How could I ever have wished such a thing? I hated Qosqo! It was filthy and ugly and unkind!

The man's angry words kept repeating in my mind: "Shut your mouth," "filthy," "served up as a meal," "your type!" Perhaps Chumpi and I were not so clean by Inca standards, but that was because we did not stand around all day, talking amiably in the road. Chumpi and I had endured great hardships in order to bring the water at the end of the world to the Capac Inca. It was the water that was important, not our appearance. And before I even had a chance to explain why I had come, I had been chased away by a fancy-dressed, ill-tempered, Inca monkey who probably luxuriated in hot water baths every day!

If it were not for Charapa being in prison, I believe I would have quit Qosqo then and there and left Topa Inca to his fate.

Then I remembered how sick Topa Inca had been that day he visited Qomermoya, how my heart had pitied him, and later how he had called back his father so he might give me the beautiful, yellow feather. I reached beneath my lliqlla and pulled out the necklace on which the feather hung. A few of the barbs were missing, but the color was still vivid. Perhaps if I had had the wits to have shown the feather to the angry Inca, he might have treated me differently.

I shook my head. The angry man would have probably acted the same. He even might have even accused me of stealing the feather. I remember general Kuntur saying not all Incas were noble. Perhaps the man who chased me away was one of those. Well, I knew of an Inca who was noble, and tomorrow I would find Anka and ask for his assistance.

I closed my hand around the feather. Why had I come to Qosqo? Because the gods had willed it. Because the fate of Tahuantinsuyu rested upon the health of a boy.

In my anger, I had failed to notice that darkness had come, though it did not seem like darkness because the sky was illuminated by the sacrificial fire in the Huacaypata. Distant sounds came to my ears: the call of a mother for her child; the clatter of cookware; the pad of sandals upon the Capac-nan, busy even at night.

Yet within the Kusipata, all was still. I was grateful for this sanctuary, for I had already decided to spend the night here. I remember the angry man saying "my type" were in the Chinchasuyu. I did not know what he meant by this. Yet had I known where the Chinchasuyu was, I did not know anyone who lived there. Even if I had, I still would have preferred the quiet of the Kusipata to a cramped wasi.

I pulled my chusi from one of the packs and laid it out next to Chumpi.

"I'll never call you filthy again," I promised, as I snuggled up against him. "I'd rather lay my head against you than upon a spotless chusi made of the softest vicuña."

Looking up through the branches of the molle tree, I could see no stars and wondered if their absence was due to clouds or to the awful smoke that filled the air of this unfriendly city.

Chapter 43

I awoke to neither night nor day, wondering if it was morning or a false dawn created by the sacrificial fire still burning in the Huacaypata. It wasn't a comforting light, such as Inti's, but unnatural and somehow menacing. I shook the dew from my chusi before tucking it away in one of my packs. I felt as if I had not bathed in weeks and knew I must amend my appearance so that when I presented myself at the Yachawasi, I would not be driven away as I had been at the Cora Cora. I led Chumpi to the river that separated the Kusipata from the Huacaypata. The current was sluggish and taikiji grew thickly near the shore. Pollen spilled from these tall reeds as I pushed them aside to drink. I thought it best not to undress and instead rinsed off my arms and legs then let my hair float upon the surface of the water. Sitting back on my heels, I wrung my hair and watched the water dribble upon the ground then run back into the river. When I leaned forward to rinse my hands, I saw my reflection. It wavered as tiny drops fell from my face, but I could see myself well enough. I had changed. My skin was tight over the bones of my cheeks with no fat to soften the sharp angles. My eyes looked enormous in my emaciated face. My nose—never my nicest feature—was a stubby projection that did not blend well with my face, like a lump of clay carelessly stuck to a pot.

In disgust, I shattered the reflection. What would Anka think, seeing me as I looked now? Maybe he would not be inclined to help. Yet I knew that Anka was a noble Inca, and having offered aid, he would not now refuse it because of my appearance.

It was too early to present myself at the Yachawasi, so I returned to the Kusipata and sat with my back up against the molle tree. I felt a little chilled, but the air temperature was nothing like the cold I had endured in the tunnel. Still, I longed for a small fire just for its friendly glow. And a cup of hot tea!

I hugged my knees to my chest, rested my head upon my arms, and dozed. When I awoke, I was surprised to see the day was well advanced, though the sky was overcast with dark, brooding clouds. Chumpi, who had been pulling up tufts of grass when I had nodded off, was gone. Alarmed, I jumped to my feet. My eyes swept the Kusipata, but I could not see him anywhere.

"Chumpi!" I cried, taking up my packs. Other people in the Kusipata turned to stare at me, but I didn't care. "Chumpi!" I yelled, running through the park.

I heard the sound of children's laughter and discovered Chumpi being fed tidbits by a small boy and girl under the watchful eye of their mother.

"Chumpi, you shouldn't run off like that!" I scolded. "You had me worried!"

"Is Chumpi your llama?" the girl said.

"Yes, though Chumpi thinks he belongs to anyone who will feed him."

"I wish we had a llama," the boy said.

"You know we have no place to keep one," his mother said.

"You're lucky," the boy said. "It must be wonderful to have your very own llama."

"Chumpi is a very special llama, though he shouldn't beg for food." On impulse, I hoisted the boy upon Chumpi's back and placed the girl behind him.

"Atakachau!" shouted the boy.

The little girl laughed. "Mother, look at us!"

As I slowly led them about in a circle, I realized their laughter was the first I had heard since coming to Qosqo.

"Look at us! Look at us!" the children commanded bystanders.

We circled about once more then, with reluctance, the children allowed me to lift them off Chumpi's back.

"Thank you," their mother said, smiling at me. "I don't believe my children have ever ridden on a llama before."

I smiled in return. "Back in my village, I have a baby brother who loves to sit atop Chumpi, though he's too young to stay on by himself."

"And where is your village?"

I waved my hand toward the southwest. "It's many days walking in that direction. This is my first visit to Qosqo. I've only come to deliver something."

"How do you like our city?" she said.

My answer must have shown in my face.

She placed a hand upon my arm. "You've come at a sad time. Everyone is worried about Topa Inca."

"I know."

"After you have made your delivery, you must come visit us so we can show you true Qosqo hospitality."

My eyes began to tear. "Yours are the first friendly words I have heard since coming here."

"All the more reason you must visit so I can introduce you to our friends." She pointed to the southwest. "We live in the Cuntisuyu, that part of the city where most of the artists live. My husband is an artist who works with gold and silver. Once you get to the Cuntisuyu ask anyone for directions to the wasi of Sampa Maki. Everyone knows my husband. Now I better go and give these two their morning meal."

"Before you go, would you tell me how to get to the Yachawasi?"

She pointed to the bridge I had crossed last night. "You go across—"

"Is there another way other than by crossing that bridge?" I did not want to go anywhere near the Cora Cora lest I run into the angry man again.

"Well, yes." She turned to point east. "Follow the river until you come to a second bridge. Once across it, you will immediately come to a crossroads. Don't go left, for that way goes to Saqsaywaman. Instead go right and you will soon see buildings enclosed by a wall. That's the Yachawasi."

"Chanka, a friend of mine, told me about Saqsaywaman. It's an area shaped like the head of the puma is it not?"

"Yes. Do not be surprised if you see many men working on the road leading up to it. The Capac Inca has ordered the building of a great temple atop Saqsaywaman. Workers are repaving the road with newly quarried stones so that supplies can be moved up the hillside more easily."

"Thank you for the directions and also for your invitation. I will visit if I can."

"Please do."

"And bring Chumpi with you!" the boy cried.

I laughed and promised I would. Once Chumpi and I got to the bridge the woman had spoken of, I realized I had failed to introduce myself or to get the names of my new friends. Perhaps the manners of this unfriendly city were rubbing off on me.

Once over the bridge, I saw the road that led to Saqsaywaman had already been repaved, and now many men were hauling a massive block of quarried stone. The great stone was bound with ropes and the men pulled upon two thick lead lines. The stone itself floated upon rollers made of stout poles. It was the job of two very strong men to carry the back roller to the front once it had been passed over. The men pulling upon the ropes used this interval to briefly rest before dragging the stone a few hand widths forward. It was arduous work, and seeing the steep hillside they still had to climb, I did not envy them their task.

Upon the tree-lined road going the other direction there were many people. I tried to blend in by tagging along behind a train of llamas, which brought to mind how Chumpi and I had entered the town of Calca. Though the pace of the train was slow, no one came to shoo us away. It was not long before I glimpsed through the trees a wall above which I counted four thatched roofs, all the same size and shape. A wide, well-worn path led to a wooden door set in the wall. Unlike the Cora Cora, this entrance to the Yachawasi was not guarded.

"Hello!" I called out, hoping someone behind the wall would hear me. I waited but got no response. I stepped back so my voice would carry better over the wall. "Hello! Hello!" When still no one responded, I realized I would have to wait until someone inside had a reason to come out. I just hoped no one would chase Chumpi and me away in the meantime.

Then the door began to open inward. I stepped forward. A boy no older than the ones I had seen the evening before stuck his head out. His anxious look quickly turned to one of disdain when he saw me.

"What do you want?" he said.

"I want to talk to Anka."

"What for?"

I wasn't going to stand for the insolence of someone half my age even if he was an Inca. I pulled the gold medallion from beneath my lliqlla. "Never you mind what for! You just tell him Yana Mayu is here!"

Seeing the medallion, the boy's eyes grew wide. "Wait a moment," he replied, then quickly added, "please." He pushed the door shut. I waited, shifting my weight from one leg to the other. How would Anka respond to seeing me again? Perhaps he had had second thoughts about being friendly with a woman who was a Hatunruna. I had little time to fret over this, for the door began to open and there stood not Anka, but Anka's brother Kacha.

"Yes?" he said. "You wish to see my brother?"

I could tell he did not recognize me at first. Then his eyes suddenly flashed with a maliciousness that turned my body to ice. But he instantly masked his hostility with a look of blandness.

"Ah," he said, "It's Anka's pet."

"Where is Anka?" I said, angry at being called someone's pet.

He looked behind me to the road. "Step inside," he commanded.

"What about Chumpi?" I said.

Kacha waved his hand dismissively. "He'll be all right where he is."

I stepped next to Chumpi. "Don't you wander away! I'll be right back."

I passed through the door and Kacha pushed it closed behind me. I didn't have a chance to look around before he confronted me.

"Do you have it?" he said.

"Where is Anka?" I countered.

He laughed. "Gone to look for you."

I could only stare at him, speechless.

"Not too clever of him, was it? He thought you were going to pass through Qosqo on your way to some tunnel or something. He watched the road for days, but when you did not pass by, he went in search of you."

My head swam. Poor Anka! How would he have known where to look? "How long did he say he'd be gone?"

"He didn't. Probably not until he gives up looking, and knowing my sentimental brother, that could be a month, maybe more."

A month! I did not have a month.

"Do you have it?" Kacha said again.

I looked into his face. Now his eyes seemed merry, almost warm. Of course, I did not trust him. Even so, I smiled slightly, and by that smile he knew that I had come with the water at the end of the world.

"Come!" he ordered, pulling open the entry door once more.

"Where to?" I said.

"To the Cora Cora, of course. To take your precious water to the Capac Inca."

I was stunned. I never thought Kacha would help me, and a part of me still doubted he would. Yet to whom else could I have now turned? Anka was away looking for me and Kacha did not know when he would return. In the meantime, Topa Inca might die, and with him would die any chance of freeing my brother from prison.

I went to Chumpi and took him by the halter then hurried to come up with Kacha who had stopped at the road.

"The Cora Cora is this way," Kacha said, pointing southeast.

I knew that already, but did not bother to tell him. As we walked along, I made sure to keep Chumpi between Kacha and myself.

"I'm sorry my brother was not here to greet you," Kacha said. "I know he was looking forward to showing you the city."

I doubted Kacha was very sorry. That said, I had more important matters to think about. When we reached the Cora Cora, I wanted to know exactly what to say, so that this time I would not be caught stuttering.

"There's the Huacaypata where the sacrifices to Inti take place," Kacha said, pointing. "Much of the smoke you see is coming from there."

Kacha seemed to be enjoying his role as guide. I ignored him and wondered if I would be allowed to be present when the water at the end of the world was administered to Topa Inca.

"And there's the Cora Cora!" Kacha said, sweeping his arm out with a flourish.

We were approaching the Cora Cora from a direction opposite from the way I had come the day before. I could not stop thinking about the angry man and his stick. When we turned the corner and I once again saw the guards, my heart started to hammer in my chest. Fortunately, I did not see the angry man.

I had to admire Kacha's ease. He walked right up to one of the guards and addressed him as if he were a mere servant. "Tell old Hatun Rinri I wish to see him."

"Since when have I gotten old?"

I spun about. My blood froze, seeing the man who had chased away Chumpi and me the day before. He still had his stick with him.

Kacha and Hatun Rinri eyed each other briefly, then Hatun Rinri spoke. "I thought you were ordered to stay inside the Yachawasi after you debauched that poor dignitary's daughter." Hatun Rinri's eyes drifted to me. "What's she doing here?"

"She's with me," Kacha said. "She carries something important. That's why I'm here. I wish to see the Capac Inca's camasca. I've brought powerful medicine for Topa Inca."

"Really?" said Hatun Rinri, smirking. "What kind of medicine?"

For once, Kacha was unsure of what to say. But he recovered quickly. "Just tell him I wish to see him!"

"Very well," Hatun Rinri replied. "If it's your wish to get into even more trouble, I'll be happy to oblige you."

Hatun Rinri turned to address the head guard. "See if the Capac Inca's personal camasca is available." The guard turned to mount the steps. "No, wait!" The guard turned back. Hatun Rinri stood for a moment, thinking.

"Not his personal camasca. Summon that old Qollowayan." Looking at me, Hatun Rinri added, "Likely this is something more in his line."

When the guard reached the door bearing Inti's golden image, it opened without him even having to touch it. He passed through, and the door quickly closed behind him.

As we waited at the bottom of the steps, Hatun Rinri eyed Chumpi, which made me even more anxious.

"Where is it?" Kacha said, suddenly beside me and whispering in my ear.

I hesitantly pointed to the pack on my back.

He nodded. "Better have it ready. You may not have much time."

I moved away and carefully got out Sumaq's jar, heavy with the water at the end of the world. Kacha, ignoring me, eyed Hatun Rinri who had walked a little distance away.

Suddenly the door began to open again. "Come!" said Kacha, motioning me to follow.

Holding Sumaq's jar tightly to my chest I quickly fell in behind him.

But as we approached the steps, Kacha suddenly turned. "You'd better let me carry the jar," he said.

I stepped back, shaking my head.

All the pretended affability left his face, and his demon eyes blazed. "Give it to me!" he hissed. "I know what I'm doing!"

"No!" I yelled.

"What's all this?" Hatun Rinri demanded, stepping forward.

Kacha pointed to me. "This wretch, whom I've entrusted to carry the medicine, now refuses to give it to me!"

"No! That's not true!"

But Hatun Rinri was not listening to me. He pointed his stick at me. "Give it to him!" he ordered.

I clung to the jar and watched the dreaded stick as Hatun Rinri advanced upon me. Suddenly Kacha tried to wrest the jar out of my arms, but I held it tightly, and we struggled over it.

"Give it to me!" Kacha screamed.

"No! You had nothing to do with finding it. You're just a weasel!"

"If you break it, I swear I'll see you hung by your hair!"

Hatun Rinri began to jab me with his stick as Kacha continued to demand the jar. Above the tumult, I heard Chumpi's anxious bleating. I tried to twist the jar from Kacha's grip and felt Hatun Rinri's stick hard in my back.

From the corner of my eye, I saw several guards advancing toward us.

It was then I knew they would take Sumaq's jar from me, but that was not why I let go of it. Rather I feared that in the struggle for its possession, the jar would be broken, and that would have been calamitous. The water at the end of the world would heal Topa Inca and revitalize Tahuantinsuyu. Without the water, all was lost.

"All right!" I yelled. Tears streamed down my face as I let Kacha have the jar containing the water at the end of the world. I hated to let it go. It was everything I had struggled for.

Holding the jar, Kacha stood over me, a look of malicious triumph in his eyes. Then he turned and started to mount the stairs.

But he did not get past the first step before Chumpi let go with a perfectly aimed kick that struck Kacha square on the side of the face, cracking his jawbone with a sound like a stick breaking.

But the cost of this sweet revenge was infinite. Sumaq's jar spun out of Kacha's arms and went end over end through the air.

"No!" I screamed, lunging after it. But I was too far away, and the jar hit upon the stone that surfaced the road, and it shattered. Suddenly there was water pouring in every direction. Frantically I crawled forward and seized the jar, but it was like a spider's egg that had been stepped upon. All the water was leaking out through the beautiful golden threads of Sumaq's jar and disappearing into the crevices between the rocks.

I placed my forehead upon the damp stone and added my tears. "No! No!"

A sudden blow to my ribs knocked me onto my back. Having kicked me savagely, Kacha stood over me, holding his jaw. Tears of pain could not hide the murderous hate in his eyes. "You filthy dog-eater!" he hissed. "I'll kill you!"

He was mad! He drew back his foot to kick me again, and before I could scurry away, he struck me square on my tailbone, and I was thrown forward. A sharp shard from the broken jar cut deeply into my hand.

Two guards seized Kacha and tried to pull him away. He raged against them, all the while spitting out vile promises of retribution. I knelt upon the stones and cradled my torn hand. Blood pooled in the palm.

And as I watched my blood spill upon the stone pavement, the gods seized my mind. Angry voices continued to rave and curse, a fallen spear clattered upon the stone, but a vision bore me away from the turmoil and freed me from time.

I saw the rapid interweaving of threads not bound to a loom. I knew not which threads were the warp or the weft, nor what pattern was being woven. Vibrant colors entwined, the colors of feathers: red and green, blue and yellow, brown and gray. There was the white of snowflakes and amber like the light that penetrates the jungle forest. A silver mist rose from a waterfall. Streams of black interwove with golden rays of Inti's light and the shimmering motes floating within it.

Voices became part of the fabric:

If you cannot find what you seek, wait. It will find you.

When the gods choose someone to do their bidding, they first make her strong.

Is the water at the end of the world in the sky? Surely, there is no land there. Or is it nearer to Pachamama's sonqo, Lake Titikaka? Nothing is clear. Who is to say where the water begins and where the world ends?

I felt Ipa's bony hand hard upon my chest.

The food you eat, the air you breathe, the water you drink all move to the center, the sonqo, the area of the heart. There the sonqo takes these elements and combines them and moves them outward to the other parts of your body through the blood.

Suddenly the threads were pulled taut, the pattern emerged, and I saw the whole of it. It was as Ipa had always told me, I had the power. I held it in my hand. Then my tears fell all the more, but this time for the wonder of it.

I had found the water at the end of the world!

Part Six

The Water at the End of the World

Chapter 44

A bony hand shook me by the shoulder, and I looked up into the faces of three men: Hatun Rinri, the head guard, and then, to my surprise, the Qollohuayan camasca who once used my offered cloth to wipe vomit from Topa Inca's face. The camasca held me not only by his hand upon my shoulder, but with eyes that seemed to be examining the very workings of my mind. Suddenly, he smiled and with surprising strength, pulled me to my feet. Blood spilt from my torn hand onto my lliqlla, and spattered upon my legs. The camasca took no notice, but hurried me toward the steps.

"Wait!" I twisted out of his grip and ran back to the head guard. "Chumpi was only trying to protect me! He didn't know better. I'm sorry he kicked Kacha, but please, please, don't hurt Chumpi!" I gripped my bleeding hand so tightly, it squirted blood onto the guard's yacolla.

To my amazement, the guard smiled. "Don't worry yourself so, little sister. Look! you're making that poor hand of yours bleed all the more!" He tore wrapping from his spear and began to wind it around my bleeding hand. "No harm will come to your Chumpi; that I promise. Atakachau! The sound of that black-hearted skunk's jaw popping was the sweetest music I ever heard!"

The camasca was back at my side, tugging at my arm. The guard quickly tied off the wrapping. "Now, you go along, and I'll watch after your Chumpi." He chuckled. "Just for seeing that kick, I'll give him a big maize cake come mealtime!"

I was hurriedly pulled up the stairs. The golden door again opened of itself. Inside, I was bustled through a beautiful courtyard toward a great square building with a steep roof of new thatch. In striking contrast to the humble thatch were the building's walls, for they were truly made of gold! Countless figures had been worked into the gleaming metal. As I was pulled past, I caught a glimpse of the image of a puma about to spring upon an unsuspecting deer.

We came to the doorway where the camasca released my arm and motioned for me to remove my sandals. Then he whisked me past two guards and into a room larger than any I could have ever imagined. There were two curtained openings: one directly ahead, one to the left. The camasca pulled back the left curtain and pushed me through ahead of him. The air in this smaller room was warm even though two narrow openings admitted outside air and light. A tall man stood looking out of one of the openings, his features indistinct in the hazy light. The warmth came from a fire, burning in a clay oven set near to where a boy slept upon a chusi. At first, I did not recognize the boy because his face was blotched with angry red blisters. Then I realized it was Topa Inca.

A woman knelt at Topa Inca's feet. She wore a long flowing lliqlla that fanned out on the floor behind her. Upon her head was a woven headdress, which fell about her shoulders, concealing her hair. Yet the magnificence of the woman's apparel was as nothing compared the beauty of her face.

Dirty, disheveled, and bloody, I felt unworthy to look upon her. I tried to fix my eyes upon the floor, but they had a will of their own, and would steal upward to gaze upon the perfect flower that was her face, exquisite even in grief. I realized I must be in the presence of the Coyamama, the wife of the Capac Inca and mother to Topa Inca.

Across from the woman, knelt a man dressed like the wilka camayocs I had seen in the Huacaypata only with the addition of a mantle made from the skin of a jaguar. I suspected he was the Wilka Uma, the high priest. His quiet chanting was the only sound in the room, save that of water trickling unseen.

Standing beside me, the camasca cleared his throat. The Wilka Uma looked up, and suddenly bristled. "What is this?" he demanded.

The man at the window turned toward us, and I recognized the Capac Inca. The Capac Inca addressed the camasca in a strange tongue. Turning toward him, the camasca answered the Capac Inca in the same language. The Wilka Uma stood up and entered into the conversation, which quickly grew heated.

I did not have to understand their words to know I was the subject of their debate. Neither did I need to be told I was unworthy to be in their presence. Yet for all that, it was I who was the chosen instrument of the gods. I had been allotted a power I could feel coursing through my veins. But for how long this power would be mine to use, I did not know.

Unnoticed by the bickering men, I knelt beside the Coyamama. My power made me bold to speak. "How is he?"

Her sudden tears were my answer.

"Here, help me lift him," I said.

Slowly we lifted Topa Inca to a sitting position, and as we did, that part of the chusi which covered him fell away, and I saw red blisters upon his arms. Topa Inca groaned loudly, which brought a stop to the argument going on above me.

"Who do you think you are?" the Wilka Uma shouted, coming to stand over me. "How dare you touch his highness!"

Topa Inca groaned again, his breath coming in small gasps.

The Wilka Uma leaned toward the Coyamama. "Sister, I must respectfully protest. This is unseemly. What could she possibly do that would be of benefit?"

The Coyamama replied in a tired voice. "And what have you done that has been of any benefit?"

"But sis—"

"Leave her alone!" The Coyamama's voice was the snap of a whip. Then she sighed and spoke less sharply. "Let her at least try."

Defeated, the Wilka Uma turned away.

I passed my uninjured hand through Topa Inca's loose unku and placed it upon his fevered chest. A strong tingling traveled along my arm and into my fingers. Topa Inca again cried out, but then he quickly relaxed, and his breathing eased. I spread my fingers and willed his lungs to pull in the air deeply and release it slowly.

I looked to the camasca and pleaded with my eyes for his assistance. He hobbled to my side. "I will need a bowl, shallow, like that used for letting blood."

It was the Capac Inca who responded. From a nearby table, he selected a clay bowl and brought it to me. As I took my hand from Topa Inca's chest to receive the bowl, Topa Inca groaned in protest. Forgetting the bowl which he held, the Inca looked down upon his son. That he loved his son was apparent in his eyes, yet there was also a look of helplessness. I realized that even the mighty are humbled by sickness.

"Wise Father," I said, "I know I am unworthy to be in your presence, yet it is the gods who command it. Now, I must work quickly while their power holds me."

The Capac Inca tore his eyes from his son's ravaged face and placed the bowl into my waiting hand.

"Please, sir, take my place and hold your son."

The Capac Inca knelt down and gently helped the Coyamama support

Topa Inca. Released, I examined the bowl. The inside was stained brown-red from past lettings. It had to be purified for what I was to do. I took the bowl to the oven and placed it upon the flames, praying it would not crack in the heat. I looked about for something to grip the bowl once heated. I saw a stack of small cloths upon a nearby table and leapt to retrieve one. In doing so, I passed the Wilka Uma who glared at me.

Returning to the oven, I used the cloth to lift the bowl from the fire. Leaving it to cool, I knelt at Topa Inca's feet and pulled back the chusi covering his legs. It was as I expected: like his face and arms, his legs were spotted with red blisters. Ipa had taught me that the places of the body had a counterpart upon Pachamama's own body, whose head was the mountains, whose arms, the highlands, whose legs and feet, the lower river valleys. Now I knew why all Tahuantinsuyu suffered, for Topa Inca's sickness involved his entire body.

I stood and walked back to the table where I had seen an obsidian knife. I took it and another piece of cloth and returned to kneel at Topa Inca's feet. The Capac Inca and the Coyamama watched as I carefully pared Topa Inca's toenails. Then I took parings from his fingernails and cut a lock of his hair. All these cuttings I placed upon the flames within the oven. As smoke rose up, I prayed aloud that the gods might carry the smoke to the four quarters where it might heal the land.

"I have already done this!" the Wilka Uma shouted.

I nodded, yet wondered if he had also tried what I was about to do. It was nothing Ipa had taught me, but something based on intuition, or more accurately, upon an idea placed in my mind by the gods. I unwrapped my injured hand and held it over the bowl. Using the knife, I reopened the wound. Pushing along the veins in my forearm, I squeezed out the blood and let it drip into the bowl. When the bowl was half full, I rewrapped my hand.

Standing, I began to slowly circle Topa Inca's body. I dribbled a little of the blood in a circle around him then came to a stop by his head. The old camasca, who had been standing apart, now came forward. He understood what I was about to do. Standing opposite, he bent over and tilted back Topa Inca's head then gently parted his jaws. I brought the bowl to Topa Inca's lips and very slowly began to pour my blood into his mouth.

Both the Wilka Uma and the Coyamama gasped. The Capac Inca seized the bowl, nearly spilling its contents. But Topa Inca, who had swallowed some of the blood, whimpered. For the first time since I entered the room, he opened his eyes.

"More," he whispered.

Hesitantly, the Capac Inca returned the bowl to my hands, and I resumed having Topa Inca drink my blood. Eventually he drank it all. As I used another cloth to wipe Topa Inca's lips, he startled us with a long, satisfied belch. The Coyamama laughed. Her laughter was like music, and in response, Topa Inca smiled. I stole a glance at the Coyamama and saw her eyes sparkling.

"Now I must hold him," I said. I sat cross-legged behind Topa Inca and motioned for the Coyamama and the Capac Inca to release him into my arms. I supported his weight with my body, but before I laid my hands upon him, I addressed the camasca. "Later, I will need fresh roots of taikiji along with hot water to bathe his sores."

"I will prepare it for you," he answered then left the room by an opening opposite to the one we had entered. As he pulled back the curtain that covered it, the sound of trickling water momentarily grew louder.

I pulled Topa Inca tightly to my chest. Though his back was wet with perspiration, he felt not as feverish as before. I threaded my hands through the opening in his unku and held him close. If anything, the tingling in my arms and hands was greater than before. Whatever this power was, I knew Topa Inca was receiving it, and that it was traveling through his body, for his feet began to twitch.

The Capac Inca sensed it also. He touched his son's leg and quickly pulled his hand away. "Atakachau!" he exclaimed.

The Coyamama also gave her son a tentative touch. With a look of astonishment, she too quickly pulled her hand away. As they repeatedly touched their son, I marveled at their playfulness, like two children exploring a small animal they had never seen before. I felt privileged to witness this, yet closed my eyes to better concentrate upon Topa Inca's breathing. I purposely matched my breathing to his, then, with slight pressure of my hands, guided his breathing in slow deep breaths as when sleeping. As our chests rose and fell in unison, I envisioned the great cavern wherein flowed the water at the end of the world. A chill passed through my body which broke the rhythm of our breathing. Topa Inca reacted by moving restlessly in my arms. Willing both our bodies calm, I accepted my return into that great cavern, where, dimly illuminated, the stream of impossibly clear water glided soundlessly over the polished stone.

Oh, how I wished I could have held Topa Inca's feverish body in that cool water! I did what I could; I placed us both there in my mind. Topa Inca drifted just ahead, and as I held his head above water, I felt the slow current pass along from my body to his. It was many things: a power I had been lent; a life force within my blood; a crystalline memory of ancient, dark waters.

The current grew stronger, yet never threatening: a gentle rising and falling. We rose to the crests on each soft intake of breath and lulled in the troughs of our exhalations. We bobbed and drifted until the current gradually weakened, and we were channeled into a still pool.

And there, feeling neither weight nor care, we both fell asleep.

Chapter 45

Slowly, I opened my eyes, squinting against Inti's light, which streamed through openings high in a wall. Alarmed, I sat up, concerned that I had failed to bathe Topa Inca's sores with an infusion of taikiji. Stupid from heavy sleep, I addressed a girl who sat nearby, studying me.

"Where is the Qollohuayan camasca?"

She shook her head and ran from the room by way of a curtained opening. I rubbed my eyes, then leaned back, my hands sinking into cloth wonderfully soft. Turning about, I saw I had been sleeping upon a thick chusi made of vicuña! Occasionally, in the mountains above Qomermoya, I would come upon tufts of this delicate fiber snagged on a branch. I had also seen the fine vicuña garments worn by the Incas. Yet never had I imagined sleeping upon such luxuriant softness.

Suddenly, the curtain was pulled back, and through the opening bounded the girl followed by a tall woman dressed in a pure white lliqlla. She was thin, yet beautiful. A touch of gray in her hair suggested age, but was belied by her remarkably unlined face. Knowing I was in the presence of an important Inca, I quickly rose to my feet and stood looking down at the floor in front of her.

Her voice was strangely low. "Paru, here, informed me you were awake. I trust you rested well."

I nodded, not daring to speak, even though many questions raced through my mind. The woman took my chin in her hand and lifted my head to study my face. Her expression was neither welcoming nor disapproving, more as if she were deferring judgment on the workmanship of a piece of cloth. She released me, and I again dropped my eyes, wondering if I had met with her approval and hoping I had, for she possessed a quality I was drawn to.

"You must have many questions. Later, I will do my best to answer them. But first, I'm sure you would like to bathe. Paru will show you where." The woman turned, and I heard the curtain being drawn back, though I did not hear her light footsteps as she left.

Looking up, I saw Paru smiling at me. She was small and pretty. Her hair was as her name suggested: golden-brown. I had never seen hair of such color, and I wondered if it had been dyed.

"What quarter of Tahuantinsuyu do you come from?" Paru said.

"I believe my village is in Chinchasuyu," I said.

Her eyes widened. "So is mine! Now I can help you bathe!" She grabbed my hand. "Come! Those of us who come from Chinchasuyu bathe in the fountain of pebbles."

I followed her through the opening, but got no farther than the covered walkway that sheltered it before I pulled away from Paru and used both hands to rub my eyes, for I could not believe what I was seeing. Before me was a garden filled with blossoming trees, flowering shrubs, and mosses of brilliant green. Not even in the jungle had I witnessed such an abundance of greenery. In addition, there were birds of every size and color perched upon the tree branches. That they were tame I discovered when Paru succeeded in drawing me forward, for they took no notice of our passing. Yet not all the birds were real. Exact likenesses had been fashioned of gold and silver. Nor were these creations limited to winged creatures, for behind bushes and beneath trees, lustrous animals stared out with bejeweled eyes. We even passed a life-sized, golden puma asleep upon a bed of silver grass.

But sight was not the only sense indulged, for the air was fragrant, and the singing of the birds, sometimes tuneful, other times raucous and shrill, was thrilling to hear. And amidst all the chattering and shrieking and piping, water gurgled merrily. If all this were not enough, rain had recently fallen, and beads of water, touched by Inti's light, glistened like gemstones.

Again, I pulled away from Paru and stood transfixed before a bejeweled butterfly feeding upon a silver, trumpet-shaped flower. "What is this place? I don't remember drinking any potion and entering the land of the spirits."

Paru laughed. "Don't you know where you are?"

I shook my head.

"You're in the Acllawasi."

I was stunned. Of course, I had heard of the Acllawasi, the house of the chosen women. Upon rare occasions, exceptionally beautiful girls from our village were chosen to serve as acllas. But as to how I should come to be here, I knew not. I remembered falling asleep as I held Topa Inca, but nothing between that and waking.

"How did I get here?" I said.

Paru shook her head. "I don't know. I've not been here long, and no one thinks it necessary to tell me anything." She took my hand again and tugged.

"But if I don't get you to your bath soon, they'll punish me by increasing my work load."

Not wishing to cause Paru trouble, I let her lead me away, though I felt as if I could have spent the rest of my life in the garden and never grown tired of its beauty. Thankfully, Paru's destination was not outside the garden, but a small pool located in one corner. It was ringed with short shrubs whose wispy branches, thick with pale blue flowers, trailed into the water. The bottom of the pool was covered with smooth, rounded stones, each one small enough to hide in my hand. But if their size and shape where nearly alike, not so their colors. The stones varied in color from the purest of white to the most vibrant of yellows, blues, even reds. Many were speckled like birds' eggs; others appeared translucent. Though the colors were different, together they were as pleasing to the eye as the intricate patterns of bird feathers or a handful of colored maize kernels.

Two women about my age approached, one carrying a bundle of folded clothes, and the other with three small jars. Like Paru, each woman was beautiful, and by comparison, I felt like a marsh weed set amid three lovely meadow flowers. As the women set down their loads, Paru reached up to pull the topu from my lliqlla.

I pulled away. "What are you doing?"

Paru stepped back, frightened. "I was only trying to help you undress so you could bathe."

"Here?" I said, pointing to the pool. I could not imagine the pool being used for anything so mundane. I looked at the two young women, but they quickly looked away. Still, I felt their contempt of my ignorance.

I closed my eyes and tried to gather my thoughts. Not since a baby had anyone helped me undress. To do so seemed silly. Yet I was in a strange place where women acted differently, and I knew I should not disrespect the customs of others. Neither did I wish to appear an ignorant rustic.

"Very well," I said, leaning forward so Paru could more easily unpin my topu. The topu removed, she began to lift my lliqlla from my shoulders. I turned about so it would be easier for her. As she laid my lliqlla aside, I hurriedly slipped off my two necklaces, noting the women's curiosity as I laid them atop my dirty lliqlla. I was not wearing sandals—I remembered leaving mine outside the Capac Inca's residence—but was not bothered by this, as Paru and the two women were barefoot also.

One of the women motioned me to enter the pool. I did so hesitantly, unwilling to disturb the pool's tranquility. The water was cool, but far less chilly than the streams I was used to bathing in. There was a carved stone for a seat, and I sat down and began to splash water over my shoulders. Seeing ripples of water moving past, I turned and was startled to see that the two women had removed their clothing and entered the water with me. Their bodies were as lovely as their faces. Their hips, shoulders and breasts were softly rounded, their skin unblemished. Seeing the myriad scratches upon my arms and legs, I was overcome by a sense of inferiority.

One of the women dipped her fingers into the jar she held. Reaching forward–as if loath to touch me–she smeared a pasty soap upon my shoulder and began to rub it about.

An unreasonable anger seized me, and I slapped her hand away. Startled, the woman dropped the jar she held. She looked at me with eyes wide before quickly reaching down to rescue the sinking jar. As she straightened up, I saw tears in her eyes. It was then I realized my stupidity. What I had assumed was the disdain of these women was actually fear. For some reason, they were warier of me than I of them. Realizing this, I felt ashamed.

"I'm sorry I slapped your hand. It was mean and inexcusably rude. It's just that, in the presence of your beauty," I motioned to include the others as well, "I feel like a mud hen among snowy egrets."

My apology broke down the barrier between us. The women smiled warmly then began to barrage me with questions.

"Is it true you cured Topa Inca?"

"Is it true you cured him just by looking at him?"

"I heard you turned yourself into a puma and tore the heart out of the evil spirit that possessed his body."

I laughed at the absurdity of this last. Then I explained, as best I could, about the power the gods had lent me. As we talked, I learned their names. The one who had carried the jars was Miski Qapay. I let her spread the flower-scented soap upon my shoulders, back, and legs while Kupa Chukcha, the one who had carried the bundles of clothes, rubbed soap from another jar into my hair. Kupa would not even let me remove the wrapping from my injured hand, but did it for me. Atatau! I shuddered to think what Ipa would say, seeing me now!

I was equally as curious about them and asked many questions about their life in the Acllawasi. I also wanted to know the ingredients of their marvelous soaps. After Kupa rinsed my hair, she rubbed a sweet-smelling oil into it then combed it until it shone like maize silk after a rain.

"I don't believe I've ever been this clean," I told them. "After this, I will hate to put back on my dirty lliqlla."

"There's no need," Miski replied. "We've brought another for you to wear."

I leapt from the water. Miski and Kupa followed, laughing. Paru met me with a towel, and feeling more comfortable with such intimacy, I let her pat me dry. Then Paru unfolded a lliqlla and held it before me. I gasped! It was woven entirely of vicuña! Reverently, I reached out to touch it. It was as soft as the down of a baby bird. As I savored its feel, I also noted the great skill that had gone into its making. Never had I seen such delicate threads, nor ones woven so tightly and evenly.

"This is far too fine for me to wear. Whoever wove it was a weaver without equal!"

"It is my work, I am afraid," Kupa said.

Surprised, I turned to look at her. She looked down at her feet. "They say I have potential to become a good weaver."

"You have more skill than I could ever imagine having." Impulsively, I said, "Would you show me how you keep the pattern so perfectly even?"

"I would be proud to share with you my small skills," Kupa replied.

Paru cleared her throat. I turned and she wiggled her arms to indicate they were getting tired holding up the lliqlla. Voicing my apology, I let her wrap it around me. It felt as nothing against my skin, and I wondered whether I would ever again be content with llama wool.

As Paru began to fasten the lliqlla with a beautiful silver topu, I gently stopped her hand. "The topu is beautiful, but I'd prefer to wear my old one." Reaching down, I retrieved my topu made of tarnished copper. "I know it is not very attractive, but it is special because my father made it for me."

Just then, above the cries of birds and the gurgling of water, came the sound of a drum being struck. It must have been a very large one judging by its low tone.

"Come!" Miski said. "That is the signal for morning meal. Paru will show you where to go."

Hearing this took away some of my pleasure, for though I was not an aclla, I was hoping to share morning meal with my new friends.

Kupa understood my thoughts. "Perhaps this evening we may have the pleasure of your company, but this morning you will be taking your meal with

Acllamama."

I quickly slipped my necklaces over my head then wrapped my hand with a strip of cloth that Miski had thoughtfully provided. The wound was healing nicely. Then as I bent down to pick up my old, dirty lliqlla, Kupa touched my arm.

"Leave it," she said. "I will take care of it. You must not keep Acllamama waiting."

Following Paru back the way we had come, I now saw that the garden was enclosed on all four sides by a high wall. A walkway followed the wall, shaded on three sides by a short roof. The roof also sheltered the many curtained openings in the walls. Paru pulled one aside and motioned me to go before her. Beyond the opening was another garden, a miniature of the one we had just left. The curtain fell behind me, and I realized Paru had not followed. Turning to find out why, I heard a voice call to me.

"Welcome, child."

I spun about and saw the same woman who had so intently examined me earlier. She patted the chusi on which she sat, indicating I should sit beside her. As I sat down, she smiled, evidently pleased at my appearance. I was likewise pleased to be clean and appropriately attired, for it helped to alleviate my discomfort of being in the presence of someone so important.

She offered me a beautiful glazed cup filled with hot tea.

"Atakachau!" I shouted, momentarily forgetting my manners and seizing the cup.

Acllamama reacted to my rudeness with raised eyebrows.

"I'm sorry," I said, "I didn't mean to shout, but it seems forever since I had a cup of hot tea."

"How is it you've been deprived of this drink?"

"I have been traveling far and carrying very little with me."

She nodded. "What is your name, child."

Most strangers reacted curiously to my name, but she did not.

"Well, Yana Mayu, I insist you tell me all about your travels. But first, you must have something to eat. You look as if a little food might do you good."

Acllamama clapped her hands twice, and three girls appeared, each bearing a large silver platter filled with food. They set the platters before us then quickly withdrew. One platter held nothing but meat: slices of llama and strips of guinea pig, but also fresh fish, still sizzling. Another held cakes made of maize and quinoa along with steaming piles of sliced potatoes, peppers, and nasturtium root. The third was filled with nothing but sliced fruit, many of which I did not recognize. I stared at the food in amazement. There was enough to feed a whole village!

Acllamama laughed at my expression. "Don't think we always eat like this. Only when we have special guests. Now, let me serve you."

From a short stack of plates, she took one and filled it with delicacies from each platter. Before handing me the plate, she placed a wide cloth across my lap.

"That is to keep from staining your new lliqlla," she said. She patted my knee. "You look lovely."

Remembering my manners, I willed myself to take small bites of my food. It was one of the hardest things I ever did. I had never tasted food so delicious, and I was so hungry, I wanted to gulp it down.

Acllamama slapped me on the leg. "You pick at your food like a sick person. Eat!"

Abandoning restraint, I stuffed my mouth with tender fish and let the fat dribble down my chin.

"And don't think you have to make conversation," Acllamama added. "My father always said eating was not the time for talking."

When my plate was empty Acllamama replaced it with a full one. "And don't let me catch you with any food left on your plate!" she ordered.

At that moment, I fell in love with Acllamama, not only for her generosity, but for her understanding and her willingness to overlook my manners as I sated my appetite.

When my second plate was empty, she took another from the stack. "More?" she said.

I shook my head. "My mouth says it wants more, but my stomach says my mouth is a liar." My hands were dripping with fats from the meats and juice from the fruit.

"Use the cloth," Acllamama said, pointing to the one she had placed upon my lap. "That's what it's for."

It seemed too fine to soil with my greasy fingers, but I did as ordered.

Looking at all the food remaining, Acllamama sighed. "Perhaps I'll enjoy a few tidbits while you tell me of your adventures." Then she filled a plate for herself.

The three girls reappeared to take away the empty plates and the silver platters.

"Tell Paru to bring us some chicha," Acllamama ordered. Turning to me, she explained, "I expect and rather hope the story of your adventures will take time to tell. You will need the chicha to moisten your throat when it gets dry."

"I hope you won't find my story dull. I'm afraid I'm not a very good storyteller, not like my brother, Charapa."

Though Acllamama smiled, her eyes appeared a little sad. "I'm certain I'll find all you have to say of interest." She slowly swept her arm to call attention to the beautiful garden surrounding us. "As you can see, there are great advantages to being an aclla, but there are disadvantages also. Those who live here either weave or serve in the temples, and consequently see little of the outside world. Sometimes this makes being an aclla feel like one is a bird in a beautiful cage."

Paru appeared with cups and a large jar of chicha.

"You took long enough!" Acllamama scolded.

"I am sorry, Acllamama," Paru said. She stood as if waiting for more instructions.

"Why do you stand there? Leave us!" Acllamama commanded.

Paru began to move away, but ever so slowly.

Acllamama sighed. "I imagine, Paru, that you will try to eavesdrop in order to hear Yana's story, and later I will have to go to the trouble of punishing you."

Paru, trying to look contrite, stared at the ground.

"I'm no longer any good at my job," Acllamama said to me. "I'm far too lenient." She sighed again. "Very well, Paru, you may stay, but don't think you're going to get out of work. Now, sit so Yana can use your back to rest against while she tells us of her adventures."

Smiling, Paru dropped to the ground then pushed her back snug against mine.

Acllamama, pouring the chicha, suddenly stopped. "Paru, there are three cups here!"

Paru didn't say anything. Acllamama, looking irritated, shook her head. But I noticed she filled all three cups. Then taking up her plate of food, she leaned back against a short wall behind her. "Now start at the beginning, Yana, and don't leave anything out. I want to know what kind of trouble you young women are getting into nowadays."

I started with the day the Capac Inca came to visit our village. It was not long before I had to tell of Charapa's imprisonment. It troubled me to have to confess this, but my story would have made no sense otherwise. The telling took longer than I expected, and hearing my own voice, I was surprised by just how much I had experienced. Still my audience did not appear to grow tired of hearing me talk, and when I told of my days spent in the tunnel, I could feel Paru's body trembling. By the time I finished, I had imbibed two cups of chicha, and was well into my third.

"Magnificent," Acllamama exclaimed, with a faraway look in her eyes. She took in a deep breath and let it out slowly. "There, Paru, wasn't that wonderful? Think of the fun you'll have retelling Yana's story to the others. That is after you've swept all the storage rooms as well as the walkways." Acllamama clapped her hands. "Now go!"

Paru sprang up and with a girlish giggle bounded away.

"I really am too lenient," Acllamama said. "I'm sure that even while busy working, Paru will contrive to tell your story to someone. By nightfall, everyone in the Acllawasi will have heard it." She laughed. "And it won't stop there. Though the women here have very little contact with the residents of Qosqo, still news somehow passes between the Acllawasi and the outside world. In three days' time, all of Qosqo will be talking about Yana Mayu."

I shook my head, disbelieving.

"Don't look so humble!" Acllamama's face revealed a hardness which, until that moment, she had kept hidden. "You should be proud of what you did. It took great courage and initiative."

I looked down at the floor. "The gods gave me the courage. They led me and kept me safe."

She yanked my chin up so she could fix her eyes upon mine. "Yes, the gods will lead people, but very few are strong enough to follow." I was frightened by her intensity. Fortunately, she relaxed and smiled. Releasing my chin, she leaned back. "Now, I told you earlier I would answer your questions. I'm sure you have many."

I was grateful she had remembered her offer. "How did I come to be here?"

"That's easy to explain. A guard carried you here, or rather to the entrance to the Acllawasi; men are not allowed inside. It seems you had fallen asleep at the Cora Cora, and they could not wake you. Neither could we. For the rest of the day and through the night, you slept like someone dead."

"But why did they bring me here?"

Acllamama thought for a moment. "I guess someone over there, the Capac Inca or perhaps the Coyamama, thinks highly of you."

"For helping Topa Inca?"

She nodded.

That brought me to my third question. "How is he?"

"Much, much better, thanks to you. Most of us have exhausted ourselves in prayer and worry over Topa Inca, not to mention the copious amount of weaving required for the sacrifices. We were starting to wonder if he would ever die."

I did my best to hide my shock at hearing this flippant comment concerning the descendant of Inti.

"Any more questions?" she said, smiling.

I thought about my brother, Charapa. I wondered if I could go visit him in prison or talk to someone about getting his release, yet I sensed these matters would be better addressed to someone else.

I shook my head. "No, at least, not for now, thank you."

"Well, you're easy to satisfy. Still feel free to come to me if you have any more questions. Now, let me explain a little more about why you're here. I said you were placed here because someone favored you. That is true. But there is more to it than that. In a way, you are now a prisoner."

I started.

"It is for your own good," she quickly added. "I'm sure the Capac Inca, having found someone so successful in treating his son illness, doesn't want her to just go walking off. But more than that, there are others in Qosqo who may not appreciate your intrusion. They may feel jealous of your success. It's for your own good that you are not readily accessible to those people."

I shuddered, thinking of the Wilka Uma who had objected to my presence before Topa Inca. I did not want to be disliked by a man so powerful, though truly I was no threat to him.

"Now, I suggest you return to your room and try to sleep some more. You still look very tired."

I nodded. I did feel tired, though it may also have been the effects of drinking so much chicha. Acllamama began to rise, and I quickly stood also.

"I will show you to your room as I am going that way," she said.

She interlocked her arm with mine and led me back into the main garden.

"You are a very special young woman," she said as we walked. "Perhaps you should become an aclla and stay here with us." Acllamama, feeling me tense, laughed. "It's just a thought. Now, here's your room." She released me and pulled aside a curtain. "Rest well."

The chusi was as soft as I remembered, and now I noticed it was scented with the perfume of flowers as well. As I sank into the luxuriant softness, I thought about what Acllamama had proposed. Was she serious about me being an aclla? And if she were, would I be content to stay here for the rest of my life? I remembered thinking I would be happy to spend my whole life just exploring the magnificent garden, yet realized that was a response to my feelings of the moment. Eventually I would miss my village and the freedom of the mountains. I would miss my family. It was to bring my family back together that I sought the water at the end of the world.

No, the Acllawasi was very beautiful, but I did not want to live in a beautiful cage.

Chapter 46

As I sat in my room in the Acllawasi, Paru suddenly entered. "A man has come for you," she announced. I saw by the angle of the light it was late afternoon.

Paru left and returned with a large bowl, half-filled with water. "To wash your face," she explained.

Kneeling, I rinsed away the effects of my earlier sleep. Sitting back, I patted my face with the soft cloth Paru had also provided, and as I did, Paru gently ran a comb through my hair. Her touch was light, and the comb upon my scalp felt delightful. I could get used to this, I thought.

"Who is this man?" I said.

She repeated a variation of an earlier response. "I don't know. I've not been here long, and no one tells me anything that's important."

I stood up. "I better not keep him waiting."

"First, put these on."

I slipped my feet into sandals so well worked, I knew they would need no breaking in.

We passed out of the main garden and into a smaller courtyard. It was heavily shaded by trees, and beneath these sat many acllas, working upon their looms. All the women seemed beautiful to my eyes. As we passed among them, I noticed a sudden silence followed by excited chatter. Taking possession of my hand, Paru skipped alongside me until we reached another curtained opening on the far side of the courtyard.

"Go through there," Paru said, pointing. I pulled the curtain aside and walked into a small room with a great wooden door opposite. To each side of the door stood a guard. Though the guards were old men, they still appeared to be very strong. I remembered Acllamama saying men were not allowed in the Acllawasi, which made me wonder if I was now outside of it.

"I was told someone called for me," I said.

In response, one of the guards opened the door and motioned for me to pass through. I found myself out upon a road with Inti's light bright in my eyes. I shielded my eyes with my hand and saw to my surprise the head guard from the Cora Cora, and beside him....

"Chumpi!" I rushed forward to embrace my friend, then skidded to a stop a few steps shy.

"Chumpi?"

In response, Chumpi shook his head, making a musical sound.

"I think he wants you to notice his new apparel," the guard said, smiling. "I tidied him up a bit."

That was an understatement. I hardly recognized my friend. His hair glowed as if brushed a thousand stokes. But that was only the beginning of his transformation. He had on a new halter made of bright red yarn. About his neck was a collar from which hung shells, feathers, and small copper bells—the source of the musical sound. But the most outlandish touch was the fact that his ears had been pierced and now bright red tassels hung down over the sides of his face.

Laughing, I pushed aside a tassel. "And I thought you were spoilt before! There'll be no living with you now. Just don't think I'm going to weave tassels for your ears once these wear out."

Chumpi seemed particularly proud of these tassels and flicked them back and forth. Impulsively, I turned to the guard and gave him the hug I had intended for Chumpi.

"There, there, little sister," he said, patting my back. "Remember, I'm captain of the guard, not a llama." Still, he gave me a firm squeeze before releasing me.

"Thank you for taking such good care of Chumpi," I said, tears filling my eyes. "He looks wonderful!"

"I'd say the same of you." The guard stepped back to look me over. "Atakachau! I hardly recognize you. Yesterday, you looked like a ragged starveling. Now look at you!"

I turned about, showing off my new lliqlla. I'm afraid I was as proud of it as Chumpi his ear tassels.

"Your new clothes suit you and befit an important visitor to the Cora Cora, where I must take you now and quickly lest I be demoted to a foot soldier."

I quickly apologized for detaining him.

"Not to worry," he replied. "But come!"

The captain's brisk pace made it difficult for me to talk to him, though I did learn his name: Chukru Makis. As Chukru strode down the road, others were quick to get out of his way, though he did not insist upon their doing so, nor even took notice when they did. Yet I knew that beneath Chukru's formidable military bearing, beat the heart of a thoughtful and kind man, and I wondered if he was someone I could talk to about my brother, Charapa.

We reached the Cora Cora just as Inti was passing behind the western mountains. I was led to the same room where I had treated Topa Inca. Standing just inside, I discerned the Wilka Uma by the light of the oven. He was kneeling next to Topa Inca, letting blood from a vein in Topa Inca's neck.

"I wouldn't do that," I said, stepping forward. Atatau! When would I ever learn to think before speaking?

"Oh, you wouldn't, would you?" the Wilka Uma said, sneering. He quickly looked me over from head to foot. "You think a few fancy togs make you an equal? Look at you! How dare you come before Topa Inca wearing sandals!"

Inwardly, I groaned. I had forgotten to remove them. I quickly kicked them aside. Looking down at the worn stones, I voiced my apology. "Forgive me, wise one. My mouth speaks before it listens to my head. That it is because I am an ignorant Hatunruna. I know I am truly unworthy to be in your presence. Forgive me."

The Wilka Uma appeared somewhat placated by my apology. For myself, I wondered if I had just uttered a lie. I certainly did not hold the Wilka Uma in the same esteem as the Capac Inca. I had only given my apology because I did not wish to be the enemy of such a powerful man, one who, it seemed to me, was not a very good camasca, if he was one at all. Could he not see Topa Inca did not need to be bled? If anything, he needed to be fed blood.

Ignoring me, the Wilka Uma placed a cloth upon the small incision he had made then removed the bowl with blood in it.

"There, your highness," he said, "that should make you feel better." The Wilka Uma cradled the bowl reverently in both hands. "I will personally see this is given to the sacred fire and the proper prayers made." The Wilka Uma slowly stood up, careful not to spill the blood. "I believe it would be wise, your highness, if you did not receive any visitors right now."

Topa Inca shook his head. "I wish to talk to her."

The Wilka Uma shrugged. "Of course, if that is your wish." The Wilka Uma turned to me. "Don't tire his highness!" Then he disappeared into the darkness of the far side of the room. This was a brief admission of twilight as he passed through a curtained opening.

Not sure why I had been summoned, I stood and waited.

"Come here," Topa Inca said.

I approached and knelt beside him. Not wanting to appear disrespectful, yet concerned about his condition, I briefly studied him by the light from the oven. He was obviously tired, yet his appearance showed great improvement. His face was free of the angry, red blisters, as were his arms. Only a few small rashes remained.

Satisfied, I looked down at the floor.

"Look at me." he commanded.

I lifted my head. Topa Inca studied me intently. I turned my head so he could see my face better in the small light.

"It was you," he said. My confusion must have shown, for he added, "The one in my dream." He wrinkled his forehead in concentration. "But I seem to remember you from somewhere else."

I was surprised he remembered. Quickly I took my necklace from beneath my lliqlla and pointed to the yellow feather. "You gave this to me when you visited our village."

He lifted his head to see the feather better. "Did I?" he said, dropping his head back onto his chusi. "I give away many things." He was quiet for a moment, then he smiled. "Atakachau! You're the one who gave me the cloth to–" he circled one finger rapidly in front of his mouth, "when I got so sick."

I nodded, smiling.

"What is your name?"

"Yana Mayu."

"Yes, I remember now." The smile suddenly left his face as something occurred to him. "You're not an Inca," he said.

I hung my head. "I am a Hatunruna," I replied.

"Stop hanging your head so I can look at you!"

I raised my head and looked into his eyes. "Perhaps I look like an Inca because of these clothes I was given to wear."

"It is nothing to do with your clothes. There is something about your eyes. They're old, like my father's. That's why you look like an Inca."

I started to lower my head, but caught myself and instead stared off into the dark side of the room. "I am a Hatunruna, and soon I hope to return to my village to be with my family."

"No!"

The sharpness of his voice startled me. I caught a look of fear in his eyes before he closed them.

"You must not leave, not for a while anyway." He took in a great breath of air and slowly released it. "I thought I was going to die. I dreamt I was walking in darkness." He pulled his chusi up over him. "It was cold, and I was very tired, tired from walking so far. Yet no matter how far I walked, I couldn't escape the darkness, and I kept running into things and hurting myself."

There were tears in the corner of his eyes. Without thinking, I reached forward and took one of his hands. He opened his eyes and looked at me.

"Then you found me. You were carrying a small light. You led me into a great cavern and showed me a pool where I could drink." His eyes sparkled. "The water was cold, and I was so thirsty! I never tasted water so delicious!"

He closed his eyes and smiled, remembering. I closed my eyes and remembered too.

"We went swimming in the pool," he said. "Atatau! It was cold! But I didn't feel afraid because you were there with me. I remember looking down into the water. It was so clear, it was as if I were floating on air!"

For a while he was silent. I opened my eyes and saw him staring up into the darkness.

"Then the pool was no longer a pool, but a great river and we were being swept along in the current. I felt it pull me under, but you reached out and held me up. Then we floated out of the darkness and into Inti's light." He turned to look at me. "That's when I woke up and found myself here, and you were holding me, only you had fallen asleep." He gave my hand a squeeze. "Tell me, was it all just a dream?"

"It was more than a dream. During your illness, your spirit decided to travel." I told him what Ipa had told me about the underground road which people travel to be reborn. I also mentioned about my finding the water in the tunnel.

"You traveled in a tunnel?" He jiggled my arm. "Tell me more!"

His eagerness reminded me of one of the children of Qomermoya, always begging Ipa to tell them a story. I realized that even though Topa Inca was the Capac Inca's son and the descendant of Inti, he was also just a boy much like any other.

I looked at him closely. Remembering the Wilka Uma's warning, I wondered if it was wise to excite him. "When was the last time you ate something?"

Now he was truly a boy, pouting. "I'm not hungry."

"You must eat if you're going to get well. A nice tender piece of llama."

He made a face. "I don't like llama. I don't like guinea pig either."

What was this? A boy not liking meat? "Well, I want you to eat a nice big piece of llama, just barely cooked, still bloody."

He made another face then said, "Well, maybe I could eat a little fish. I like fish."

I shook my head. "No, llama, and bloody."

He lifted himself up. "Who are you to order me? You're just a Hatunruna! I'll eat what I want!"

It was true. He was Topa Inca, the heir to the throne, and I but a fancy-dressed Hatunruna. But I was older than him, and since he insisted upon acting like a spoilt little boy, I decided to treat him like one.

"Would you like to hear how the birds led me to the entrance to the tunnel. It was behind a waterfall!"

His eyes lit up. "Yes! Yes!"

"Then you'll have to eat llama, bloody."

"I can order you to tell me the story!" he countered.

I pulled my hand from his and cupped it around my ear. "Did you hear that?"

He listened a moment. "I don't hear anything."

"I'm sure I heard someone calling my name. I had better go."

I started to stand, but he grabbed my hand. "Please, Yana, don't go! Tell me about the waterfall!"

I hesitated.

"I'll eat llama."

I raised my eyebrows.

"All right, bloody!" he said, gritting his teeth.

I knelt back down. "Good. It will make you feel better."

Now that I had my little victory, I realized I did not know how to go about having food brought to Topa Inca. Then in the back of the room the curtain was pulled back, and someone passed to the outside. A sudden chill passed through my body. Someone had been sitting in the back of the room, listening. He had heard everything that had passed between Topa Inca and myself.

I looked at Topa Inca, but he just shook his head. He either did not know who it was, or was not telling.

The curtain was again swept aside, and a woman entered holding a lit candle. I had not often seen candles, which were made from llama fat, a food too precious to waste on candles. The woman held the curtain back while two other women entered, both carrying trays of food. They set the trays down beside Topa Inca along with a silver jar containing chicha then quickly withdrew, leaving the candle for us to see by.

Topa sat up then selected a slice of llama and bit into it. "Mm, good!" he exclaimed, feigning enjoyment.

"But not very bloody," I said, laughing.

He finished chewing then swallowed. "Actually, this is not so bad. I must be hungrier than I thought."

I nodded, pleased to see him eating the meat and enjoying it.

He reached for another piece of llama, then stopped. "Join me."

I shook my head. "I don't think it would be right for me to eat with you, your highness."

He made a face. "Don't call me that! Only my uncle, the Wilka Uma, calls me that." He leaned forward and whispered. "I don't like him."

I did my best to keep my face expressionless, yet inwardly was glad we both felt the same way about the Wilka Uma.

"Now eat!" he said, waving the meat in his hand.

"Is that an order?" I said, smiling.

"It is a request," he said, smiling in return. "Orders don't seem to work very well with you."

I picked up a small potato and bit into it. I was hungry even though I had stuffed myself at morning meal. Topa did not talk while we ate. I was pleased to see he had an appetite, especially for the meats. I left them for him while I enjoyed the potatoes, maize cakes, and fruit. I realized if I continued to eat like this, I would soon regain all the fat I had lost and then some.

When he was satisfied, Topa pushed aside the trays. Taking up the jar, he poured chicha into two small golden cups then offered one to me. I was heavy from the food and knew if I also drank chicha, I would get sleepy. Still I wanted to hold the cup because it was made of actual gold. It was polished to a shine and was as smooth as ice, though without the cold. Topa drank deeply, then, setting his cup aside, emitted a big, satisfying belch.

"Now tell me about the waterfall," he said.

"First let me straighten your chusi so you can lie down and be comfortable." I set down the cup and began to brush the crumbs of food from his chusi. As I did, the curtain in the back of the room again opened and closed. I suspected that our earlier, unseen visitor had returned. This troubled me, yet I also felt a little excited, for I realized another person—perhaps an important one—would also hear of my adventures, and that might be to my advantage later.

I looked down at Topa, now lying upon his chusi. "Do you want to hear about the waterfall, or should I tell you of all my adventures starting at the beginning?"

"Are they very interesting?"

"Well, I did encounter a dragon."

"No!"

"Yes! A dragon and dancing rocks and pink birds, and I nearly fell from a bridge into a deep chasm and—"

"Yes! Yes! Tell me everything!"

"It will take a very long time, and I certainly won't get to the waterfall tonight."

"That's all right. That means you'll have to return."

I smiled. "Well, my story really begins when you and the Capac Inca came to visit our village. All the people of my village were—"

"Yana?"

"Yes, Topa?"

"Will you hold me like you did in my dream?"

"Of course."

He sat up and I moved to sit cross-legged behind him. I pulled him tight into my chest. Some of the tingling was there in my hands and fingers, though not as strong as the day before. Topa sighed.

"Are you comfortable?" I said.

He nodded.

"All right. Now, where was I? Oh, yes. It all started on the day you and your father came to our village...."

Thus began my telling to Topa Inca of my adventures. I did not get very far that evening, for he soon fell asleep. For a while, I continued to hold him, feeling the gentle rise and fall of his chest. It was comforting and made me sleepy. But I did not want to fall asleep again and have to be carried like a baby to the Acllawasi. Slowly, so as to not wake him, I gently lowered Topa then tucked his chusi tightly around him. I found my sandals and, carrying them, tip-toed to the entryway.

Outside stood a guard, someone other than Chukru Makis.

"Topa Inca is asleep," I whispered.

He nodded. "I will escort you back to the Acllawasi."

I wished Chukru had been my escort, for I wanted to talk to him about Charapa. To this other guard, I said nothing. As we walked along the road, Qillamama's bright face was intermittently revealed by the clouds that raced before her. A chill wind carried moisture with it, a sure indication that rain was imminent.

At the entrance to the Acllawasi, the guard pounded on the door with his fist. It was slowly opened by one of the old men I had seen earlier. Words were passed that I could not hear, then my escort motioned for me to enter. I said nothing to the guards, but quickly passed into the inner courtyard where I saw Paru sitting upright, asleep. A candle, half consumed, burned beside her.

"Paru?" I said, gently shaking her shoulder.

She was slow to awake.

"I am sorry if I have kept you up," I said.

"That's all right," she replied. "I am not important. It is nothing that I should have to clean the Acllawasi all by myself then stay up half the night."

I smiled. I did not remind her that it was not all that late. I was beginning to wonder if Paru was going to like being an aclla. She did not seem quite to fit in.

"Did you see Topa Inca again?" she said.

I nodded.

"Tell me about it!"

"Perhaps tomorrow. I think it is time we were both asleep."

Sighing, Paru picked up the candle. "This way."

To my surprise, there was another candle burning in my room. Paru set hers down and started to help me undress.

"I can do that myself. I've kept you awake long enough."

She gave me a grateful smile and took up her candle. Pausing near the entrance she said, "You will tell me about your visit with Topa Inca, won't you?"

I nodded. "Tomorrow, if I can."

I waited until she was gone then blew out the candle. It seemed an extravagance to waste it. I could certainly undress in the dark.

Chapter 47

It was my second day as "prisoner," and I did not know what would be required of me. I drank tea with the other women, then accompanied them as offerings were made to the gods whose images were set in a special huaca within the garden. In honor of Urcuchillay, there was an exact likeness of a vicuña made entirely of gold. Urcuchillay was particularly revered in the Acllawasi, for he watched over the vicuñas that provided the delicate wool for the fine cloth.

Offerings were also made to a lovely wooden carving of Pachamama holding an ear of maize nearly as big as she was. Acllamama also said a prayer, thanking Intuillapa for the much-needed rain that had again fallen in the night. Looking up, I saw dark clouds that promised more rain still.

After these observances, Kupa led me to a small room where her weaving materials were kept. But she had no sooner started instructing me in the finer techniques of weaving then Paru came to tell me I had another visitor.

"It's bad enough I have all my work to do," she grumbled on the way toward the entrance, "but I also have to be your message deliverer and escort."

"That's because you're new here," I replied "and are not important."

Paru spun around, a look of hurt upon her face. Seeing that I was only teasing her, she laughed along with me.

"I know I complain too much," she said, taking my hand. "I'm sorry."

"Don't be. It is I who should be sorry for taking up your valuable time." We had arrived at the courtyard beyond which was the entrance to the Acllawasi. "I now know the way to the entrance, so you won't need to escort me from now on."

She clung to my hand. "Oh, I don't mind, really," she said, then added in a low voice, "It's all the work that I object to." She spoke as if the maintenance of the entire Acllawasi were her sole responsibility.

I thought how much Paru reminded me of my brother Charapa. Perhaps that was why I was drawn to this precocious child.

"Remember," she said, "you are going to tell me about your visit last night with Topa Inca."

"If I am able," I replied.

The guard at the entrance opened the door as I approached. I was hoping my visitor would be Chukru Makis accompanied by Chumpi, but it was the old, Qollowayan camasca along with two guards.

"Come with me," he ordered.

We walked until we reached the river where we sat down beneath a large huayau tree. The guards stood apart from us, looking attentively about, though there was no one else I could see. The river was the same one I had washed in my first morning in Qosqo. It was not sluggish now, but swollen from the recent rains. The half-submerged taikiji quivered in the swift current.

I slapped my forehead. "I forgot to treat Topa Inca's sores with an infusion of taikiji!"

"Do not worry," the camasca said. "I did it. In fact, I have been treating his sores with taikiji every day for the last two months, but it was not until you came that he showed any signs of getting better."

"How is he?"

"His improvement is nothing short of miraculous."

He turned away from me and studied the water flowing past. I followed his gaze. The rain, which had swollen the river, was much needed, and I hoped it was falling upon the fields of Qomermoya as well.

"How is it you came to have this power?" the camasca said.

I turned to look at the camasca, who studied my face as I talked. "I suspect I've always had it."

"Has it always been so strong, like when you first placed your hands upon Topa Inca?"

I shook my head. "No, nothing like that. I believe this power was awakened in me by the water I found in a great cavern, though I am not sure how this could be."

"Is it the same water you had in the jar, the one that was broken?"

I nodded.

"Where did you find this water?"

Knowing he did not care to hear all of my adventures, I only related to him my experiences in the tunnel. When I finished, he nodded, as if my telling had explained something to him.

"You discovered a great achachila," he said.

Occasionally, Ipa had spoken of achachilas. They were special, sacred places of great power. Yet an achachila was not just a place, but a living force with its own personality. Ipa always talked of an achachila as if it were a person.

"Did you meet anyone else in the tunnel?" he said.

I shook my head.

"Were there signs that others had been there recently?"

"It seemed no one had visited there in a very, very long time. I saw no footprints and dust was upon everything."

The camasca rubbed his forehead, looking disconcerted.

"What troubles you, Father?" I said.

"An achachila that is not cared for soon loses his power. An achachila must be fed and certain rituals performed in order to keep him strong. When an achachila is neglected, he becomes angry and will hurt those who approach him."

"So why was I not hurt? Why was I given this power?"

"I don't know, and that is what troubles me."

It was then I remembered the giant in the cave. "There was someone else in the cave, though he was no longer living. I found a giant sitting in the center of the tunnel not far from the place of the water. I think he had been there a long time, warning travelers not to enter the tunnel he guarded."

"A giant, you say?"

"Yes, I could look directly into his eyes, even though he was sitting, and I was standing."

The camasca was clearly excited. "Before Wiraqocha created man, he created a race of giants. Perhaps the man you saw was one of those. Perhaps it is his spirit that guards the water and keeps the achachila from becoming angry." He nodded. "You have given me much to think about. I must go to this place soon so that I can learn more about it. When you are able, I would like you to take me there."

I shuddered.

The camasca noticed my reaction. "What bothers you about this request?"

"The tunnel holds great terror for me. I was hoping I would never have to enter it again."

"Perhaps it would not be necessary for you to enter the tunnel. Is the entrance very hard to find?"

"Yes, but only because it is hidden by thick bushes." I gave him directions for finding the tunnel, concluding, "I made a fire of the remaining burning stones to thank the gods for delivering me from the darkness. The remains of the fire may still be there, though the recent rains might have washed them away."

He sat very still, thinking. Finally, he spoke. "Perhaps I will go there without you. Something tells me it is important that I do this soon, and you may be a long time taking care of Topa Inca. There are certain soldiers who can track the footsteps of others even after a rain. I will take one of those with me."

Having made this decision, he stood up. "Come," he commanded. "I will take you back to the Acllawasi."

I stood and waited for him to lead the way. Instead he placed one hand upon my shoulder. "The gods are wise, yet that day, outside the Cora Cora, when I first looked into your eyes and saw what lay behind them, I was surprised that they had entrusted so much to one so young. Yet hearing of your experience in the tunnel, I now understand. It is not just courage you possess, but love. You love the gods and honor them. Yet I sense it was for the love of another that you undertook this burden."

I nodded. "In a way, it is because of you I was forced to seek the water." I explained about Charapa hearing the voice in the fire when the camasca performed his healing ceremony in Tambo Puquio, and how Charapa's going to look for the water at the end of the world resulted in his imprisonment. "The desire to change his own life was what tempted Charapa to search for the water at the end of the world. Yet surely imprisonment was not the type of change he was looking for." I sighed. "My brother Charapa has always been a dreamer. That is why he got in so much trouble."

The camasca shook his head. "Your brother is not the dreamer. You are."

"I do not understand."

"There are two types of people in this world. There are the dreamers, and there are those who are dreamed upon. Dreamers work to bring about something good of their dreams. Those who are dreamed upon think they are dreamers when in fact they are caught in the web of another's dream. For them, nothing turns out as expected.

"But now, let us go. I want to talk to someone about finding a tracker."

As I followed the camasca back to the Acllawasi, I thought about what he had said. I had never thought of myself as a dreamer, and wondered if the camasca was not mistaken. I also realized the camasca was the second person

I had told about my brother, yet neither he nor the Acllamama had offered to help make contact with him, even though it was obvious that his freedom was my great concern. I hoped I would get a better response from Chukru Makis, if and when I got an opportunity to talk to him.

Within the Acllawasi, I once again resumed my weaving lesson with Kupa. Part of her success was the vicuña wool she used, for it was much finer than llama wool and spun into a very delicate thread. Suggesting that I should begin by spinning this soft fiber, Kupa gave me a basket filled with carded vicuña wool and the use of a drop spindle. Since the rain had held off, I took these into the garden and spent the rest of the morning and most of the afternoon spinning. It was very pleasant work, for not only was I surrounded by beauty, but I was doing something useful.

Late in the afternoon, the rains came again. I hurried from the garden and returned the spindle to Kupa along with two balls of spun vicuña. In response to my request to assess the quality of my work, she unwound a long section of thread. I immediately saw a tiny lump in the thread made by a burr that I had failed to remove. Kupa was kind enough not to comment upon this.

"Before I was chosen to be a aclla," she said, "I lived in a small village noted for the quality of its woven cloth. To maintain this reputation was a great incentive for me, and I spent many hours combing and combing the llama wool in order to have long fibers to spin into thin thread." She began to rewind the thread I'd spun. "But never did I get nearly so fine a thread as the very first time I spun vicuña."

"It is a wonderful fiber." I ran my hand down the front of my lliqlla. "I've have only worn this for little more than a day, yet I wonder if I could wear anything else."

"I know exactly what you mean." She handed me a ball of yarn. "Here is some thread I have recently spun."

I unrolled an arm's length. "Atakachau!" I exclaimed "This is wonderful!" The thread was as slender as a spider's and as perfectly even. By comparison, mine looked like coarse rope. "And I thought I had done well!"

Kupa smiled. "For the first time working with vicuña, you did very well. I'm sure my first efforts were not nearly as good."

I doubted that, but appreciated her tact, nonetheless.

It was then we were interrupted by my message bearer.

"I've been told that the captain of the guard is here to see you again,"

Paru said.

I thanked Kupa for her instruction, then quickly made my way toward the entrance, anxious to have an opportunity to speak to Chukru Makis about my brother. Paru skipped along beside me, even though I had told her it was no longer necessary for her to accompany me. As I drew back the curtained opening that led into the guardroom, I chanced to look back. Paru stood looking at me wistfully. I was reminded of two other children, Imayoq and Huchuq Uma, who had accompanied me as far as they dared along the road to Pisac. I did not wave to Paru, as I had to Imayoq and Huchuq Uma, for that would have seemed to say that I was going where she could not. In fact, even closing the curtain behind me seemed hurtful.

Outside it was raining steadily and Chumpi, though still attired in his finery, did not look nearly so elegant, for his wet ear tassels drooped sadly. Chukru Makis permitted me a few moments with my friend. I offered him a nice piece of nasturtium root, saved from morning meal. To my astonishment, Chumpi turned his nose up at it.

"Atatau! What have you been eating that you would turn down a such a nice tidbit?"

I looked at Chukru Makis, who quickly looked away "There were a few maize cakes left over from the guards' morning meal," he said, then cleared his throat. "Not many. Five... maybe ten, something like that, I forget."

I laughed then poked Chumpi playfully in the stomach. "Between your maize cakes and my vicuña clothes, both of us will be very unhappy to return to the simple life of our village." I reached up and squeezed water out of Chumpi's ear tassels.

"Let us go," Chukru Makis said. "We must not keep Topa Inca waiting." He smiled broadly. "Word has it he's been clamoring all day for you to come and tell him more of your adventures."

As I hurried to keep step with Chukru Makis, I summoned the courage to ask about my brother. "Chukru, do any of your duties concern prisoners?"

Looking straight ahead, he replied. "No, thank Inti. Nasty work, that." Then he turned and looked at me. "Why do you ask?"

I began to explain about Charapa, and as I did Chukru's steps slowed. Still, we were almost to the Cora Cora by the time I concluded. For the rest of the way, Chukru said nothing, and I wondered if by telling him about my brother I had overstepped the bounds of our new friendship.

He pointed the way up the steps to the golden door. "You know the way," he said, looking distracted. As I mounted the steps, I felt a heaviness in my heart that more than matched the gloom of the gathering darkness. The great door opened, and I trudged on towards the entrance to Topa Inca's chamber. No sooner had I removed my sandals and entered his room than Topa Inca called out to me.

"Watch!" he said, pointing to a slice of llama, dripping with blood. Topa stuffed the bloody meat into his mouth and chewed vigorously. The meat consumed, he let out a tremendous belch.

I laughed. He was obviously in good humor, and this did much to dispel my sadness, that and the fact that Topa Inca's uncle, the Wilka Uma, was nowhere to be seen.

"I am pleased to see you are feeling so much better," I said, sitting down.

"I feel great!" he said, popping a small potato whole into his mouth. "Atatau!" he cried. "Hot!" To cool his tongue, he drank chicha straight from a silver pitcher. With chicha dribbling down his chin, he motioned me to join him in eating.

I chose a piece of llama meat and slowly chewed it. I was glad to note my appetite was beginning to return to normal. Still, I enjoyed Topa's food, for the women who prepared it were excellent cooks. We ate in companionable silence, and I was gratified to see Topa not only devouring most of the llama, but seeming to relish it. When he was sated, he poured chicha into the two golden cups and offered one to me. I took a sip to clear my throat, preparing to resume the story of my adventures.

But to my surprise, Topa did not ask to hear more of the story, but to see the yellow feather he had given me. I took off my necklace and handed it to him. He examined the yellow feather very closely, rubbing it with his fingers.

"You haven't taken care of it!" he scolded.

"I am sorry, Topa. Someone told me I should rub oil into the feather to keep its luster. I will do that as soon as I can."

Topa shook his head. "I think it's too late for that. I think I should throw it away."

Without thinking, I pulled the necklace from his hand. Topa looked startled and not a little angry.

Ashamed, I hung my head. "I am sorry, Topa. Once again, I have acted without thinking. It's only that the feather is very precious to me, and even though it is not as it once was, I would be very sad to part with it."

Topa smiled. "Perhaps what the feather needs is some company."

I looked up and gasped. Topa held a necklace of not just one feather, but hundreds, and not just yellow, but all the colors I had seen on the birds at the mineral lick.

"It is a gift," he said. "Put it on."

Trembling, I took it from his hands. It was more of a collar than a necklace, for the cord that bound the feathers was just long enough to encircle my neck.

Topa nodded, looking pleased. "It looks very nice on you."

I gently stroked the feathers with my fingers. "I am unworthy of such a gift."

"You are worthy," he replied. "and also, you are my friend."

I smiled. To be considered his friend was more precious to me than the beautiful necklace.

He opened a polished wooden box in which a circular depression had been carved. "This is to keep the necklace in when you're not wearing it."

I started to remove the necklace, but Topa shook his head. "Leave it on. I want to look at it as you tell me more of your story." He set the box aside then leaned forward anxious for me to begin.

I started where I had left off the night before. As when I told my story to Acllamama, the telling took time, and more so now, for I included more details which I thought Topa might find interesting. As he listened to how I nearly fell from the bridge, he picked at his unku nervously until he had made a little mound of fibers on the floor. And when I described how I eventually reached safety, he clapped his hands together, delighted.

Then I told him how I was forced to spend the night in the company of prisoners, and how I was protected by general Kuntur. At the mention of the general's name, there was a brief rustling at the back of the room, and I realized, once again, I had a hidden listener.

"I've heard about general Kuntur," Topa said. "He was one of my father's best generals."

I wondered why if general Kuntur was one of his father's best generals he had been sent to the coca plantation. But of more immediate concern was the identity of the listener hidden in the darkness. What if he were the Capac Inca? How would he react to my favorable comments concerning the general? Perhaps I would be better off not to mention the general again. Yet this seemed a betrayal of the man who had befriended me. I decided it was best that I tell my story the way it happened and live with the consequences.

By the time I told Topa how I crossed the mountain pass and descended into the jungle forest, it was getting late, and though Topa's face still reflected a keen interest, his body sagged with fatigue. Briefly I told him of the bird who made himself to resemble the dead tree and showed him the feather the bird had dropped for me to find.

"And now I think it is time you went to sleep," I said.

"No! tell me more!"

"I would not be a very good camasca if I let you get overly tired." I realized it was the first time I had ever used the word "camasca" in reference to myself.

Topa pouted, but did not put up much resistance. I think he suddenly realized how tired he was.

"You still haven't told me about the waterfall," he said, lying down.

"Tomorrow," I promised, as I pulled his chusi up around him. I removed my necklace and carefully laid it within the box that was made for it. Then carrying my magnificent gift, I quietly left the room. Outside of Topa's room was not the guard who had met me the night before, but Chukru.

"Put on your sandals and follow me," he commanded.

The gloom descended upon me again, for Chukru seemed not the kind protector so fond of Chumpi. He led me across the road where there were many smaller buildings. Lifting back the curtain that covered the entrance to one of these, he motioned me to precede him.

"Try to be quiet," he said in a whisper, "the others are sleeping."

Though it was too dark to see, I heard the sound of men snoring.

Chukru took me by the arm. "This way," he whispered. He pulled back another curtain to reveal a smaller room lit by the light of a candle. As I entered, Chumpi, who had been lying in one corner, stood up.

"Chumpi!" I said, much too loudly. I put my arms around his neck, drawing comfort from his familiar smell. I looked at Chukru whose stern demeanor had been replaced with a look of embarrassment.

"Well, I couldn't very well have Chumpi sleeping outside on a night like this, could I?"

My thanks was answered with a brief nod. He motioned for me to sit down then he joined me, leaning up against the wall opposite.

"It's been a busy night," he said, wiping the rain from his face with his hand. "I had my men going to all the prisons."

My heart began to hammer in my chest.

"There are more than you might think," he continued. "The upshot of it was what I expected. Your brother was not in any of them."

Thinking the worst, I covered my face to hide my sudden tears.

"Don't take on so!" he said. "That your brother is not in any prison is good news."

I looked up. "Doesn't it mean he's been executed?"

"Executed! What for? A little thing like thinking some water had special curing powers? The Capac Inca is a just ruler and he instructs those who serve him to mete out punishments in accordance to the nature of the crime." He chuckled. "The problem is there's been so many others just like your brother. Nearly as many as fleas on a llama." He quickly added, "Not on Chumpi, of course."

I shook my head. "I don't understand."

"Do you think that your brother was the only one who thought he had found the water at the end of the world?"

"But few knew about it."

"Few? Everyone in Tahuantinsuyu had heard of the water that would cure Topa Inca. The jails have been packed with these charlatans, even though the judges have been passing sentences upon them almost every day."

"Sentences?" I said.

He shrugged. "Usually doesn't amount to much. Just a whipping on the back of the legs with a stout rope. Just enough to give the offender something to remember on his long walk home. To my way of thinking, we ought to have met every jar-toting youth that entered the city and given them a whipping right then and there. Saved the trouble of jailing and feeding them."

"So where is my brother?"

"Home in your village, I imagine. I found a jailor who remembered Charapa because he was one of first to claim he'd found the water at the end of the world. The jailor remembers your brother hanging around after his punishment was given. At bit of a nuisance he was, though the jailor liked him well enough. Gave him a job, taking care of other prisoners, which lasted until someone from your village came to fetch him."

Suddenly, I felt dizzy. I leaned forward, nearly falling on my face.

Chukru reached out an arm to support me. "What's the matter, little sister?"

I could not help the sob that broke from my lips.

"There, there," Chukru whispered, "what's to carry on about? Your brother's safe now, and all has worked out for the best."

But Chukru did not know what all I had gone through: being buried under rock, days spent in the darkness and cold of the tunnel, all the loneliness, all the fear. And for what? I could have just as well have stayed in Qomermoya.

If you cannot find what you seek, wait. It will find you.

Oh, why hadn't I just waited in my village? Charapa would have come home, and I would have been spared all the pain and struggle.

Then I remembered the words the camasca had spoken earlier about those who are dreamers and those who are dreamed upon.

Wiping my eyes, I sat up. "The camasca was wrong. I am not a dreamer."

"Eh?"

But I did not share with Chukru my thoughts, that it was I who had been caught in another's dream, only in my case, it was the dream of the gods. And as the camasca had said, nothing turns out as expected when caught in another's dream.

"I should have just stayed in my village!" I said.

Ignoring this, Chukru picked up the box that held the necklace and opened it. "Atakachau! This is a pretty thing." He passed a rough finger across the feathers then closed the box and set it aside. "Well, Yana Mayu, I, for one, am glad you didn't stay in your village."

I shrunk back a little as his eyes bore into mine.

"I saw you the day that blackguard kicked you out there on the road. I saw how he hurt you. But then I saw the look that came in to your eyes. The gods gave something to you, and it wasn't just to get your foolish brother out of jail.

"And look what's come of it! Topa Inca is like a boy reborn. And because of that the rains have come, and soon the crops will grow, and there will be plenty of food in the colcas again. No, I'm glad you left your village." He pointed to the box containing the necklace. "And it looks like someone else is glad, too. And if all this isn't enough, if you hadn't come, I'd not have had the chance to share my room this evening with Chumpi."

I stifled a laugh so as not wake the other guards. Smiling, Chukru stood then reached down to help me up. "Now, I better be getting you back to the Acllawasi."

I held onto his hand. "Thank you for finding out about my brother.

Knowing he is safe relieves me of the worry I have carried for a very long time."

Chukru nodded and tried to pull away, but I would not let go.

"When I first came to Qosqo, I thought it a very unfriendly place. But I met a woman who told me I was wrong. Having met you, I now know she was right."

He smiled, gave my hand a pat before pulling his free. As we moved to leave, Chumpi, who had lain down again soon after we had entered the room, made motions to stand up. Chukru pointed a warning finger at him. "You stay right there! I don't want to have to dry you off two times in one night."

Walking back in the rain, thinking about what Chukru had said, I felt ashamed that I should have felt anger toward the gods. Truly Topa Inca's recovery was more important than anything Charapa and I had endured. Yet Chukru had also reminded me there had been more at stake than Topa's recovery. Topa's body and that of Pachamama were as one; one could not be sick without the other being also. And now, like Topa Inca, Pachamama was returning to health. I tilted back my head to feel the rain upon my face, certain it fell not only upon Qosqo, but upon all Tahuantinsuyu. For this, I said a prayer of thanks.

We arrived at the Acllawasi and Chukru banged on the door. "I'll be picking you up tomorrow, same as usual," he said, then added, "I'll be bringing you back as well. I'm wanting to hear what's going to happen when you find that waterfall."

I suddenly had a picture of Chukru standing outside Topa Inca's chamber his ear to the curtain. "You were listening?"

Chukru smiled. "Well, perhaps I didn't spend all evening checking out reports from the prisons."

Chapter 48

My days settled into a routine. During the morning and afternoon, I practiced spinning and weaving under Kupa's tutelage, and each evening, just before Inti passed behind the western mountains, Chukru came to escort me to the Cora Cora.

After a few more visits, I finished telling Topa of my adventures. Then he insisted I start all over again. The retelling took even longer, for he peppered me with questions about the most insignificant details. His was an active and probing mind, and I was challenged to gratify it. Yet Topa was also a cheerful boy, much inclined to laughter and relentless teasing. He nicknamed me Pallqa Wawa, meaning baby fingers, as if I were the one who had dropped Sumaq's jar on the day Chumpi had kicked Kacha. With a pout, he accused me of purposely depriving him of a taste of the mysterious water, then laughed at my frustrated reaction. Yet his ceaseless questioning about the breaking of the jar and what happened afterward showed me that even his keen mind was having difficulty making sense of it all. These were not matters I could help him with, for they remained a mystery to me as well, even though I often pondered them as I sat in the garden of the Acllawasi with my spindle.

Yet it thrilled me to hear Topa's infectious laughter–even if I was the object of it–for it showed me just how well he was feeling. Only his tendency to tire easily indicated he was not completely restored to health.

All told, my life was very pleasant. Nevertheless, I grew restless. It seemed I was always behind walls, and I longed to go out and explore Qosqo. I mentioned this to Acllamama, but she shook her head and told me it was still not safe for me to be wandering outside the walls of the Acllawasi.

One clear morning, I took my spindle and went to the garden. I sat upon my favorite rock next to the wall, out of the wind. The air was chill, but beneath Inti's light, I was comfortable. The quality of my work was improving, and Kupa had entrusted me with vicuña wool dyed red using the juice of the insects that live on penka, a succulent plant which grew on rocky hillsides where little else grew. As my spindle revolved, I tried to think of ways to color the story of my adventures so Topa would not grow tired of it. While thus absorbed, I heard an ocarina's sweet voice carried by the wind over the wall. The familiar melody drew my thoughts back to the day I was in Tambo Toco during the celebration of Urpito's recovery.

I took my eyes from the spindle and listened more carefully, for I knew the melody. Suddenly the ocarina stopped, and a well-remembered voice began to sing.

> Two doves,
> Two snow-white doves,
> Winging the skies as one—

I sprang from my seat, sprinted down the walkway that bordered the wall and flew across the small courtyard, startling the astonished acllas at work at their looms. I surprised the guards with my speed and had the door open before they could stop me. I raced along the wall and tore around the corner. Then I saw him still singing to the silent wall.

Anka turned at the sound of my footsteps, and I threw myself into his arms. He spun me around in circles. Our chins touched and we rubbed them together. Our passion shocked us, and for a moment we separated, wide-eyed with the wonder of it. Then we laughed and joined hands and danced merry circles to the beating of our joyous hearts. A Hatunruna and an Inca cavorting shamelessly in the public eye! I did not care. In truth, I did not even think about it, for we were two doves reunited.

The appearance of a sturdy figure recalled us to the ongoing world. We looked into the stern face of one of the guards.

"I was not supposed to leave the Acllawasi," I explained to Anka.

In response, Anka held me tightly, his eyes defying the guard to intervene. The guard took a step forward, and, fearing a confrontation, I gently removed Anka's protective arm.

"Walk back with me," I said, taking his hand.

Reluctantly Anka let me lead him, the guard following close behind. As we approached the entryway to the Acllawasi, the door suddenly flew open, and there was Acllamama along with the second guard. When she saw me, her look of worry turned to one of anger.

"Yana, I told you not to leave the Acllawasi!"

Her commanding presence did not intimidate Anka. "I am Anka," he announced. "My father is an important amauta at the Yachawasi. How is it that Yana has been made an aclla?"

The two faced off and I trembled for fear of what might happen. Then Acllamama broke into a smile. "She's not an aclla. The offer was made. Now I see why it was not accepted."

I sensed Anka's body relaxing. "Then, with your permission, I would like to talk to Yana awhile."

Acllamama looked to the guard, who stood like a wall behind us, then back to us. "I suppose it will be all right providing you promise to stay near. I'm responsible for Yana's safety."

"Thank you. We will sit right here," Anka said, pointing to the ground beside the door.

Acllamama returned to the confines of the Acllawasi along with the second guard, who closed the door after them. Our protector positioned himself so we were between the wall and his broad back.

Anka was wearing a yacolla over his unku. Removing his yacolla, he spread it upon the ground. "Sit on this."

I was grateful for this courtesy, for I did not own the beautiful clothes I wore. Yet when I started to sit down, Anka stopped me.

"Let me look at you first." He stepped back. "You are even more beautiful than I remember."

I shook my head. "It is my clothes which are beautiful, and they do not belong to me."

Anka stepped forward and rubbed my cheek with his smooth chin. "I was not looking at your clothes," he whispered. He then sat down and pulled me down beside him. There was just enough room for both of us upon his yacolla if we sat close together.

"Your brother told me that you went to look for me," I said. "I'm sorry I have caused you so much trouble."

Anka held my hand as he spoke. "The trouble was of my own making. When you did not pass through Qosqo as I expected, I got very worried and not a little angry. After waiting three days for you, I returned to Tambo Toco and demanded of Chanka that he tell me where you'd gone. He obliged me. Of course, by then, you already had several days' head start on me.

"It was not hard to follow the route you took, for there were many who saw your passing. It only became difficult, when I left Calca, for there was no one I could ask of you. As matters worked out, I never would have discovered the entrance to the tunnel if I hadn't found your sandal."

"My sandal?"

He released my hand and took from the woven bag he carried a dirty and battered sandal, my size.

"Where did you find this?" I said, taking it from him.

"The road in the jungle crossed a fast-flowing stream. It was at the edge of the stream that I found your sandal."

I shook my head in amazement. "I threw my old sandals into the stream when they were no longer of use. The current must have carried them away."

"Seeing that sandal, I feared the worst, especially when I discovered you had tried to pass behind that thundering waterfall."

"But how could you have known that?"

He laughed. "The vegetation to one side had been torn up as if someone had fallen down the slope."

I nodded, for that is exactly what had happened.

"I could not imagine why you would do such a thing until I climbed up after you and saw the opening behind the waterfall." He shuddered. "Seeing that convinced me you were dead, carried away by the waterfall when you tried to pass behind it. Still, I had to be sure. I waited until the wind held back the curtain of water then dashed behind it." He shook his head. "It was a very dangerous and foolish thing to do, but I guess you know that."

I took Anka's hand and pressed it to my cheek. I never imagined he would have gone to such lengths to find me. Now I felt doubly ashamed, for I had also caused him to risk his life. "I'm so sorry," I whispered.

He leaned in close to me. "It was your life I feared for. Imagine my relief when I saw your footprints in the wet ground behind the waterfall. And then, I found this."

He handed me Akakllu's ocarina, which I had left at the tunnel entrance as an offering to the gods. I took it from him, amazed to see it now returned to me.

"But you didn't follow me into the tunnel, did you?"

"Of course! Chanka gave me a good supply of those burning stones." He made a face and waved a hand in front of his nose. We both laughed, remembering the acrid smell.

Then the humor left Anka's face. "Now I know Chanka had been right to dissuade me from going with you. In the tunnel, I would have been a rope around you, always trying to pull you back to the light. My brother and I once found a tunnel not far from here. We did not stay long inside it, for the darkness and the silence felt like a weight crushing us.

"Atatau! How did you stand it, Yana? The first night, when I stopped to rest, I hardly slept at all. The next day—there was never any day there—I forced myself to continue on, and with each step I prayed I would meet you returning. After I had walked many, many tupus, I came to a place where dust hung heavy in the air and I found my way blocked by recently fallen rocks. It was then I became certain of your death. The dragon had once again buried you, only this time too deeply for me to dig you out. I thought my heart would break, yet, if I'm honest, I must admit a small part of me was relieved that there was no longer a reason to be in the tunnel. I said a prayer for the safe journey of your spirit then walked back to the place where the roof of the tunnel had collapsed and Inti's light flooded in. Unable to endure a moment more in the tunnel, I stacked rocks one upon the other until I could reach the opening and climb out. I found my way back to the waterfall and there spent three days in mourning. Eventually I walked back to Qosqo, but very slowly, for there seemed no longer a reason for my returning."

Anka squeezed my hand. "What a joy it was to return and find you were still alive. And not only that, you had cured Topa Inca of his sickness!"

"The gods did that," I said, squeezing his hand in return.

"But how did you escape from the tunnel?"

"By the help of the gods and my llama, Chumpi. I hated the cold and darkness as much as you. Like you, I always wanted to turn back. But then the dragon brought down the rocks. Thanks to the gods, I was not buried or seriously hurt, but the way back was blocked." I explained how I was forced to continue on and how I found the cavern which contained the clear stream. "When I emerged from the tunnel, I discovered I had actually walked beneath the mountains and was only a day's walk from Qosqo."

"Where my brother gave you a warm welcome," he said, the smile gone from his face.

"Each of us has had a role to play in the gods' plan," I said. "Kacha included."

"So, what has been my role?"

I thought before answering. "After many days in the tunnel, I became sick, and this only increased my fear. There were several times when I was sure I would die. It was then I tried to imagine the faces of my family so that I might, in my mind at least, say good-bye to them. But always it was your face I saw." I laid Anka's hand upon my chest. "More than anyone, it was you I wanted to say good-bye to, and it was my feelings for you that helped me continue on in the darkness."

Anka put an arm around my shoulders and pulled me close. We sat in silence, staring at the back of the unmoving guard. A little later, the door to the Acllawasi opened, and the other guard signaled for me to return. Against our wills, Anka and I parted.

"Do you think I'll be allowed to see you again?" I said.

"I'm going to come here every day, and I dare even the Acllamama to stop me from seeing you." And with that, he quickly walked away.

As I entered the Acllawasi, I was met by Paru.

"Is he handsome?" she said.

"How did you know I was with Anka?"

She waved the question away. "Is he handsome?"

I laughed. "Yes, he is very handsome."

"Are you going to marry him?"

I very much wanted to marry Anka, but knew it was not possible. "He is an Inca," I replied. "I am a Hatunruna."

"Then become an aclla. The Capac Inca often gives acllas as wives to Inca lords. Perhaps he will give you to Anka."

I shook my head. "I would not want to take a chance he might give me to someone else. Besides, I don't think I was meant to be an aclla."

Paru's response was a great sigh that spoke much. Obviously, she did not think she was meant to be one either.

Chapter 49

The afternoon passed with me volunteering to help Paru with her work, cleaning out the colca where vicuña wool was stored. This gave me the chance to tell Paru of my visits with Topa Inca. I was grateful for Paru's company, for she kept me from thinking about the impossibility of marriage to Anka. Paru's curiosity was boundless, and she kept up a steady stream of questions about Topa Inca. Yet even with all our talk, we managed to clean the colca and restack the bundles of wool before Chukru arrived to escort me to the Cora Cora.

That evening, I found Topa's room empty. Gone was the oven, which had taken the chill from the room. Even the chusi on which Topa Inca slept had been removed. Not knowing what these changes portended, my heart pounded with fear.

Then the curtain covering the opening at the far side of the room was lifted, and a woman, one of those who had attended to Topa Inca, beckoned me to follow. The woman's smile seemed a good sign, but did not completely dispel my anxiety. Yet I also felt a little excited, for ever since I first had entered Topa's room and heard the sound of trickling water, I had wondered what lay beyond the opening.

Reality far exceeded imagination, for I entered into a magnificent garden wherein water gushed out of a large rock and flowed away through four opposing channels cut into the stone. I could see this because of the countless lanterns hanging from poles or suspended from branches. These bright lights made me think the garden even more lovely than the garden of the Acllawasi.

The woman allowed me a moment to take in the beauty before leading me along a stone pathway overhung with ferns and flowering shrubs. Our feet stirred up the fallen petals thick upon the pathway. The air was heavy with the scent of flowers and the delightful smell of Pachamama after a recent rain. The voices of insects, frogs, and night birds added to the magic. My heart ached with the beauty of it all.

I lagged behind my escort who suddenly turned from the path. Hurrying to catch up, I entered a small, grassy clearing upon which a large cloth had been spread. And there, sitting upon a low bench, sat not Topa Inca, but the Capac Inca himself, surrounded by trays of food.

"Ah!" he exclaimed, "my guest has arrived!" He pointed to a place on the cloth near to him. "Come! Sit!"

With eyes fixed upon the ground, I crept forward, my arms extended in obeisance.

"Stop that!"

His sharp command was like a slap on the face. I looked up into eyes like two dark stones.

"It is not necessary for you to grovel like a conquered foe." His eyes softened, and a tired smile appeared upon his face. "You are my guest, and I want to be able to look my guest in the face. Tonight, we will act as if I am your father and you my daughter, which, in a way, I feel you are. Now, come, sit and enjoy this food before it gets cold."

As soon as I was seated, the Capac Inca lifted a silver tray and offered me the choice of its contents. Though my appetite had abandoned me, I took a sweet maize cake out of politeness. I wondered the reason for this meeting, and why Topa Inca was not here with us.

The Capac Inca read my thoughts. "You are probably wondering where Topa is."

I nodded as I bit into the maize cake that tasted as nothing.

"Topa has a friend, a cousin whom he has not seen since becoming ill. Because Topa's health is so improved, I decided to let him spend the night with this cousin. Do you think I was wise in this?"

The Capac Inca asked this in all seriousness, as any concerned parent might of his camasca. I sat up tall in an attempt to merit the respect he accorded me. "Topa appears to be fully recovered. Lately I have done little more than provide him company." Hedging a bit, I added, "Still he should get lots of rest and not overdo his activities."

The Capac Inca nodded. "Tomorrow he will be here, same as usual, when you come. He says he wants to hear you tell of your adventures again."

I could not help but laugh. "I will have to search my mind for additional details to amuse him, otherwise I'm sure he will be bored."

With a half-smile, the Capac Inca stared off at something unseen. "It is a good story that loses nothing in its retelling." He quickly added, "Or so Topa tells me."

At last I knew the identity of the listener in the shadows. I tried to hide my reaction to this knowledge by making a pretense of studying the tray of fruit before making a selection. When I looked up, the Capac Inca was staring at the tray containing slices of llama, the meat sitting in a pool of its own reddish juice. I was reaching for some more fruit when his question stopped me.

"Why was it you had my son drink of your own blood?"

As I withdrew my hand, the Capac Inca lifted the tray of fruit and offered it to me. I took a lucuma, but held it in my lap. "Ipa, my great aunt, is a wise camasca, who often urged me to follow in her footsteps. She says a good camasca trusts her intuition. Something just told me to give my blood to your son."

The Capac Inca nodded, yet I sensed my explanation did not satisfy him. Neither did it me. I tried to gather the words to express what had gone through my mind while pondering upon this very question in the garden of the Acllawasi.

"When the jar broke that contained the water at the end of the world, I thought all was lost. But as I knelt in the road, I heard in my mind Ipa's voice asking me where the world ended and where it began. I even felt the flat of her hand pressing upon my chest as she asked this question. Many images like threads shuttled across my mind: rivers, mountains, a pool of water within a cavern.

"I do not know how to explain this, but I did not see these things as being outside my body. Instead, I saw them inside of me, as if my veins were rivers and my heart a liquid pool. Ipa once told me the water at the end of the world was nowhere and everywhere. But there is more to it than that. I realized that everything I saw with my eyes was false. There is no world outside separate from what is within me. There exists but a river of blood, Pachamama's life force, and nothing else.

"It was then I realized the water at the end of the world was in me." I shook my head. "No, that's not correct. The water at the end of the world was me, is me. And when I discovered this, suddenly, I felt its power. I don't know whether it was necessary for your son to drink my blood. Perhaps touching him with the power I felt was enough. I only acted as I thought was right when the power was upon me."

"I felt that power," the Capac Inca said, "and so did the Coyamama. It was a strange tingling not altogether pleasant. Do you feel that power now?"

"No, it was strongest right after the jar broke. In the days that followed, the power waned. As I said, lately I've done little more than provide Topa with company. And yet the time the gods allowed me the use of this power seemed sufficient; Topa is nearly recovered."

"Do you think the power will return to you?"

"The gods have shown me that I am a camasca. I pray they will again entrust me with this power, for it seems a great force for healing."

The Capac Inca looked again at the slices of llama. He selected a piece and chewed it thoughtfully. Then he poured some chicha from a silver jar into a golden cup and drank. Setting aside the cup, he cleared his throat. "I am planning a great celebration in honor of Topa's recovery, and you are to be the guest of honor."

I gasped.

"Don't look so surprised. If it wasn't for you, my son would be dead."

"If wasn't for the gods," I corrected.

He nodded. "Yet they chose you. It is to honor them that I honor you." He leaned forward to emphasize what he was about to say. "I have many sons, but Topa is special to me. When I die, he will rule Tahuantinsuyu. His sickness nearly took my reason. I tried everything to cure him. I ordered special ceremonies in which I implored the gods to save my son. I commanded that, day and night, llamas be offered upon the altars of every temple in Tahuantinsuyu. I consulted with all the best camascas. I took Topa to baths known for their healing waters. I neglected my duties as Capac Inca in the pursuit of a cure for my son.

"Yet despite all my efforts, Topa only got sicker. Finally, I promised the gods I would give anything in my power to the person who cured my son." Smiling, he leaned back. "I never imagined that person would be a young woman."

I sat, stunned.

The Capac Inca picked up the silver jar and filled my cup. "Have some chicha. You look like you could use some."

Gratefully I lifted the cup and took a large swallow. Sputtering, I quickly set the cup down and hurried to cover my mouth. The chicha was stronger than any I had ever drunk.

The Capac Inca laughed. "This chicha is made with molle berries. It is much stronger than chicha made from maize."

Unable to speak, I wiped tears from my eyes.

"But it put the color back in your cheeks." He drank from his own cup and set it aside. "Now, Yana Mayu, tell me how I can fulfill my promise to the gods. All my power is at your command. How can I reward you for what you have done?"

It was as if my head was suddenly full of whirling birds. How could I respond to such an offer? I could not ask for my brother's release from prison, for Chukru had assured me he had been sent back to Qomermoya. I thought about my father. The Capac Inca could release him from his service. And there were the many people who had helped me on my journey to discover the water at the end of the world. Now I could repay them for their kindness. But in what manner would it be best to thank them?

I didn't realize I had been quiet for so long.

"Perhaps you will need more time to think upon this," he said.

I nodded. "Your offer is beyond anything I could imagine." Yet one desire blazed in my heart hotter than any other. "Wise Father, is it possible for a Hatunruna to become an Inca?"

My question surprised him. "Why do you ask?"

I lowered my head. "I love someone…"

"Ah, and that person is an Inca?"

I nodded.

The Capac Inca lifted my chin. His eyes revealed the tenderness I had first seen in Qomermoya, seeming ages ago, when he had looked upon his sick son.

"There are Incas who are Inca by birth, and others who are Inca-by-privilege. To become Inca-by-privilege, a man must do something extraordinary. He must be a soldier who acted very courageously, or someone whose idea caused something to be built that was unimaginable before. You, Yana Mayu, have shown both by your courage and by your abilities that you are an Inca. It is something you made of yourself." He released my chin. "Still I can do something so that everyone will recognize you as being an Inca."

Then, to my amazement, the Capac Inca took off his headdress and began to unwind the red cord of which it was partially constructed. When he had the length that he wanted, he drew his knife and cut the cord.

"Lean forward," he commanded. He encircled my head with the cord. "Only an Inca is allowed to wear a red llautu. Now everyone will know you are an Inca." He tied the ends together and released me. "I have never seen a llautu worn by a woman, but on you, it's fitting, and I will allow it. Then everyone will know you are special in my eyes."

My eyes blurred with tears.

"Why do you cry? Is it too tight?"

I laughed and shook my head. "Wise Father, you have made my deepest wish possible."

He waved his hand as if brushing away a fly. "I have done nothing. Now think of ways I can really reward you. This ceremony for Topa will take time to plan, at least a month, but don't take that long to decide what it is you wish. Take until Qillamama has hidden her face. Then we will meet again, and you can tell me of your wishes. Now, are you going to eat that lucuma?"

I looked down. The lucuma still lay in my lap.

"And have some of this fish," he said. "It was caught just this morning in Lake Titikaka."

The fish was rich in oil and tasted incredibly delicious. Yet I wondered whether it was the merry delirium in my mind that now made all food seem like ambrosia.

As I ate and drank, the Capac Inca talked of many things: of the nations he planned to conquer, of the temples he intended to build. He even gave me a lecture on the best way to support his armies with provisions. I hope I was a good listener. I remember nodding a great deal and even making some verbal responses. But mostly I remember how my heart felt: filled with gladness and hope.

After the trays of food were cleared away, the Capac Inca excused himself, saying he would return shortly. I was glad of this interruption, for it gave me a chance to pen in my racing thoughts. I closed my eyes for, as much as I loved to look upon the garden, my mind was already overwhelmed. Breathing deeply, I first said a prayer of thanks to the gods. I felt undeserving of the Capac Inca's munificence. I had only tried to do the gods' bidding. Many others must have done similarly, yet never received the reward I was being offered. I vowed I would honor the gods by this opportunity, and thinking this, my mind calmed. I was once again aware of the sounds of the night. A chorus of insects and frogs rasped a rhythm soothing by its repetition. The gurgling of the fountain reminded me of the stream that ran through Qomermoya.

I opened my eyes and saw that Qillamama had risen; her rays of light were like silver spider threads cast straight from overhanging branches. How quickly she had changed, for now nearly half of her face was concealed. Hatunrunas have always held a special place in our hearts for Qillamama, for her softer radiance seemed more approachable than Inti's brilliant light. Her comings and goings were not as ordered as Inti's. The Incas admired Inti for his precision; the Hatunrunas loved Qillamama for her caprice.

But I was no longer a Hatunruna. I was an Inca. I looked into the face of Qillamama and realized that I too had changed. Not long ago, all I wanted was to have my family reunited. Though I still longed for that, now I also wished to marry Anka. Yet by accepting the llautu and marrying an Inca, I was walking down a road that diverged from the ordinary life of a Hatunruna. Where, I wondered, would that road take me?

Perhaps it was my sudden status as an Inca that caused me to accept the uncertainty of my future without my usual fearful reaction. Instead, a sweet sadness entered my heart and pushed out the wild elation which was the result of the Capac Inca's offer of reward.

When the Capac Inca returned, he did not stay long. He released me with a reminder to think of many ways he could reward me. Dazed from the rich food and drink, as well as all the excitement, I stumbled after the woman who came to lead me back through the garden and Topa's room.

I had expected Chukru to comment upon my llautu. He only asked if I was ready to return to the Acllawasi. Following close behind him, I concentrated upon negotiating the steps, for I was a little intoxicated. At the bottom of the stairs, Chukru stepped aside.

Looking up, I saw a beautiful litter covered with cloth bold in its design and colors. Beside the litter stood eight sturdy young men, four to each side.

"These men will have the pleasure of returning you to the Acllawasi tonight," Chukru said.

I stared at the litter, disbelieving.

Chukru, smiling broadly, stepped forward and pulled aside the curtain which covered the entrance to the litter. With sweep of his other arm, he motioned for me to enter.

I don't remember my legs moving, but suddenly I was inside the litter. No sooner was I seated than the men hoisted the litter upon their shoulders and moved out, walking in unison. I don't know if it was the state of my mind, or the gracefulness of their step, but I felt as if I were floating upon a cloud. I held the curtain back so I could see out. I was a bird winging along at the height of the trees. We passed by a shorter wall, and I saw over it into a garden where a pool of water reflected Qillamama's light. Then we came upon a patrol of soldiers, and they scurried to get out of the way. I nearly laughed at the absurdity of it: that they should have to yield the road to me!

My magical ride ended too soon. The bearers carefully lowered the litter outside the Acllawasi and waited for me to exit. I thanked them for their efforts, but not one of them spoke a reply or even looked in my direction. They stood impassively until I had walked away a few paces then quickly lifted the litter and disappeared into the night. I stood and listened as their footsteps faded. Eventually, all was quiet save for a tree frog croaking nearby.

It had been a night beyond my wildest imagining. I realized if nothing were to follow, I would still have the wonder of it to cherish for the rest of my life. But I wanted more to follow. I wanted to be able to tell of this night to my children, to Anka's children. I could not wait for the morrow when I could show Anka my llautu.

And with that thought, I knocked upon the door to the Acllawasi. I realized it was the first time there was no guard to do it for me.

Chapter 50

The next morning, I bathed in the fountain of pebbles even before the stars began to fade. I had not slept much, being anxious to tell Anka of my evening spent with the Capac Inca. Wishing to look my best when Anka arrived, I considered wearing the necklace Topa had given me. It seemed an adornment more suitable for someone like the Coyamama. I decided to leave it in its beautiful box; the simple llautu would make me feel conspicuous enough. Yet thinking of the necklace reminded me I had forgotten to return Anka's to him. I spent the morning braiding a new cord for the medallion.

When the drum announced morning meal, I went along with the other women. During my time in the Acllawasi, I had made many friends, and now several greeted me and upon seeing my llautu voiced their approval. That they already seemed to know how I came by it did not surprise me.

As we came to the area where morning meal was taken, Paru intercepted me and told me I was to join Acllamama. Holding hands, Paru and I walked toward Acllamama's private garden.

"I heard that the Capac Inca made you Inca-by-privilege," she said.

I touched my llautu. "He made this for me, using a part of his own headdress."

She squeezed my hand. "Now you and Anka can be married." We arrived at the entrance to Acllamama's garden. "I want to hear all about your evening," Paru whispered.

"I will tell you, when I can," I whispered back. It seemed I had spoken those same words to her many times.

"Paru, quit pestering Yana so she can have her morning meal," Acllamama scolded from behind the curtain.

Paru quickly released my hand, and I entered the smaller garden. Acllamama was seated next to an oven whose fire took the chill from the air.

"Good morning, Yana. I understand you had quite an evening."

"Good morning, Acllamama." As I sat down, two acllas appeared bearing trays of food. As I recounted the events of the night before, one of the women held back, listening, and Acllamama, perhaps absorbed in my recitation, did not dismiss her. I was not aware of her either until, just after telling how the Capac Inca fashioned the llautu for me, I reached for my cup of tea to moisten my throat. The woman, seeing my cup empty, rushed to fill it. But as she handed the cup to me, it slipped from her fingers, and fell into my lap. With a shout, I jumped up, for the tea was scalding. I held my lliqlla away from my skin, which prevented the tea from burning me further, but the beautiful cloth was now permanently stained.

"Wayronqo!" shouted Acllamama, standing. "How clumsy of you!"

Wayronqo rushed to capture my cup and refill it.

"That will be enough!" Acllamama said. "Leave us!"

Wayronqo set down the cup and the jar of tea and quickly retreated.

"I'm sorry," said Acllamama, brushing my lliqlla with a dry cloth.

"It is all right. I was not really scalded."

"But your lliqlla is ruined. Don't worry, I will have another one sent to your room." She tossed aside the cloth in anger. "Are you too wet, or can you sit with me a little longer?"

"I am hardly wet at all. I just feel sorry for Wayronqo, that she got yelled at because of an accident."

"Accident?" Acllamama looked at me with arched eyebrows. Then she threw back her head and laughed.

I wondered what I'd said to draw such a response.

Acllamama resumed her seat and motioned for me to do the same. "You have much to learn about being an Inca," Acllamama said. "That was no accident. Wayronqo spilled the tea on you because she is jealous."

I shook my head, disbelieving.

Acllamama rapped my knee with her knuckles. "Listen to me! Life as an Inca is not all nice clothes and rides in litters. Though most people will respect your status, others will hate you for it, and they'll show their displeasure in sly ways difficult to defend against."

I wondered what had I gotten myself into.

"The price of entering a wider world is an increased awareness," Acllamama said. "Sometimes you will not like what you see. My advice to you is to not let it trouble you for, on balance, the wider a person's world, the richer it is."

Hearing her words, I reflected how the places and events on my journey had enriched my life. I was glad of those experiences, even though they had been acquired through hardship.

"Now, I have some good news," she said. "You may now come and go as you please, providing you return here each evening in time to be escorted to the Cora Cora. I suggest, however, that you don't range far until you get to know Qosqo better."

I beamed at this news. "Anka promised to show me around the city."

"Did he? Why does this not surprise me? He will be here today, no doubt."

"I'm hoping he will call for me this morning."

"Then you best go change." She stood up, and I quickly stood also. She placed an arm around my waist and escorted me from her private garden and along the walkway outside. "You know, Wayronqo is not the only one envious of you. So am I."

The sudden tension in my body caused her to laugh.

"Don't worry, I won't spill hot tea on you. But I envy you the wider world you will know. Enjoy it. Cherish it. And don't worry that it will make you something you are not." Stopping outside the entrance to my room, she placed a finger upon my chest. "In there, the goodness that is you will not change." She tugged at my lliqlla. "It's this that needs changing. Now go change before Anka arrives."

Forgetting my wet lliqlla, I threw my arms around Acllamama and hugged her. She sighed and patted my back before pushing me through the curtain.

I found another lliqlla had already been placed upon my chusi. I had thought the one I wore luxurious, but it was as nothing compared to this new one. It had a checkered border, and each row of squares was alternately colored. Even the lliqlla Chanka had given me had not been so elaborately decorated. Such intricacy in design was only for the clothes of certain people: the Incas.

"And now I am an Inca!" I said aloud.

I quickly shed my wet lliqlla and slipped into my new one. Then I sat upon my chusi and combed out my hair. Finally, I carefully retied my llautu around my forehead. Preparations made, I waited for Paru to announce Anka's arrival. While I waited, I tried to recall additional details of my adventures so I would have something new to tell Topa. After I grew tired of this, I got my spindle and spun thread while I waited.

And waited.

I waited the time it takes to cook potatoes twice then stood to shake the chill out of my body. I went to the curtain, pulled it back, and looked for

Paru. I only saw two women, hurrying from the garden where the rain was falling heavily. I went back to sit upon my chusi and spin some more. Feeling sleepy, I lay down and dozed. When I awoke, the morning had passed and Anka still had not come. I got up and went for a walk under the covered walkway. I stopped to chat with Kupa, but found her busy weaving a cloth with an unusually intricate pattern. Not wishing to distract her, I returned to my room and once again took up my spindle.

I had never known time to pass as slowly as it did that afternoon. I started at every footstep outside my door, or every time the wind blew hard against my curtain. I dozed and awoke and dozed again. And still Anka did not come. Finally, late in the afternoon, Paru arrived to tell me it was time to go to the Cora Cora. Outside the Acllawasi, eight men waited alongside the litter. My ride did not give me as much pleasure as before, for I was troubled that Anka had not come for me. By now he must have heard I had been made Inca-by-privilege, for nothing remained secret for long in Qosqo. Perhaps now that our marriage was possible, Anka was having second thoughts. Perhaps he preferred to marry a woman born Inca.

I quickly dismissed this thought, for I knew, in my heart, Anka loved me.

Arriving at the Cora Cora, I hurried out of the litter and ran up the steps, for the rain was now torrential. Once inside, I brushed the moisture from my lliqlla before entering Topa's room. That evening, I told Topa some of the stories Ipa used to tell me, and he appeared to like them nearly as much as the story of my adventures. We also played a board game called chuncara, using colored beans. Topa was a very good chuncara player, and I rarely beat him, which made him happy.

When it was time to return to the Acllawasi, I was met by Chukru outside Topa's room. As we walked along toward the way out, our sandals made a slapping sound, for, though the rain had stopped, the ground was still wet. I asked after Chumpi, and Chukru assured me he was spending the evening snug and warm in Chukru's room.

Chukru sensed my somber mood. "What's troubling you, little sister?"

Though I was now Inca-by-privilege, I was grateful Chukru still thought of me as his little sister. "My friend Anka was supposed to visit me today. I hope something bad has not happened."

"Is he not the brother of that blackguard who kicked you?"

I nodded.

Chukru hesitated before answering. "Probably he had some job he couldn't get out of. I'm sure he'll visit you tomorrow."

As I rode in the litter back to the Acllawasi, I tried to push away my troubled thoughts so I might enjoy the ride. Behind torn clouds, Qillamama showed her face. I said a prayer, asking her for Anka's safekeeping.

When I returned to my room within the Acllawasi, I found a candle had been lit for me. I wondered who had done this kindness, for since that one other time, I had not had the use of one. This time, I did not blow it out immediately, but sat and watched the shadows upon the wall as the candlelight flickered and wavered. Chukru was right, I told myself, Anka probably had some responsibility that prevented him from visiting; he was, after all, the son of an important amauta. No one in Tahuantinsuyu could avoid his duties, not even an important young Inca like Anka. But this opened up a disturbing area of thought. Sometimes duty required that a person marry someone other than the one he wished to. In our village, Weqo Churu sometimes decided which couples were to be wed. What if Anka's father had decided his son should not marry me, but someone else, someone more important?

With a groan, I lay upon my side. Why did I torture myself with such thoughts? I remembered my bridge and told myself to take one step at a time and not think of the future. I closed my eyes. Light and shadow played across my eyelids. I turned away from the candle and eventually fell asleep. When I awoke, the darkness told me the candle had burned itself out. I rose and made my way to the garden in order to look at the stars and determine how much of the night remained. But as I looked up, a gentle rain fell upon my face. I returned to my room and tried to sleep, but I could only turn restlessly upon my chusi. Finally, I got up and once more stole into the garden. The rain had stopped. I waited for my eyes to adjust to the darkness then made my way to the fountain of pebbles where I removed my lliqlla and sat in the pool. The water felt warmer than the chill air, and I stayed in it for a long time. When I finally emerged, the sky was beginning to grow light. Having brought no cloth to dry myself, I shivered in the cold air, but at least I felt wide awake after a troubled night.

I returned to my room, and to occupy my mind, considered the Capac Inca's offer and tried to think of ways I could reward those who had befriended me on my search for the water at the end of the world. This required much thought, and it seemed no time until I heard the beating of the drum and the soft patter of feet as acllas made their way to morning meal.

I was not hungry, but decided to join the others in order to keep from thinking about Anka.

As I sat with the women, I realized how harmoniously they lived together. Around me, there was much cheerful banter. Whenever an older woman reprimanded a younger she did it with gentle humor; and the younger women were always quick to assist the older acllas. Maybe being an aclla would not be so bad, I told myself, if marriage to Anka was impossible.

After morning meal, I returned to my room and to my thoughts concerning the Capac Inca's offer. I became so absorbed in this, I did not notice the running of feet until Paru burst into my room without first announcing herself.

"He's here!" she cried.

Chapter 51

I sprang to my feet then took a moment to still my racing heart, for I did not wish for Anka to see I had been worried. His absence had undoubtedly been for a good reason, and he might not understand my being upset over it. I drew in a deep breath, then forced myself to walk slowly toward the entrance. But Paru, in frustration, grabbed my hand and yanked on my arm. I laughed as she dragged me through the courtyard. As I pulled back the far curtain, I saw, as usual, the guards, one to each side of the outer door, looking as impassive as ever. Yet when one of the guards opened the door for me, he actually smiled. I took this for a good sign.

I did not see Anka at first. The sky was gray, the clouds very low, and mists floated along the nearly empty road. Anka stood some distance away, leaning one arm against the wall of the Acllawasi, his face studying the ground. I walked toward him with a feeling of misgiving. He did not look up until I had nearly come up to him.

When I looked into his face, all my hopes shattered like Sumaq's jar when it hit the stone. I had never seen his eyes hold such sadness. At least, I would have that, I thought. He too sorrows that we will not be able to spend our lives together.

"Can we walk a bit?" he said. "I must talk to you."

I nodded. I could not speak. It took all my courage not to cry.

He did not offer to take my hand, but shuffled along, staring at the ground. I walked beside him as he led me toward the river. There he stopped and motioned for me to sit beneath a huayau tree. He sat beside me and leaned back against the tree. He closed his eyes and ran his hands through his hair repeatedly then placed both hands atop his head, as if trying to keep it from floating away.

I could not look upon him and still hold back my tears. I looked at the swollen river instead. It had risen even higher. Sodden branches and putrid foam lined its edges.

"Kacha is dead," he whispered.

I spun my head toward him. "What? How?"

It was difficult for Anka to speak for his heart was in his throat. "An infection… his jaw broken… thought he was getting better… then, the night before last."

The horror of it seized me. "Oh, Anka, I am so sorry! It's all my fault!"

He looked upon me with sad, loving eyes. "No, Yana. My brother's death was of his own making." He took my hand and squeezed it once for each of his next three words. "You–are–good," He released my hand. "And my brother was bad. But, oh, Yana, to die like that!

"The day before yesterday, when I left to meet with you, I was sure he would be fine. Though the cut on his face was slow to heal, his jaw had nearly mended. But when I returned to the Yachawasi, Kacha could not move his mouth." Tears began to flow down Anka's face. "And yesterday, my brother could not move any part of his body. It was as if he had turned to stone!

"Then, last night, just before he died… the most awful thing. His body arched up with only his feet and the back of his head touching the floor. We tried to ease his agony… relax his body… like a bow tightly drawn." Anka covered his face with his hands. "Oh, Yana, they had to break my brother's body to get it into the position of death!"

Convulsive sobs racked his body and tore at his throat. I rested my head upon his and placed one arm around his quivering back. The people of Tahuantinsuyu rarely cry, particularly the men, for life is hard and tears a waste. Yet when we lose someone we love, we are not afraid to express our grief.

I held Anka until he stopped shaking, and his tears ceased to fall. Then he told me of the times when he and his brother were boys and the adventures they had shared and the joy they had known. When Anka had talked himself out, he leaned back against the tree, and together we watched the water flow by.

"Tomorrow, we will place Kacha's body in a nearby cave," he said. "I want you to be there when we do this, for it will ease the pain in my father's heart if I could reintroduce him to his future daughter-in-law."

I gasped.

Anka turned to look at me. "Why do look surprised?" His expression fluctuated between concern and anger. "You didn't doubt we would marry, did you?"

I gently placed my hand upon his cheek. "I never doubted your love, only… there seemed many obstacles to marriage."

"I would have married you even if you had not been made an Inca." For the first time that morning, he smiled. "I don't know how, but I would have!"

It was good to see him smile. The release of his tears had emptied a place for his cheerfulness to return. Still smiling, he stood and pulled me up. We walked along the river for a while, holding hands, but talking little. A little later, he returned me to the Acllawasi.

"I will come for you tomorrow, sometime in the morning." As he started to walk away, I called him back. Taking off the necklace he had given me, I held it out to him. "I've been meaning to give this back to you, but keep forgetting. I no longer need it to find you, for soon we will always be together."

Smiling, he took the necklace and slipped it over his head then hurried away. I watched until he was lost in the mist. It takes much work to prepare a loved one to walk the underground road, and I was grateful Anka had taken time to come and talk to me.

I returned to the Acllawasi, where I was not surprised to be met by Paru.

"Are you going to be married?" she said, skipping along beside me.

Even with the sadness I felt concerning Kacha death, I could not keep from smiling. "Yes, I am."

Hugging herself, Paru spun in circles. "Oh, I wish I could be there to see you get married!"

As I watched her spin about, it occurred to me that perhaps she would.

Chapter 52

The next morning, I was again particularly attentive to my bathing, for it dishonors the dead to appear before them less than scrupulously clean. Acllamama had heard of Kacha's death by way of her mysterious communication system, and she provided me with a green paint made from fat and herbs which I smeared on my forehead and temples as a sign of respect and mourning. As for my clothes, the occasion demanded that I wear something plain, and in this, the clothes I arrived in were more suitable. Thankfully, Kupa had washed them for me. Wrapping myself in my old lliqlla, I smiled at how coarse it felt.

Anka, meeting me outside the Acllawasi, smiled his appreciation of my preparations. Together we walked toward the Yachawasi where the funeral procession would begin. We did not hold hands on that solemn day, but happily we brushed together occasionally. Ironically, on this day of mourning, the day was sunny, the blue sky sprinkled with small clouds–remnants of the departing storm. When we arrived at the Yachawasi, we waited outside in the company of other mourners. Soon a wail of mourning was heard, and the entry door was pushed open. Anka's father emerged at the head of a procession. His wife did not accompany him, for she had preceded Kacha in death several years earlier. Behind Anka's father came Kacha's body borne on a simple litter by six young men whose faces and bare chests were painted brown.

Seeing Kacha sent an involuntarily shiver through my body. Even in death, Kacha emitted a malevolence. As his bearers passed, I joined Anka as he entered the procession behind them. Though it was an ungracious thought, I was relieved that I did not have to view Kacha's face as we made our way toward the cave in which he was to be interred.

The crowds in the streets of Qosqo parted to allow our procession to pass. Strangers stood with heads bowed. Women, mouthing prayers, scattered handfuls of quinoa upon the ground before the litter. Old men poured out offerings of chicha from their coveted jars. Everyone was respectful, for death looks over every man's shoulder.

Outside the city, the procession moved toward low hills. I glanced back. Many people followed, for Kacha's father was an important man. The mourners made a long line as many of the elders could not keep step with the young bearers. When we drew near to the hillside, I saw it contained many caves though they appeared dug, not natural. Kacha's body was placed in the largest of these. The litter bearers lowered Kacha to the ground, then quickly cut away the lashings and carried away the poles, leaving Kacha sitting upon a cane frame covered with a dried llama hide. Kacha's treasured possessions were then laid about his body so that he would have the use of them in his next life. Anka's father placed a golden cup at his son's feet. Anka draped a well-used aillo over his brother's folded arms. Food and drink were also placed beside Kacha so he would not go hungry upon his journey to be reborn. Then a young man, his voice high and resonant, began to sing.

> Like a mountain flower, I have bloomed.
> I have basked in Inti's light.
> Opening to the wind,
> The cold gave me strength.
>
> Since I bloomed like a mountain flower,
> Spring has turned to summer.
> With me, my friends, laughing,
> My brother by my side.
>
> Since I bloomed like a mountain flower,
> Little have I thought of winter.
> Swiftly falls the snow.
> And now my body lies frozen.
>
> Mourn not!
> Look for me in the spring.
> By a mountain lake will I bloom again.

I had never heard this heart-stirring song, and thought it likely composed as a singular honor to Kacha. From the corner of my eye, I saw large tears coursing down Anka's face. I slipped my hand into his and could feel him trembling.

The singer then placed a small statue of a hunter alongside the golden cup. The statue was made of clay mixed with all the cuttings of Kacha's hair and the parings of his nails collected during his lifetime.

Next, someone began to tap on a drum. Taking turns, different people spoke over the constant beat, each recalling Kacha's talents and achievements. When it was Anka's turn, he sang of his brother's deeds of daring. Yet there were other qualities spoken of by others. I was surprised to learn that Kacha had been, at one time, a good scholar and engineer, that he had great gifts of memory, and that he told a good story. The drumming continued for as long as people wished to tell of their memories of Kacha.

When the drumming finally ceased, an old man came forward, carrying a burning torch. Behind him came two girls, each bearing garments which Kacha had once worn. They made a pile of the clothing near to Kacha's feet, and the old man ignited the garments. As the smoke rose, the old man slowly circled Kacha's body three times. Stopping at Kacha's side, he held the torch high which caused Kacha's eyes to be shadowed by his forehead. Under the steeply angled light, Kacha appeared alive, a young man sitting before a fire, drawing visions from the flames. In a voice that belied his years, the old man asked Pachamama to receive Kacha and return him to Inti's light. I said a silent prayer, asking that she first drive out the demon that had lived in his heart.

Then a mourner, chosen for the strength of his voice, began an ululating wail that caused the hair on the back of my head to rise. Others joined in. Added to this was the pounding of drums, the trill of pipes, all this to scare away the evil spirits so they would not accompany Kacha as he walked the underground road. The sound rose louder and louder until I thought the din would cause the cave to collapse. Suddenly, the drums stopped, and without them, the wailing quickly faded and died, leaving a silence in which blood throbbed in my ears.

The mourners stood awhile in silent reverence, but as the flames slowly died they began to return to the city. I went to stand outside while Anka and his father remained with Kacha until the fire burned down to ash. In the sky, clouds were tiny white boats, skittering before the fresh wind. I think many hearts were lifted by this beauty and thought it a good sign for Kacha's journey.

After a while, Anka and his father emerged from the cave. I joined them, and we walked back to the city, not speaking until we reached the Yachawasi. There Anka reintroduced me to his father.

"Father, this is Yana Mayu, whom you met once before. Yana is to be my wife."

A smile appeared on the tired face of Anka's father. He pointed a bent finger toward me. "I knew there was something special about you the moment I saw you that day by the Apurimac River. My sons thought so too and couldn't stop talking about you." This reminded him that one of his sons was dead, and the smile disappeared. "I'm sorry I cannot give your marriage my blessing on a day less sad."

I touched his arm. "Father, I am sorry Kacha is dead. In part, I feel responsible." Since learning of Kacha's death, I had wondered whether I could have used some of the power the gods had granted me to aid him. Yet I knew Kacha had hated me and probably would not have accepted my help.

"Please, do not be troubled about that," Anka's father replied. "The gods act for the best. Perhaps it is good that Kacha died when he did. Now tell me, did you really turn yourself into a puma in order to heal Topa Inca?"

This change of subject took me by surprise. Then I caught the twinkle in Anka's father's eyes. He began to laugh, and Anka and I joined in. People turned toward us, not knowing what was so funny, but smiling all the same.

"Join hands," Anka's father instructed. He placed one hand upon Anka's shoulder and one upon mine. "May you have a long, happy life together, and may the gods give you lots of children." Pulling us to his chest, he added, "And me lots of grandchildren." He released us. "Now, I'm tired. If you two will excuse me, I think I'll go rest."

Anka turned to me. "I will not be able to see you until the three days of fasting are over."

I nodded, understanding.

"I want you to join us when we celebrate the ending of the fast. That way you can meet my friends and relatives."

"I'm so glad your father is happy with our plans to marry."

Anka took me in his arms and brushed my forehead with his chin.

"You now have a green chin," I informed him when he stepped back.

Smiling, he wiped his chin with the back of his hand. "I will come for you in the morning, three days from now."

As I watched Anka enter the Yachawasi, I realized I did not have to return to the Acllawasi and was seized with the desire to explore Qosqo in the company of Chumpi, whom I'd not seen in over two days. Hurrying to Chukru's room near to the Cora Cora, I found Chukru about to go on duty.

"I thought I would take Chumpi and wander about the city for a while,"

I told him.

"Good! He's been restless and the exercise would do him good." He pointed toward the guards' sleeping quarters. "You'll find him in a pen behind the barracks. Is there any part of the city you're wanting to see in particular?"

"I thought I'd visit the Cuntisuyu."

"That's a pleasant quarter. Many artists live there."

"Have you heard of one named Sampa Maki?"

Chukru raised his eyebrows. "How do you know Sampa Maki? He's one of the best goldsmiths."

I explained how I had met his wife in the Kusipata my second day in Qosqo. "Do you know where he lives?"

Chukru shook his head. "Not offhand. But once you cross over the Huatanay River just ask. Someone will know."

As I turned to go Chukru called me back. Circling a finger about his face, he said, "Little sister, you may want to wash first."

I had forgotten about the green paint I had applied for Kacha's funeral. Not yet being a member of his family, there was no longer a reason for me to wear it. I went to the river, washed my face, then hurried to find Chumpi. Though he was no longer wearing his ear tassels, he still looked handsome in his new halter and collar.

I lifted away the poles used to pen him in. "I'm sorry, Chumpi, for not visiting, but I have been penned up too."

The Cuntisuyu was easy to locate as there were four major roads in Qosqo each named after the quarter they passed through. I crossed a bridge over the swollen Huatanay River then approached an old woman sitting next to the river washing an infant. She instructed me on how to find Sampa Maki's wasi. It was not difficult to follow her directions as all the roads in Qosqo are like the straight warp and weft of threads upon a loom.

Sampa Maki's residence was more than just a wasi. As I approached, I saw an additional walled-in yard out of which smoke rose. There was also the sound of hammers pounding upon metal. Seated before the wasi was the woman I had met in the Kusipata. She was weaving, and her daughter sat next to her, picking burrs from llama wool. I wondered if they would remember me. I need not have worried. Seeing us approach, the girl jumped up, shouting, "Chumpi!"

Her cry summoned her brother. "Chumpi! Chumpi!" he cried, running after his sister.

Chumpi trotted toward the children and nuzzled one then the other until the boy produced a piece of maize cake.

"Can we go for a ride?" the girl said.

"Easy, now," their mother said. "Our friend has only just arrived." She set aside her loom and came forward to meet me. "I see you were able to find us. You're certainly looking much better than the last time I saw you. Did you make your delivery?"

Before I could answer, a woman older than the children's mother emerged from the wasi.

"What's all the ruckus?" she said. "I was trying to sleep."

The mother turned to the older woman. "We have a visitor, Kiro. This is—" The mother turned back toward me. "I'm sorry, I never got your name."

"It's Yana Mayu."

It was like I had cast a spell, turning them all to stone. They stood staring at me.

The boy was the first to speak. "Are you the one who cured Topa Inca?"

"Only the gods could do that," I said, "but I helped. Now before you ask, let me tell you that I can't turn myself into a puma. I won't even be able to turn into a better weaver without a lot more practice."

"Atatau!" the boy exclaimed. "I was hoping to see a puma!"

Our laughter broke the spell.

"I am Sumapayay," the mother said. "And this is our son Khirkinchu, and our daughter Munaycha."

"Would you tell us how you cured Topa Inca?" Munaycha said.

"Wouldn't you and Khirkinchu rather go for a ride on Chumpi?"

Brother and sister looked at each unable to choose.

"Let me help you decide," I said. "Chumpi needs exercise. Let him take you for a ride, and maybe later, if there's time, I will tell you about how I helped Topa Inca."

Brother and sister readily agreed to this. I led them along the nearby roads. Chukru was right, the Cuntisuyu was home to many artists. I saw men working with metals, some fashioning objects out of gold and silver while others used copper and bronze. Beautiful creations of life-like animals sat upon wooden shelves about their work areas.

But there were more than just metal workers in the Cuntisuyu. We passed a large yard with row after row of bowls, plates, and jars, all skillfully made of clay and set to dry in the warm air. There were also basket makers, and musical instrument makers, and men who sat behind little tables upon which they fashioned exquisite jewelry using gold, silver, and colorful gemstones.

When we returned to Sampa Maki's wasi, I told Sumapayay of all the beautiful artwork I had seen. She smiled then motioned for me to follow her. She led me through the opening in the wall and into the work area of her husband. I counted five people working. A young man was feeding air to a fire by blowing through a long tube. Upon the glowing coals, sat a small cauldron half filled with molten metal. Three other young men were hammering lumps of gold into flat sheets. In the center of the yard sat an older man, working upon a cup nestled within a large piece of wood. Oblivious to the racket of the hammering, the man used a metal chisel to etch a design into the soft metal. Everyone was so preoccupied, no one noticed us.

"My husband is very busy right now," Sumapayay said, pointing to the older man. "He's gotten an important commission he must finish soon."

I watched with fascination as Sampa Maki drew curling threads of gold from the cup, using his chisel. He stopped and held the cup up to examine it. The cup sparkled in Inti's light.

"That is the second of two identical cups ordered by the Capac Inca. The first is already done. Only the jewels remain to be fitted, and those are being cut and polished by a gem maker as we speak. Ah! my husband has seen us."

Sampa Maki's expression indicated he did not wish to be disturbed, but that did not stop Sumapayay from approaching him with me in tow.

"Sampa, I want you to meet the woman I met in the Kusipata, the one who gave Khirkinchu and Munaycha a ride on her llama. Yana Mayu, this is my husband Sampa Maki."

Upon hearing my name, Sampa Maki's expression suddenly brightened. He looked questioningly at his wife, and Sumapayay nodded, smiling.

"Here, let me show you what I'm working on, Yana." He held the cup toward me. "What do you think?"

As Sampa Maki held the cup, I examined it closely. The cup was very different from those used in the Cora Cora. Except for being made of gold, the cups used by the Capac Inca were little different in design from ordinary cups made of clay or wood. But Sampa Maki's cup was unique. The top was a small bowl from which a stem descended to a square base. Though his design limited the amount the cup could hold, it gave a grace to the piece which was pleasing to the eye.

"It looks like it weighs no more than a feather," I said.

Sampa looked pleased. "Here, hold it."

The cup was heavier than it appeared, though the weight was mostly in the base, which would make it less likely to tip over.

"It is the most beautiful cup I've ever seen." I said.

He shook his head. "I've hardly started to work on it. Let me show you the one I've finished."

From a small wooden box, he took an object wrapped in cloth. He unwound the fabric until the cup was revealed. I gasped. I never would have believed such an object could have been made by human hands. Looking closely, I realized why Sampa Maki had been removing threads of gold from the other cup. The finished cup had two serpents coiled about the cup's stem. Upward they climbed until they separated, each to opposite sides of the cup. The serpents, who were important symbols connoting alliance, looked out with just the back of their heads attached to the cup.

"Would you like to hold it?" Sampa Maki said.

"I'm afraid I'll ruin it," I replied. "My hands are dirty."

"Don't worry. I will have to polish it again after the jeweler sets the stones."

I lifted the cup and turned it slowly. I had always enjoyed holding the cups used by Topa Inca and his father, but this one gave me a far greater pleasure, for all joy of the creator for his craft could be felt in the cup.

"Jewels will go here and here," Sampa Maki said, pointing to the eyes of the serpents, "and larger ones here and here." He pointed to a flat place on opposite sides of the cup.

"The serpents seem alive," I said. "As I turn the cup, they seem to be climbing up it." I returned the cup to his hands. "The gods have blessed you with a great skill."

"And he's worked hard to develop it," Sumapayay said.

Sampa Maki beamed. "Now I'd better do more of that hard work, or I'll not get the other cup done in time. I'm glad I got the chance to meet you, Yana. I hope you will have the opportunity of visiting again when I have more time to talk."

We left him to his work and went out of the yard. The children, who had been feeding Chumpi tidbits of food, came running toward us.

"Tell us about how you cured Topa Inca!" Khirkinchu demanded, pulling on my lliqlla.

I looked inquiringly at Sumapayay.

"Can you stay to tell us your story?" she said

"I would like to. I don't want to go back to the Acllawasi yet."

"The Acllawasi? You are a mystery, Yana Mayu, and I would like to know all about you and how you came to be in Qosqo."

"To tell all would take a great amount of time," I explained.

"It would make my work go easier to listen to you," she said, pointing to her loom.

"Is there something I can help you with as I talk?"

Sumapayay thought for a moment. "You could spin wool, but that might be difficult for you to do and tell your story at the same time."

I shook my head. "I'm good at spinning while talking."

Sumapayay turned to her daughter. "Munaycha, go get a spindle for Yana and that llama wool you cleaned yesterday. Yana's agreed to tell us her story."

"Atakachau!" Khirkinchu shouted.

As I began to tell of my adventures, Chumpi lay down near to us, content to chew his cud. Kiro appeared and listened as she ground kernels of maize in preparation for making chicha. It was then I put small things together in my mind and realized Kiro was probably Sampa Maki's first wife, for she was about his age. The Capac Inca occasionally gave a man a second wife as a reward for outstanding contributions to Inca society. Surely Sampa Maki's talent with gold made him deserving of such a reward.

I had already told my story several times, and I thought I was getting good at the telling, though I knew I would never be a storyteller like Ipa or Charapa. Still my listeners appeared interested. The children never fidgeted or grew restless, even though the telling consumed the whole afternoon. No one spoke when I concluded. It seemed all were holding onto some incident in the story and reliving it with faraway looks.

"Atatau!" Sumapayay cried, suddenly. "Look where Inti is, and I haven't started to prepare evening meal!"

I jumped up, alarmed.

"What's the matter?" Sumapayay said.

"I'm supposed to return to the Cora Cora soon, and I first must bathe!"

Munaycha pressed about my legs. "Don't leave us!" she cried. Khirkinchu joined her, and I laughed as I tried to disentangle myself from their clinging bodies.

"Children," Sumapayay scolded, "leave Yana alone, or she will never want to come back."

"You will come back, won't you?" Munaycha asked.

"I would like to," I answered.

Sumapayay smiled. "Please visit us again soon and bring Anka with you so we can meet him."

"You don't even have to bring Chumpi, if you don't want," Khirkinchu said.

I rubbed his head. "Coming from you, that's a great compliment. Now I must run or I'll be late. I'm sorry I could not help you prepare evening meal. Come, Chumpi."

I led Chumpi away at a trot. I returned him to his pen with the promise to come for him on the morrow. Then I ran to the Acllawasi, hurried to my room, grabbed my good lliqlla, then walked quickly to the fountain of pebbles. It was fastest bath I ever took. I had just enough time to dress, comb my hair, and fasten my llautu before Paru announced the litter was here to take me to the Cora Cora. I took several deep breaths to calm myself then walked with her toward the entrance.

"It must be fun to ride in a litter," Paru said.

I nodded. "Perhaps someday you'll will ride in one."

She snorted. "Not likely!"

As I sat in the litter, I wondered how much longer I could expect to enjoy that privilege. I reasoned my rides would cease after I met again with the Capac Inca. I sighed, thinking how I would miss not only the nightly rides, but the evenings spent in Topa's company and the walks in the magnificent gardens of the Acllawasi.

I had to laugh at myself. What did I expect? That it would all go on forever? Even if it could, I would not have wanted it to. I wanted to marry Anka and raise our children in our own wasi.

I looked to the west. Small clouds were flames in Inti's fading light. Seated high up in the litter, I could see the silhouette of a majestic peak to the southwest. Closer were the glow of cooking fires within the city. Atakachau! It truly was fun being high up like a bird!

That evening, for the first time, Topa and I shared evening meal in the garden, for it was a beautiful night, and a fire in an oven kept away the chill. After we ate, we walked through the garden, and Topa showed me his favorite replicas of animals. He also told me about his life. Listening, I realized the life of the future Capac Inca involved little play and much work. His days were mostly spent in study with special amautas. Rarely was he able to play with his cousins or his older brothers who, like him, had their own duties to attend to. The most frequent contact Topa had with other boys was when he was practicing martial skills. With so few friends, he was a lonely boy, and that explained why he valued the time we spent together.

After our walk, we returned to his room and played chuncara until it was time for Topa to go to sleep. When I got back to my room in the Acllawasi, I collapsed upon my chusi, for I was very tired. But I had to smile. It had been a very pleasant day, considering it began with a funeral.

Chapter 53

The next two days passed quickly. With Chumpi for company, I explored more of Qosqo. I spent time in the Kusipata, watching as people traded goods. Trading was a slow process. The two barterers sat in silence, and every once in a while, one or the other would add to or subtract from the quantity of goods offered until, eventually, an agreement was reached.

My status as an Inca allowed me to enter the Huacaypata where I observed more closely the rituals conducted by the priests. I thought of Kupa as, once again, I saw beautiful fabrics placed upon the fire as an offering to the gods.

But in all my wanderings, it was Inti's temple, the Coricancha, that astonished me the most. It consisted of six buildings, five of which formed the borders of a large square. Enclosing the buildings was a high wall built with the same skill as the wall which surrounded the Cora Cora. Also like the Cora Cora, the buildings were covered in gold and embellished with the images of animal figures. But more astounding were the paintings within the main temple. Artists had used bright-colored paints to depict scenes which told stories, only for the eyes rather than the ears. The first scene depicted Wiraqocha creating all the diversity of life; the next how Manka used the staff Wiraqocha gave him to discover the fertile valley where Qosqo was built. This was followed by a depiction of Manka trapping his evil brother, Kachi, in the cave. Lastly, there was Inti giving Manka the magnificent golden yacolla to acknowledge him as Inti's son and the first Capac Inca.

"Now I realize why Tuku had called Qosqo the most beautiful city in the world," I told Chumpi, when I went to untie him from the Pisonay tree where I had left him. "Qosqo is more than beautiful; it's magical."

And something else I discovered to be true: the people of Qosqo were very friendly. Many surprised me by addressing me by my name, and several times I was given gifts of flowers and sweet-smelling herbs. Even Chumpi was welcomed and fed bits of squash and potatoes. Of course, my red llautu identified me as the one who had helped Topa Inca. Yet it was not just to me that they showed kindness. As I watched friends greeting friends with smiles and the sharing of chicha, I realized I was witnessing what the people of

Qosqo were truly like when they no longer worried about Topa Inca or about crops drying up for lack of rain.

The third day following Kacha's funeral, I rose early in order to bathe ahead of the acllas. As I sat in the fountain of pebbles, my head cushioned by a fern, I looked up at Intuillapa's river in the sky. The last few days had been sunny, which had allowed the swollen rivers to subside and the ground to soak up the recent heavy rains. Still I prayed to Intuillapa that he not let too many days pass without his gift of rain, as more would be needed to assure a bountiful harvest.

Back in my room, I took my time dressing, for I knew Anka would not come for me until Inti was well in the sky. I decided I would wear the necklace Topa Inca had given me. I justified this bit of vanity by telling myself I should look as nice as possible so that Anka would not be ashamed to present me to his relatives. Of course, the truth of the matter was that it was I, not Anka, who wished to impress them. Either way, I need not have worried, for upon arriving at the Yachawasi, I was greeted as if I were already a member of Anka's family. It was a genuine acceptance that had nothing to do with my appearance, though many women complimented me on the beauty of my necklace.

Though it was a day to honor Kacha and to celebrate his having completed his journey upon the underground road, Anka and I received many congratulations upon our engagement as well. One of Anka's favorite uncles even told me how my recent service to the Capac Inca had brought much honor to Anka's family. In response, I hugged this uncle so fiercely, I caused him to spill his chicha. Laughing, he went to refill his cup.

"I already feel a part of your family," I told Anka.

"Then come dance with me."

We joined with others, forming two circles around the musicians. One circle spun in the direction opposite the other. If this looked dizzying to the observer, it was much more so for those dancing, especially for the ones who had drunk much chicha. Eventually someone fell down and this tripped up more of the dancers, and the two circles came apart with all of us laughing.

Then two men entered the dancing area to perform a purucaya, a special dance to pay tribute to Kacha's warrior spirit. The men were dressed in feathered garments and had painted their faces so they were hardly recognizable as men. Indeed, they looked more like fiends conjured up by a sorcerer. Each man had two ropes tied about his waist, and the ends of these ropes were held by women.

As drums pounded out a blood-stirring rhythm, the men circled each other, yelling ferociously and threatening each other with the aillos they held. The purucaya was frightening to watch, for the men, whirling the aillos above their heads, seemed sure to kill each other. When the men got too close and seemed like to bash in each other's skulls, the women would pull them apart, using the ropes. This heart-thrilling spectacle went on until I thought the men would surely die just from their exertions. But when they grew tired, the women fed them coca leaves, and the men went after each other again. Eventually the drums stopped pounding and both men fell upon the ground, each pretending they had been struck down by the other. As they lay upon ground with chests heaving, we roared our approval of their masterful performance. The men slowly rose up to acknowledge our appreciation before they were led away by the women.

In the calm that followed, Anka signaled the musicians to accompany him. Standing before an unlit pile of firewood, he began to sing.

> Above the snow top mountain
> Look! There Inti rises.
> He chases from Pachamama's face
> The shadow of night.
>
> Beneath her jagged brow
> her eyes slowly open.
> Out hops the viscacha
> to drink of her tears.
>
> It is a new day.
> The condor rises with the first wind.
> The delicate blossom unfurls.
> And from tears are the spirits reborn.

I had heard this song many times, yet never with such emotion as Anka expressed. Tears fell from my eyes, and as I looked around, I saw many were likewise crying.

By custom, there had been no fire in the Yachawasi since Kacha's death. But now an older man, carrying a torch, ignited the pile of wood. Then two young men set a basin of water before the fire. Anka's father was the first to wash away the mourning paint he still wore. He was given a small piece of cloth to dry himself with. When he was finished, he placed the cloth upon the fire.

Anka repeated this cleansing ritual, followed by the other relatives in order of the closeness of their relationship to Kacha. Once all had washed and the cloths had been consumed by the flames, the basin with its tinted water was used to extinguish the fire. Yet even as the steam rose from the sizzling embers, a second pile of wood was ignited, and the flames quickly grew.

The drowning of the flames marked the end of the mourning period for Kacha; the second fire was the signal to resume the celebration. As the musicians broke into a lively tune, people rushed to refill their cups with chicha. Taking my hand, Anka led me away from the celebrants. We walked slowly along the wall that enclosed the Yachawasi. Past the main buildings, there were several rows of wasis. Stopping, Anka pointed. "This is the wasi of my family. I have many pleasant memories of nights when Kacha and I would lie awake, waiting until my parents were asleep so we could jump the walls and go explore Qosqo."

He took a deep breath and slowly released it. "My father believes I am ready to become an amauta. I think I'm ready too."

"Then we will live here in the Yachawasi?"

Anka turned to look at me directly. "Could you bear to live within these walls?"

"I could live anywhere so long as I'm with you." It was Anka I worried about. Could such a free spirit be contained within walls?

This same question must have been in Anka's mind. "My brother and I promised each other that one day we would explore all Tahuantinsuyu together. But the gods have decided otherwise."

"Will you be happy as an amauta?"

"I think so. I have always wanted to follow in my father's footsteps. Besides, now Yana Mayu is my Tahuantinsuyu. I want to live with you and learn of your mysteries."

He looked at me with such love, my heart rose to my throat. I put my head upon his chest and he encircled me with his arms. Yet as we held each other, I felt his head turn, and looking up, saw him staring at the wall.

"Perhaps we should go back," I said. "The others must be wondering what happened to us."

We returned to the celebration. I ate little, but danced much. I drank just enough chicha to pacify my thirst after dancing, for I did not want to arrive later at the Cora Cora in a state of intoxication. When Inti drew near the mountains to the west, Anka accompanied me back to the Acllawasi, promising to return early the next day, for he wanted me to share morning meal with him and his father.

I was never so happy as that evening when I was carried upon the litter to the Cora Cora. Not only was I to be married to Anka, but, having given much thought to the Capac Inca's offer, I now knew how I might show my appreciation to those who had helped bring me to this happy moment. It was timely knowledge, as I was soon to find out.

Chapter 54

When I entered Topa's room it was the Capac Inca who greeted me.

"Good evening, Yana. Come, sit here." He pointed to a place on the floor not far from where he sat upon his short bench.

I walked forward, blinking my eyes, for I had never seen Topa's room so illuminated. It seemed there were as many candles burning as there were stars in the sky. The pleasure I felt at what this might portend was countered by the sight of four elders who sat two to each side of the Capac Inca and looked as if what they just ate did not agree with them.

"I've ordered special foods for this evening," the Capac Inca said. Immediately four women entered bearing trays. "Please enjoy yourself."

The candles wavered as Topa Inca rushed into the room, carrying a small wooden chest. Throwing himself down next to me, he slapped me on the leg as if to say, "Watch!" Then taking a piece of llama, dripping red, he stuffed it into his mouth.

I could not help but laugh, and the Capac Inca's eyes sparkled as he watched his son's antics.

"I have much to thank you for, Yana Mayu," the Capac Inca said, "and that's why we are all here." He gestured to the men sitting beside him. "Don't let these old carcasses frighten you. They are just here to listen and to ensure that your wishes are recorded and carried out."

One of the men must have been a quipucamayoc, for he fingered long quipus with different colored strings.

"Have you considered the ways I can reward you?" the Capac Inca said. I nodded.

"I hope there are many, otherwise, I've kept these old fellows from their sleep for no reason. Now, what is your first wish?"

I took a deep breath and began. "I would like a guinea pig so that I may sacrifice it to the gods."

One of the wizened observers actually smiled. "One guinea pig?" he said. "Why not one thousand?"

"I promised the gods I would give them a guinea pig when I could. I made this promise when I was a Hatunruna. To a Hatunruna, one guinea pig is a great sacrifice."

The Capac Inca nodded approvingly. He turned to the quipucamayoc. "Make a record of that. One guinea pig."

The quipucamayoc made a small knot in his quipu.

"What besides one guinea pig?" the Capac Inca said.

"The chieftain of our village, Weqo Churu, I'm afraid my brother and I have caused him much trouble. I would like to give him something as a way of apologizing. Perhaps a—"

The Capac Inca cut me off with a raised hand. He turned back to the man immediately to his left. "Send him a wife," he instructed, "Someone young and beautiful."

I swallowed. I was going to suggest a llama.

"And one hundred llamas. Also, for every member of Yana's village, including the children, two new sets of clothing. Also, this village will not have to pay tribute to me for as long as I, or my son, Topa, lives. They may use my fields in any way they wish."

My heart leapt. How my people would rejoice when they heard this!

The Capac Inca turned back toward me. "What is your next wish?"

Now came what was closest to my heart. "I would like my father released from his service in the army."

The Capac Inca stared at me with dark, penetrating eyes. To the quipucamayoc, who had started to work his strings, he said, "Leave that for now."

I tried to swallow my disappointment. Why had the Capac Inca disregarded my request? I studied his face, but it was inscrutable.

"What is your next wish?"

"I would like for my brother, Charapa, to become a student at the Yachawasi."

The Capac Inca leaned forward. "Does he have your courage?"

"He has the courage to speak his mind, which often gets him in trouble. He also has an uncanny ability with numbers."

"Very well. If we can't make a soldier out of him, perhaps he can work designing buildings or something. What next?"

"Many people helped me on my journey to find the water at the end of the world. I would like to reward them for their kindnesses. First, there is Mana Chanka, the camasca of Tambo Toco. I would like for him to attend the celebration of Topa's recovery. Unfortunately, one of his legs is bad, and it prevents him from walking long distances."

"In that case, I will send a litter and bearers to carry him to Qosqo."

"There are three others from Tambo Toco who I would also like to attend the celebration. They are Urpito and his mother Sumaq Ñawi and a wonderful musician named Akakllu. I ask that Akakllu be allowed to play with those you have chosen to provide music for the celebration."

The Capac Inca smiled. "Do they all require litters?"

I shook my head. "They can walk except for the boy who is very small and recovering from a head injury. I would like for him to ride upon the back of a gentle llama."

The Capac Inca chuckled. "Did you hear that?" he said, addressing the quipucamayoc. "A *gentle* llama."

The old men laughed, and I did too. The Capac Inca was obviously enjoying himself, and I was feeling less anxious.

"Next is Chogñi and her son Huchuq Uma and her daughter Imayoq. I would like for them to attend the celebration also."

"Chogñi. I deduce from her name she is partially blind. Perhaps I better send a litter for her as well."

I nodded. Blindness was not Chogñi's problem, but I thought a litter a good idea anyway. "I don't know the name of their village, but it is located where the Huatanay and Wilkamayu Rivers join."

"Very well. What next?"

"In the town of Calca, there are three brothers whose names are Atoq, Kumari, and Ruwayniyoq. They were very fond of my llama, Chumpi, and took care of him for me. I would like to send them a llama that looks like Chumpi. The hair about the middle of this llama must be darker than the hair elsewhere."

I watched as the quipucamayoc's fingers quickly made knots in the strings. I had not forgotten Kaka, the boys' blind uncle, but had thought to include him in another request.

The Capac Inca shook his head. "So far all your wishes have been simple and easy to grant. Isn't there something greater you want? Something that will challenge my powers?"

I took a deep breath. Now is the time, I thought. "I would like General Kuntur released from his sentence and returned to his former position in the army."

The smile vanished from the Capac Inca's face. The quipucamayoc dropped his quipu. Two of the old men, who for the most part had sat quietly, now erupted. Talking at the same time, they vehemently protested my request. Leaning to one side, then to the other, the Capac Inca listened to their objections, then with a slash of his hand, cut them off. The Capac Inca leaned toward me, his wide shoulders blocking the light of many candles.

"General Kuntur has displeased me. Why do you make this request?"

"He befriended me, and he protected me. I have never known anyone with so much courage. He is an honorable man who I know will always be loyal to you."

The Capac Inca's dark eyes bored into mine. I trembled, yet did not look away. In my heart, I knew I was right in what I was asking.

Suddenly, the Capac Inca threw back his head and roared with laughter. The old men stared at him anxiously, then at each other. "Atakachau!" the Capac Inca cried. "The ways of the gods are wondrous indeed. Very well, Yana, I will honor your request."

Again, the two men voiced protests, and again the Capac Inca cut them off with a slash of his hand. He looked at me, smiling. "I did ask you to challenge me, Yana, but perhaps you better go back to making simple requests."

I nodded. Looking down, I ran my fingers across the scar still vivid in the palm of my hand. "Chukru Makis, the captain of the guards, has been very kind to me. Among other considerations, he has watched over Chumpi, my llama, while I have been in the Acllawasi. I think he has become attached to Chumpi, and I would like for Chukru have a llama of his own."

The Capac Inca chuckled. "Chukru with a llama? Likely he'll end up eating it, but I'll have another llama found that also has a dark band about its middle. What else?"

I placed one hand upon the necklace Topa had given me, "I would like a necklace, similar to this, given to Acllamama. She has taught me what it means to act like an Inca. Also, there is an aclla named Paru. She is about Topa's age though, like Topa, she thinks and acts much older. I don't believe the Acllawasi is the best place for her, and I would like for her to be reassigned here, perhaps as a companion for Topa."

Topa, who had been listening with interest, now looked eagerly at his father.

The Capac Inca rubbed his chin. "For the time being, she will be permitted to attend the Coyamama. Then we shall see whether she would make a fitting companion for my son."

I nodded, pleased, for I knew that once given the opportunity, Paru would surely capitalize on it.

I then took off my old necklace and held it high so all could see the three tattered feathers. "The gods have given me so much. They gave me these feathers which helped guide and protect me. Now I feel obligated to return them to the jungle where they originally came from. I realize it is small thanks compared to all the gods have done, nevertheless, I would like permission to do this."

No one spoke. The quipucamayoc lowered his quipu and stared at me.

"Also, by returning these feathers, I can stop in Calca and see a blind man. He loves to hear stories, and I can repay him for his wise counsel by telling him of my journey."

"But what of yourself?" the Capac Inca said. "All these things are for others. What can I do for you, Yana Mayu?"

I smiled. "As you probably know, wise Father, I am to marry Anka, the son of an amauta. Anka's brother Kacha has recently died. It had been the brothers' dream to explore Tahuantinsuyu together. Having seen many wonders during my journey, I now appreciate this dream, and though I cannot equal the adventurous spirit of Kacha, nevertheless, I would like to be Anka's traveling companion on a journey to see all of Tahuantinsuyu."

The Capac Inca's eyes lit up. "Excellent! An excellent wish! How long will you be gone?" Before I could answer, he decided. "Three years. You must take at least three years." The smile disappeared. "But how will I be able to find you if I need you?" He glanced at Topa, and I understood his concern. "You must promise me to keep me informed of your whereabouts always. Use the chasquis to send messages."

I nodded.

Turning to the quipucamayoc he said. "They will need porters. They will need two litters plus twelve carriers for each litter. And guards. Say fifty—no, better make that a hun— What?" said the Capac Inca, seeing the look of dismay upon my face.

"Please, wise Father, we would prefer to go alone with just a couple of llamas to carry our supplies."

The Capac Inca considered this. With seeming reluctance, he consented. "Very well. I will give you tokens that will allow you to draw from the colcas for your needs. You can also sleep at the tambos. In this way, I can also keep track of your whereabouts."

"Thank you. This is the greatest wedding present I could possibly imagine. I can't wait to tell Anka."

The Capac Inca nodded in response to my appreciation. "What else?"

I shook my head. "That is all, wise Father."

"What?" He pointed to the quipucamayoc. "He's hardly done any work."

Feeling bold, I said, "I'm sorry he had to lose sleep for no reason."

Everyone laughed, including the quipucamayoc.

The Capac Inca then addressed the quipucamayoc. "Have you made a record of Yana's requests?"

The quipucamayoc tied the last of his knots then nodded.

"Then I, the Capac Inca, descendant of Inti, Supreme Lord of all Tahuantinsuyu, command that Yana Mayu's wishes, as here recorded, be carried out."

Topa, who had been anxiously fidgeting, got his father's attention.

"I believe my son has something he would like to give you, Yana."

Topa handed me the chest he had carried into the room. "It is a wedding present for you and Anka."

I opened the lid of the small chest which had hinges made of gold. Inside, nestled in vicuña fibers, were the two cups I had seen Sampa Maki making. With a trembling hand, I lifted one out so all could see. I had thought them magnificent before, but now, with gems set in them, they were bedazzling. To think that Anka and I would have the use of these treasures for the rest of our lives! I wiped away the happy tears that coursed down my cheek.

"You are crying," the Capac Inca said. "Perhaps these cups displease you?"

Topa also teased me. "I will send them back and have them melted down and made into something else. Perhaps a necklace for Chumpi."

Laughing, I shook my head. "I cry for their beauty and for the joy I feel. I will remember this day every time I drink from one of these cups."

"Drink from one now," the Capac Inca said. He lifted a silver jar and filled one of my new cups with chicha. Then he filled two other cups and gave one to Topa. But before drinking, he addressed the four men still sitting beside him. "Gentlemen, thank you for your service. You may now go sleep."

Laughing, the four old men slowly rose up. As soon as they were gone, the Capac Inca drained his cup in one long pull. With a satisfied belch, he set his cup down and began to refill it. He motioned with his free hand for me to drink. I took just a sip from my beautiful cup, for I was already brimful with happiness.

The Capac Inca cleared his throat. "Yana, about your father…"

My fickle happiness evaporated.

"I know I said I would grant you any wish within my power, but there are some things even the Capac Inca cannot do. I am sorry."

I tried to swallow the lump in my throat.

"You see," the Capac Inca continued, "I cannot release your father from his service…" He motioned and the curtain at the entrance was pulled aside. "…because I have already done so!"

Into the room walked Ipa, Charapa, Weqo Churu and my father!

Chapter 55

Miraculously, my cup did not spill all its contents as it slipped from my hand. Then I was up and running. My father stepped forward, and I flew into his waiting arms. Now that he was here, the joy of my brim-filled heart spilled over.

Then there was Ipa by my side. I released my father and hugged the woman who was a second mother to me.

"Atatau!" she complained. "Don't squeeze so hard! Have pity on my old bones."

Reluctantly, I released her. "Where's Kusi?"

"Can you believe they put him to sleep on a chusi made of vicuña? The child will be spoilt for life!"

I laughed. That was my old Ipa.

She ran her hand down the sleeve of my fine lliqlla. Was it disapproval I saw in her eyes? I realized how different I must have looked in my new lliqlla, feathered necklace, and red llautu. Embarrassed, I dropped my head.

But Ipa would not allow that. She took my chin in her bony hand and lifted my head back up. I looked into her eyes and saw an acceptance of my new status—more than that, an approval. She released my chin and ran a finger across my necklace. "This looks good on you," she said.

I smiled as tears coursed down my cheeks.

Behind Ipa, Charapa and Weqo Churu still lingered near the entrance. I quickly pulled my brother forward.

Staring at the floor, Charapa mumbled, "I'm sorry to have caused you so much trouble, Yana."

I squeezed him affectionately. "You did act selfishly," I chided, "but look at all the good that has come of it!"

To this, Weqo Churu snorted loudly. I looked and saw an anxious look appear upon Weqo Churu's his face, as if he feared he overstepped by venturing disapproval within these lofty surroundings. As I moved to welcome him, Charapa held me back.

"Yana, did I hear right? Am I going to be a student at the Yachawasi?"

I nodded, smiling, but before I could say anything more, the Capac Inca interrupted.

"Come, good people. Don't hang back. Share with us our meal!"

He clapped his hands twice, and women appeared, carrying jars of chicha along with extra cups.

"Come!" he again ordered. He motioned for my father to sit beside him. "Old soldiers should sit together!"

I purposely maneuvered Charapa to sit beside Topa Inca. The boys eyed each other, unsure of what to say. Topa was the first to make an overture by lifting a plate of sliced llama and offering it to Charapa.

"Yana makes me eat this stuff," Topa complained.

"She *makes* you?" Charapa said, taking the thickest slice.

Topa explained his dislike of all meats except fish, and this led to a discussion of favorite foods, a topic Charapa could discourse upon at length. Then they talked of other matters important to boys: games, toys, music, and the like.

I looked at my father sitting next to the Capac Inca. Both possessed a strong, proud bearing not uncommon among warriors. I remembered that same demeanor in general Kuntur. My father listened as the Capac Inca explained about the difficulties he was having with rebellious citizens in some far-off place. The Capac Inca asked for an opinion and my father responded in a voice too low for me to hear. Yet I could tell by the Capac Inca's attentiveness that he valued my father's comments. It seemed there was no one, even a common soldier, from whom the Capac Inca did not try to learn.

To my left, Weqo Churu, looking ill at ease, picked at his food. I noticed he had not touched his chicha. "Try the chicha," I said. "It's particularly good."

Weqo Churu picked up his cup and took a large swallow. Sputtering, he quickly set down his cup. Ipa patted his back as he wheezed. All conversation ceased as Weqo Churu gasped for breath. "Strong!" he said, as tears ran down his cheek.

Everyone laughed.

"That's because it's made from molle berries," I said. The Capac Inca looked at me and winked.

The chicha's strength did not keep Weqo Churu from drinking it. When his cup was empty, I quickly refilled it. The Capac Inca, the consummate host, motioned for Weqo Churu to move closer and join in a discussion about llamas. I listened for a while as the Capac Inca talked about the problem of mange. Here was a subject Weqo Churu could discuss at length.

Watching Weqo Churu gesturing dramatically with his hands, I wondered if he had heard he was to receive a new wife. I was glad for him, for his first wife had been dead many years.

I moved to sit closer to Ipa.

"You would think we were all one big family," I said.

Topa and Charapa, having each produced a top, had moved off to spin them upon the floor. The Capac Inca, while listening to Weqo Churu, checked to see the cups of the men were full. Then he laughed at something Weqo Churu said.

"You know, Yana," Ipa said, "I never believed you would find the water at the end of the world."

My jaw dropped.

"Don't look so surprised. It wasn't your brother I was thinking about when I encouraged you to look for the water. I figured Weqo Churu would take care of Charapa." She took a piece of fish from one of the trays and began to pull it apart. "What I was hoping for was that a little time by yourself would make you a little wiser, a little more mature. I really didn't think you'd be gone more than a day or two." She dropped the bits of fish back on the tray. "Atatau! I was just trying to get you to grow up!"

Ipa looked at me to see if I understood. She pushed a loose strand of hair off my forehead. "But I didn't realize how determined you'd be, or maybe I forgot how much you love your brother." She moved her hand down to straighten a few feathers of my necklace. "I heard how you cured Topa Inca even before they sent for us to come here. You wouldn't believe the stories!"

Before I could respond, Ipa jabbed her finger hard into my chest. "See? I told you, you had the power!"

I grasped her finger, for it was hurting me. "Yes, Ipa, you were right. Like you, I am a camasca."

"Like me? Better than me!" She leaned in close, a mischievous glint in her eye. "For I heard you cured Topa Inca by turning yourself into a jaguar!"

"Please, Ipa, it was only a puma."

We both laughed, and the men briefly stopped their conversation to look at us.

"I also heard you are to be married," Ipa said in a quiet voice.

I swallowed, then nodded.

"Is he a good man?" she said.

"He's a wonderful man, Ipa. He is kind and strong, and when he laughs he makes me—"

"Atatau! And here I thought you had grown up!" Ipa tried to pinch my waist, but could find to nothing grip. "You're too skinny! But you know what I'm asking. Is your future husband a hard worker?"

"He's the son of an amauta. Like his father, he's going to be an amauta also."

"So, your new husband is an Inca." She looked up at my llautu. "Like you."

I nodded.

She sighed. "Does that mean you will live here in Qosqo?"

"In the Yachawasi where Anka will teach. Charapa will live there also."

"Yes, I heard something about him being a student. Well, that's good. He will be happier here."

Ipa looked sad. I rested my hand upon her arm. "And you will come and live here in Qosqo too."

"Atatau!" she exclaimed, pulling her arm away. "And live like a guinea pig stuffed in a pen?" She shook her head. "Besides, what would happen to the people of our village without me to care for them?"

Now, I was the one sad. Though I thought it unlikely she would choose to live in Qosqo, still, I had hoped.

Ipa placed her hand upon my arm and squeezed. "I'm very proud of you, Yana."

It was true, she was proud; I could see it in her eyes. "It was the gods who cured Topa Inca. I was only their tool."

She shook my arm. "I'm not talking about Topa Inca or the gods. I'm talking about you. I'm proud of you for growing up. I'm proud that when the moment came, you realized you were more than just a water bearer, but a true camasca. And I'm proud of you for acting like one."

"But how do you know these things? You were not there."

I followed her crooked finger as she pointed at Topa Inca, who, along with Charapa, was laughing as they jumped over the spinning tops. "The last time I saw that boy, he was near to death. Now look at him. He didn't get that way by sipping water!"

That's true, I thought. And yet—

Something was moving past me, an important thought that I did not wish to lose. Ipa had just told me I had grown up. Into my mind came a picture of

Kusi laughing as I sprayed him with water warm from my mouth. Then he was screaming and shaking, for Ipa had flung icy water upon both of us. She was angry, for she wanted Kusi to grow up to be hard, not soft. Was that what it was to be an adult? To be hard? I did not feel hard.

I glanced at Ipa who was studying my face as if following the trail of my thoughts. I closed my eyes to think better.

I recalled being in Topa's room for the first time, how sick Topa had looked. I had helped to heal him, using the power the gods had granted me. Yet helping him had not felt like something I chose to do, rather the other way around; I had been chosen. So how could that experience have caused me to grow up when I felt I had done so little?

I shook my head. This trail of thought was leading nowhere. I started again this time on a different path.

Why had I gone to find the water at the end of the world? Because I wanted to free my brother from prison; because I wanted my family back together.

I opened my eyes and looked at Ipa. "Now that he no longer has to be a soldier, where will Father live?"

"Atakachau! You have given your father a great gift! As long as he was in the army, it was impossible for him to remarry."

"Remarry!"

Smiling, Ipa nodded.

I looked across at my father who sat listening to the Capac Inca.

Ipa followed my gaze. "He is still a young man," she whispered, "still vital."

I was upset. I had never dreamt of my father having any wife other than my mother. Yet, reluctantly, I acknowledged the truth of what Ipa said. My father was a vital man. He had always worked hard and deserved the affection and care only a wife could provide.

"He could find a wife here in Qosqo," I said. "Perhaps the Capac Inca would give him one."

Ipa snorted. "A stranger for a wife?" She leaned in close and whispered. "I think he'd like to marry Huchuq Wepaq."

Appalled, I shrank away from her. Huchuq Wepaq was a widow in our village whom I'd always thought stupid.

Ipa cackled. "Not good enough, is she? Well, you're wrong! She'll make your father a good wife, and she'll be a good mother to Kusi."

I swallowed. "Well, they can still live here in Qosqo."

Ipa shook her head. "Your father would not be happy here anymore than I. Qosqo is too crowded. Your father is an important man in Qomermoya, respected as a brave warrior and a hard worker. But here, in Qosqo, he'd just be another ant on the ant hill."

Tears stung my eyes, and I closed them.

Ipa placed her hand upon my knee. "I think I know what you're thinking, Yana." Her voice was surprisingly gentle. "All your efforts to bring the family together have come to little."

But she was wrong. I was not thinking that. I had known for a while now that I would fail to reunite my family, and not because of Charapa's restlessness or my desire to marry Anka. Within me a change had begun the day I stood on the mountain above Tambo Toco and watched the clouds passing overhead. There I had felt myself being pulled into a wider world, one of alluring beauty and wonder. It was the first hint of my betrayal. Yet how could I go back to our village after what I'd seen and all I still wished to see?

And my tears were not tears of sorrow, but of acceptance. Well, perhaps some sorrow. I would miss not living with my family. Yet I was fortunate, for now that I was an Inca, I could come and go as I pleased and would always be able to visit Qomermoya.

So, what of my heart, the one with all the pieces missing? Well, I now had a new heart, a much larger one, waiting to be filled by Anka and the children we would have, and I would not trade this new heart to piece together the past.

Now I reached the end of my trail of thought. This, to me, was what growing up meant: an acceptance of the new life the gods had given me. Only two events remained to complete my maturity: becoming a wife, and becoming a mother.

I opened my eyes and picked up my cup. It was empty. I grabbed Ipa's cup, but it was empty also.

"What are you looking for?" Ipa said, annoyed.

"I'm looking for cold water so you can throw it in my face one last time."

We both laughed. Weqo Churu and my father were deep in conversation. Only the Capac Inca noticed us laughing. He looked at us curiously.

Ipa slapped me on the knee then addressed the Capac Inca. "My daughter has grown up!"

The Capac Inca nodded. "Yes, your daughter is now an Inca." He looked up at the narrow openings in the wall. "It has stopped raining. Let me show you my garden, Ipa."

I quickly stood to help Ipa up, but she slapped my hand away. When, however, the Capac Inca stepped around the half-empty trays to offer his hand, she willingly accepted it. Placing his strong arm around her shoulder, he led her through the entry way on the far side of the room. My father and Weqo Churu went to join them. Charapa was undecided whether to follow or stay with his new friend. Curiosity won out, and he passed through the curtain, followed more slowly by Topa.

I chose to remain alone with the sputtering candles. I sat back down, closed my eyes, and breathed deeply. Heady elation had given way to deep contentment. I recalled the words of the Qollowayan camasca concerning the person who is dreamed upon: for such a person, nothing turns out as expected. How true! Yet I also remember what Ipa said: the gods always act for the best. Truly everything had turned out better than I could have dreamed.

Suddenly, Charapa stuck his head back through the curtain. "Come, Yana!" he cried. "You've got to see this!"

I did not tell him I had already seen the garden many times. I stood up and hurried to him. Placing my arm through his, I said, "Show me!"

The End

GLOSSARY

achachila: sacred site, place of great power.

acllas: the chosen women. Those who served in the temples and wove cloth used as offerings to the gods.

Acllawasi: residence of the acllas. Men were forbidden from entering it. Punishment was death by hanging by the hair.

aillo: a bola. A weapon made by attaching two or three fist-sized rocks together with a short section of rope between them. The aillo is thrown at prey to entangle its feet.

Akakllu: woodpecker.

Allallanka: lizard.

amauta: a teacher who instructed the sons of Inca noblemen in the Yachawasi, an academy in Qosqo.

Anka: Kestrel (*Falco sparverius*).

apacheta: an earth shrine found at high mountain passes. Travelers placed rocks or quids of coca upon the shrine, offerings for the removal of fatigue and the restoration of strength.

Atakachau: an exclamation. How exciting!

Atatau: an exclamation. Disgusting!

ayahuasca (*Banisteriopsis caapi*): a hallucinogen still used today by practicing shamans.

Bilyea (*Psoralea pubescens*): perennial shrub with dark purple flowers. Its leaves make a nutritious, non-caffeinated drink.

camasca: healer. A person with knowledge of healing plants and an ability to use drug-induced visions to discover the nature of an illness.

camasto (*Nicotiana tomentosa*): a bush that is a member of the tobacco family. Its leaves are used as an acaricide.

Capac Inca: the Inca were the ruling lords. The Capac Inca was first lord, the emperor of Tahuantinsuyu.

Capac-nan: the royal highway that ran throughout the highlands of the Andes.

Capuli (*Prunus capuli*): a mid-sized tree with lance-like leaves. Its red berries are sweet and delicious.

Chachacomo (*Escallonia resinosa*): a short tree tolerant to drought. Worms that develop beneath the bark can be used for food.

chamana (*Dodonaea viscosa*): a short bush with small seeds. The wood is oily and burns readily.

Charapa: turtle.

charqui: dried meat usually of llama or guinea pig.

chasqui: official messenger. Always young male runners.

checche (*Berberis spp*): A short bush with sharp points on the leaves. A laxative can be made of its roots.

chicha: alcoholic beverage usually made of maize though sometimes of berries.

chilca (*Baccharis latifolia*): a bush, one to two meters, that grows in abundance along rivers. Its ash is combined with other ingredients to make llipta which is chewed with coca leaves. Rheumatism is treated with poultice of chilca leaves.

Chumpi: a wide, woven belt.

Chinchasuyu: the northern quarter of Tahuantinsuyu. The city of Qosqo was also similarly quartered and the sections called by the same names. Chinchasuyu: the northern quarter; Contisuyu: the east; Collasuyu: the south; Antisuyu: the west. Related to this are the four fountains within the Acllawasi of Qosqo. Each flowed toward one of the four quarters of Tahuantinsuyu: Chinchaysuyu–the fountain of pebbles; Antisuyu–the fountain of the water weed; Collasuyu–the fountain of algae; Cuntisuyu–the fountain of frogs. The acllas bathed in the fountains according to what quarter they had been brought from.

Chogñi: blind-in-one-eye.

Chukru Makis: hard hands.

chuncara: a type of dice game in which colored beans are advanced along a board with holes in it depending on what number comes up.

chuño: freeze-dried potatoes. Freeze-drying is still used today to preserve potatoes.

chusi: long blanket woven of llama wool. Half is used as the bed and the other half folded over the sleeper as a blanket.

coca (*Erythroxylon coca*): a plant grown in the foothills of the eastern Andes above the Amazon basin. It is a stimulant with a wide variety of uses. A tea made from coca leaves soothes the stomach and relieves altitude sickness. Chewing the dried leaves combats fatigue and hunger.

colca: storage house.

Cora Cora: the residence of the Capac Inca.

Coricancha: the temple to Inti, the most magnificent edifice in Qosqo.

Coyamama: the wife of a Capac Inca. Often his sister or step-sister.

Coya Raymi: the month corresponding to September. The festival marked the beginning of the rainy season when villages and cities were purified to rid them of disease associated with the coming of rain. The work of cleaning was done by the men.

Cuntisuyu: the southwest "quarter" of Tahuantinsuyu. Also, one of the four divisions of Qosqo.

guayyaya: a dance in which men and women joined hands and formed a line. It was dignified and solemn.

hanca: (*Solanum ochrophyllum*): a bush of up to five meters that grows in ravines. An infusion of its leaves is used to clean the wounds of animals.

Hatun Rinri: big ears.

Hatunruna: a commoner, as opposed to the ruling class, the Incas.

hiwaya: punishment whereby a heavy stone is dropped upon the offender's back, often resulting in death or permanent injury.

huaca: a sacred place either of outstanding natural beauty or of significance because of what had occurred there. They were often marked with a man-made shrine.

Huanacauri: a mountain outside of Qosqo. It was upon this mountain Manka supposedly first saw the valley where he would build his city.

Huacaypata: "holy place." The square in Qosqo where ceremonies and sacrifices took place. Only Inca nobility could enter.

huarachicoy: boy's puberty rite in which he is given his adult name.

huaranhuay (*Tecoma sambucifolia*): a bush that grows to three meters with clusters of bright yellow, tubular flowers.

huayau (*Alnus jorullensis*): a riparian tree that grows to 20 meters. An alder tree.

Huchuq Uma: small head.

Huchuq Wepaq: narrow waist.

ichu (*Stipa ichu*): coarse bunch grass.

Ichuq Maki: left hand, implying the person is left-handed.

Imayoq Chanka: hollow leg.

Inti: the sun; the most important god of the Incas.

Intuillapa: god of thunder, second only to Inti. From the river in the sky (the Milky Way) he drew water and flung it upon the earth as rain.

Kacha: axe.

Kaka: uncle.

kantuta or kantu (*Cantua buxifolia*): A tall bush with red, tubular flowers.

Kiro: tooth.

Kullku: turtledove.

Kumari: an abbreviation of Ukumari, the spectacled bear.

Kuntur (*Vultur gryphus*): the Andean condor.

Kupa Chukcha: curly hair. Very rare among the Incas.

Kusi, Kusisqa: Happy.

Kusipata: "the happy place." A square of approximately 20 acres where commoners celebrated religious festivals. It was also used as a marketplace.

Llakato: snail.

Llama (*Lama glama*): a camelid. The coarser fibers of its hair were used for weaving blankets. Valued primarily as a pack animal, but also used for meat.

llaulli (*Barnadesia horrida*): a pink-flowered bush with long thorns.

llautu: a red braid the width of a finger wound around the forehead. Only worn by Inca men.

lliqlla: a long blanket that wraps around the shoulders and is fastened at the neck with a topu. Worn by women.

llipta: a resinous ball made from the ashes of burnt plants (quinoa, chilca). It facilitates the extraction of the alkaloids in the coca leaves and freshens the mouth after the bitterness of the coca.

locro: a stew made with dried meat, potatoes, chili peppers, and other vegetables.

lucuma (*Lucuma obovata*): a tree that grows to 16 meters. The fruit has a thick, green shell but a deliciously sweet orange, fibrous meat. Today it is used to flavor ice cream.

Mana Chanka: bad leg.

Miski Qapay: sweet aroma.

molle (*Schinus molle*): a medium-sized tree with red berries. The berries make a strong, alcoholic beverage, while resins from the tree were used to embalm mummies.

Munaycha: beautiful.

motepatasca: a stew made from whole kernels of maize and flavored with chili peppers.

mutuy (*Senna birostris*): short bush with bright yellow flowers. Its root is used as a yellow dye.

ocarina: a small, oviod flute made of clay.

Pachamama: the earth, a goddess.

Pakpaka: likely *Aegolius harrisii*, the Buff-fronted Owl.

Pallqa Wawa: baby fingers.

paqpa (*Furcraea andina*): the maguey plant, a large, spikey succulent. Its leaf fibers are used to make rope, and the root is pounded and used for soap.

Paru Chukcha: gold-brown hair.

penka: (*Opuntia ficus-indica*): a cactus with broad, flat joints and clusters of sharp thorns. The delicious red fruits have smaller thorn clusters.

Penqali: bashful person.

Piki: flea.

pisonay (*Erythrina edulis*): a leafy tree with bright orange blossoms. Native to the cloud forest of the eastern Andes, it was acclimatized by the Incas to survive in the highlands.

puma (*Puma concolor*): mountain lion.

purucaya: dance in which two men dressed in feathered garments appear to combat each other in a stylized manner.

puturutu: horn made from a conch shell.

Qallo: tongue.

Qapia Weqe: soft cry.

Qillamama: the moon, a goddess.

Qilli Chukcha: dirty hair.

Qollowayans (Kallawayans): A nation of people who for millennia have resided near Lake Titacaca. Even today, they are known for the skill of their healers. The Capac Inca always traveled with a Qollowayan camasca.

Qosqo: Cusco. The "navel of the world" and the capital of the Inca Empire.

Qomermoya: green pasture.

queuña (*Polylepis spp.*): a scrubby tree with small, dark green leaves in groups of three. Grown for a windbreak.

quicochicoy: a celebration of a girl's passage into womanhood when she is given her adult name. It is celebrated after the girl's first menstruation.

quinoa: a small grain native to South America. It has a nut-like taste.

quipu: a means of recording information using a series of attached strings of various colors. Knots tied on the strings represented the amount of food harvested, the number of llamas, number of deaths, births, etc.

quipucamayoc: a record keeper whose means of recording information was a quipu.

quishuar (*Buddleia longifolia*): a tree growing up to 14 meters. It was used to carve idols which were sometimes incinerated as offerings to the gods.

ratuchicoy: the ceremony conducted when a child reaches the age of one year. The child is given his first haircut and the name he'll be known by until he reaches adulthood.

Ruwayniyoq: able.

Saqsaywaman: Pachacutec Inca Yupanqui, Topa Inca's father, designed for Qosqo a vast complex of walls, buildings, and religious shrines called Saqsaywaman. The city of Qosqo was built in the shape of a puma and Saqsaywaman was the head of the puma, and by extension, the source of the great power of the Inca empire.

Sampa Maki: light hands.

sanco: a porridge made with partially-ground maize kernels. During the Coya Raymi festival, sanco was smeared on faces and clothing as well as the entrances to wasis as a preventive against diseases prevalent during the rainy season.

Senqa Qilli: ugly nose.

sonqo: the heart, lungs, and central organs. The area of a person's life force.

Sumapayay: exemplarily behaved.

Sumaq Ñawi: pretty eyes.

Sumaq Uya: pretty face.

taclla: wooden foot plow.

Tahuantinsuyu: the four quarters, the Inca empire.

taikiji kawayu (*Equisetum giganteum*): horse tail. (This word is not Quechuan but from the language of the Kallawayans.)

tambo: waystation to serve those traveling in official capacities.

Tambo Puquio: refers to a waystation where there are springs.

Taruka (*Hippocamelus antisensis*): the Andean huemul, a relative of the deer. It is short-legged and barrel-chested.

topu: a stick pin of metal with a thin, round head which is sharp enough to use as a small cutting tool. Used to fasten a lliqlla.

tokoyrikoq: official inspector. Today, he would be called a health inspector.

Tullu: slender.

tupu: a distance equal to 7.5 kilometers.

Ukumari (*Tremarctos ornatus*): spectacled bear.

unku: a sleeveless garment for men made from one piece of cloth folded and sewn together along the edges with a hole through which the head was inserted. It usually came down to just above the knees.

Urcuchillay: A constellation and a god. He protected llamas and his eyes were Alpha and Beta Centauri.

Urpito: little bird.

vicuña (*Vicugna vicugna*): a camelid. Of the five types of camelids found in South America, the vicuña is valued for its fine hair.

viscacha (*Lagidium peruanum*): a long-eared, bushy-tailed rodent with a body length of 37cm that lives in rocky crevices and talus slopes of the Andean highlands.

wasi: small, one-room house used for sleeping.

Wayronqo: bumble bee.

Weqo Churu: crooked beak.

wilka camayocs: members of the priesthood.

Wilka Uma: high priest. The head of the priesthood. He was often brother to the Capac Inca.

Wiraqocha: the creator of life. The Incas lessened his importance to that of Inti.

yacarca: a diviner who could summon the voices from fire. The Capac Inca always traveled with a yacarca.

Yachawasi: an academy for young Inca nobles.

yacolla: cape worn over an unku.

Yana Mayu: Black River.